DARE SERIES BOOK THREE

IF YOU DARE

BESTSELLING AUTHOR
SHANTEL TESSIER

For more information about the author and her books,
visit her website- www.shanteltessierauthor.com. Editor:
Jenny Sims
Proofreader: Amanda Rash
Formatter: CP Smith
Cover Designer: Tracie Douglas with Dark Water Covers.

To Author K. Webster. When I decided to write Deke's story, she was the first one I spoke to about it. I had two very different directions I could take it. One was safe. The other was not. She was the little devil on my shoulder who whispered in my ear to do it. And I never looked back. I thank her for that.

Playlist

Deadset Society – "Like A Nightmare"
Starset – "My Demons"
No Resolve – "What You Deserve"
My Darkest Day – "Nature of The Beast"
Valerie Broussand – "Trouble"
Seven Day Sleep – "Down"
Memory of A Melody – "Things That Make You Scream"
Adelitas Way – "Invincible"
Sin Shake Sin – "Can't Go to Hell"
Memory of A Melody – "Darkest Hour"
TheUnder – "Ready To Die"
Zero – "Left Alone"
MISSIOS – "I Don't Even Care About You"
Halsey – "Nightmare"
Nina Nesbitt – "The Best you Had"
Redlight King – "Boneshaker"
The Score – "Legend"
Yungblud & Halsey – "I Will Follow You into the Dark"

DARE SERIES BOOK THREE

IF YOU DARE

PROLOGUE

DEKE

DEATH IS A debt we are all born owing.

It's something that money can't buy nor can it be traded.

You can't bargain for more time. When it's up, you accept it like a fucking man.

I've never been afraid to die. Or to love, for that matter.

Aren't they the same?

You surrender to a fate you have no control over. You don't get to choose when or how you die, just as you can't choose when and who you fall in love with.

Some couples get a happily ever after while others are toxic for one another.

My love was like that.

She lied; I believed every word.

I hurt her; she forgave too easily.

It was a vicious circle of deceit and sex wrapped in a pretty black bow. Neither one of us could quit.

I wrapped my hand around her throat, and she begged me to breathe.

She stabbed me in the heart and demanded I bleed.

She might as well have been fucking poison, but I would have drunk her anyway.

That was the kind of obsession I had for her.

I knew how it would end—total devastation.

A war zone of broken bones and bleeding souls.

I should have hated her, but that's the funny thing about love—it's out of your control. And even when it leaves you with two black eyes, you beg for more.

People are afraid of the unknown, but I never feared death, and love was no different.

She was going to destroy me, and I was going to let her.

It was a game that could only end one way—a slow and torturous death.

ONE

DEKE

I DARE YOU

A little game my friends and I have played since we were kids. Every Sunday, we get together and write a dare, and the lucky son of a bitch whose turn it is gets to pluck one from the glass bowl and fulfill it. You have a month to complete it; once your time is up, you must face the consequence if you haven't. Each dare has one, but none of us has ever refused the dare. Some are harmless. Others illegal. Just depends on whose dare you get and what their mood is at the time.

My best friend Eli dared our friend Cole to ride a skateboard down a hill. He did it, of course, but ended up with bruised elbows, scraped knees, and bloody hands. After we all ran down the hill to help him stand, we found him sitting on the ground with a smile on his face. It was as though he enjoyed the pain and the sight of the blood. And from then on, we found ourselves daring one another to do something that could either get us killed or thrown in jail. We didn't care. Nothing scared any of us, for that matter. But as we got older, the dares got more dangerous and then turned illegal. Girls got involved and … well, let's just say the game went from eight boys fucking around to five friends trying to figure out how we ended up haunted by our past.

We fucked up along the way. Some of us fell in love with the wrong girl. And some of us would die at the hands of others. It was a sick game we were going to end. And finish it is exactly what we had to do. Even if that meant killing one of our own. We were sharks and not all sharks can swim with others.

Sixteen years old

For the second night in a row, I find myself standing in Bennett's parents' basement. We threw a party here last night that ended in several fights. My best friend Cole got his dick sucked by Trenten's girlfriend in the closet, and Kellan somehow started a fight between Cole and Trenten. It ended with Cole throwing some punches and me getting jumped from behind. Some fucker hit me in the back of the head with a glass cross. Once shit settled down, Cole took me to my sister's to get it stitched up even though I assured him I'd be fine.

Now here we are. It's Sunday, and we're back to draw a dare. It's my turn.

"Kiss Becky Holt." I read the three words written on a folded-up piece of paper out loud. "Or you have to record yourself dancing naked." I snort. I'm sure videos of me in my birthday suit are out there somewhere and didn't even involve a dare.

Someone snickers, and I look up at my seven friends. Each and every one of us known as the Great White Sharks. The small, rich town known as Collins, Oregon, has been calling us sharks for years. Some say it started because we are all on the high school swim team and dominate in the water, but others say it's because we're ruthless. Just like some of our fathers. Some believe killers are born that way, but few will argue they are made. I'm not sure which one is correct anymore. I just do it for fucking fun. But a couple of my friends do it because they crave it—the blood, the rush, and the flat-out terror in someone's eyes when they get too close. They thrive off it. And I don't blame them because it can be quite a rush.

"Really?" Cole looks over at Eli, wearing a look of boredom on his face. He's holding a beer in one hand and his cell in the other.

"Since when do we do dares that involve chicks?" he asks, then looks at me. "Not like Deke can't get his dick wet on his own." Cole craves the blood. The fight. He always has. His darkness is a hole that will one day swallow him whole if he allows it.

Eli lights his blunt and takes a long drag, his cheeks caving in as he lounges on the couch before his eyes meet mine. "What? We all know he has a crush on her." He winks at me, a grin now playing on his lips. "This just gives you a reason to make your move. And nowhere did the dare mention him shoving his dick into her. Just a harmless kiss." Eli does it for fun. Both of his parents are dead, so he lives with his older sister and her piece of shit husband. He does whatever the fuck he wants, and no one tries to stop him.

"Who says I haven't already?" I ask.

He throws his head back, laughing. "Come on, Deke. You're no Casanova. I'm doing you a favor. Now go get that taken care of."

I rip up the piece of paper and throw what's left of it into the glass bowl.

Kellan sits in the recliner. I can feel his eyes boring into me, but I ignore him. He hasn't said much since last night. I used to think he did this for the hell of it, but it seems he has an agenda. I just can't figure out what it is yet.

Maddox and Landen quietly talk to each other as they lounge on a futon up against the wall, and Cole finishes off his beer before lighting up a cigarette.

Walking over to the couch, I take the joint from Eli and bring it to my lips. Pulling in a long drag, the taste of citrus fills my mouth. I lean my head back and blow it out, feeling the burn in my chest. "Shit, your sister has some good weed," I say, handing it back to him.

He grunts. "Yeah, Jerrold only buys the good shit." Eli can't stand her piece of shit husband.

"Quit stalling," Bennett finally chimes in while he sits cross-legged on his parents' basement floor with an open laptop in front of him. The guy lives on that thing. He's obsessed with hacking shit. He's not much for getting his hands dirty, but the guy does pretty well behind the scenes. "She's up at the school."

"Know her schedule, do you?" Is my friend into the girl I like? They all know how I feel about her. And they also know to stay the fuck away.

He shrugs. "My mother is on the PTA. Says she sees her up there with the cheerleaders."

I frown. "Becky doesn't cheer." She doesn't play any sports. She's too good for that. Wouldn't want to sweat her makeup off or mess up her perfect hair.

"No. But Demi does," Eli informs me.

I never pay her little sister any attention. "And how do you know that?"

"I like staring at her ass in the short skirts they wear." He smirks.

Cole chuckles, looking over at Eli, but he doesn't say anything. He seems to know something the rest of us don't.

I ignore it and snap my fingers at Eli. "Let's go."

I pull up to Collins High and park my SUV. I look across the almost empty lot and spot Becky's car, a white Mercedes E400.

Eli points at the football stadium. "There she is. All by herself."

I follow his line of sight and see a blonde sitting on the bleachers. She leans forward with her elbows resting on her knees while she looks out at the squad on the football field. "Wait here," I order, getting out.

"Aww, man I wanted to hold your hand ..."

I slam my door, cutting him off, but I give him the bird when I see his body shaking with laughter through the windshield.

As I walk across the parking lot, she rises to her feet and starts to descend the stairs. I slow my steps but don't stop. She keeps her head down, typing away on her phone, totally oblivious to what is going on around her. Stupid girl. Don't their fathers warn them of guys like me and my friends? The ones who see a situation where they can take advantage and seize it. We're all the same. If a guy tells *you otherwise, he's lying. We all stare at your tits while we imagine fucking them. We all look at your ass. And we're all thinking about you on your knees while sucking our cocks. It's all about what we can do to get you undressed and underneath us.*

Becky Holt is a mystery. She doesn't have many friends, if any, yet she's popular, if that makes sense. All the girls hate her, and the boys want to fuck her.

I pick up my pace when I see she's headed straight for me. I should say her name or place my hands out—anything to prevent what I know is coming—but I don't. Instead, I let her run right into me, knocking herself down.

"Are you okay?" I ask, looking down at her sitting on her ass that's now covered in dirt.

The dust fills the air around her, and she coughs. "What …?" She looks up at me, blinking from the sun shining in her face. She lifts her hand to her forehead to shade her ocean blue eyes.

"I didn't see you there," I lie, giving her a kind smile.

"It's okay." She sighs heavily.

"Here. Let me help you up." I offer her a hand for assistance.

She takes it, and I yank her to her feet. I use more force than necessary, causing her chest to hit mine. Her breathing picks up when her blue eyes meet mine.

I've had a crush on Becky for a while now. I've known her all my life, and we've grown up together. My parents always invite hers to their Christmas parties and birthday celebrations on their yachts. Collins, Oregon, isn't a big town, but the wealthy only party with the wealthy. No matter how much I've wanted her, I have never touched her. Never pursued her.

The ass in our school is too easily given, so why chase a bitch down for it?

"Thanks," she mumbles and pushes away from me.

"What are you doing out here?" I ask, placing my hands in my jeans pockets as my eyes drop to her tits. They look bigger than usual today. I've undressed enough girls to know they either stuff their shit or they spend too much money on bras to make what little they have

look three times bigger. As if we're not going to notice the difference once you're naked.

We do.

"Waiting on my sister to be done with practice." She dusts off her skinny jeans.

"Want some company?"

She tilts her head to the side, pulling her bottom lip between her teeth as she contemplates my question. Since a pair of black Aviators shades my eyes, she can't see the way I'm looking her up and down. I linger on her thighs and wonder just how hard it will be to get her to spread them for me. "Yeah ..."

"Becky!"

She spins around at the sound of her name. Demi Holt, her little sister, comes up to join us dressed in a pair of black spandex shorts that barely covers her pussy, a bright pink sports bra, and tennis shoes. That's it. If I was their father, I wouldn't let her leave the house looking like that, let alone parade around the school. Even if it is Sunday. She has her long, bleach blond hair up in a high ponytail with a black ribbon tied into a big bow around it. She's a walking Barbie doll. A total high school cheerleader cliché.

Demi places her hands on her narrow hips, her already flat stomach sucking in, making her ribs even more pronounced as she takes a deep breath. She glares up at her sister, and I don't miss the thin layer of sweat that covers her chest and face because the sun makes her glisten. "I'm done and ready to go." Then, without another word, she stomps off toward the parking lot.

Becky looks at me. "Sorry, I've got to go."

Not yet, baby.

Stepping forward, I smile down at her. "Shame," I say, and her breathing picks up at my closeness.

Becky isn't a virgin, not by any means. Boys talk in the locker rooms. On campus. At parties. And she's already had quite a few of them. They all said she wasn't that good of a fuck, but what her cunt lacks, she makes up with her mouth. I'm up for testing that rumor.

She doesn't say anything, but her blue eyes stay on mine as if I hold her in a trance. "I wanted to spend some time with you." I reach up and take a strand of her blond hair and twirl it around my finger. "Alone."

Her breath hitches, and I know I have her right where I want her. It's sad, really, how easily these girls believe our bullshit. Leaning down, I trail my lips along her jawline, just letting them graze her delicate skin. I slowly give her a chance to push me away, but she won't. No one turns down Deke Biggs. The ones I fuck consider themselves lucky to catch my attention. They just never keep it long.

When I reach her lips, my free hand slides into her soft hair, and I tilt her head back, pulling away just enough to look down at her. "Guess a kiss will have to be enough for now." Then I press my lips to hers.

She opens up for me like all the others do and then moans. I wrap my other hand around her waist and pull her into me, gently grinding my hardening cock into her lower stomach, letting her know that we can go as far as she wants. Right here and now. The fact that we're on school property hasn't stopped me before.

Her hands wrap around my neck while her tongue dances with mine. Her kiss tastes like strawberries, and I know it's her lip gloss. The same one that all the girls wear. I swear they pass that shit around to one another. It's step one in how to be a slut.

Her fingers dig into my hair, and she moans loudly. I groan in response, holding her tighter against my achingly hard cock. I go to pull away, to look down at her, but she won't release me. And I can't push her away. My feet work on their own, and I'm pushing her backward. She whimpers into my mouth when her back hits what I'm guessing is a wall, stopping our movement.

I pull away quickly. We both stand, breathing heavily, and I look over her heavy eyes and parted, wet lips. I run my thumb over them while my eyes drop to the blue shirt she wears. It matches the color of her eyes. Her tits rise and fall fast as she continues to pant from our kiss.

I cup her face, then run my fingers down over her chin and to her neck. Her pulse races under my touch, and I lick my wet lips, wishing

I could carry her off to my SUV and fuck her in the back seat because I want more. What can I say? I'm a greedy motherfucker. I don't like to wait for something when I know I can have it. And I can have her. Now. But instead, I take a step back, then turn and walk away from her. Always leave them wanting more.

Making my way back across the parking lot to my Range Rover, I ignore my hard fucking dick straining against my jeans and catch sight of Eli leaning up against the passenger door talking to Demi. She has her head thrown back in laughter when I approach them.

"What did I miss?" I ask.

Her laughter cuts off, and her blue eyes settle on me. I watch them turn hard as stone. She ignores me and looks at Eli. "I'll see you around." She slaps his chest playfully and then walks off.

I make my way around the front of my car. "She's too young for you, man."

He laughs at that, but his eyes stay on her bubble ass as she sashays across the parking lot with her long blond ponytail bouncing across her back. "The best ones always are." Then he turns, gets into the passenger seat, and winks over at me. "That's what makes them so much fun."

TWO

DEKE

Present- Eighteen years old

I PULL MY Range Rover into the driveway and look down at my phone ringing in the passenger seat. *Fucker* lights up my screen, but I press ignore just as I have the other hundred times he's called me. I have nothing to say to my father. And I know he has nothing to say to me either. He just hates that I won't answer him—my lack of respect for him knows no bounds.

Grabbing my phone, I get out of my SUV and walk into my best friend's house. I live with him, his little sister, and his fiancée. We all moved to Austin, Texas, three months ago after high school graduation. Cole and I attend the University of Texas on swimming scholarships. Austin, his fiancée, is still trying to decide what she wants to do with her life.

I throw my gym bag down at the front door, and call out, "Cole?"

That stupid Halloween decoration Austin put out makes a noise when you activate its motion sensor. The fucker gets me every time I come in late, drunk off my ass. Pretty sure I threw it away last weekend, but she found it and put it back. Its red eyes glare up at me with its ugly mouth open, showing off its vampire-looking teeth and growling at me again. The first time I saw it, I thought the damn thing was a ghost, but I'm not even sure what the hell it's supposed to be. Austin seems quite attached to it, but I'm hoping to get rid of the thing before Halloween next year.

"Kitchen," he answers.

Walking down the hallway, I take the first right, entering the kitchen to see him bent over at the stainless fridge looking for something to eat. "I've got plans for us tonight."

He groans. "I don't feel like going to a party."

"Even better."

Straightening, he shuts the door and turns around to face me. His blue eyes give me a pointed look as he tears open a container. My best friend hasn't been himself lately. His temper is shorter, and his mood darker. Worse than usual. Cole Reynolds has always been a ticking time bomb, but there's more to it now. And I hate that he hasn't come to me about it. Things just haven't been the same since we left Collins.

"I'm not going to a strip club," he deadpans.

I smile at him. Tits and some ass in my face are exactly what I need, but I shake my head. I'm trying to get him out of the house, and I knew he would never go for that. Plus, I don't want to be on Austin's shit list. And taking Cole to a place like that will get my name at the motherfucking top of hers. I'm quite fond of my balls, and they would be the first thing she'd go for. "Although that is a fantastic idea, it's not what I have in mind."

He sets the container on the countertop next to him and crosses his arms over his chest, arching a dark brow. "I'm waiting."

I open my mouth to fill him in, but it closes the moment Austin enters the kitchen, and she's not alone. Becky is with her. *My ex.*

The girl who I fell in love with. What started as a dare and ended up being so much more. I wish I would have known then what a lying whore she was. I guess a part of me knew. I just thought I'd be the exception. *Fuck, when did I turn into a chick?*

Junior year

"Dude, let her go," Eli all but growls as he sees what I'm drooling over.

"She's with David now." I say it like it fucking matters. It doesn't.

"Let him have her ass. You can do better."

I frown at his tone. Since when does Eli hate Becky?

When I say nothing, he turns his attention to Cole and Maddox as they walk up after leaving the cafeteria.

I lean up against my locker and watch the blonde come down the hallway. I kissed Becky last year by the football field because Eli dared me to. And now I can't get her out of my mind. It didn't happen suddenly. No, it was more like a sickness. She slowly took over my mind and body with no cure in sight. Maybe it's because I know she's unavailable now. Three months after that kiss, she started seeing David, and now that he has her, I want her. I watch her in class and at parties. And I catch her watching me too. She comes to swim meets but doesn't speak to me. Instead, she ignores me completely. Just like we agreed.

Her boyfriend, David, comes up behind her and places his hand in hers. She looks up at him but doesn't smile. He's too busy talking to Maxwell, his friend walking beside him. I feel my heart begin to beat faster as she approaches me, but he brings her to a stop and then says a few more words to his friend. Once Maxwell walks away, David turns to face her. He leans down and kisses her, pulling her body into his, and her arms come up and wrap around his neck. Just as they did when I kissed her last year. Then just as quickly, he lets go of her hand and walks away, leaving her all alone in the middle of the hallway.

As if she feels my eyes on hers, she looks up at me. I remain leaning against the locker, trying to play it cool as though I couldn't care less what she does, but it's all for show.

I care, and she knows it.

I'm jealous that he gets to kiss her, touch her, and fuck her for all to see.

I want a piece of Becky. More than what she already gives me. I want her to be completely mine, but for now, I'll settle.

Fucking pathetic.

"Deke, there's a party at Luck's this weekend. Cole, Maddox, Landen, and I are thinking about going after the meet. You wanna go?" Eli asks me.

I just nod at him, not taking my eyes off hers. "Of course." I'm always down to get drunk and pretend I'm not obsessed with the blue-eyed blonde.

She walks past, looking me up and down before her tongue darts out and runs along her pink-painted lips. They still glisten from his kiss. "Hey, Deke," she purrs, then watches me over her shoulder before turning the corner and walking out of my sight.

I slap Eli on the chest, cutting off whatever nonsense he was telling Cole. "I'll see you all at practice later." I push off my locker before they can stop me.

I turn the same corner she took and open the first door on the left. Mr. Tomson always leaves his door unlocked. Stupid fucker.

A hand grabs me from behind, and I spin around to see Becky leaning up against the now closed door. "Hey, baby." I smirk, stepping into her.

She reaches behind her and locks it. "I don't have much time—"

"Then what are you waiting for?" I cut her off.

Grabbing my shoulders, she spins me around and shoves my back into a wall. Then she falls to her knees before me.

As I place my hands in her blond hair, she goes to work on my jeans to free my already hardening cock. I grip her hair and prepare to fuck that mouth he just kissed. I'm going to come all over her lips and watch her lick them clean.

I should have known then that she didn't have a loyal bone in her body. But I never had the chance to think about it. After that, things changed. They all went to that party Eli mentioned. There was a car wreck, and three of my best friends—Eli, Maddox, and Landen—died. Cole was the only one who survived. Or so I thought. Cole had taken full responsibility for that accident at the time but just recently confessed he was not the one driving. It was Becky. And she was with them that night because she was fucking Eli. I still can't decide if I'm more pissed at her or my dead friend who knew how I felt about her. Too bad I didn't know she was fucking him sooner. I would have never given her the time of day, much less allow myself to fall in love with her. That's why he tried to tell me to stop wanting her—so he could have her.

Her blue eyes widen the moment she notices I'm in the kitchen with Cole, and she comes to a stop. I didn't see her car outside, which means Austin must have brought her over here earlier. I don't see her all that often, thank God. But her best friend is my best friend's fiancée, and I live with them, so it's bound to happen. Whenever the situation presents itself, I completely ignore her. It's as if she doesn't exist. Because she no longer does to me. She's as dead as my best friend buried six feet deep in a wooden box.

"Thought you were going back home for the weekend?" Austin asks me as she goes over to Cole. He uncrosses his arms and wraps them around her shoulders, pulling her back to his chest and resting his chin on top of her head.

Shelby, my older sister who still lives in Collins, called me yesterday and said that she had picked up a weekend shift at the hospital. As a trauma nurse, she always works crazy hours, so I decided to stay here. She was the only reason I was going to spend two days in Collins. Any chance I have to stay away from my father, I take it. "Plans changed," I answer.

The room falls to an awkward silence. Austin's green eyes drift from me to Becky. Then to Cole. Almost as if she's secretly asking us to go have our conversation in another room—preferably outside.

I jump up and plant my ass on the kitchen island, smiling at her. Austin's disappointment shows when she lets out a heavy sigh.

"What do you have planned for us tonight?" Cole asks me. He knows I'm not going anywhere, no matter what his soon-to-be wife wants. He's the one who has to kiss her ass, not me.

I may like to avoid Becky, but I also like to make her feel uncomfortable. I hold all the cards here. She has no clue who I have told her secrets to, and I want to watch her sweat for a while.

"I got us tickets to Silence," I answer.

Austin's brows pull together. "What is Silence? And can Lilly go?"

"Only the scariest haunted house in Texas." Becky answers her, and Austin's face lights up like fucking Christmas. "No, Lilly can't go. It's not a place for children," she adds.

Austin looks up at Cole with a big smile on her face, silently begging him. He shrugs, telling her, "It's up to you, sweetheart."

She turns her attention back to me. "I'll call and see if Misty can watch Lilly for a few hours. If she can, then we'll go." Looking at Becky, she asks, "You can go, right?"

I refrain from growling because I wanted Becky to be the babysitter. I can't stand to be around her for five minutes, let alone spend an evening with her. We keep our distance for a reason.

"Sure," she answers. "When are we going?"

"Tonight," I say, and everyone's heads turn toward me when the word comes out a little too snappy.

"Okay." Austin spins around in Cole's arms so she can face him. "I'll call Misty …"

He doesn't even let her finish before he leans down and presses his lips to hers. His hands go to her hair, and she lets out a moan when he pulls her head back to give himself better access to her mouth. Becky exits the kitchen, rolling her eyes.

I stay where I'm at, being the pervert that I am. Plus, it's not like I haven't ever seen them kiss. Hell, I once recorded them fucking in a bathroom while at a high school party and then posted that shit online for all to see. All because he told me to do it. That was before he fell in love with her, though. And also because I can be an asshole.

"Austin?"

She pushes Cole away, breathing heavily when Lilly enters the kitchen. "Yes, Lilly?" she asks, breathlessly.

The cute little six-year-old smiles up at her. She is Cole's little sister, and he's raised her since the day she was born. Celeste, Austin's stepmother, killed Cole's mother by shoving her down a flight of stairs when she was pregnant with Lilly. Lilly survived, but their mother did not. "I don't know where my phone went."

Austin takes her hand and pulls her own cell out of the back pocket of her jeans. "I'll call it."

"I think it's dead." She frowns.

"We'll find it," Austin assures her before they walk out of the kitchen.

"Need a moment?" I ask Cole, jokingly.

"More like an hour," he answers.

I turn to face him, and he has his hands in the pockets of his jeans. Things have been awkward around us since the night he told me all his secrets in Collins. He thinks I'm mad at him, but I'm not. He did exactly what I would have done, so I can't fault him for being like me. But I hate that I'm still keeping my own. Maybe he's pulling away from me because he knows I'm not being honest with him. And it makes me think of Eli. How close we all once were, but how many secrets we had among us. Were we all ever really friends? I think that's the hardest part about all of this. I was loyal to the sharks. I may have been an ass to most, but I would have laid my life down for any of them. Even Kellan. But in the end, I helped Cole kill him. Would Cole have helped me kill Eli if he hadn't died that night in the car accident? Would Cole have dug with me to get the answers I needed? Still want? I'm not sure. And I hate that I'll never know. You can't kill someone who is already dead. But the unanswered questions still eat at me.

He finally looks away from where Austin exited the kitchen with Lilly, and his eyes meet mine. "You gonna be okay with Becky tonight? I can tell Austin I don't want to go—"

"No," I interrupt and wave him off. "It'll be fine. How bad can it be?"

His dark brows rise at my question as if to say *really? You gonna ask that? Because we both know just how bad shit can get.*

Austin pops her head back into the kitchen. "Found the phone and Misty is gonna come stay with Lilly."

Neither one of us says anything to her.

Her green eyes narrow, and she walks over to me. "Please be nice." I open my mouth, but she continues, "It's just one night."

I grind my teeth but nod once because that's the first time Austin has ever asked me for anything. And I love that girl like my own sister. Even if I did once aim a gun at her, planning on ending her life in the middle of a cemetery. But now that's water under the bridge and all that. "One night." I've put up with worse in my life.

She smiles and looks over at Cole. "I'm going to take a shower and start getting ready." Then she turns and walks out of the kitchen once again.

And no surprise, Cole all but runs out of the kitchen to follow her up to their room for a little *shower* time of his own. He's been on her ass more than usual and doesn't let her out of his sight. If it were anyone else, I would say their relationship has gone from extremely toxic to a tad unhealthy, but I know the loss that he has suffered and the scare he had with her five months ago. Hell, even I'm protective of her now.

I walk over to the fridge and grab a bottle of water, and when I turn around, Becky is standing there. I bump into her on accident, and it pushes her backward. Instinct has me reaching out and grabbing her upper arm to keep her standing. I should shove her ass to the floor, but I don't.

Her blue eyes are wide as they look up at me, and I realize the last time I was this close to her was three months ago. When I stormed into her bedroom back at her father's house in Collins and told her I knew all her secrets. That she had been fucking my best friend, Eli, and that she had lied to Cole and wasn't really pregnant. She begged me to love her, to want her, but it didn't work.

"Wait! Please?" she begs. "I can fix this."

"No. You can't." Things have gone too far, and there's no going back now.

"Deke? Please? I can't lose you," she cries.

"You already have." I reach for the door handle, but she places her hands on my back, gripping my T-shirt and causing the collar to choke me.

"I'm sorry. Is that what you want me to say?" she grinds out. "I lied. And I've felt terrible about it. Austin is my best friend. And I love

you. You love me."

"Not anymore." I shake my head.

"I don't believe you," she argues. "There has to be something I can do. Please ... tell me." The desperation in her voice makes me smile.

I turn around and cup her tear-streaked face. She sucks in a long breath, and her body presses into mine, now interested. Funny how women turn to sex when they're desperate for forgiveness. "Unless you plan on falling to your knees and opening that mouth of yours so I can fuck it, I have no use for you."

"I don't believe you," she whispers again as new tears run down her face.

"That's your problem. Not mine." Her eyes stare up at mine, silently begging me to forgive her and tell her that it's all going to be okay. That I love her. I'll die before I ever say that to her again.

When she licks her wet lips and falls to her knees like an obedient slave, I look at her with disgust. I'd always held Becky to a higher standard because she continually held her head high and didn't care what others said or felt about her. Cole was not driving the car when it wrecked and killed three of our friends—she was—and she allowed him to take the fall for it. Though I can't blame her for that part. I understand firsthand that when Cole makes up his mind, you can't change it. I'm just like him in that aspect. But she lied to him when she told him she was pregnant. She wanted him to feel sorry for her and tell her to run, and it worked. She played him, and then she kept it from me because she knew I could tell him the truth.

I'm a killer. But I've never lied without a reason, and that purpose is rarely just to save my own ass.

She looks up at me, tears running down her face, and she pulls her shoulders back as though she has a backbone. "I'll prove it to you." Her voice doesn't waver with her renewed determination. As if sucking my cock is going to make me fall in love with her all over again.

She's not the first girl to suck my dick who I didn't fall in love with. And she won't be the last.

"Deke?" Her shaky voice pulls me out of that memory. Her hands are on my chest, and she breathes heavily.

I love that I still have this effect on her. After three months of nothing, I can still turn her into a fucking puddle of water that I can stomp through. I once loved Becky, but now I hate her with a passion.

My fingers dig into her arms. "Yeah, baby?"

She bites her bottom lip at my words. I avoid her like the plague, but maybe I shouldn't. Maybe she could be more useful than I thought. If I told her to drop to her knees right now and suck my dick, would she do it? Only one way to find out.

I let go and run my hands up her arms. Her breath hitches when I move them over her neck, being as gentle as I can when I really want to fucking break it. Watch her perfect fucking lips open as she tries to breathe while the life drains out of her pretty blue eyes.

I can be a fucking heartless bastard.

Her blue eyes look up into mine, and I see it. That same desire she used to have for me. I wonder how much she faked. Did it make her sick when I touched her? When I kissed her? How about when I fucked her?

I'd love to make her hate herself as much as I hate her now. I can make her believe I love her again. That I've forgiven her.

My hands slide into her hair, and she licks her painted pink lips. "I've missed you," I lie.

A shiver runs through her body, but she says nothing.

"Have you missed me, baby?"

Her eyes close and her lips part. The act reminds me of that last memory when I allowed her to suck my cock. The hopefulness she had in her eyes as tears ran down her face from my force. Those boys in high school were wrong—her mouth didn't make up for what her cunt lacked. But when you love someone, you're blind to their every flaw. Now that I hate her, I see much clearer. The fog is gone, and I see Becky for who she really is—a slut I can use to my advantage.

Sweet fucking revenge. I'm an expert at fucking someone over. No one plays that game better than I do.

I lean down, pressing my lips gently to hers, and she opens up immediately, but I don't take the bait. Not yet. Why rush this, when I can have some fun and draw it out?

I pull back, and she opens her heavy eyes. "Deke—"

The doorbell rings, interrupting whatever she was about to say.

I let her go and walk out of the kitchen. I open the front door to see the neighbor kid Misty standing there with her dark hair up in a ponytail. She reaches up and pushes her glasses to sit higher on her nose. She's a fourteen-year-old girl with three older brothers. I sometimes play basketball with them out in the driveway.

She smiles at me. "Hi, Deke. Austin called and said she needed a sitter tonight."

I step aside for her to enter. "She's upstairs in the shower right now, but Lilly is in her room."

"Thanks." She walks inside, bouncing down the hallway to find Lilly.

When I return to the kitchen and find it empty, I take my ass up to my room to get ready for the night. I'm going to seduce Becky. And she's going to realize she's weaker than she thought when it comes to me.

THREE

DEKE

Two hours later, "Like a Nightmare" by Deadset Society plays inside my SUV as I drive us to Silence. The sun has officially set, and we decided to go earlier rather than later to beat the crowd and traffic since it's a Friday night.

Austin leans forward from the back seat and taps Cole on the shoulder. "Turn that down for a second, please?" He does as she asks, and she begins to read something to us off her phone. "Did you know they can touch you? I'm on their website, and it says that you should not wear open-toed shoes or nice clothing. That you may have to crawl, jump, or run to get free. And that you may have *blood* thrown on you."

Cole stiffens in the passenger seat at the mention of blood. And I wonder if he has the same thought as me.

Five months ago

Cole pulls up to the Lowes estate and doesn't even bother turning his car off. He jumps out, and I follow him up the stairs, and he barges into Bruce's house. Celeste, Austin's stepmother, lies dead at the bottom of the stairs. Neither one of us gives her any thought.

"Austin?" Cole yells, pulling the gun out of the back of his jeans.

I'm holding mine down by my side, and it's ready with a bullet in the chamber. "Austin?" He shouts again, running down the hallway.

He follows the blood trail down the hall, and my throat tightens at what we're going to find. It won't be good.

He takes a sharp right, entering the kitchen. "Austin?" I hear him choke on her name, and my heart begins to pound. What did he find?

I enter behind him and gasp. "What the fuck?"

Austin lies in a pool of blood on her father's marble floor. Fuck! She's bleeding too much. Her shirt and her jeans are soaked. Her once sun-kissed skin looks pale, and the pool of blood underneath her slowly gets bigger. The smell alone almost knocks me off my feet. Kellan still holds the gun in his hand. Why did he shoot his best friend's girl? I don't understand.

"Take him," Cole calls out, not looking up from her body. He goes to touch her but then pulls back.

She's dead. I've helped him kill enough people to know what a lifeless body looks like. "She needs help," I argue. Looking over her with narrowed eyes, I know there's not much we can do for her at this point. Kellan killed the only thing Cole has ever loved. And Cole will make Kellan suffer in ways he can't even imagine.

"Take him!" Cole barks this time. "Help is on the way." He turns his attention to Austin, dismissing me.

I look over at Kellan leaning up against the countertop with a knife stuck into his side. He smiles, looking over at Austin lying on the floor. Fucking prick. I grab him by the back of his neck and rip the gun out of his hand, before yanking him away from the countertop.

I'm not sure how Cole would handle seeing Austin covered in blood again. Even if he knew it was fake.

"For the ones who think they are fearless, they have a 'blackout' attraction where you are given a glow stick to navigate your way out." She goes on to read about Silence.

"Pass," Becky says.

I smile to myself. She's avoided me since I played with her in the kitchen back at the house. She stuck by Austin's side while she got ready. It's like she's afraid to be left alone with me again because she doesn't trust herself with me. Silly girl. *Space won't save you from me.*

"I think that sounds like the most fun," Austin argues.

I watch Cole relax into his seat and smile at Austin's words. *She isn't afraid of anything.*

"You have to sign a waiver for that, though," Austin adds.

"I'm not signing shit," Becky mumbles to herself.

"Silence was once an insane asylum that was shut down back in 1984 due to a patient being killed. She died by strangulation. She managed to get out of her straitjacket and hung herself by the straps."

"God," Becky whispers.

"Afterward, the place was bought by the Thompson family. Over the years, they have added new attractions to Silence, but the part that makes it stand out from all the other haunted houses in Texas is the fact that it is actually haunted."

"I should have stayed home," Becky whines.

Austin continues, "Silence sits on a hundred acres and has over 200,000 square feet of attractions. That does not include the original underground tunnels that the staff used to transfer dead bodies from one building to another …" She pauses for a second and then looks up at the back of Cole's head. "I wonder if we get to walk in the tunnels."

"You can't be serious?" Becky asks.

"I mean, wouldn't that be awesome?" Austin goes on. "If the tunnels were the *blackout* attraction?"

Cole and I both chuckle. "What?" Austin finally directs her attention to Becky. "Halloween is one of my favorite times of the year. Bonfires and ghost stories. Some apple cider with a little rum. Scary movies and haunted houses."

"The only part I want to participate in is the one where we get drunk off that apple cider and rum." Becky smiles at her.

"We're here," Cole announces as I pull up to a wrought-iron gate.

We enter, and buses line the long driveway to an opening. Men in yellow vests holding flashlights navigate the long line of cars. One guides me to a parking spot in the middle of a field that is quickly becoming full. We exit and turn around to see what looks like an abandoned castle that's been painted black and has boarded-up windows. The tallest part stands at five stories high in the center with an even taller clock tower. Red lights on each side of the building make it glow.

To the right is another gate and the ticket booth with a Ferris wheel and roller coaster in the distance. You can hear people screaming from here as it takes a loop.

"It has a carnival?" Becky observes.

"It has a scarenival," Austin corrects her. "I read it on the website as well. It has a maze, a mirrored fun house, and ..."

I tune her out and remove the tickets from my pocket before handing them to Cole. I had only purchased three, so Becky is going to have to buy her own once we get up there.

Austin has moved on in conversation and is now talking to Cole about what she wants to do on Halloween in two weeks when Becky groans at her cell going off.

"What?" Austin asks her.

"My sister is here."

Great!

She quickly types away. "With her boyfriend," she adds, not pleased with the situation.

"Do they wanna join us?" Austin asks her.

Cole throws me a look of sympathy. This was supposed to be the three of us. With my newfound idea to seek revenge, I don't mind Becky tagging along, but now I've got her bitch of a sister to deal with.

Fucking fantastic!

"Yeah." She sighs heavily. "She's gonna meet us over by the wristbands." At least she sounds about as thrilled as I am.

Cole takes Austin's hand, and they lead us through the crowd to the ticket booth. We fall into line, and Austin shivers. "It's freezing." Her teeth chatter as she wraps her arms around her chest. "The news said it wasn't gonna get below fifty-five tonight."

"It'll be warm inside," he tells her.

"I hope." She laughs, rubbing her hands up and down her long-sleeve shirt.

"Probably be cold as death," Becky mumbles.

"Here." Cole pushes Austin away so he can unzip his black hoodie.

"No. You'll be cold," she protests.

He wraps it around her shoulders and yanks the hood up over her head. She looks up at him with a smile on her lips.

He snorts at her statement. "I'll be fine, sweetheart." Then he pulls her back into his side, and she snuggles into him.

It's sickening how cute they are together. But I can't deny that I've seen my friend turn into a different person since she came along. A better version of himself. But I can tell he's been a little off and in a funk lately, and Austin knows it too. She watches him closer and makes sure to give him more one-on-one time when I take Lilly out to a movie or shopping for some new toys. I think she's afraid of losing him to the darkness that he was in when she entered his life. I'm not sure how far he is from that at the moment, but I know it won't take much to push him over the edge.

A scream has us all turning around to look. A guy lifts a girl dressed as a naughty nurse with fake blood covering her costume and throws her over his shoulder. She screams out again playfully and slaps his ass over his jeans while his hand slides up her short skirt to grip her ass.

When we all turn back to face the line, a blonde stands before us with big blue eyes and her hands on her narrow hips. Demi Holt is the spitting image of her sister, and both girls look just like their mother. I'm pretty sure all three use the same amount of bleach, shade of makeup, and brand of perfume. Neither girl knows who they really are. All they know is who their mother has told them to be.

Such a waste of a good piece of ass.

A guy by the name of Seth stands next to Demi. *What are the odds?*

"Hey, guys," he greets us, shaking Cole's hand and then mine. "Didn't know you were gonna be here."

"You know them?" Demi asks with a look of disgust on her face.

If Becky can be a bitch, Demi can be a fucking mega bitch. They're not close. They've always disliked one another, and somewhere over the years, it's turned to hate.

She looks the same as when I saw her three months ago. Her bleach blond hair is down and in soft waves. Where Becky wears a lot of makeup, Demi barely has any on tonight. Her blue eyes are narrowed, and her usual plump lips are now thin and coated with a shiny gloss.

Seth nods, answering her question. "We attend the University of Texas together. English Lit."

"Forgot you guys went there," Demi mumbles.

Liar. She knows where we go to school. She just doesn't care. About anyone. Another quality she and her sister share.

"I want some popcorn," Becky announces, looking over at the popcorn cart to the right of us. "It smells amazing."

"Then get some," Demi tells her, tossing her hair over to one shoulder. Seth goes to place his arm around her, but she pulls away from him. He doesn't seem upset in the least.

I wonder if he's ever tried to fuck that stick out of her ass?

Becky's face falls. "I left my purse in the car." She holds up a twenty-dollar bill. "All I have is enough to get in."

"Why?" Demi asks.

"I didn't wanna carry it in here. Not after Austin said I may have to run or crawl for my life." She shivers at that thought, and Austin laughs.

"Just go and get your money," Demi suggests, rolling her eyes.

"We parked too far away. I don't wanna make you guys wait for me." She sighs. "It's fine."

Gotta give a little to get a little, I tell myself. "I'll get it for you." Becky looks at me with wide eyes. Austin gives me a soft smile, but Demi looks at me suspiciously as if she's on to my plan. "Anyone else want some?" I ask, not taking my eyes off Becky's. I am trying to be nice tonight.

"I'll get my own," Demi announces while everyone else tells me, *"No thanks."*

Walking over to the popcorn stand, I stand behind the only other two people in line. I'm not a fan of the shit. It gets stuck in your teeth, and they never give me as much butter as I like. So, I pull a piece of gum out of my pocket and pop it in my mouth.

"Still her little bitch boy, I see."

"Excuse me?" I turn around to find Demi standing behind me in line with her arms crossed over her chest. Her blue eyes glare up at me.

"Gotta say, I admired your lack of empathy. Until now."

"What are you talking about?" I growl. Demi knows nothing about me.

She pops her right hip out. Her blue eyes drop to my tennis shoes and slowly run up over my jeans and T-shirt before meeting mine again. "Men always think with their dicks," she says.

I give her my back, dismissing her. *She's a child.* And someone I don't like, so I'm going to ignore her the rest of the night.

I get the popcorn and return to my friends, not bothering to wait for Demi. Becky gives me a mumbled thank you. I return it with a smile, and she looks up at me suspiciously. *Yeah, baby. I'm feeding you full of bullshit, and I'm gonna cram it down your throat until you choke on it.*

We get our wristbands that allow us into the first attraction and make our way over to the black building with a banner that reads *Fright Night* on it. As we walk through the entrance, Austin sneaks up behind Becky, places her hands on her sides, and screams in her ear. Becky jumps so fucking high she could have dunked a basketball had she been on a court.

"I think she pissed her pants." Seth laughs, throwing Demi's now empty bag of popcorn in the trash can as we pass it.

Austin covers her mouth to muffle her laughter. "Sorry …"

"No, you're not." Becky pulls away from her.

"I don't even know why you came," Demi growls. "You hate anything even remotely scary." Then her blue eyes slide to mine before looking away.

What was that for?

"Watch what you say and where you look. For it may blind your sight and take your voice," a creepy man sings while he stands in a corner and gestures to a hallway on his left.

We enter a makeshift room no bigger than the entryway to Cole's house with black walls and ceiling. Creepy Halloween music plays softly through the hidden speakers. The girls are standing there, waiting for us to pack ourselves inside. Cole walks up behind Austin and places his arms around her chest. Seth pulls Demi into his side, and she looks like she wants to push him away but won't due to the cramped space. Becky stands next to me awkwardly, biting her lip nervously.

We all stare at a girl who sits in a white clawfoot tub against the opposite wall. Water black as night, not allowing you to see through it, fills the bath, coming all the way up to the sides. She's wearing a dirty, cheaply made replica of a straitjacket, and the wet fabric clings to her small frame. You can tell she isn't wearing a bra because you can see her hard nipples poking through the thin fabric, showcasing a set of big tits.

A man who looks to be about our age kneels beside the tub. He gently runs his hand down the back of her wet, dark hair. "Did you learn your lesson?" he asks her sternly.

Her body shakes uncontrollably, her lips are blue, and her eyes are red from crying. She has tears running down her face, leaving black streaks in their wake. She turns to look at us; gray eyes meet mine, and she whispers. "Help … me …"

He grips a fistful of her hair, and a scream erupts, cutting off her words. Rising to his feet, he bends at the waist and shoves her face-first into the black water. It splashes us, and the girls jump back, but Becky is the only one who screams in surprise.

He holds her under the black liquid surface as she thrashes around, water continuing to splash onto the floor. He yanks her back up, and she gasps for breath. He lowers his face down to hers, pulling her head back by her hair as she openly chokes and weeps. His other hand grips her chin tightly. "You will either learn, or you will die," he says simply.

"Please … don't—"

"The choice is always yours." He shoves her head into the water once again.

A door to the left opens, and Cole pushes Austin through it, entering a hallway. She's trying to look over his shoulder at the girl still submerged. Once we're through the door, it slams shut behind us.

"I wanted to see how long she could hold her breath." Austin pouts, disappointed.

"Long enough," he tells her.

The hallway curves to the right, and we follow it. It's narrow and only allows you enough space to walk single file. Cole grabs Austin's hand, taking the lead, so I take up the back. She rolls her eyes and then bumps into his back when he takes another turn and comes to a stop.

We've reached an opening. A man stands before us in a white lab coat covered in blood. His arms lie against his chest and cross at his wrists. He lifts his eyes to us, and a light that he has around his forehead shines on us. "Separate," he demands.

The main hallway splits, leading to the different doors. Cole drags Austin through the one closest to them. Demi and her boyfriend go through the second one, leaving me and Becky alone. She bites her bottom lip nervously, and I refrain from smiling.

I can do far worse things to you than anyone in this haunted house could possibly think of, baby.

I gesture for her to enter. "After you."

She sighs heavily and then enters. It's dark, but the light that comes through the seams in the makeshift wall is enough for me to see where the hallway leads us.

"Where do we go?" she asks, and her voice shakes with fear of what is to come.

She thinks something is going to jump out at us, grab her, and drag her to hell. I laugh at that thought. *Honey, I'm the closest to hell you can get.*

A scream erupts from the left, behind the wall, and she jumps, bringing her hands to her pounding chest.

"Here, let me get in front of you." Reaching out, I place my hands on her shoulders and push her behind me. She grips my upper arms and doesn't let go. Another sound to my right has my head whipping in that direction. It's a door, and a light shines from the room on the other side of it. A man dressed in all black stands there. You can't see his face through the black mesh mask over it.

Becky shrieks, pressing her body into mine. "Please don't touch me," she begs.

I nod to the guy and push open the door, leading us into a new room. A woman lies on what looks like a hospital gurney. She wears a dingy gown that has been torn. Her wrists and ankles are strapped to the bed with brown leather straps and blood drips from the restraints. She tries to sit up, but the straps across her chest and stomach prevent any movement. A man stands next to her, his back toward us as he faces a white table.

"Okay, Beatrice. Do you know why I have to do this to you?" he asks.

She stares up at the ceiling, no longer struggling. The only movement is her chest rising and falling slowly. "Because I survived," she whispers, and Becky stiffens against me.

"Very good," he praises her. "But why did you do it?" he asks.

She swallows, and whispers, "Because the voices told me to."

I look at the dirty floor and see a bloody razor blade by the bed. The blood running from her bound wrists suddenly makes sense. She's suicidal. She told him that voices told her to kill herself, and now she's being punished because she survived.

He walks to the head of the gurney and stands, wearing the same black costume as the man out in the hall sans mask. She arches her back, looking up at him longingly as though they're lovers. "Don't worry, I'm gonna make them go away." He snaps a brown leather belt between his fists, and she opens up her mouth for him. Her hips rise, and she moans as if it's turning her on. He places it between her teeth and runs his knuckles gently down the side of her cheek. She lets out a muffled groan, and then he reaches over and grabs two paddles, pressing them to her temples. The lights flicker on and off as her restrained body thrashes in the bed.

Becky buries her head into my chest. "Jesus, this place isn't scary. It's fucked up."

I smile. Yeah, it is. I like it.

I grab her hand, and we exit the door to the right and come to a new room with two more doors. Austin and Cole come through the one to the left. Demi and her boyfriend to the right. Austin is smiling like a kid in a candy store. Demi looks bored.

A door opening to the right has Becky jumping back, causing Demi to laugh at her expense. We follow each other into the next room. The floor and all four walls have tiles that once were white, but now are brown and have been stained with blood on them.

A small woman stands with her nose to the far wall, her back to us. She's completely naked. Scratches run up and down her back and thighs. Blood trails down them and pools at her feet. Her blond hair is tangled and dirty. A man stands behind her holding a hose. He turns it on and sprays her, and she screams as the water hits her skin and splashes us. Smoke instantly fills the room so you think it's steam from the hot water. Becky grips my shirt as it quickly engulfs the space, making it hard to see. I cover my mouth and push through a door just as Becky lets go of me. The lights shut off, leaving us in complete darkness, and a small body runs into my back. "Shit." I hear her hiss.

"Here." I reach back and take her hand. Putting my free hand on the wall to the right of me, I slide it across the area. It curves to the right, and I follow it, pulling Becky behind me. She doesn't say anything or try to pull away.

My hand comes to a new wall, and it's right in front of me. "What the fuck …?" *It's a dead end.* I sigh. Silence meets me. No more music plays from above, and I don't hear any screams off in the distance. "Cole?" He doesn't answer. "Austin?" Still nothing. "Guess it's just us." I turn around to head back to where we came from and run right into her. We both trip over our tangled feet and her back hits a wall. "Becky," I breathe. My body is up against hers, pinning her in place.

Her heavy breathing fills the silent hallway. I have to remind myself why I hate her so much and how this is just a game I intend to win.

My hands grip her wrists, pinning them down to her mattress. She arches her neck, and I kiss my way up the soft skin to her ear. "I love you," she whispers.

I pause and pull away to look down at her. Blue eyes fill with tears, and she sniffs. "I love you, Deke—"

"I love you too, Becky," I interrupt, then kiss her.

I make love to her, showing her just how much she means to me. Her face is flushed, her hair a wild mess, and her lips swollen. She looks absolutely fucking perfect. "Tell me again," I order, pushing my hips forward. She no longer belongs to that fuckface David. He went off to college and dumped her like the ass I knew him to be. Cole is busy playing with his new toy, Austin. Becky is all mine, and she fills the hole left in my heart from my three dead friends. She makes it go away. I'm never going to let her go now that she's all mine.

"I love you." She gasps, licking her lips. "I love you ..."

I slam my lips to hers again.

This fucking bitch never loved me. We slept with each other and with other people for a long time to hide how we really felt for one another, so I'm not innocent in this situation. But I believed it would be me and her in the long run, and then she played me. If I were an honest loser, I would bow and tell her good fucking job. But I'm a sore loser. Especially at my own game.

Her hands come up to my chest, and I smile in the darkness. *That's right, baby, come to me. Let yourself think I'll save you from the darkness when I'm really gonna drown you in it.* Mine go to her hips, and I slide my fingers in the belt loops of her jeans.

"Deke, I'm ..." She whispers so softly that I barely hear her, but the sound travels straight to my dick, and it goes hard on its own. Fuck, I want to pin her down and fuck my hate out on her. She gasps when I rub my hips into hers.

"I know, baby." She can't deny it anymore. She wants me, just not like I want her.

My hands leave her jeans and trail up her sides and then my

knuckles skim over her breasts through her shirt. Her heavy breathing fills the confined blackness we have found ourselves in alone. I run my hand over the skin of her neck, and I can feel her pulse racing. And like before, she doesn't stop me and makes no move to push me away, so I push a little further. My hand fists her hair, and I gently pull her head back. She's panting when I skim my lips against hers. My other hand cups her face, and I can feel the tremble in her body pushed up against mine.

I smile to myself.

"I'm gonna kiss you now," I give her one warning. One chance to push me away or kick me in the balls. If she doesn't, who knows how far this will go right here and now. I've got three months of pent-up aggression for this woman, and I'll make her like every fucking moment of it.

Her hands fist my shirt, and I chuckle before pressing my lips to hers. Her body goes stiff against mine. I move my hand on her face down to wrap around her waist and grip her ass over her jeans, rubbing my hips into hers again. She begins to soften. Her hands come up to wrap around my neck, and my kiss grows frantic when her tongue sweeps over mine. She tastes different. She used to remind me of fresh air—the woman I loved. A woman I planned to spend the rest of my life with. Silly, right? Now she tastes like betrayal and bitterness—the lying little slut I know her to be. And for some reason, that turns me on even more. No more pretending. No more lies. I can fucking hate her while making her love me.

My hand tightens in her hair, and she whimpers into my mouth. She pulls away from the kiss, and I spin her around to face the wall I had her back pressed up against. She gasps as I press her chest into the wall. I push my hips forward, letting her feel my hard dick rubbing on her ass. She never gave that up to me, but she will this time. My right hand still holds her by her hair, and the other comes around her waist to undo the button on her jeans. She sucks in breath after breath as I slide my fingers down into her lace underwear. When I make it to her shaved pussy, she whimpers. I can't help but chuckle to myself because she's so fucking wet.

That's something no woman can fake.

I smirk in the darkness and lean down to kiss her neck when I pull her head back. She wears the same perfume that reminds me of cherries, and it makes my mouth water. "Miss me, baby?" I nip at the skin, pushing two fingers into her. Her breath hitches as she squirms under my touch. I pull them out and then slide them in again. "I missed this fucking pussy wrapped around my cock … sitting on my face …"

She tilts her head back farther, twisting in my grasp, and her lips find mine. She's frantic, nipping my lips with her teeth and sucking on my tongue. She twists in my arms, and her nails dig into my neck. My fingers work in and out of her while she bucks her hips. Yanking her head back, she sucks in a deep breath and one of her hands goes to my hard dick. She presses on it through my jeans. I expect her to take it out and start stroking it, but she doesn't. I add a third finger, and a strangled cry rips though the darkness as her pussy tightens around my fingers. "Fuck, baby. Come for me," I order, panting myself. "Show me how much you've missed me."

She pulls my lips to hers again, and I feel her body shudder against mine while my thumb massages her clit, and then she's coming all over my fingers. She whimpers into my mouth, her shaking body clinging to mine, and her nails digging into my skin as I hold her to me. I knew it wouldn't be hard to make her weak.

I'm just about to undo my pants and fuck her right here inside this haunted house when her hands hit my chest, and she shoves me back. When I reach out, all I feel is wall. "Becky?" I reach to my right. Nothing.

I spin around as a light shines in my eyes, and I blink quickly at the invasion. "Hey, man. Sorry about that. We're having some electrical difficulties in this building. Everyone has to exit this part of the tour." It's the guy from the first scene. The one who was giving the woman in a straitjacket hydrotherapy. His jeans and shirt drip water onto the floor. He smiles at me and gestures to a door behind me with his flashlight, that I hadn't found earlier.

"Thanks," I grumble, readjusting my hard dick.

I shove open the door and look across a courtyard to see Austin and Cole talking to Becky and Seth while they stand next to a few vendors.

Cole looks up and spots me walking toward them. "Where the hell have you been?" he asks.

"Got lost." I look at Becky, and she doesn't even acknowledge me. Just bows her head and takes a drink of the Coke in her hand.

I smirk. *She's embarrassed.* Cute.

"How did you get lost?" Austin asks. "They kicked us out the moment the lights went off."

"Huh?" I question, looking away from Becky to her.

Austin pops some Sour Patch gummies in her mouth before answering. "The lights went out. I thought it was the blackout attraction." She frowns, clearly disappointed. "But a guy grabbed Cole and ushered us all out here."

I look at Becky. Her drink is almost gone. And I frown. *How did she ...?* "How long have you been out here?" My question is directed at her. She gives me her back, turning to face Austin, still ignoring me.

I roll my eyes at her. So, we're going to pretend I didn't just get her off in a haunted house.

"Oh, there you are, babe," Seth calls out.

We all spin around to see Demi coming toward us. Her blond hair is now up in a messy bun on top of her head, but she has a smug smile on her face. Not her usual scowl. It makes me frown.

"Where did you go?" he asks her. "I've been worried."

I look back at Becky, and she still faces away from me. My eyes scan over her jeans and tennis shoes. Then I look over her shirt and notice she's wearing a jacket. She didn't have that on a minute ago. Maybe she went to my SUV and got it. But then I realize I have the keys in my pocket.

I start to get a sickening feeling in my stomach. *Oh, God no ...* I look back at Demi.

Her blue eyes meet mine before returning to her boyfriend. "Restroom." Then she blows a bubble.

"Hey, I asked if you had gum earlier, and you said no."

Her eyes find mine again. And my entire body goes rigid as fear creeps up my spine.

"I didn't. Borrowed it from a friend."

"Have any more?" he asks her.

"Nope. But you can have this one." She puts her finger in her mouth, twirls it around and pulls it out with the gum on the end. He places her finger in his mouth, and he sucks it off.

I think I'm going to vomit. Was that my gum? Did I kiss and finger Becky or was it fucking Demi?

Fuck! Fuck! Fuck! This can't be happening ... No! It was Becky. No doubt in my mind. It was Becky! *Wasn't it?*

"Mmm, cinnamon," he says, nodding his head.

FOUR

DEMI

THE LOOK ON Deke's face is priceless. The bastard really had no idea who the fuck I was. How did he not know I wasn't Becky? I told him earlier that guys only think with their dicks, and I just proved myself right. All he needed was a willing body, and he pounced. It didn't fucking matter who I was.

My eyes go to Cole who stands next to Austin with his hands in the front pockets of his jeans, staring at me and Deke. I smile sweetly at him, but he doesn't return it because he knows something is up. That's Cole Reynolds for you. Always fucking watching. Always aware of what is going on around him. He has to be three steps ahead of everyone and ready to pounce if need be.

Everyone else is oblivious to Deke's unease and my smug smile. All in their own little world talking about pointless shit.

"Aww, man. I'm out." Austin pouts, crumpling her empty bag of gummies.

"I'll get you some more." I take the opportunity to walk away and make my way over to the somewhat long line while everyone decides if we're going to stay at this pathetic freak show or call it a night. This place just doesn't do it for me. I like to be scared. I like the thrill—heart racing, paralyzing fear—and this place doesn't give me that. Throw spiders on me or chase me down with a knife. Hell, lock me in a tomb and make me think I was buried alive. If I wanted to watch a woman being drowned in a bathtub, I would stay home and watch a Lifetime movie about a jealous boyfriend.

I just pull my cell out of my back pocket to check the time when I'm spun around. Deke stands there, glaring down at me. His blue eyes shimmering with rage. *Guess the shock has worn off.*

"What the fuck was that?" he demands.

"That was an orgasm," I answer. "Thanks, by the way." My legs are still wobbly. I had to take a minute for myself after I came. I ran to the bathroom and cleaned myself up the best I could, but my underwear is still soaked.

He shoves his hands through his dark hair aggressively, making it look sexier than it already did. The muscles in his arms stretch his white shirt to the point I think the seams may burst. His arms fall to his sides, and he takes in a deep breath. "Why the fuck didn't you stop me?" he growls.

That is the million-dollar question. *I could have.* But why would I? I can't stand either one of them. I wanted him to think he was getting a piece of his ex. And hell, he got me off. I'm not going to lie, that was a surprise. Who knew Deke wouldn't have any problems in that area? I always saw him as just one of the other self-absorbed GWS who only cared about what he got out of it. "I tried to tell you who I was."

"Bullshit," he snaps, and the girl behind us narrows her eyes on him. "You took my gum ... then stuck it in your boyfriend's mouth." His dark blue eyes widen. "Fuck, your boyfriend ..." he trails off.

"Eww," the girl says in disgust.

I smile. "And?"

"And ... and ... and fuck, Demi! I thought you were your sister!" His pretty blue eyes look pained as they stare down at me at a total loss.

"Gross," the girl adds.

I bite my bottom lip to keep from laughing but fail. My body shakes with it. I've never seen Deke Biggs so furious and confused at the same time. It's a good look on him. "You dumped her," I remind him.

"Yes, but ..."

"If I remember correctly, back in Collins, you told her unless she planned on falling to her knees and opening that mouth of hers so you could fuck it, you had no use for her."

He opens his mouth, but the girl behind us gasps. "You're such a pig."

"Then get the fuck away from me," he snaps at her, then turns back to me. She huffs but doesn't leave the line. "You were listening to us?" he demands.

I shrug. "Thin walls." Lie. Of course, I was. My sister was finally getting what she deserved. She's a manipulative bitch who spreads her legs for anyone with a dick. She's a male version of them. The GWS. Well, Cole has seemed to change. And the huge rock on Austin's finger proves that.

"I can't believe this," he growls, running a hand down his face.

Placing my hand on his chest, I feel his entire body stiffen. I'm pretty sure he quits breathing as he towers over me. I step into him, pushing my hips into his on purpose to see if he's still hard. He's not, and a part of me is disappointed at that. "You liked it," I tell him, and he says nothing. "You *were* hard," I add.

"Demi ..." He growls my name in warning, and his chest rises slowly as if he's finally taking a deep breath.

"And ..." I lean in, standing up on my tiptoes, and I press my lips to his ear. The smell of his cologne makes my pussy tighten. Deke may be a fucking ruthless dick, but he sure is mouthwateringly delicious. "You would have fucked me if I had told you to."

He pulls back from me as if I've slapped him. He grips my upper arm, his fingers digging into my sensitive skin, and yanks me out of line to drag me behind the vendor trailer. People walk around with their faces painted like skeletons, and girls flaunt their bodies in little costumes to show the sluts they really are, but no one pays us any attention.

I giggle. A speaker on the back of the trailer plays "My Demons" by Starset. "Round two ...?"

He shoves my back into the trailer so hard that it takes my breath away for a second and cuts off my words. Pressing his body into mine again, he places both hands flat against the truck on either side of my head. His blue eyes cloud over like a storm moving in on a sunny day and darkening the world. His lips thin, and his chest rumbles against mine with a growl.

A slow warmth runs up my spine and neck, making me hot even though the night air is cool. Deke Biggs has a side I actually like. Who would have known? My eyes drop to the black belt around his dark jeans, and my fingers itch to undo it just to see how far he'd let me go now that he knows I'm not my sister. I have a feeling I wouldn't have to push him much. My eyes find his again.

"Want me to please you this time?" I lick my lips.

"You will keep your mouth shut!" he orders, ignoring my question. "About what you heard me and Becky talking about. And what we just did!"

I give him a slow and innocent smile and decide to push him. How much will it take before he snaps? "How are you gonna keep me from running my mouth, Deke?" Lifting my right hand, I run my finger down his shirt. He's shaking with anger, and his muscles flex. Fuck, his body is as hard as a rock. I bite my bottom lip and lower my hand to cup his limp dick over his jeans. He doesn't budge and just goes still as a statue like a minute ago when we were in line. "Gonna fuck it?"

"Jesus!" he hisses. Stepping away from me, he turns away, giving me his back, and grips his dark hair.

A girl dressed as a slutty Little Bo Peep walks by and eyes him up and down while she holds the hand of a guy dressed as the Grim Reaper. Deke doesn't even look at her. All of his attention is on me, even if he isn't looking my way. I'd bet anything he's thinking about what we did when he thought I was Becky. Would he do it again now that he knows it was me? Absolutely not. And that thought disappoints me.

I smile at the look of him. So undone. Nothing like the pathetic boy who fell to his knees for my sister. "Afraid I can't keep a secret …"

He spins back around, and his hand wraps around my neck, cutting off my words before I can finish. "You'll keep your goddamn mouth shut 'cause I told you to," he growls.

His face is so close to mine that if I puckered my lips, I'd kiss him. I can still smell the cinnamon on his breath from his gum. My thighs tighten, remembering the way he kissed me back in the haunted house. He was rough and unapologetic, and I liked it. He thought I was Becky, and he was angry with her. He meant to hurt her, and that turned me on.

Hurt me, Deke.

"Demi!" He barks out my name when I don't acknowledge his order.

Slowly, my eyes look over his sharp jaw and parted full lips. He's so full of rage he's panting. I think the guy wants to snap me in half. I wonder what it would feel like to have him on top of me, holding me down and fucking me. I've heard him fuck my sister, but I thought she was faking it. She's always been a good actress.

I could be better.

"Demi, I swear to fucking God …"

My eyes finally meet his, and his words cut off. My heart begins to pound as I stare into the most beautiful blue eyes I've ever seen. But Deke Biggs is more than just a pretty boy. There's a darkness that covers him in madness and lust.

I feel it.

I see it.

I want it.

My silence pisses him off more, and his hand tightens around my throat, restricting my airway.

I don't fight him. His anger just turns me on, making my already soaked thong even more so. I always thought he was too soft for Becky. The kids in Collins feared the sharks, but that was because of Cole. They were all capable of terrifying things, but Deke and Becky? He was a pussy when it came to her. It was pathetic. Maybe she didn't challenge him. Not like I can. She held him back when I would set the monster free.

Chase me.

Hurt me.

Fuck me.

My tongue peeks out between my parted lips, and I run it along my lip. His eyes follow the movement like a moth to a flame. Just as my lungs scream for breath, and tears begin to prick my eyes, he releases me and steps back. I take a deep breath, swallowing roughly.

"Fuck! You're underage," he mutters to himself.

I laugh at that. "I'm not even a year younger than Becky." Our mother couldn't keep her legs closed for long after she had my sister. Less than eleven months after Becky was born, I arrived. A month early.

"That's not the point," he snaps and spins back to me. He points his finger in my face as though I'm an unruly child.

The thought pisses me off. He thinks he can treat me differently than her, but what makes her so goddamn special and me nothing? I've never been close to my sister, but I've hated her the last couple of years. Ever since she tried to take something from me, I vowed I was going to make her pay. No matter what I had to do, I was going to break her fucking cold, dead heart. And this is it. The man standing in front of me is what I've been looking for. He doesn't know it yet, but I'm about to make him exactly what I need. The last piece in my own personal game to destroy my sister. So, instead of showing my anger, I give him a soft smile.

I open my mouth and lean forward. He stands before me; body stiff and eyes wide as I take his pointed finger into my mouth all the way up to the knuckle. The same one that still tastes like me because it was just inside me twenty minutes ago. My eyes stay trained on his, and I watch as his pupils dilate when I wrap my lips around his finger, then run my tongue along the bottom and slowly suck until it pops out. Then I lick my lips. "Wanna kiss me now, Deke?"

He doesn't answer. He doesn't even blink. Blue eyes burn into mine, and there's a tic in his jaw. My eyes drop down to his jeans and bingo! He's fucking hard. Because of me.

"Deke?"

He jumps at the sound of his name before looking away from me. Cole stands to the right, behind the trailer with us, holding Austin's new bag of gummies in his hand. "Everything okay?" he asks. His blue eyes narrow in suspicion as he studies us.

Deke doesn't answer. Instead, he just storms off, leaving me against the truck without so much as looking back.

Cole watches him leave, then his eyes come back to mine, void of any emotion. For as long as I've known him, unless he's angry, he looks bored. I always thought he and Deke could pass as brothers, but where Cole is lean, Deke is bulkier. They're the same height with blue eyes and brown hair, but Deke's is a little darker. They've worn the same cut for as long as I can remember—short on the sides, long on top, and spiked to perfection. It was the GWS way. It's as if all the guys on the swim team at Collins High said *let's look the same and make the girls beg us for attention.* It worked. Fucking bastards.

I push off the trailer and wink at him as I walk by. "It was good seeing you, Cole." Then I laugh.

BECKY

I look up from my phone just in time to watch Deke storm by us. I spin around to see Demi also walking our way with Cole right behind her carrying Austin's gummies.

What is she doing with him?

"What's wrong with Deke?" Austin asks Cole with a frown as she looks over her shoulder and watches him stomp away from us, headed toward the parking lot.

Yes. We're leaving.

My sister was wrong earlier when she said I hate anything scary, but I didn't correct her. She's just a bitch who likes to piss me off. I came tonight to get on Deke's good side. He almost kissed me in the kitchen back at Austin's house, and I know he planned to seduce me.

Of course, I'm going to lie down and give it to him. Deke and I have this love-hate kind of relationship. Even back when we were fucking and I had a boyfriend, I knew I loved him. I just couldn't be with him and him alone. It was … complicated. Now things are in damage control. I fucked up, and I've got to redeem myself.

It's possible, but it'll just take a lot of work. Possibly a lot of time on my knees. But a girl's got to do what a girl's got to do.

"We're leaving," Cole snaps. He takes Austin's hand and begins to drag her toward the parking lot.

I start to follow them.

"See you later, sis," Demi calls out.

I turn and give my sister a tight smile. She stands with her arms crossed over her chest and a fucking smile on her face. What the fuck is she up to? Ignoring her, I toss my hair over my shoulder, then I turn and walk off after them.

By the time I make it to Deke's Range Rover, he's already got it started and shifted in reverse. I jump into the back seat behind him. The tires grip the gravel, and he backs us out of the spot.

Austin pouts beside me. "I really wanted to do the blackout attraction."

"We'll come back," Cole promises.

I'll make sure to stay home for that one. Putting myself in a situation where I can't see is not my idea of fun. Especially with Deke.

Austin shoves some gummies in her mouth and then pulls her cell out of Cole's hoodie pocket that she's still wearing. "Have I shown you Lilly's Halloween consume?" she asks me.

I refrain from sighing. This is her life now. Lilly and Cole. Cole and Lilly.

I really like Austin, even if I was forced into a friendship with her. She was fun and always up for a hit or a drink. But now that we've moved to Texas, she's changed. Ever since she almost died, Cole keeps her on a tight leash. As if someone still plans to hurt her. She waits on the guys and Lilly nonstop. She makes them breakfast, lunch, and dinner. She takes Lilly to and from school. I popped by yesterday when I knew the guys were in class to ask if she wanted to go to the mall, and she turned me down. She said she had to finish laundry and then clean the kitchen. All before running Lilly to ballet.

She has become a fucking mom.

It's a total disappointment.

I honestly don't know how she ended up with Cole. Well, that's not the truth. I've read her deepest, darkest secrets. She doesn't know that, but what's that saying? What you don't know can't hurt you? She's so full of life, and Cole is just a black hole.

He's hot. I've always had a thing for him but never went there. His loyalty to Deke is unwavering, and I have a fear of being alone with him. The guy has death vibes, and I don't want to die.

I thought she could change him, but I think he ended up changing her more. But my question is why? Is it because of money? She came from a poor druggie mother. Her father was wealthy, but she didn't have access to it until she came to live with him at the beginning of this year. I'm not sure what she plans on doing with her life. Be his fucking housewife? Raise Lilly and whatever kids they plan on having?

She could be a stay-at-home mom and live whatever kind of life she wants because he has money too. His mom died when he was twelve, and she left him her millions when he turned eighteen. If I was Austin, I'd have jumped on that too. Hell, her engagement ring is around fifty thousand. I know because I googled that shit. It's some kind of rare ruby. Talk about a reason to lie down and spread your legs. The sad part is her expectations are so low that she would have been fine with a rubber band. She has no idea how much it cost him, and she would never ask him because she couldn't care less. And he'd never tell her because that's just Cole.

"It's a bee." She beams, showing me the picture.

Lilly's standing in a dressing room with a bumble bee costume on. Her blond curls up in pigtails and her hands on her hips.

"Adorable." I nod my head as if I fucking care.

"Isn't she?" She tilts the screen toward her and smiles down at it.

I roll my eyes and look out the window. I was supposed to move in with them but decided against it after Deke told me Cole ratted me out. He disclosed to Deke and Austin that I was the one driving the car the night their three friends died. He also snitched that I was fucking Eli. Well, that was only half the truth. I hadn't quite made it that far yet.

That fucker.

He only ever does shit in his best interest. After Deke told me he had enough information to *bury me,* I decided against living under the same roof as a killer. I chose to move in with my mother and stepdad. And of course, Deke moved in with them instead.

It's not awkward when it's just Austin and me, but whenever Cole is home, I tense, waiting for him to get me alone and tell me he's going to make me pay for the lie I told him. When I lied that I was pregnant.

Junior year

Cole's car is upside down. Smoke makes it hard to see anything. My entire body aches, and I feel dizzy.

"Eli?" Cole coughs. "Mad ... dox?"

Pain slices through my stomach, and I cry out.

"You okay?" he asks, coughing again.

We're both hanging upside down—our seat belts keeping us in place. The smoke has cleared, and I can see that the entire windshield is gone. I feel blood running from my nose. "I don't know ... what happened," I cry. One minute, I was driving, then the next, the car was flipping.

"We gotta get out of the car," he says. "Eli? Landen?" he screams, making me flinch.

I sob. What did I do? I've been drinking, but I don't feel drunk. Had I had too much? I thought I could drive.

I hear Cole feeling around, then he places his hand on the ceiling and releases his seat belt. He falls on his face. "FFFUUCCCKKK!" he growls. He gets out of his broken passenger side window and stumbles over to my side. He gets down on his knees and looks at me through where my window once was. "Cover your face." He stands, kicking what's left of the big pieces off the edge. "I'm gonna have to undo your seat belt. Put your hands on the ceiling."

I continue to sob as he gets me out. I fall to my knees and grab my stomach. My crop top is ripped, and I'm bleeding. My hands shake.

"Eli? Maddox? Landen?" He calls out, but no one answers. "I gotta call 911." He pats down his pockets. "Fuck!" he growls when he can't find his phone.

I continue to sob, and he drops to his knees beside me. "Are you okay? What hurts?"

I look up at him. "I ... I ..." I don't know what to say. I can't get caught with them. Not like this. My father will kill me, and my mother will make me move to Texas to live with her. And I refuse to give up my life here.

"What is it?" he asks.

Cole is a fucking shark. A twisted soul. But I've never seen his blue eyes filled with so much concern. The guys have to be dead. They weren't in the car with us, and they're not answering when he calls out to them. And I can't go down for that. I can't go to jail.

So I take advantage of this rare side of Cole and wrap my arms around my stomach. "I'm pregnant."

Silence falls over us. An eerie calmness. Like the calm before a catastrophic storm that is going to level everything in its wake. Fresh tears run down my cheeks, and he places his hand on my back. I begin to shake.

"Go," he says.

I look up at him. Could it be that easy? I pretend like I have a conscience. "But ..."

"Go, Becky," he orders. "I'll take care of this. You need to get out of here." Then without saying another word, he stands and begins to walk along the street, looking for his dead friends.

I knew if I told him I was with child, then he would tell me to run. I didn't want to get caught up in that bullshit. My parents would have killed me if they knew I was driving drunk and wrecked Cole's car. They all thought I was sober, and that's why I drove. Big fucking mistake. But I wasn't about to take the fall for it.

But when Cole confessed that truth to Deke, he knew I had lied about being pregnant. Cole hasn't mentioned that to me yet, which can only mean one thing—Deke hasn't told him the truth. That's what gives me hope that we can still have a future. That he doesn't hate me completely yet. He's keeping my secret as if it's his own.

He's protecting me. A part of him still loves me, and that's all I need to know to move forward with my plan to win him back.

My phone vibrates, and I unlock the screen to see I have a new message.

You still coming tomorrow?

Me: Yes. My flight leaves at 6:45 in the morning.

I turn the brightness down on my phone, so it doesn't draw attention.

Do they know you're coming?

Me: Nope.

Good. I'll see you then.

I lock my phone and smile as I look out the window. I've been back to Collins a few times since we've moved to Texas. I hate that place, but I have unfinished business there.

Deke pulls up to Cole and Austin's house and jumps out, still not saying a word. It's obvious he's pissed. I need to try to smooth things over with him. I ignored him earlier when we were with the others at Silence because I didn't want them questioning me. Austin would be all over that. She still thinks we can work through our problems, but my sister would just tell me I'm a stupid fucking bitch.

They both need to understand that I don't give a fuck what they think. I don't want their opinions or need their advice.

We enter the house, and Misty greets us.

Reaching into his jeans pocket, Cole grabs his wallet and pulls out some cash. "Here you go …"

The teenager waves him off. "Mr. Biggs already paid me before you left earlier."

"Deke," he growls.

"It was my idea," he mumbles before storming up the stairs and slamming his bedroom door.

"Thank you, Misty," Austin tells her. "I'll walk you over to your house."

"I'll do it," Cole interjects, and she doesn't argue.

Austin turns to face me. "Want me to take you home?"

I look up at the top of the stairs and then at her. "Yeah." Tonight is not the night to try anything with Deke. I'm not in the mood to kiss his ass or suck his dick. Plus, I've got an early flight out in the morning.

"Wait until I get back and I'll drive you guys," Cole orders Austin.

"I can drive myself, Cole." She sighs.

Just when I think he's going to argue with her, he bends down and kisses her forehead. "Hurry back, sweetheart."

"Deke was being nice tonight." Austin speaks once we're alone in her car. "Until he wasn't."

"Yeah," I mumble. "He can be like any other man. Hormonal."

She laughs. "Things will work out."

"I know." Because I'm going to force them to. Just like Cole forced me into being friends with her.

I walk through the back door and step out onto the patio of the Reynolds' house. I stop when I see Cole swimming laps in their Olympic size swimming pool. I knew he'd be here. Even before the car wreck, he lived in the water. It's only been six weeks, but it hasn't slowed him down. Now he uses it for his physical therapy because he can't afford to lose his position as captain on the swim team.

"What You Deserve" by No Resolve plays through the outside speakers while he swims his laps.

He stops and pops his head out of the water. I know he feels me watching him. I shouldn't have come, but he's been ignoring my phone calls. Running both hands through his hair, he steps out of the pool and looks at me.

"Isn't it too soon to swim?" I ask, sitting on one of the chaise lounge chairs under the awning.

He doesn't answer. Taking the towel off the table, he wipes his face.

I hang my head. "I've been texting you. I came up to the hospital."

"I didn't want to see you then, and I don't want to see you now," he snaps and rolls his shoulders.

Tears instantly spring to my eyes. "I lost someone too, Cole. Eli was my friend too ..." I lie. He wasn't my friend. I barely knew him, but I'm too ashamed to say that out loud. And now I can't let anyone find out I was there or what I had planned that night.

"No, you were just another girl he was fucking."

His words sting, even if they aren't true. I jump to my feet. "You don't know ..."

He wraps his hand around my throat and pushes me back against the wall of the pool house. He's in my face, growling, "You have no fucking clue what I lost! What I did for you!"

I take in a shaky breath. "I'm so sorry." Tears run down my cheeks. I'm not sorry for walking away from the accident. I'm sorry for ever being there. "You shouldn't have taken the fall." I've never known Cole to be a good guy. I don't know why he took the responsibility for me that night, but I know it will cost me in the long run.

"You shouldn't have been there at all!"

My eyes narrow on him. Then why did he let me walk away? "I was responsible—"

"You wanna owe me, Becky? Huh? Is that why you came here? To tell me that you're fucking sorry that my friends are dead?" he interrupts me.

I swallow nervously against his hand that holds me hostage. I knew he'd make me pay in some way. Cole Reynolds does nothing for free. Hell, maybe he saw this coming and knew he could use me.

"I owe you, Cole," I whisper after a long second, accepting my fate.

"When I need you for something, you will do what I say?" he asks, arching a brow.

I give him a slow nod, and whisper, "Whatever you need."

"I don't wanna talk to you or fucking see you until then, do you understand?"

I'll gladly stay the hell away from him. "Yes." My shoulders physically shake, and I can't stop the tears that run down my face.

"Good. Now leave." He lets go of my neck and takes a step back from me. I rub my sore throat as he turns and dives back into the

pool.

"The three of us should get together soon." She breaks through my thoughts.

"Three of us?" I ask.

"You, me, and Demi."

"Why?" I can't help but wonder. "We never hung out with her back in Collins."

She shrugs. "I don't know. She just seems … sad. Maybe she didn't want to move here."

"She didn't have a choice." My mother decided that when I was moving to Texas so was Demi. She hates me for that, but I don't give a fuck.

"Then it's settled. We'll all get together. Maybe have a girls' night."

Like Cole would allow her to do that, but I nod. Hell will freeze over before I'll have a girls' night with my sister.

Placing my head against the window, I think back to the day Cole decided it was time for me to pay up. My payment could have been much worse than the woman sitting beside me.

I stand in the kitchen of the Reynolds' house. Cole is throwing a party tonight during Christmas break before we all go back to school in a few days. I was tired of being holed up in my father's house. I've avoided Cole since he wrapped his hand around my throat months ago, telling me I owed him. I knew Deke was going to be here tonight, and I need to talk to him. See him. I take a drink and set my cup down when I hear my phone go off. I open it up to see I have a text from Cole, and my stomach drops.

Cole: Ready?

I begin to type out what do you mean but delete it. Instead, I settle on just a question mark.

Me: ?

Cole: A friend of mine is coming tonight. You would make a great friend for her too.

Her?

Me: You don't have any girls who are friends.

Who the fuck is he talking about? Cole isn't like the rest of the GWS. He doesn't hang all over girls. He doesn't even speak to them. He only shows interest once he decides he wants to fuck you. And then after you spread your legs for him, he moves on. The girls always try to get more out of him, but it never works.

Cole: Her name is Austin. Brunette. Green eyes. Probably wearing something red. Text me when she gets here.

Austin? Who the hell is that? Collins isn't a big town, but it's also not tiny. Who the hell is she, and why does he want to know when she arrives?

Me: And why do you want to know that?

Cole: It's time to pay up!

Fuck!

I take another sip and then pour myself a new one. Pay up? How the hell am I going to pay up with a girl named Austin? What could he possibly want me to do?

I'm downing it when I catch sight of a brunette entering the kitchen. She's wearing a red sweater that hangs off one shoulder, showcasing a black tank top underneath it with black skinny jeans and matching heels. Her dark hair curls down her back. I've never seen her before, so it has to be her. She picks up a red Solo cup and pours some Fireball into it before tossing it back. Then she pours another one. No one seems to notice her, letting me know that no one else knows her either.

I take out my phone and text him.

Me: She's here. Kitchen.

He reads it but doesn't respond. I take a deep breath and walk over to her, needing to know as much as I can about her before he comes down here. "Hi."

"Hello," *she says with a nod of her head. She's pretty, but I can't say she's Cole's type 'cause he really doesn't have one.*

"I've never seen you here before." *I hold out my right hand.* "I'm Becky."

"Austin. And I just moved here."

How the fuck does she know Cole? "Oh, how exciting," *I lie and grab a new Solo cup. "Are you going to Collins High?" She looks about my age.*

"Yep."

This doesn't make any sense. Maybe his dad is dating someone, and this is her daughter, but even I know that's reaching. His father doesn't really date anyone around here. He just fucks them all. "I'm a senior. How about you?" I pry.

"Same," she answers and pours herself another shot.

"I wonder if we'll have any classes together." Even though I don't know her, it would be nice to have a clean slate. To make a new friend who doesn't really know the real me.

"Who the hell throws a party on a Monday?" she asks, avoiding my previous statement.

"Cole Reynolds." I roll my eyes when I answer, trying to feel her out. I pause to see if she says anything about him, but she doesn't. So I add, "He and the Great White Sharks do whatever they want, whenever they want." I give her a fake smile. Fuck the sharks. Well, all but Deke. "But they do throw some awesome parties."

"Where are their parents?" she asks.

"Never around. They are all socialites in this town with big careers. Always busy and not enough time for their children." I'm rambling and possibly telling her too much. She obviously knows nothing about Cole and the guys, and she said she is new to town. I take a drink to try to calm my nerves.

Where is Cole? He throws these parties all the time, but he stays up in the game room with the rest of the sharks. They very rarely grace us with their presence, and if they do, he ignores everyone. He thinks he's fucking God.

"I see." She nods once.

How does he know her? I've grown up with the GWS, and he's never lived anywhere else. "Where are you –?"

"Austin?"

I look up to see Kellan standing in the kitchen. His brown eyes are narrowed on her, and she arches a brow at his tone.

Fuck ...

"Cole is looking for you," he snaps. "Let's go."

She turns back to look at me, rolling her eyes. Her eyes meet my surprised ones, and she asks, "What?"

I just shake my head 'cause I'm not sure what to say to her. Whatever she's done, it wasn't good. And they will make her pay for it. She ditches her cup and grabs the bottle of Fireball and walks out behind him.

A phone ringing brings me out of that memory, and I look over to see Austin press answer for her hands-free. "Yes?" she asks in greeting.

"Have you dropped her off yet?" Cole's voice fills the SUV.

I roll my eyes and block out their conversation. While Cole told her and Deke that I was driving when we wrecked, he also told them I was forced to befriend her. She might have easily forgiven me for that, but if she knew the other things I did, she'd probably kill me. If Cole didn't beat her to it.

"Thanks," I mumble as she drops me off. I walk up the stairs to my mother's house and walk inside. I make my way up the left staircase to my room when I hear a man whispering.

"Yeah, I told you later."

I come to a stop and look over the balcony to Demi's room. Her bedroom door is cracked open. I tiptoe over to it and peek in. Seth stands at the end of her bed, pacing with his cell to his ear. "I'm only gonna be here for an hour. Then I'll meet you there. Okay. See you then." He pockets his phone just as my sister exits her en suite bathroom. Looking over at her, he plasters a smile on his face.

I yank back so they don't see me and run over to my room, softly shutting the door with a smile. Well, isn't this interesting?

FIVE

DEKE

I SIT AT the kitchen table with my head down and the lights off. It's got to be almost two a.m. After the incident at Silence, we all decided to go home. Well, I stormed off to my Range Rover and the ones who rode with me followed. No one argued or asked what was wrong. I think they could feel the tension and the change in my mood.

I didn't say one word on the way home.

And thankfully, Becky didn't linger. I didn't want to be around her. My plans for the night had backfired, and I had a hard time wrapping my mind around that.

I went straight to my bed, but when I couldn't sleep, my ass came down here and sat. My mind's running circles around itself, getting me nowhere.

The lights come on, and I lift my head to see Cole walking to the fridge wearing his black board shorts with a towel hanging around his neck. His shorts and hair are wet, letting me know he's already been in the pool.

Grabbing two bottles of water, he sets one in front of me before falling into the seat across from me. I refrain from sighing. Usually when he's up late like this, he heads straight back up to his room to be with Austin as soon as he's done with his laps.

But once again, tonight proves to not be on my side.

"What's going on?" he asks.

"Nothing."

He snorts and twists the lid open on his bottle. "Really? You think I'm gonna believe that bullshit?"

I don't answer.

He takes a drink and then sets it back down. "You're fucking Demi."

Jesus! My teeth clench, and my eyes meet his, but I don't say anything to that. It wasn't a question.

He nods once, taking my silence as confirmation and then takes another drink. "Does Becky know?"

If I wasn't so pissed, I would laugh at that. Instead, I shove my chair back and jump to my feet. "It was an accident." Was it? Even that sounds like a lie to me. I knew something felt different, felt off, but I kept going with a smug smile of satisfaction on my face, thinking I was really winning and had got one over on her.

But instead, Demi Holt fucked me. Just not in a good way.

Leaning forward, he places his forearms on the table. "How do you accidentally sleep with someone?" he asks curiously.

"I thought she was Becky." She had acted so willing in this very room just hours before that, that I didn't question her decision to spread her legs for me after going three months without even speaking a word.

Guys only think with their dicks.

Yeah, Demi, I did. But I was hard for your sister, not you, you little bitch.

His brows rise to his hairline. Then he sits back and pushes his wet hair off his forehead. "How did you …?" He pauses, searching for the right words. "I didn't know you and Becky were still fucking."

"We aren't!" I begin to pace. "At Silence, right before the lights shut off, we got separated. I thought I was with Becky. Long story short, I finger-fucked her right then and there while the power was out in the hallway. Then after she came, she split."

"That's why you were so surprised when I told you that we had been outside for a while."

I nod. "That's when Demi showed up, and she had my gum. I started to panic. Then I followed her over to get Austin's gummies, and she confirmed it was her."

"Shit," he whispers.

I nod. "Yes. Shit is right." I look at him. "I called her Becky. She had every chance to stop me, and she didn't. Why the fuck didn't she?" I demand as if he has the answers.

I can't figure out what her angle is. Demi doesn't like me enough to talk to me, let alone allow me to finger-fuck her in a public place. It doesn't make any goddamn sense. Then she acted like I could have fucked her while we stood behind the trailer. And the problem? I wanted to! Fuck, I thought about it. That alone makes me want to throw fucking bleach in my eyes in hopes to erase the memory. I'm still thinking about it.

"So, what's the issue?"

"It's Demi!" My eyes bug out as if that's enough reason to panic. He just stares at me. So I add, "She's underage." That's just one reason out of many why this is so fucked up.

"Legal age of consent in the state of Texas is seventeen." He shrugs before taking another drink. "She's seventeen."

She is but ... "How do you know that?" I ask, coming to a stop. Since when does Cole know Texas law?

A dark look clouds his eyes when he answers. "My dad brought it up back in Oregon regarding Austin and me. And after what I saw between you and Demi earlier, I looked it up. Just to make sure she couldn't get you in trouble."

Even he thinks she was setting me up for something. The sad part? I fell for it. Who knows what I would have done if he hadn't shown up when he did. I run a hand through my hair. "That fucking bitch played me. Then she laughed. As if it was some kind of game to her."

"What are you gonna do about it?" he asks.

Placing my hands on the table, I lean over and look down at my best friend. "I want to show Demi just what kind of game I like to play."

A slow smile spreads across his face, the one that tells me he's up for whatever I want to do. It's been a long time since I've seen it. Whatever Cole is dealing with right now, this could be his distraction. I'm always willing to help my friend out.

He nods. "Let's play."

That bitch doesn't want to fuck with me. I've got all kinds of tricks up my sleeves. I watched the look of satisfaction in her eyes and her smug smile when she sucked on my finger. Fuck, it made me hard. And I tried so goddamn hard not to think about it. Not to feel it. But in the end, she won that round. She thinks she can push me to touch her, to fuck her? She's about to realize she can push me, all right, but it won't get her the result she wants.

DEMI

I lie in my king-size bed, my back propped against the padded white headboard while I watch the documentary *Serial Clown Killer* on YouTube. A serial killer who lived in Illinois known as Pogo the Clown. Hired to perform at birthday parties, he would sexually assault the boys, strangle them with rope, and then bury their bodies under his house. He was put to death in 1994 after being found guilty of thirty-three counts of murder.

Murderers and psychopaths have always fascinated me. I've always wondered how a mind of a serial killer works. What makes them want to kill? And what makes them choose their victims? How do they not get caught? I can see someone getting away with one or maybe two, but more than that? Thirty-three fucking murders before finally being arrested. No way. That would never happen these days. The technology we have now would make it difficult for anyone to slip through the system.

That's what you think, my mind taunts. You know a killer, and he's not locked up in prison or on death row.

Deke told on himself. I overheard him confess what he did to my sister three months ago. I've never cared for the bastard, but it made me respect him a little.

I lean up against my bedroom wall at my father's house, listening to my sister and her boyfriend fight. He looked pissed when he stormed into her room and ordered me to leave.

"I'm sorry ..." she cries out.

"You will be," Deke says, and I snort.

I quickly place my hand over my mouth, hoping they didn't hear that. But honestly, come on? What the hell would he do to her?

"Please, Deke," she begs, and I roll my eyes at the desperation in her voice. "It's not like you haven't kept secrets from me."

"What I did was none of your business," he replies simple as that.

It's how all the sharks work—they can do whatever the fuck they want.

"You lied to me!" she screams. "You killed Kellan!"

Whoa! What the fuck? His friend Kellan has been missing for two months now. After the news broke of him shooting Austin Lowes and killing her stepmom, the authorities have had a manhunt out for him but haven't had any luck finding him. Now I know why.

"I have." He doesn't deny the lies. "Want to know the truth, Becky?" I press my body more into the wall to listen since he's lowered his voice. "I'm a murderer," he admits with no shame. "I've killed five people."

Holy shit! The town is afraid of the GWS, yet my sister always bitched about how harmless they were. I knew they were untouchable. Evil. That's what fascinated me about them the most. They played a stupid game of dare that always went too far and landed them injured most of the time. Or in trouble with the law. But a group of kids whose parents have endless pockets mean you never have to pay for your actions.

"Do you wanna be my sixth?"

She gasps.

And I can just see her body trembling in fear right now.

"You ... What ...? Why, Deke?" she rambles.

"It doesn't concern you," he answers.

She was terrified for a few seconds. Then when she realized he was really going to leave her, she dropped to her knees and sucked his dick like the pro she is.

Why isn't the guy in jail? I know he had help from the GWS. How did they do it and not get caught? And why hasn't my sister turned them in? She has to know more than she is letting on. She must have evidence to put Deke and his fucking pathetic sharks away, right? Maybe she's keeping her mouth shut for Austin since she is engaged to Cole. He was arrested for killing her stepmother and shooting her, but I didn't believe it. Cole isn't that stupid or that careless. He's a fucking time bomb, but he wouldn't do something to get caught. No, they're all smarter and more calculated than that. So, after being questioned, he was released. And a body was never found to prove what the cops already knew.

I turn off my TV and get out of bed. All I wear is an oversized T-shirt of Seth's and a pair of boy shorts. I walk down to the kitchen to grab a bottle of water and a banana. I notice the clock on the wall reads 10:35. I'm home alone on a Saturday night. My mom and her husband are at some fundraiser for his job in New York, and they won't be back until Monday. Becky's out doing who knows who at the moment. She's never here. I don't know where she goes or what she does, but I never ask, and she never offers. The hired help my mother keeps on the property have been sent home for the weekend. My only friend here in Texas is at some party tonight that I refused to go to because it's at some bitch's house that I don't like. She tried that *I'll come visit you instead of going* shit, and I waved her off. I don't need her to coddle me. Or pretend she'll pass up free booze. And Seth is … well, I know he's busy.

I shut off the kitchen lights and make my way back to the foyer. My mother bought this house after my parents divorced. I was twelve at the time. I managed to stay in Collins until just a few months ago. *I hate Texas!* I loved Collins, Oregon. It was smaller, but that's what I liked about it. It didn't take hours to get somewhere due to traffic. Even though she picked to live in Austin, she associates with the same people: stuck-up billionaire snobs. My mother owns a lingerie line, and she's in stores all over the world. Some would say she's a big deal, but I think it's stupid. She makes slutty little outfits so housewives can dress up to try to seduce their husbands who are already fucking someone else on the side. The ironic part? I bet my life that their "secrets" are also dressed in the same lingerie and look better.

I walk past the round glass table that sits in the middle of the grand foyer and take the right set of stairs to my room on the second floor. I enter and notice that my windows are open. The soft wind blows my violet curtains around, giving my room a cold chill from the outside air. "Hmm." That's weird. They weren't open a minute ago. My bedroom light is off how I left it, but since the window is open, the lights on the side of the house give my room a soft glow.

I walk over to them and look out the open windows. The Victorian mansion sits on five acres in a secluded neighborhood. You have to have a gate code to access the property, so it's not like you can just pull up to our house. If someone doesn't have the code or clearance to get in, the guard shack will phone us for approval. My mother thinks she's some kind of celebrity and needs protection from the outside world.

I look over the manicured lawn. Holly trees line the area below my windows—big shrubs that have pointed leaves on them. I've cut myself on their sharp edges before, and they sting like a bitch. I'm pretty sure my mother put me in this room so I can't jump out and escape. Becky's doesn't have anything outside her window, but she's always been allowed free rein. She comes and goes as she pleases. Plus, when we lived with our father, the parent who wants to be your friend more than a parent, he allowed her to do whatever the hell she wanted. That's why she begged our mother to stay there when they announced their divorce. Thankfully, my father talked her into letting me stay too. But he was just as strict on me as our mother is.

I place my knee on the white cushion of the alcove and pull both bay windows closed, then flip the latch. I turn around, and a scream erupts from my mouth when I see a guy sitting on the opposite side of my bed with his back to me. He has his head down, facing the floor. A black hood pulled up, so I can't see the back of his head. With matching black jeans. He sits with his hands in the pockets of his hoodie.

I've fallen onto the bench, pressing my back up against the windows. My heart races in my chest. He sits perfectly still—like a statue. Swallowing nervously, I try to remember any survival skills, but I've got none. The thought crosses my mind of the serial killer documentary I just watched and how I'm about to be raped and hacked into a million fucking pieces before they're buried under some psycho's house. *I'll never be found.*

By the way his broad shoulders pull against the black fabric, I'm guessing the guy has at least a hundred pounds on me. I'm five feet three and weigh a hundred and twelve pounds. I can't fight off someone that size.

I sit paralyzed, waiting for him to stand. To turn and show me his face. The fact that he's hiding from me has to be a good sign, right? I've seen enough documentaries to know if they hide their face, they don't want you to be able to identify them. If they do show their face … well, then they've already decided you're going to die.

I swallow nervously and push myself up when he just continues to sit there. I will my shaky legs to tiptoe over to my bed and snatch my phone off the nightstand to call 911. But it's not there.

My stomach drops. I know I didn't take it downstairs with me. That only leaves one other possibility—he has it.

"What … what do you want?" I ask and swallow the knot in my throat. I'm here all alone. Why isn't he doing anything? Did Becky send him? Is this some sick joke she's playing on me? It wouldn't be the first time she's tried to scare me. And since I made fun of her getting scared at Silence, I wouldn't put it past her to retaliate.

A thought hits me, and I release a long, shaky breath. Halloween is coming up. My hands come to rest on my pounding chest. "Seth, knock it off." The guy likes to scare me because he knows how much I enjoy it. Last year on Halloween, I just happened to be visiting my mother in Texas, and he dressed up as Jason and hid in the back seat of my car. When he popped up, I had just merged onto the highway and almost killed us both, barely missing the center median. We laughed about it afterward.

He swears he's going to scare the shit out of me. My eyes narrow on the back of his hoodie when he continues to just sit there. "Seth …"

The hallway and outside lights go out, cutting off my words and leaving us in complete darkness and total silence. I blink and suck in a deep breath, trying to slow my racing heart. Blood rushes in my ears, momentarily deafening me. *What the hell is going on?* Looking around, I notice that even the green light to my DVR is off. He's cut the power. But how? It isn't storming outside. The stars were out when I looked out my window a minute ago.

"This isn't funny," I snap, my chest aching from my heart beating so hard.

The silence swallows me, and I blink, trying to adjust myself to nothing. You know when you imagine a spider crawling on your arm, and you scratch at it as though it's really there? That's how I feel right now. I get that feeling creeping up my spine that has my fear rising again. *It's not Seth.* He messaged me earlier that he had plans tonight when I asked him if he wanted to come over and watch a movie.

I don't move. I don't breathe. Seconds pass before I hear footsteps. But they're outside my bedroom door not inside. The banister creaks as they grip it with their hand, making their way slowly up the stairs. *Oh, God no.* There's more of them. That's why he hasn't moved. He's waiting for help. "Please …" I say as tears begin to sting my eyes, and my anger rises at how hopeless I am. "Just go …"

"Can't do that," a voice whispers from my right.

I jump and slap my hand over my mouth to keep from yelping in surprise. A hand gently touches my side, and I begin to shake. "WHAT DO YOU WANT?" I scream this time.

Voices chuckle, and I try to catch my breath. I spin around in a circle. *How many are in my room?*

"To play a game," a male voice says softly, right up against my ear. And I jerk away. My body heat rises at the closeness of a stranger in my room, and my hip runs into the corner of my nightstand. *Shit!* That's going to leave a bruise.

I reach over, wrap my fist around my lamp that I know sits on it, and throw it across the room. Seconds later, you hear it shatter against a wall. Not wanting to stand here like a sitting duck, I run for my bedroom door. If I can get downstairs or outside ... but just as my fingers wrap around the doorknob, a hand twists in my hair, yanking me to a stop. I cry out, my hands flying to the one that holds me. I claw at the hand as my scalp stings from them fisting my hair. "Please ... don't ..."

My back is pulled into a hard body and another hand comes up and slaps over my mouth. I try to catch my breath through my nose, but it's not working.

My chest rises and falls fast, and I cuss myself for not wearing more clothes. I'm your typical cliché in every horror movie. The one I laugh at when she ends up getting stabbed or dismembered in a brutal fashion.

A warm breath hits my ear as the person who holds me leans down to whisper. A shiver of fear runs through me at the same time my thighs tighten. "I thought you wanted this, *Becky?*"

My entire body stiffens at his words. And not because of how he called me by my sister's name but because of who said it.

Deke!

My fear is doused like fucking water thrown on a fire and replaced with anger. I start to squirm in his hold and try to twist around to punch him, kick him, anything. When it gets me nowhere, I lean my head forward the best I can and then slam it back. I smile when it makes contact with something, and he growls.

He removes his hand from my mouth, and I suck in a deep breath. "You motherfucker ..."

He lets go of my hair, and before I can run to the door again, he wraps an arm around my waist, picks me up like a rag doll, and tosses me onto my bed, face down. My fists grip the already tangled comforter, and I try to crawl away, but he jumps on top of me, straddling my ass, and his force makes my headboard slam against the wall. His weight pushes my body down into my mattress. I try to push myself up with my hands, but he grabs them and yanks them behind my back.

"Deke ..."

He crosses my wrists and wraps something hard and rough around them, and then I hear the zipper as he pulls it tight. *Shit!* The zip tie pinches my skin.

"Stop!" I fight him. He shifts, and then I'm rolled onto my back. I cry out as my hands get smashed underneath our weight.

He slaps his hand over my mouth again. This time pressing the back of my head into the bed and digging his fingers into my cheeks. I whimper just as my legs tighten, and my pussy begins to throb.

This can't be happening ...

His breath hits my face, and it smells like his gum that I had stolen from our kiss last night. His lips run along my jawline, sending a jolt of electricity up my spine. "Last time, you didn't tell me to stop." Deke's voice skims over my skin like a warm blanket—one he's going to smother me with.

He removes his hand from my mouth, and I suck in a long breath.

I hear a chuckle behind me, and I know it must be Cole. I pant and then snap at him. "Get off me, Deke!"

His body shakes against mine with his laughter.

This fucker!

"But I wanna play. Don't you want me to play with you?" He places both of his hands on my hips and slides them upward, pushing my shirt up a little in the process. Even though his fingers are as soft as a feather, they set my skin on fire.

"Deke ..." I pause, my heart pounding and stomach tensing. I close my eyes, and that familiar burning sensation licks my skin.

"Yeah, Becky?" his soft voice says. Almost lovingly.

Again, calling me by her name is like he's dunking me into ice-cold water. "Fuck you, Deke!" I snap.

"I know you want me to fuck you, princess. I'm ready. Are you as wet for me this time, too?" He moves his hips, grinding them into mine, and he's hard. *Motherfucker* ... Just like last night at Silence.

My breath hitches, and my pussy begins to throb. They say that the reaction your body has to fear is similar to what you feel when you're sexually aroused, like an increase in your heart rate, breathing, and blood pressure. And I feel all of them right now. It makes my head spin. The fear of what he will do to me, and the arousal of what I want him to do to me.

Heat runs up my spine, and suddenly, what little clothes I have on are too many. The dark room too hot. "Oh God," I whisper to myself. What is he doing to me? Will I stop him? I allowed him to touch me at Silence because I liked that he thought I was Becky. I wanted him to think she gave in to him and that she actually still cared. I liked the look of surprise and confusion on his face. Now … now … he's come to play, and I don't know this game.

He chuckles in the darkness. "I can be your God, princess. Wanna get down on your knees and worship me?"

He grinds his hips into mine again, and I lift my hips to him. Needing more. Wanting more.

I've always been the girl who loved scary movies. The hunt. The kill. They fascinate me and turn me on. My mother tells me I'm sick and need to watch more Disney movies, and I tell her I don't want to live in a fantasy world. I want to live in a dark one. But maybe she's right. Maybe I'm sick and need help. Because Deke breaking into my house, pretending to hurt me and tie me up should not turn me on, but fuck if it does. I'm so fucking wet for him right now. The way his hands grip my body like he owns it. His weight on top of me, pinning me down. And fuck, the way his cock presses the roughness of his jeans against my swollen clit. I could come right now.

A light flashes in the room, making me blink, but then it's gone. "What …?"

He grinds his hips into mine again, and I forget it.

Is this how it was for him and Becky? Did they pretend to be someone else? Is that how he was able to put up with her for as long as he did?

He slides my shirt up farther, and a strangled moan leaves my lips when I feel the pads of his thumbs brush over my nipples. The cool air still lingers in my room, and the feel of his hands makes them harden.

I shudder.

"Deke." I pant, my boy shorts soaked. My arms are still pinned underneath me, and they're starting to go numb. He remains silent. The room is full of my heavy breathing, and I think I'm getting dizzy. It's hard to tell because I can't focus on anything due to the lack of light.

Another flash of light. *What the hell is that?*

I bite my bottom lip to keep from moaning when his right hand comes up and wraps around my throat. His free hand slides down my hip, his fingers setting my skin on fire before it dips between our bodies and to my boy shorts. He pulls them to the side, and I gasp when he slides a finger into me.

No warning and no asking for permission. It's like he thinks he fucking owns me.

You're allowing it, my mind shouts. I can't tell him to stop. I can't … "Fuck …" I arch my back, and my breath gets caught in my lungs when he adds a second one.

He's so rough, it hurts, but in a way that makes me like it.

You're sick, my mother would say.

I am. I'd have to agree.

"So fucking wet. Just like last time. Does this turn you on, babe? A stranger in your room? Taking advantage of you? You didn't put up much of a fight. Or is it just me? Is it the fact that I call you Becky?" Someone laughs from behind me, and my face heats with embarrassment.

"Cole!" I growl, knowing who it is.

Deke chuckles. "He's not gonna help you. He's my soldier. And if you plan on going to war with me, you're gonna need an army. 'Cause you can't fight me on your own."

I try to wiggle my arms, but it just makes the zip tie dig into my skin, and I cry out. Deke ignores it. "Tell me, princess. Do you want my mouth or my cock this time?"

He removes his fingers and then adds another, making me arch my back as I let out a strangled cry. It's painful in the best way. His free hand is still wrapped around my throat, but it's not cutting off my air. I'm panting and so fucking wet for this monster.

"Why do I have to choose one?" I mumble, my hips grinding against his fingers as they slow. I pump my hips, not wanting him to stop. I don't give a fuck that Cole is here. Or the fact that I hate Deke

Biggs. It feels too good. My body wants it. My mind is screaming for it. And it's just one step closer to pissing my sister off.

She'll hate me when she finds out he's touched me. More than she already does. *Perfect.*

His thumb brushes over my clit, and I whimper.

"Greedy." He kisses my stomach, and my body begins to shake. "I like that." His lips pull away at the same time he removes his fingers. My body sags into the bed in disappointment. "Open," he orders, his voice hardening, and I blink up at the darkness confused by what he means. But then I feel his fingers on my lips. Pushing my head back with his free hand, I open, and he shoves two fingers into my mouth. I suck on them like the good girl he wants me to be and taste myself, hoping he'll reward me with another orgasm like last night. He lets out a growl as I lick them like they're his cock. That thought makes me moan. Then suddenly, he removes them, and I pant, licking my wet lips.

His laughter fills the cold and dark room. My face flushes with embarrassment, and I'm thankful they can't see me. He shifts his weight, and I feel his lips brush against mine. I suck in a nervous breath and don't move. "You get neither," he tells me with satisfaction.

Then he pulls away from me, and I hear his footsteps along with another walk out of my room and down the stairs, followed by the front door opening and shutting. Seconds later, I'm still lying on my bed looking up at nothing when all the lights come back on.

I roll over onto my stomach, panting. Knowing that he damn well left me here with my arms still tied behind my back on purpose. My underwear wet. My shirt shoved up to my neck and my hair a tangled mess. I catch sight of my phone lying next to me, and I realize what those flashes of light were. Cole took pictures of me and Deke because one of them is showcased on my screen.

"Fuuuuccckkk." I think I just started a war with Deke Biggs. But what he doesn't know about me is that I'm not like Becky. She can't play like I can. She can't think like I can. And she sure as hell can't seduce him like I can.

Game on.

SIX

DEKE

"HAVE A NICE night." I nod to the guy who sits in the guard shack.

He looks up from his phone and smiles at us. "Have a good night, boys. Cole, tell Austin I said hello."

"Will do." Cole pulls onto the road and hits the gas, shifting gears in his M4. I sit back in my seat and readjust my hard cock inside my jeans.

"She's gonna be pissed you left her wrists tied." Cole breaks the silence, but I hear the amusement in his voice.

"I know, but she'll figure out how to get herself out of it." I turn and throw my black bag into the back seat that I had dropped by her front door when we entered her house. I thought about using my handcuffs but then decided against it. I'd have to relieve her of those, and I had no desire to leave Demi Holt how I found her—free.

If she wants to be a little bitch, then I'll give her a reason to. It wasn't hard to find out what I needed to know. A look online showed me that her mother and stepdad were in New York for business reasons. The pic that graced social media had them dining at an expensive hotel a few hours ago. And a look at Becky's Facebook assured me she was not at home—she was back in Collins. She may have deleted me as a friend, but she keeps all her shit public. It's like she wants me to get jealous that she allows men to hang all over her. Like I fucking care who she spreads her legs for. That time has passed.

"You know I've always got your back," Cole starts, "but I'm curious. What exactly are you trying to accomplish by playing with her?"

"I don't know," I say honestly, running a hand down my face. "Just wanna let her know where she stands." Demi needed to be thrown off her high horse she rides with a smug smile. I think leaving her pussy wet and her wrists restrained in her bed is a good start.

I liked the way her voice shook when she thought I was there to hurt her. The fear I heard when she asked what I wanted. It matched the same fear Becky had when she found out I knew all her secrets. I held all the cards and had all the power.

She needs to remember that I do.

She thought I was Seth at first, and that pissed me off. Knowing that she had allowed me to touch her when she was clearly unavailable makes her just like her cheating, lying sister. But still, I can't help but wonder, is that how they do it? He dresses up as a burglar and sneaks into her room before taking advantage of her? She plays the role of victim, fighting him off, but she eventually gives up and lets him win?

I could totally get into that.

Fuck!

Don't think that way. She is off-limits. Untouchable. I just wanted to scare her. I wasn't going to force myself on her because I'm not a rapist. But I wanted her to know that I was the one who made that decision, not her. I had told myself it was nothing sexual. To get in, scare the shit out of her, and get the fuck out. But shit, she got turned on. More so than when she was at Silence last night. I wasn't even planning on touching her in any way, but when she moaned, I went hard. Then she lifted her hips, silently begging me for more. I fingered her again—as though she belonged to me—when I had no right to touch her.

Why didn't she stop me?

She's messing with my mind more than Becky ever has. Why am I allowing her to do this? I'm supposed to be the one in charge, but am I playing her game? Or is she playing mine?

Something tells me that Demi is a much better player than Becky could ever be. And that thought turns me on even more.

"You okay?" Cole asks, giving me a glance before looking back at the road.

I grunt. "Yep." She got my warning. She'll stay away, and I'll go back to my plan of seducing Becky. She has to fall in love with me all over again so I can break her fucking black heart. Demi can't get in the way of that. I *won't* let her.

"Where did you guys go last night?" Austin asks, stepping out on the patio with Lilly. She sheds her little towel with fairy wings on it to showcase a pink bathing suit.

I have come to find I like the Texas weather much more than Oregon. It's the middle of October and still nice enough to swim. Even though the pool is heated, it's not needed yet. The temp doesn't drop until the sun goes down.

"Uncle Deke," she screeches when she sees I'm already in the pool and runs, jumping in. I pull her head up from under the water and put her on my shoulders. Her little feet kick water up in my face as she splashes.

"We had to take care of something," I answer Austin.

She pulls her shirt up and over her head, her green eyes glaring down at me. "What did you need to take care of?"

My eyes fall to her scar from where Kellan shot her, but I don't answer.

She looks at Cole who sits on the third step staring up at her. He's leaned back, his elbows resting on the second step. His blue eyes run up her body slowly as if he'd rather have her naked and alone at the moment.

"Cole?" she urges.

His eyes make their way up to hers, but he says nothing.

She looks at me when she realizes he's not saying shit. "What did you guys do?"

"We just had a little fun," I decide to say in answer.

She looks back and forth between Cole and me for a second. "And?"

"We were just playing. Harmless fun," I tell her.

She rolls her eyes. "Oh God, not this again."

"What?" I feign innocence while Lilly pounds her little hands into my cheeks excitedly, her feet still splashing me.

"You know what?" she snaps and then bends over to remove her shorts. "I know what your definition of *play* is, and it's not fun."

Yeah, Austin was once something Cole played with. The moment he laid eyes on her, she became his prey.

Nine months ago

I stand in an abandoned cemetery over the bloody dead guy who my friends and I just killed. He was our revenge. Cole wanted him to pay, and we all played our part in making sure he got it.

A phone ringing slices through the silent night. "Hello?" Kellan answers. "Yeah." He nods to himself. "Be there soon." Hanging up, he pockets his cell. "I gotta go."

What the fuck? Where in the hell does he have to go that is so important right now? He's been acting fishy for days. More than he usually does. He didn't even want to be a part of this tonight. But I think Bennett talked him into it at the last minute.

"Get out of here," I tell him, trying not to show my frustration toward him at the moment. "Cole and I will wrap this up." Where did he go anyway? We heard a noise, and he went to check it out. It was probably some wild animal. No one comes up here anymore.

"Let us know when it's done," Bennett tells me, turning on his flashlight to light the way back to his car.

"Will do." I nod, and they turn and begin to walk down the hill to where we parked our cars. I wait a few seconds before I call out his name. "Cole?"

"Over here," he answers. His voice doesn't sound far away from me.

I pull out my flashlight, making my way down the hill so I don't trip over any tree limbs. I see him down on his knees, straddling someone dressed in a pair of jeans and a black hoodie.

"You sorry son of a ..."

"What did you find?" I ask, cutting off the girl as I come up next to them. My light shines down on her. A pretty brunette lies on the wet ground. Cole straddles her hips, pinning her arms under his legs. "Oh, a toy. Where did she come from?" What the hell is she doing in this abandoned cemetery this time of night?

"Not sure," he answers.

"Are there more?" I ask, taking a quick look around but don't see anything. He has one; I want one too.

"Fuck you," she spits out.

I laugh. "I like when they have a dirty mouth."

She arches her back, letting out a scream of frustration that rings out in the dark, rainy night.

"No one can hear you out here," he tells her, his free hand coming up and wrapping around her throat. The blood from the guy we just killed on his hand covering her sun-kissed skin. "There's no one to come save you."

She whimpers.

"I love it when they scream. Go ahead, sweetheart," I say softly. "Scream for me." I kneel next to them. Reaching out, I wrap her brown hair around my bloody hand, and I jerk her head to the side to face me. She bares her perfect teeth, sucking in a breath, but she doesn't cry out from my force. Both of our lights stay on her face, and she squints her pretty green eyes, trying to see.

In the distance, I hear an engine roar as Shane, Kellan, and Bennett leave. "What were you doing out here all alone?" I ask her.

"Watching you murder someone," she snaps.

I throw my head back, laughing at the fucking bitch. I find her truth refreshing. "Like to watch, do you?"

She bucks her hips, trying to throw Cole off, but no such luck. He's twice her size, so she's not going anywhere.

"What a coincidence. So do I," I continue with a dark laugh.

She stiffens, and I look at my best friend. "Go ahead, Cole. Give me a show. I earned it. We gave her one, after all."

"Don't," she whispers as her lips part, and she sucks in a ragged breath.

Cole smiles down at her, his hand loosening around her neck to run along her collarbone, pulling down her oversized hoodie in the process. His bloody hand leaves a trail. The sound of her ragged breathing fills the cold night.

"You know how much I love to perform," he tells me, fucking with her.

"Please," she pleads while his finger runs over her shoulder, pushing her black bra strap off and watching it disappear into the sleeve of her hoodie.

I slap Cole on the back. "She's begging you already, Cole. Fuck! That's some kind of record, right?" I whistle. But not really. All the women beg to get in his pants. Every girl wants a piece of a GWS.

The wind picks up and tosses her hair around her face, causing it to stick to the blood along her neck and chest. "Red is your color," he tells her.

"Orange is gonna be yours," she growls, lifting her chin.

He smiles at her words.

I laugh it off, then have a thought. How much did she see? What the hell is she even doing here? I've never seen this girl before. Does she know who we are? Is she related to Jeff, the guy we just killed? As far as I know, he only had one relative—Jerrold. And that fucker is next on our list. "She may have recorded it."

Cole sighs. "That would be very stupid of you," he tells her.

He drops the flashlight beside her head. Letting go of her shirt, he sits up, freeing her arms, and she begins to fight him. Her hands slap at his body, and her nails dig into his naked chest before he pins her hands above her head. "Check her pockets," he orders me.

She screams as she tries to fight him. Her hips buck, and she kicks her legs out, but I pat her pockets and find a cell phone. Fuck! "It's locked."

"What's the passcode?" he demands.

She clamps her mouth shut, and her pretty green eyes narrow.

"Either you give me the passcode, or I take it from you. What's it gonna be, sweetheart?" he threatens.

"I didn't ..."

This bitch isn't gonna play this game with us. Not tonight. "That's not the only thing we're gonna take," I say, cutting her off. I bend down and unbutton her jeans, then lower her zipper. Knowing her biggest fear and using it to my advantage.

"No!" she cries out. "It's retina ... it's a retina scanner," she says in a rush.

"Fucking technology," I growl. "What happened to the good ole days where you just flipped the phone open, and it fucking worked?" Why would this chick need a retina scanner? I highly doubt she has anything important on her phone that she doesn't want others to see.

I hold the damn phone up to her face, Cole's flashlight lies on the ground next to them, shining on her face. It unlocks the phone, and the first place I go to is her photos. They're the typical girl selfies with the duck face. I go to her videos, and she has none. Strange, but also smart for not recording us.

But who the fuck is she? And why the hell is she hanging out in a cemetery in the middle of the night? On New Year's of all nights? She should be at a party. Drunk or high. I exit out of her videos and go to her Facebook app. I stare at her name for a few seconds, then frown and squint. This can't be right ... I exit out and then open it back, thinking it will change. It doesn't.

Shit! I grunt.

"What is it?" he asks, clearly hearing me.

"No videos or pictures, but there is something interesting." I may not know this girl, but I know my best friend. And she is about to become as fucking dead as Jeff is.

"I tried to tell you. I didn't record it," she says, panting.

"What did you find?" he asks, ignoring her.

I take in a long breath and say two words. "Austin Lowes."

"As in Bruce Lowes?" he asks her.

Silence follows.

He chuckles. "Well, well, well, I didn't know he had a daughter."

"We don't have time for this," I growl. She's useless to me at this point. We could have had some fun with her but not anymore. She's the daughter of the man who raped Cole's mother and got her pregnant. He's wanted to make that bastard pay for years, so he'll make her pay. Not only because of who her dad is, but because of what she saw. I stand and pull my gun out of the back of my pants. "Let's just kill her." She's already dead anyway. He won't let her walk away. Not after what she saw.

"Put the gun away," he orders.

He can't be serious. "But ..."

"Now."

I tuck it back into my pants, biting back a growl. "Let's take her with us. I don't trust her not to call the police afterward."

"I'm not going anywhere with you," she snaps.

"You'll do whatever the fuck we say," I reply flatly.

"She won't call them," he tells me as if he knows what this bitch will and won't do. "Will you?"

She clamps her mouth shut.

I snort. "You don't fucking know that."

"No one will believe her," he says. "She's covered in his blood. It's underneath her fingernails from where she scratched my chest. It's on her clothes. In her hair. As far as they're concerned, she will be an accessory to murder."

"You fucking bastard—"

"What did you guys do with the body?" he interrupts her, asking me.

"Kellan got a call and had to leave; he rode with Bennett, so they all left. I told them we would take care of it."

"Perfect. Call my phone with hers."

I all but roll my eyes. What is he up to? "What? Cole, we don't have time ..."

"Call my phone with hers, Deke," he snaps.

I let out a huff but look down at her phone and see it's still unlocked. I type in his number, and seconds later, it starts ringing in his pocket, but he doesn't answer it.

I don't expect him to explain himself.

He stands up, and she takes the opportunity to try to scramble away, but he grips her hoodie and yanks her to her feet. Wrapping his hand around the back of her neck, he starts shoving her forward up the hill. She twists in his grip, and his hand slips, allowing her to get a few steps ahead of him.

What the fuck is he doing?

He runs after her, fisting her hair to pull her back against his front. Wrapping his free hand around her waist, he says, "We're not done, sweetheart."

"Where are we going?" she demands.

He doesn't answer her, and I don't say shit 'cause I have no fucking clue what he's doing. Maybe he plans on burying her with Jeff's body. Anything is possible when it comes to Cole.

He walks her over to where he knows we had Jeff. And I shine my flashlight on the body. She shows no sign of fear as she stares at the dead man. She saw everything we fucking did. How did she know where we were? How long had she been following us? The Lowes estate is just down at the bottom of the hill, but it's over a hundred yards away. There's no way she heard us.

"Hold her," he demands, shoving her into my arms.

"Let me go, you son of a bitch!" she screams as she bumps into me.

Her small fist makes contact with my face. "Fuck," I hiss. "She punched me," I say, irritated with this turn of events. She's like a fly I want to flatten under my hand.

I grip her hair with one hand, dropping my flashlight, and wrap my now free hand around her neck. I choke her, taking away her air. I'm not gonna go easy on this bitch. I don't care what Cole plans on doing with her. She tries to fight me, but just like when Cole held her, she has no chance.

I hear him digging into our black bag, and he pulls out the knife. "Pin her to the ground. Face down."

I smile and shove her to her knees with my hand in her hair. She grunts and cusses me as I force her to her stomach with my knee in her lower back.

Cole grabs his flashlight and shines it down on her. I straddle her ass, her hands pinned in mine against her back.

He kneels beside us and yanks her sleeve up. "What are you doing?" she asks in a rush.

"Insurance," he replies and then drags the blade against her forearm.

She cries out in the cemetery as the skin gives and blood starts to pour from the wound. He then takes the knife and stabs Jeff in the chest. "Now your DNA is in him with the murder weapon."

I chuckle. This bastard ...

"You go to the cops. They dig him up and investigate his murder, and you go down with us."

"Fucking ..."

"And you called me. More proof that we were communicating the night of the murder. Around the time of death."

Her body lies stiff under mine, and her breathing is labored.

"Return her phone and let her go so we can bury this body," he tells me.

I release her, and then I stand up, hovering over her. She crawls away from me, and I toss her phone to the wet ground. She stands up on shaky legs, holding her arm where he cut it. We both shine our lights on her.

"Get the fuck out of here before I change my mind," he growls.

She turns and runs.

"We should have killed her," I say, not really knowing what the fuck he's doing with her. She could still talk.

"That wasn't part of the plan," he argues.

I fist my hands. "I don't fucking care about the plan. What I care about is not going to prison. We should, at the very least, have taken her with us." Even I knew that wasn't a possibility, but what other choice did we have other than killing her? Bruce Lowes is a fucking evil bastard. How do we know his daughter isn't just like him?

"Did you want to take her home?" He arches a brow. "Keep her as a pet?" Then he shakes his head. "She won't say anything."

"She will ..."

"She won't. She's Bruce Lowes' daughter. We kill her, and they start looking for a missing girl. Then that brings questions."

"They'd never find her body, and you know it," I add. It may be the first time we've ever committed murder, but we know what we're doing. Our fathers have trained us for times like this. We were raised to be fucking sharks. Just like them.

"I wasn't worried about them finding her body."

"Then why not let me shoot her?" I growl, confused by what the hell he is doing. *"Two birds with one stone."*

"Not yet," he responds.

I run a hand through my hair, finally understanding his intentions. *"You want to fuck with her."* I chuckle. He wants a toy. *"This will be fun."*

He smiles.

Oh, Austin Lowes, he's gonna make you wish he would have just killed you.

That night was the beginning of her torment and our fun. One thing after another, he put her through hell. Who knew she would survive it? Or that Cole would fall in love with her? I sure as hell didn't see that coming, but even I can't deny that they were made for one another.

"Ah, come on, baby." She glares at me. She hates it when I call her baby, but I don't care. "You had fun. It's okay to admit it."

"Cole." She growls his name.

He gets out of the water and walks over to her. Placing his hands on her hips, he remains silent. "Did you hurt her?" she asks him, knowing exactly what I meant by *had some fun.*

He shakes his head. "I didn't do anything. Just stood there."

"You didn't try to stop him?" Her mouth falls open.

He doesn't respond because he already answered her once.

She sighs. "Do I know her?"

"No." We both lie in unison.

She pulls away from him. "You said you were done."

"I am." He nods.

"But now you're playing some sick game with someone."

"It's not what you think," he argues.

She places her hands on her hips. "Then explain it to me."

"Not my place."

She looks at me, and I give her a big smile. "I'm a rock, baby." I'm not telling her anything. Can't take the chance she'll run off and tell Becky. I don't want to have to deal with her more than I already do. I want to fuck her, not listen to her bitch. And I think my warning was very clear. Demi will keep her mouth shut, and she'll stay the hell away from me.

Austin leans over to pick up her clothes and then storms off into the house.

Cole turns and looks at me over his shoulder. "You got her?"

I nod. "We'll be fine. Won't we, Lilly?"

She giggles. "Let's dive for rings."

He turns back to the house and goes in after her. I have no doubt they'll be fighting it out with her on her back and him between her legs.

An hour later, I'm in the shower washing away the chlorine water when I hear a knock on my bathroom door. "What?" I ask.

Cole clears his throat, and I pop my head out of the frosted door to look at him. "You have a visitor."

My jaw tightens. It'd better not be my father. I'm still avoiding that fucker, but I don't put it past him to show up here in Texas to make me talk to him. "Who?"

He gives me that Cole Reynolds smile that I know all too well. His previous argument with Austin forgotten, so I know he told her. He didn't have to say it, and I didn't ask. Austin can be relentless when it comes to wanting to know what's going on. It's better for her to know than to bother me twenty-four seven. "She's downstairs in the living room waiting on you." He slaps the bathroom door. "We're on our way out. You have the house to yourself for at least three hours. Make them count."

DEMI

I sit on Cole and Austin's couch scrolling through Facebook on my phone. I've been waiting for over twenty minutes in silence. Cole and Austin left with Lilly. Austin looked at me strangely when she answered the door and I asked if Deke was here, but she didn't question me. At first, I thought it was pity and then confusion. I didn't want to get into it with her. I would prefer her to not tell my sister that I was here. Maybe she thinks my visit involves Becky. That I'm here to save her from the big bad wolf. Maybe I'm here to tell Deke to leave Becky alone.

If only.

"Well, well, well. I must say I'm surprised to see you here." Deke enters the living room dressed in nothing but a pair of gray sweatpants. I look away as my face heats. I hate that after he left me lying on my bed last night, horny as hell, I finished what he had started. "Come to play some more?" He plops down across from me in a white leather recliner.

I take a chance to look at him, and he has his muscular arms crossed over his smooth and defined bare chest. His skin tan from spending so much time out in the pool over the summer. His dark hair is wet and pushed back off his forehead. His baby blue eyes twinkle as they look me up and down. My legs tighten, and my breathing hitches when he stops on my chest. I remember his lips … my eyes drop lower, scanning over his defined abs. I've never seen a boy look so much like a man. It's hard to believe he's only eighteen and a fucking bastard.

His eyes move to my bruised wrists. "I'm a little disappointed." Then they return to mine. "I'd hoped your hands were still tied behind your back."

My heart begins to race at his words, and my body heat rises. God, it's like I just walked into a sauna. Sweat breaks out across my forehead, and I rub my hands against my denim-clad thighs. "I came to call a truce." The words burn my throat as if I just downed a shot of acid.

He tilts his head to the side. "Truce?"

"Don't act stupid, Deke. We both know you're not." I roll my eyes, ignoring the throbbing between my legs.

I'm testing him. And myself. I've always been a competitive person by nature. I have to win. And that is exactly why I'm going to take Deke away from my sister. He doesn't know it yet, but she wants him back. They're playing this little cat and mouse game right now, but she has no idea she's got competition. Neither one of them will ever see me coming. Not until it's too late.

He smirks and stands. My head falls back to rest on the cushion in order to look up at him, towering over me. His stomach muscles flex when he lifts his hands, running them through his wet hair. A smirk plays on his lips while he watches me take him all in. My eyes drop to his sweatpants and the fabric leaves nothing to the imagination—the outline of his impressive dick clearly visible—and he's not even hard. My mouth begins to salivate. He steps forward, placing his hands on both armrests. Leaning into me, he lowers his face until it's inches from mine. The smell of his masculine body wash hits me, and I bite my inner cheek to keep from moaning.

"You're right." He lowers his voice and licks his lips. "I'm not stupid. And neither are you. I knew you'd fold. I don't call you *Becky* for nothing."

"What the fuck does that mean?" I demand. My hands itch to slap him across his pretty, perfect face to see what he'd do. Instead, I clasp them together. *Don't show all your crazy at once, Demi.* You've got to leave a little surprise.

His blue eyes drop to my chest. I suck in a breath when they linger. Is he thinking what I am? Did he like what he felt last night as much as I did? My boobs aren't small, but they're not as big as my sister's. Did he like mine more or less?

He smirks to himself before pushing off the chair and walking out of the living room and down the hall, ignoring me. His back muscles on full display. I stay transfixed on the way they ripple at his movements. His gray sweatpants sit low on his hips, and my mouth waters at the way the fabric pulls against his round ass. I know he came down here to see me only half-dressed on purpose. He knows how to play the game. It's also the same reason I dressed up for him. He dated Becky, after all. He likes girls who look a certain way. Even if it's not the real me, I can pretend.

"Deke?"

"I'm guessing you can see yourself out," he calls over his shoulder before he turns and walks up the stairs.

"Deke?" I growl, only to hear the door to his room slam, and my fists tighten. *Don't follow him.* That's what he wants you to do.

That's what Becky would do, and you're not Becky.

But that's why I'm doing this. That's why I allowed him to touch me in the first place. To make him look like a fool. Walking out the front door means he wins, and I'm not about to give in.

"Nature of The Beast" by My Darkest Days begins to play loudly from upstairs, and I grind my teeth at his choice of song.

I take the stairs two at a time and open the first door to my left. A black wooden framed king-size bed sits up against the wall with a deep red comforter. Black glittery pillows decorate the bed along with a couple of others that match the bedding. A large picture of Cole and Austin hangs above the headboard. She's wearing a beautiful red dress, and he's dressed in a black tux with a bow tie that matches her. Nope. Definitely not Deke's room. The moment I open the next door, I don't even get a chance to look around because I'm yanked inside, and my back is slammed into a wall.

"Curiosity killed the cat." Deke chuckles.

He was expecting me. "Are you gonna kill me?" I almost smile.

He tilts his head to the side and bites his bottom lip as he contemplates that idea. My body heat rises like it seems to do when I'm around him. "Is that what you want?" he asks, reaching out and taking a lock of my hair. He rubs it between his fingers. "Want me to hurt you, Demi?" I swallow nervously because I know this man would do exactly that. I'd have to give him a reason, but once I pushed him to that limit, he wouldn't think twice. "Is that why you keep coming around me?" He chuckles, and I don't miss the innuendo.

"No." My answer is nothing more than a whisper. Not true, but not totally wrong.

I come around you because I hate you. And I want my sister to smell my perfume on you. I want her to know I've been near you. Touched you. I want to watch her go crazy knowing I have taken something from her. Something she was so sure would be there when she decided to quit being a fucking whore and come back.

The corners of his lips turn up. "Liar." My heart begins to pound, and he leans forward, his lips now inches from mine. "You're more fucked up than I originally thought," he whispers.

"Excuse me?" This coming from a monster. *We're more alike than you could ever imagine, Deke.*

"I stood outside your room while you watched that documentary. Into murder, are you?"

"I don't know what you're talking about ..."

"You lie as bad as your sister does."

I hate that—the way he compares us—more than anything.

"Is that why I turn you on?" he asks, and his eyes leave mine to admire my lips.

"You don't—"

He chuckles, cutting me off. "Another lie. I bet you're wet right now, baby." His knee pushes between my legs, easily spreading them apart. I'm panting at his closeness. His free hand comes up and cups the side of my face. His touch so soft, it has to be fake. There's nothing tender about this man. I know he's fucking with me, but my body isn't getting the memo. I lean into him, wanting more. Wetness pools between my legs when he lowers his lips to my neck and kisses the sensitive skin there, sending a shiver up my spine. But I feel it's a threat. He's pretending to be gentle just to get close to me. He can strike easier from here. Rip my throat out with his teeth. Too bad I don't care.

I reach out and grip the waistband of his sweatpants as his lips trail up my neck to my ear. He laughs when I moan.

My hands fist the material. My knuckles skimming the smoothness of his defined V. I have a thought of pulling them down just to see what he'll do from there. I doubt he'll be laughing then. "You are such a fucking …"

My words are cut short when his lips slam on mine. He doesn't ask for permission, and I don't push him away. His hands hold my face in place as his tongue enters my mouth. He tastes just as good as the other night at Silence. Like sin and cinnamon. It stirs something in my stomach, and I pull him closer to me. A moan escapes me as I open my lips, wanting him to take my breath away.

But he draws back and runs his knuckles over my cheek. His blue eyes hold a hint of amusement, reminding me this is just a game to him. I'm panting and so goddamn wet. And losing.

"Go home, Becky."

My teeth grind and I snap. "Quit fucking calling me that!"

He laughs. "That's what you want, right? To be like her?" His hands grab mine, ripping them from his sweatpants, and before I can stop him, he pins them above my head to the wall. He presses his body into mine once again. Fuck, he's hard. My body begins to shake with need, but he ignores it. "You want me to want you like I wanted her."

"Deke," I warn, but my knees threaten to buckle. Every time I'm around him, he overpowers me in some way.

I like it.

Throw me on the bed, rip off my clothes, and pin me down. I'll be your good little whore.

That's obviously what he's into— a girl who's *easy and stupid.*

"You want me to fuck you like I did her?" His brows pull together as if he can't quite understand the thought of that. Allowing himself to want me would be beneath him. He thinks she's so much better than me.

And fuck, I can't understand it either. I hate him as much as I do her, yet here I am, panting and wet all because he is touching me. Silently begging him to fuck me. "Stop," I growl as though it's his fault I came here. What the hell did I expect? Deke Biggs is ready and willing to play. He made that crystal clear when he showed up at my mother's house last night. And I couldn't stay away. I'm literally using myself as bait. And men like him, the GWS, don't ever pass up a chance to draw blood—to eat you alive.

He lowers his head to the crook of my neck, and he kisses me softly just like before. The hairs on the back of my neck stand up at his tenderness. It's another trap. He has figured out that's my spot—my weakness—so why am I falling for it?

I moan loudly and then bite my lip to keep from begging for more.

"You want me to treat you how I do her?" he whispers.

I fight to free my hands from his hold, but it doesn't work. I know he still sees her. He proved that when he thought I was her at Silence.

"Tell me, baby. Did it turn you on when I ordered her to her knees so I could fuck her mouth?"

My breath hitches.

"Did you listen to her suck my cock like the desperate woman she was?" he asks amused.

"Yes," I answer shamelessly.

I thought she was as weak and pathetic as he did. Now I understand why she so willingly fell to her knees to try to convince him to stay. But unlike my sister, I know, no matter how much time you spend staying on your knees, you don't win Deke Biggs over. There are too many other girls out there willing to do the same thing.

His lips trail over my collarbone, and he bites it through my shirt. I whimper as the feel of his teeth makes my pussy throb.

"Do you want to be useful to me?" he asks. "Take her place?"

"Stop!" I growl, getting pissy. "I'm nothing like her." *I want you to want me for me.* Fuck Becky and what he felt for her!

He steps back and drops my arms. They fall to my sides like dead weight, and I hate the distance he's put between us now.

"You're exactly like her." He looks me up and down, his blue eyes full of hatred, his lips pulled back with disgust.

For the first time, I see how much he truly hates her. How much I must remind him of her. We both have blond hair and blue eyes, but I'm smaller than her in height and overall size. Becky has always been runway ready with her long legs, but I prefer an oversized

T-shirt, no makeup, and a pint of ice cream in my lap while I stay home watching some frightening shit on Netflix. She likes to go out, get drunk or high, and show off everything she has in a tiny skintight dress with heels.

We may look alike, but our similarities stop there. He'll never believe me, though. And I'm not about to try to make him understand.

But if he hates her so much, then why did he do what he did to me at Silence, thinking I was her? My only guess is a power trip. He thought she wanted him, and he was going to take advantage of the situation. Then he realized it was me, and he was disgusted. He may hate my sister, but I'm nothing to him. Insignificant. And that's a hard pill for me to swallow.

The fact that I hate Deke is no longer an issue because my hatred for my sister is far greater. So I'm going to do what I watched her do all those years and use what God gave me.

"Get the hell out of here." He nods to the closed bedroom door.

SEVEN

DEKE

She stands there, back still against the wall, looking every bit of pissed and turned on all at once. Ignoring her, I go to my walk-in closet and grab a shirt off the hanger. I feel like going out for the evening, and there's a party on campus that I can hit up. I need to get drunk and hook up with some stranger because all this pent-up aggression I have for Demi is giving me a headache. Not to mention blue balls.

When I walk out, she's still standing there, blue eyes glaring into mine and arms now crossed over her chest.

"I'm better than her."

The bitch is convinced. I'll give her that. A part of me wants to believe her, but I know the truth. She's just another spoiled Holt who thinks she deserves every little fucking thing she wants.

I snort.

She lifts her chin. "At everything."

I toss my shirt onto my unmade bed and smirk, looking her up and down. Wanting to really look at her. Is there a difference? She wore a pair of skinny jeans, cuffed at the ankles with a plain black T-shirt that's just short enough to show me a little sliver of her tan stomach and a pair of black heels, giving her every bit of an extra five inches. Just as Becky would. But it doesn't suit her. I found her much more attractive in the oversized shirt and underwear she had on last night. With Demi, less is better. But her words don't match her actions. She looks identical to Becky in every way.

Her eyes go to my shirt on my bed and then back to mine. I watch her anger toward me build in them for every second I just stand here, letting the silence linger between us. She hates me so fucking much. I want to wrap my hand around her elegant neck and demand she tell me why she's here in my room. Is she trying to prove to me that she isn't Becky?

What is it that she wants from me? Whatever it is, she isn't going to get it.

I walk over to her, and she squares her shoulders, preparing herself for whatever I'm about to throw at her. "How are you better?" I press my body into hers again, and of course, my cock is hard. But it's not her, it's the game. I get off on fucking with people. The challenge.

Right.

I lower my lips to her ear. She stands perfectly still with her hands hanging down by her side. "Can you lie on your back longer?" My right hand grips her hair and yanks her head back. It hits the wall with a thud. Becky was made to be loved. She may have been a whore, but she needed to feel like she meant something—cherished. She didn't like a hand around her throat or to be spoken to like a cheap fuck. Demi is going to be the same way.

Little Miss Priss wants a prince to save her, but this monster will rip her apart. It's hard to smile when you no longer have a pretty face. Ever heard of the saying beauty is only skin deep? Rip Demi of her expensive name-brand makeup and fake tan, and she'll shatter every mirror she comes into contact with because she won't be able to stand the sight of herself.

Her eyes fall closed. Long, dark lashes fanning her cheeks. When they open, she looks up at me and sighs my name. "Deke …"

I hate how it makes my hard cock twitch with longing. Just as it does when her sister says it. "Can you spread your fucking legs farther?" My left hand comes up, and I run a finger over her parted lips, and I lick my own, still tasting our kiss. She tasted sweet like honey. I wonder if her pussy tastes as good. Her breath quickens. "Can you suck my dick harder?"

Her eyes narrow on mine. "Yes."

Fuck, I'd love to shove her to her knees right here and now and have her show me. But I don't plan on touching Demi. *Ever.*

I smirk and pull away from her. "Go home." I reach over and open my bedroom door. "I don't play with little girls." Her hands fist, and I don't miss the marks that the zip tie left from me binding her wrists behind her back. I wonder how long it took her to find a pair of scissors and get free. It couldn't have been easy. I should have stayed and watched the show.

"You had no problem *playing* at Silence," she growls.

"That's because I thought you were your sister. I would have never touched you otherwise." I've never thought of Demi sexually in any way. And even though my cock is hard, that doesn't mean I'll do anything about it. I have some restraint.

"And last night?" she grinds out.

I give her a smug smile and lean up against the open door. "That was to teach you a lesson, princess."

Now she's the one who smiles, and it makes her look like the evil fucking bitch I know she is. She steps into me, and her bright blue eyes light up with excitement when they meet mine. When she places her small, soft hands on my bare chest, I tense. "Want me to teach you something?" She leans up on her tiptoes and places her lips by my ear. Her breath skims over my skin, and I bite the inside of my fucking cheek to keep from growling.

I should push her away, but I'm afraid if I place my hands on her, I'll be throwing her onto the bed and not out the door where she belongs.

"I know all your secrets, Deke …" Her hands run down my chest and stomach. I think she's going to pull down my sweatpants, but instead, she taps my hard dick, making me jump.

I grip both of her wrists in my hand, and she hisses in a breath at the sensitive skin. My eyes narrow down at her. "Are you threatening me, *Demi*?" I call her by her first name because I'm no longer playing.

"Maybe." She runs her tongue over her bottom lip seductively. "What would you do to keep my mouth shut?"

It's the same question she asked me at Silence. And my first thought is to tape that motherfucker shut. I should throw her on my bed, tie her hands behind her back, and gag her. That'll show her what kind of guy I can be. But I have a feeling it'll just turn her on. She's pushing me to see just how far I'll go.

And it's working.

My blood begins to boil. I don't know what all Demi heard me say to Becky those two nights in her room, but I'm not about to let this bitch think she can play me. Pretending to be Becky was fucked up, but to threaten me is the dumbest thing she could do.

I lean down, and whisper, "You think you're being cute, Demi, but believe me when I say I have no fucking limits when it comes to protecting myself." I pull back, and the smile has dropped off her face. "Don't fuck with me because you won't survive it." What the guys and I did to Kellan was not a fucking game! And it no longer involves just me and what's left of the GWS. Austin was a part of that as well, and I'm not taking that chance. I will protect my sister just as I will protect my brothers. And that's all she could possibly know.

"Are *you* threatening me?" she asks, tensing.

"Absolutely!" I growl.

She rips her hands from my hold. "Don't threaten me, Deke." Her blue eyes glare up at mine. "I keep telling you that I'm nothing like my fucking sister. I'm not going to fall to my knees to suck your cock while begging you to love me. And I'm sure as hell not afraid of you."

DEMI

I storm out of his bedroom and down the stairs. I all but run out of the house and make my way over to my black Audi R8. I yank the door open and fall into the driver's seat. When I start it, "Trouble" by Valerie Broussard blares through my speakers. I look up to see Deke standing at the front door. He has his right hand in the front pocket of his sweatpants and his left clenching the doorframe. His completely rigid body shows off his bulging biceps and six-pack. He's too perfect for my sister.

I smile at him. This fucker thinks he can scare me, but he's wrong. I look away, throw the car in gear, and take off, squealing my tires.

I adjust myself in my seat and tighten my hand on the steering wheel as his words turn in my head.

Don't fuck with me because you won't survive it.

He thinks he's fucking God and holds that much power. It makes me think that is why my sister hasn't done anything about it. Maybe he said something to her that I didn't hear that night. Or since then. I don't know how often they speak. I know Becky's only friend in this town is Austin, and Deke lives with her and Cole, so they have to see each other on the regular.

I jump on the highway and head toward my mother's house as the song changes to "Down" by Seven Day Sleep. I cut into traffic and ignore the guy who blows his horn at me and hit the gas. I've got shit to do.

Thirty minutes later, I'm pulling up to my mother's gate, and it opens. I get out and enter the house. I take the left staircase and barge into Becky's room. Her walls are a beige color. Her peach comforter and white sheets lie wadded at the end of her bed, unlike my room that I keep clean at all times. She has clothes thrown on the floor and draped over her computer desk by the windows. I almost trip over a shoe, making my way over to her walk-in closet. I start ripping the boxes open that she brought with her from Collins. She left quite a bit back at our dad's, so I know whatever she did bring is important to her.

One is full of sweaters. I shove it to the side and pick another one. I rip it open to find a backpack and school shit. "Goddammit." I hiss and push it aside as well. Then I come to a third box. I rip it open, and there's a black and white notebook in it. I pick it up and flip through the pages. It's a journal.

Funny. My sister has never kept one before. That I know of.

I go back to the very front and look at the first page.

He hit me today.

Not the first time. But it hurt like all the others.

He tried to put his hand up my skirt. I pushed him away, and he slapped me across the face. My mother saw the whole thing and all but shoved some weed in my hand and then pushed me out the front door.

I can't wait to get the fuck out of here. I'm going to go live with my father. I'm not sure how that will be much better, but at least I know he'll ignore me rather than touch me.

I flip the pages and then stop on a new one that has *HELL* scribbled across the top. Whose is this? My sister has horrible handwriting. I remember my dad used to make her erase her homework and rewrite it until it was readable. Whoever wrote this has beautiful handwriting. The cursive is easy to read. My sister's looks like chicken scratch.

The devil doesn't come to you as an ugly monster with fire breathing out of his ears. No. He is sent wrapped in a breathtaking smile and pretty eyes that can see to your soul.

Cole Reynolds is what was sent to me.

He is ugly on the inside but pretty to look at. He just dropped me off from Shelby's house. He had her stitch up my arm. That he cut while in the cemetery last night. Where I watched him and four of his friends kill a guy.

"Shit." I hiss. This is Austin's. Why the hell does Becky have it?

He caught me watching them. He cut my arm without a thought and then placed the bloody knife in the body. Said if I turned him in, I'd go down with them. The fucker is too smart for his own good, but what he doesn't know is that I'm better.

I burned that motherfucking body and then took a hammer to what bones remained before scattering the ashes into the ocean. They can try to pin it on me all they want. I won't lie down and let some punk ass kids take what little life I have away from me. I'm going to record every little thing I hear and see from now on. Consequences if I get caught, be damned.

"Holy fuck." I like Austin more already. How did she end up being friends with my sister?

But my other problem is his friend Deke. He's the only other one who knows I saw them. He wanted to shoot me right then and there, but Cole stopped him. What will they do when they tell the others? I'm not sure, but I know I won't quit fighting them.

"Demi?"

"Shit!" I hiss when I hear Becky's voice shout out my name, followed by the front door shutting.

I shove all the boxes closed and push them up against the wall. Then I cram the notebook into the back of my jeans and run out of her closet. I get out into the hall and see she's down in the grand foyer placing her purse on the glass table and a small suitcase down by her feet. *Where the hell has she been?*

"Demi?"

I duck and run across the walkway that overlooks the foyer and into my room. I yank the notebook from my jeans and shove it into my backpack that sits next to my bed as my bedroom door flies opens.

"I've been hollering at you!" she barks.

I stand straight and spin to face her. "What?"

Her blue eyes look me up and down as I breath heavily. Crossing her arms over her chest, she takes in my skinny jeans, black top, and matching heels. I never dress like this. It's just not my thing. Not even for Seth. He doesn't give a fuck what I wear, and I never have either. But Deke noticed. Just as I wanted him to.

"What were you doing?"

"Nothing," I lie. "What do you want, Becky?"

She pushes her right hip out in a typical Becky stance. "Austin and I are going to take Lilly to the movies in about an hour. She told me to invite you." She rolls her eyes.

"You're inviting me?" I can't hide my surprise. And why does Austin want me to go? She just saw me at her house not even an hour ago. She could be setting me up. I don't want Becky to know I was there. Not yet. If Austin says something, I can play it off. Make up some bullshit about how I'm trying to protect Becky from Deke. Austin would believe it. I can be convincing. But my sister? Since when do I give a shit what she thinks?

She has nothing to say to my previous question.

I smile. Clearly, she didn't think it was a good idea to ask me. That just made my mind up. "I'd love to."

She turns, exits my room, and slams the door shut. I plop down on my bed and look down at my backpack. I have a feeling that Austin Lowes just gave me all the information that I need to scare the shit out of Deke.

EIGHT

BECKY

Austin has decided she wants to be friends with my little sister. *Just fucking fantastic.*

I can't ignore it. It was on the tip of my tongue to lie and tell Austin that Demi had something to do. Or make up something about how my sister doesn't like her. But that would just cause more problems, and as much as I can't stand this new Mommy Austin, she is my only friend. And my only way to stay close to Deke.

If I push Austin away, then my chances with Deke go from low to nonexistent. Cole isn't going to be my friend or invite me over. So instead, I said I'd love to ask my sister to come hang out with us. It's a movie. Not like I have to talk to her for hours.

We enter the theater, and I see Austin at the concessions with Lilly. And I think back to the day Austin had that bomb dropped on her. The day she found out that Cole's half-sister is also her half-sister.

Seven months ago

"I don't ..." she trails off. "Why would my dad want to hurt Cole?"

Cole stares at her but remains silent as he sits on the couch in their clubhouse. She stands next to me, and I silently cry. Deke filled me in on the way here about why Cole skipped school today. He found out that the car accident was no accident. The brakes had been tampered with. I almost fainted. Cole has kept my secret for so long. This was it. He's going to out me right here and now that I was with them. That I was driving.

It's going to ruin everything!

"We don't know for sure, but we have a guess." Deke sighs.

"Which is?" she asks.

"Lilly," Deke answers.

Her frown deepens, and even I have a moment of confusion. What are they talking about? What does Cole's little sister have to do with this?

She looks at Cole. "Why would he want to hurt you because of Lilly?"

But Deke is the one who answers her, running a hand through his hair. "Because Lilly is Bruce's daughter."

Bruce as in Bruce Lowes? Austin's father? Holy fucking shit! Cole's sister is somehow Austin's sister too? I never knew this.

"Your mom and my dad had an affair?" Austin asks, trying to do the math in her head. Her dad and her stepmom have been married for ten years now. Lilly is six.

He fists his hands, and his jaw sharpens. "No."

"Then how do you explain …?"

"Bruce fucking raped her," he interrupts Austin.

That's when things changed. She took on a new role of mother, and the rest was history. It was as if Lilly filled this hole that she didn't even know she had. And her blackmailed relationship with Cole took a jump off the deep end. She walked out of that clubhouse with her head held high even though she had tears in her eyes. I was proud to call her my friend, even if she didn't know my commitment to her wasn't real.

I would betray her more than once. And even now, she would push me away if she knew the truth. What I've done. How much I've lied. Hell, I wouldn't even be friends with me. But that doesn't mean I'm going to turn myself in willingly. You don't see any of the GWS shouting from the rooftops about all the illegal shit they've done.

Why should I? They shouldn't be the only ones who can cover their own asses. And that's why Deke and I belong to one another. We are one and the same.

I just have to remind him of that.

I pull my cell out of my pocket and send a quick text to him.

Me: Can I see you this weekend? We need to talk.

Sometimes you have to swallow your pride, or a dick. And for Deke, I'll do either.

It vibrates immediately. My heart begins to pound when I see it's from him.

Deke: Sure.

Sure? What the hell kind of response is that? I take a quick look to see if my sister is watching me, but her eyes are on Austin and Lilly standing at the concession stand.

Me: I miss you too.

I read over the text three times and then decide to delete it. He had told me he missed me while we stood in the kitchen of Austin's house. I didn't tell him then, but now isn't a good time. Instead, I write:

Me: Can't wait to see you.

I watch him read it, and my heart pounds in anticipation to see how he responds. But after several seconds, I know he won't when I don't see those three dots jumping around. Then I look up at his activity, and it shows he was active one minute ago.

And it does nothing for my already sour mood.

He used to be the first one to text me in the morning and the last one to message me good night. And we'll get back there. I just have to do what I did before—show him what I want him to see. The good girl who fell in love with him.

DEMI

"How about Skittles?" Austin asks Lilly as we come up behind them.

She shakes her head, blond curls bouncing.

"Hmm, okay, how about M&M's?"

She shakes her head again.

"How about all of them?" Becky announces, and Austin turns around.

"Hey." She smiles at us. "Demi, I'm glad you were able to come."

I just nod at her.

"I thought you and Cole had plans tonight?" Becky asks her when she puts Lilly down.

"We did, but something came up," she answers.

I look over her while she talks to my sister. Austin is pretty in that whole I-don't-know-it way. Her dark brown hair is down and a little wavy as though she let it air dry and didn't bother to straighten or curl it. It's so long that it drapes over her chest, almost reaching her belly button. Her makeup isn't caked on like my sister's, but she doesn't seem to need much. She has dark green eyes and a diamond stud in her nose. She reaches up to push some hair behind her ear and I run my eyes over her right arm, looking for what she had mentioned in her journal. And I see it. It's faint, but it's there if you know what you're looking for. A cut about three inches long across her forearm. The very cut that Cole gave her that first night in the cemetery.

"Demi?"

I blink and look up at her eyes. "Hmm?"

She gives me a soft smile. "Do you want something?"

"Yeah." I look up at the menu.

"What would you like?" She turns, giving me her back to face the man who patiently waits for her order.

"Oh, I can get it—"

"Nonsense," she interrupts me. "I'll get it. I owe you anyway. You got my gummies the other night at Silence. What do you want?" She begins to order for her and Lilly.

I scan the menu, and say, "A large Coke ICEE. Please."

Lilly grabs my hand and looks up at me. Her brown eyes wide in excitement. "That's Austin's and my favorite."

"So, what did Cole have to do?" my sister asks, being a nosy bitch as she pops a piece of popcorn in her mouth from the bucket the cashier just placed on the counter.

"He didn't say, and I didn't ask. Deke called him, and he said he had to go."

I stiffen. *Is she gonna rat me out that I was just there earlier tonight when her and Cole were leaving?*

"I'm sure it has to do with swimming. Or maybe their classes." Austin shrugs.

And I try to slow my racing heart.

My sister looks at me, and I swallow nervously, looking away from her. Austin may not have told on me, but did Deke? Did he call Cole the moment I left to tell him that I know his secrets? That I threatened to out them? Fuck, Cole cut Austin's arm, so I wonder what the hell he would do to me if he knew I had the power to destroy them? Plus, Austin mentioned in her journal that Deke wanted to shoot her. I wasn't all that afraid of Deke until after I read that. Cole always had that I'll kill you and store your dead body in my basement kind of vibe. If they worked together, I'm sure my body would never be found.

"Here, Lilly." Austin hands her a small ICEE. "Don't drop it, okay?"

She nods. "I won't." Then she takes a drink of it.

I feel eyes on me, and I can't help but look up. My sister is still staring at me, but now she's glaring. I pull my shoulders back and narrow my eyes at her. I won't bow down to Deke, so I'm sure as hell not going to bow down to my sister.

"Okay, we're ready," Austin announces and turns, handing me my drink.

"Thank you," I say to her.

She grabs Lilly's hand, and we make our way into the theater and walk up the stairs until we are at our seats. But Austin doesn't sit down. "Let's go use the restroom before the movie starts."

"Okay." Lilly gets up and follows her back out.

I sit back in my seat, place my phone on silent, and take a drink of my ICEE.

"What the fuck are you doing?" my sister growls from three seats over. I sat so Austin and Lilly are between us.

"Excuse me?"

She eyes me. "I saw the way you were looking at Cole at Silence."

I laugh at that. She thinks I'm hung up on Cole. Priceless.

"And then when you went to get Austin her gummies, he had to go track you down to get them from you."

So she paid enough attention to see that Cole left the group and returned with Austin's gummies but not enough to notice that Deke was gone as well. "You don't know what you're talking about." Maybe she is the one with a crush on Cole if she's watching him that closely. Wouldn't surprise me. My sister has to prove to herself that every guy wants her. That's why she willingly throws herself at all of them.

She looks at me with suspicion. "I know that whatever you're trying, it isn't gonna work."

Oh, it will. I'm sure of it.

"I'm nothing like you, *sis*. I'm not into spreading my legs for every guy who looks my way."

Her mouth opens in a gasp, but she doesn't have a comeback for that.

I just smile, and she sits back in her seat as Austin and Lilly come walking up the stairs.

NINE

DEKE

B ECKY AND I crash through the front door to her house. "Where is your dad?" I ask, my hands already yanking her shirt out of her jeans.

"Out. He'll be gone until tomorrow." She undoes my belt.

I run my lips up her neck. "And David?"

"Away ..." She sucks in a long breath. "Looking at a college." I grip her ass and pick her up. She wraps her legs around my waist, and her hands go to my hair. "We're completely alone."

I climb the stairs, hanging onto her and shove her door shut with my foot. Walking over to her bed, I toss her onto it, and she giggles. I reach up and remove my shirt before crawling on top of her. I grip the hem of hers, and she leans up, allowing me to pull it off. But the moment it's up and over her head, I pause. Blue eyes look up at me, but they're brighter. Rounder. Becky's are almond shaped. This body is smaller under me, and her hair a tad lighter. "Demi?"

"Yeah, Deke." She whispers my name and runs her tongue across her plump nude lips. Becky always wears pinks. "You want me to be her? Does that turn you on? Go ahead, Deke. Call me Becky."

My cock twitches inside my jeans, and she reaches out, undoing my zipper. "I can be anyone you want." Reaching inside my jeans, she pulls my achingly hard cock free. Wrapping her fingers around *the base, she begins to stroke me. Her thumb running over my pre-cum. I lean forward, burying my head into her neck, and she releases me.*

"You smell like her," I growl, hating it.

"Make me smell like you," she whispers, running her hands down my back. Her nails lightly scratching my skin. It makes me shiver. "Who do you want me to be?" she purrs.

"Yourself." No! I don't want you at all.

She chuckles. "That's no fun, baby."

I pull away and stare down at her. I blink several times, hoping she'll disappear, and that Becky will be the girl underneath me. The one I'm hard for. But Demi remains.

She moves her hands to my bare chest. Her blue eyes follow them as they skate along my skin before her eyes meet mine. "Pretend I'm her, and I'll pretend I love you."

"Demi," I say her name in warning, but I'm not sure what I'm trying to warn her of.

She seems to understand because she smiles. "Wrap your hand around my throat and show me how much you hate her."

"Deke?"

I hear a familiar male's voice off in the distance, pulling me out of my dream. Nightmare. I'm not sure what it is at this point. I ignore it, trying to push myself back into it.

"Come on." She lifts her hips to meet mine. "Do it. I promise I can take it."

"No."

Her arms fall open on the bed, and she arches her back, exposing her neck to me, and releases a laugh. The sound so loud and condescending, it makes my jaw tighten.

"She makes you so fucking soft." She relaxes back into the comforter and looks up at me. Narrowing her eyes, she spits out. "She always made you weak. That's why she did to you what she did. Because you let her."

I lift my right hand and wrap it around her delicate throat. Her smile grows to full victory, but I tighten my hold, and her eyes widen.

Her lips part, and she tries to suck in a breath. "Isn't this what you want?" I ask, tilting my head to the side as I watch her pretty eyes change from triumph to full-out fear. It turns me on. "Becky?"

She digs her heels into the comforter, and her hands slap at my chest. I sit up, my legs pinning her hips to the bed. "Becky never could handle what I liked in bed. And you're no different."

She struggles to no avail. "Look at you now, Becky," I taunt. "I get to choose if you live or if you die." I smile. "And too bad for you, your life no longer matters to me."

As if she accepts her fate, she stops fighting me, her body relaxing once again. Her eyes softening, her nipples hardening. I watch in complete fascination as her body comes alive before me. Her hands come up to cup her breasts, and she arches her back. But I don't let go. I want to see just how far she'll let me go.

How long until she loses consciousness? Time seems to slowly tick by, but she doesn't push me away again; instead, she takes it. Like a good girl or a love-struck fool. Her pretty eyes roll back into her head, and her lips turn blue. When I finally decide to let go of her neck, she doesn't move. She doesn't breathe. I did exactly what I threatened I'd do. I killed her.

I wait for her to turn back into Becky. She's the one I really wanted to hurt. But she stays Demi. And I start to panic.

"DEKE!"

I sit straight up in bed.

"What the fuck, man? Wake up," Cole snaps, standing next to my bed with a look of rage in his blue eyes. "Get your ass out of bed and meet me downstairs," he demands before he walks out of my room, but not before he flips the light on and leaves my bedroom door open.

"Fucking prick," I mutter.

I bow my head and close my eyes. What the hell was that about? Did I kill Demi in my dream because she was trying to be Becky?

Why the hell was she there in the first place?

I run a hand through my hair and jump out of bed. Throwing on a pair of sweatpants, I make my way down the stairs to find him pacing the kitchen. "What's wrong?" I ask through a yawn after noting that the clock on the oven reads a little after three a.m. I just got home twenty minutes ago. After Demi left, I had called Cole because his father had called me looking for him. He ended up coming home, and I went out to a college party. I had just gone to sleep. And dreamed of both Becky and Demi. That can't be a good sign. "This better be good …"

"I got a text."

Sighing, I pinch the bridge of my nose. I was hard for Demi, but I was pretending she was Becky. And I would have fucked either one of them. *Fuck!*

"So?" I know Cole isn't all that into technology, but a text is nothing new to him.

He snatches his cell off the kitchen counter and shoves it into my bare chest. "Fucking read it."

The light is too harsh, so I blink a few times waiting for my eyes to adjust. He turned my bedroom light on but not the one here in the kitchen. "What is it?"

"Pretend I'm her, and I'll pretend I love you."

"Just read it!" he orders.

Blinking rapidly, I put it up to my face. "This is a Facebook PM," I note, realizing it's not a text. "I didn't think you used your Facebook?"

"I don't!" he answers, continuing to pace. I know he had our other friend Bennett delete Austin's, but I thought he had gotten rid of his as well.

What the hell has him so wound up? And what am I going to do about that dream? "This is to you?" I ask, trying to get my mind off it.

"To us!" He yanks the phone from my grip when he realizes I'm not catching on as quickly as he wants me to. He points at the top of the screen. I didn't see that my name was involved in the chat too.

I pull my phone out of the pocket of my sweatpants and look at it. Sure enough, I have a message, so I open it up. "Who …?" My voice trails off when I see who it's from. "No way," I say, shaking my head in denial. "It can't be."

"When was the last time you used it?" he snaps.

"I don't know."

"Fucking think!"

"Uh … months," I answer honestly as I try to get my head in the game and out of that nightmare I just had. "Back when we were in Collins." I close out of my account and try to log in to my spam account that I've had for a few years now. "Shit!" I hiss and then my eyes meet his. "I'm locked out. Someone got access to it and changed the password."

"Goddammit!" he shouts.

"Cole?"

We both look up to see Austin enter the kitchen. She flips the switch on the wall, making us both squint at the harsh light. She runs a hand through her tangled dark hair. Wearing a pair of Cole's basketball shorts and a T-shirt, she yawns. "Why are you guys down here yelling? In the dark?"

"Go to bed," he orders, ignoring her.

That seems to perk her up. Her green eyes widen, and her brows lift. "Cole, what are you …?"

"Go back to fucking bed, Austin!" he shouts.

Even I am surprised at his tone. I haven't seen him talk to her like that since he first met her. Back when she was just a game to him. Something to destroy.

She storms into the kitchen and reaches for the phone in his hand, but he snatches it back before she can get her hands on it. "No!" She crosses her arms over her chest. "You're gonna tell me exactly what the fuck is going on. Right now!"

He shoves his hand through his disheveled hair and then storms out of the kitchen and down the hallway.

I know exactly where he's going. You hear the sliding back door open and slam shut a second later. She goes to follow him, but I reach out and grab her upper arm, pulling her to a stop. "Don't."

Her worried green eyes meet mine. Cole has always been a hothead, but things haven't been the same since our friend Kellan tried to kill her.

"Something is wrong."

"I'll take care of it." I always do. Always have. Cole is my brother. He's been through some shit, and I'm always there for him. "Just go back up to bed."

She looks like she wants to argue, but I turn and open the fridge. I grab a bottle of vodka that I was saving for this weekend and then a pack of cigarettes and a lighter out of our junk drawer and leave her standing in the kitchen.

I exit the house and step out onto the back patio. Cole's shirt sits on the ground next to the pool with his sweatpants. He has "Things That Make You Scream" by Memory of a Melody playing softly from his phone through the outside speakers. And I wonder if it's a sign from God regarding the dream I just had. Which is crazy because I'm not religious.

I plop down in a chaise lounge chair and unscrew the cap on the bottle. Breathing in the cool night air, I take the new pack of cigarettes and slam the end into my palm. After the whole Demi and Becky thing, I could use a fucking joint, but they drug test us at the university. The only downfall of being an athlete.

He pops his head out of the water and takes a deep breath.

"It's not her fault," I tell him.

"No. It's mine."

I can't argue that. "I can't let you take all the blame," I counter with a smile, trying to lighten the mood. He doesn't return it.

"I'm not doing this, Deke," he growls, running his hands through his wet hair to shove it out of his eyes. "I said I was done, and I meant it."

I nod, lighting the cigarette. Taking a long drag, I blow out the smoke. I don't normally smoke, but I need one right now. "I don't think it was talking about Austin."

"Then who was it talking about?" he barks.

"Maybe Becky," I offer.

He snorts. "Why her?"

"It could have been the fact that she walked away from the accident." At the mention of her, I take a swig of the bottle. *I need to tell him* ... Maybe I'm having fucked-up dreams because I'm not being truthful to my best friend.

"How would they know?" he demands. "I only told you and Austin."

Hmm. True.

I offer. "Maybe someone else was there …?"

"No!" He shakes his head. "There was no one for miles. And if there were, they wouldn't wait until now."

True.

I take another drag from the cigarette.

"Well … I guess, maybe …" He trails off, rethinking that option. "But what about what happened to the baby? She had to have gone to the hospital. I'm guessing she lost it."

I stiffen at his words as I'm thrown back into the conversation I had with Becky three months ago at Mr. Holt's house in her bedroom.

The first tear runs down her face. I watch it in complete fascination, thinking it's a good look on her. That I should have made her fear me more than try to make her love me.

"Was it mine?"

No one knows how far back Becky and I go. Cole believes I'm in love with her, and a part of me was, but we started fucking long before he told me she had broken up with David. I had to pretend I didn't fucking know. That just gave us the green light to go public. And the fact that Cole went all alpha for Austin, making the entire school aware he was claiming her, took the attention off what Becky and I were doing. The few whispers I did hear were shut down quickly for her sake. But we had been fucking for months prior to that. David be damned.

"So, keeping us a secret had nothing to do with you and David. It had to do with you and Eli." Until he died. I get it now. Fuck, I was stupid for her. "Was the child …?" I begin to ask again, but my voice trails off. I chuckle. This bitch! "You weren't even pregnant."

"Yes …"

"No." I shake my head. Of course. How could I have forgotten? "You weren't." She swallows nervously. "I remember us hooking up the weekend before that in my parents' pool house, and you were on

your period." Her face falls. "Don't you remember, baby?" I ask, reaching out for her. I pull her shaking body toward me. "You told me that I couldn't fuck you 'cause it was that time of the month"—I lower my lips to her ear—"and I told you blood didn't bother me." Fuck, this bitch has told so many lies. "I can't believe you let him take the fall for you." I understand why Cole did what he did. I would have done the same thing, but this is why she never wanted me to find out. Because she knows that I can prove she lied to him. And no one wants to be on Cole's bad side.

"Cole." I sigh and take another quick drink from the bottle. He was man enough to tell me, so I need to do the same. I just hate that it's like this. I should have done it the moment I realized she had lied to him.

"She was bleeding. Pretty badly. She had to require medical attention," he continues as he stares down into the water that he loves so much.

"Becky was never pregnant," I blurt out before I lose my nerve.

He frowns, his eyes meeting mine. "Yes, she was." I shake my head. "She sat there in the middle of the road, next to my car, holding her stomach, crying and told me she was pregnant."

My teeth grind. That fucking bitch … "She lied to you."

A silence falls over us, and he just stares at me. A look of nothing on his face. The old Cole would be furious. This is the new Cole. The one who is unpredictable.

I lean forward, placing my elbows on my knees. "I went to her house after you told Austin and me that Becky was the one driving and that she was pregnant." I start to explain. "And I demanded to know about it. I thought it could have been mine." His eyes widen with my confession. "We were sleeping together …" I run a hand through my hair. "And had been for a while at that point. Then I remembered that I had been with her the weekend before the accident, and it was her time of the month. She couldn't have been pregnant." I take another drink of the vodka, but the words I just spoke burn more than the alcohol. "I'm sorry, man—"

"None of it was your fault," he interrupts me.

"She lied to you," I grind out.

"Doesn't matter."

He can't be serious. "But it does," I argue.

"It doesn't change anything."

"I know, but …"

"It doesn't fucking matter, Deke!" he snaps. "I don't give two fucks about Becky! What matters now is that we got a text that puts Austin in danger. And I'm not gonna allow that." He climbs out of the pool, picks his shirt up off the ground, and dries off his hands before holding it out to me. "Let me see your phone."

I pull it out of my pocket.

He dials a number and then places it on speakerphone before dropping it onto the round glass table next to me. I take a quick look to see who he's calling and refrain from sighing.

It rings once, twice, three times. After a few more times, it goes to voicemail. "You've reached Bennett …"

Cole hangs up and dials it again.

"Heellloo?" Bennett's groggy voice answers after the second ring this time.

"Wake the fuck up!" Cole snaps at him.

"I'm up … I'm up …" I hear the rustling of covers. "Everything okay?" He clears his throat. "What time is it?"

"Late," I answer.

"Who is it?" a woman's soft voice asks in the background.

"Tell your fuck to pack her shit and get out," Cole orders coldly. "We need to talk to you!"

I expect Bennett to argue, but instead, he sighs heavily. "Give me a second."

Cole paces before me, water dripping from his boxers, his entire body rigid. I feel sorry for him. For what he has gone through with Austin. Finding the woman you love dead changes a man. I don't care who you are. Especially when you were the one who wanted to hurt her in the first place.

"I'll call you later," Bennett says after a long second. "Okay." He returns to the line. "What is going on?"

"Deke and I just got a text. That's what's up!" Cole explains.

"A text?"

"It was actually a PM through Facebook." I clarify for Bennett.

"A message?"

"Did you fucking send it?" Cole snaps at him.

"What? Why would I send you a message?" he growls, getting defensive.

"Because it was sent to us from Evan Scott."

Silence falls over us again as Bennett takes that in. Evan Scott is my spam account. I used to use it for several things. None of them were good.

Bennett is the first one to speak clearing his throat. "What? How is that possible?"

"I don't know," I answer. "But I can't log in to that account. Someone has gone in and changed the password. I'm locked out."

Bennett sighs heavily. "And you think I did it?"

I go to answer *no*, but Cole beats me to it. "You're the only one I can think of who has that kind of knowledge. You crack passwords. Change emails. You knew who was behind it, and you know how to get into it."

"Listen, Cole, I didn't change anything, and I sure as hell didn't send you a message. And it doesn't take a genius to change that shit. A Facebook page isn't that untouchable …" His voice trails off.

"What?" Cole demands after the silence lingers.

"Hang on," Bennett tells him.

I take a hit of my cigarette, and Cole begins to pace some more.

"I got one too," he growls.

I blow out the smoke and sit up straighter. "You got a message? From Evan Scott?"

"Yeah. What the fuck is this cryptic shit?" he barks.

"What does it say?" Cole growls.

"I see you, but you don't see me. I know who you are, but you'll never know me."

"Hmm," I say to myself. *His is different than ours.*

"Does it have the address at the end of the message?" Ours had a time and place here in Texas for tomorrow evening.

"Yes," Bennett answers. "Why the fuck would I go to Texas?"

Cole snatches the phone up off the table and places it in front of his face, keeping it on speakerphone. "Pack a bag and get your ass to the airport."

"What …? Cole, I can't …"

"I wasn't asking you, Bennett." He growls.

"I have class," Bennett argues.

"Fuck class! Pack a bag and book the first plane to Texas."

Bennet sighs. "Cole."

"Send the info for your flight, and Deke and I will pick you up at the airport. And don't forget your laptop." Cole leaves no room to argue.

"Cole …"

He hangs up on him before Bennett can finish speaking.

I sit back and let out a sigh as I tip the bottle back. "What do you think it means?" I ask Cole.

He doesn't answer right away. Instead, he stands there, his scarred knuckles fisted down at his sides as he stares off into space. No doubt thinking about what all he's been through in the past year. And all that he's lost. What he has to lose now.

"I think it means that once again we're gonna have to do whatever it takes to make sure no one can touch us." Then he looks down at me, arching his brow in question.

Am I in? Do I agree?

"I've got your back," I say without hesitation, then bring the bottle to my lips again.

Without saying another word, he turns and dives back into the pool.

TEN

DEMI

MONDAY MORNING, I walk into my first period at Westlake High and plop down on my seat. This is my first year here. My third month into the first semester. My mother made me move from Oregon to Texas for my senior year, and I hate her so much for it. I had gone to Collins all my life. I had friends. I had been on the cheerleading squad since fourth grade. Then when my sister told my mother she wanted to move to Texas to be with her friend Austin, my mother told me that I no longer had a choice. That there was no one there to look after me anymore. She completely forgot the fact I have a father! He even went to bat for me. Tried to talk my mother into letting me stay there living with him.

"Angelica." He sighs. "She will be fine. Her junior year is almost over. She can finish off her senior year here." He paces the living room while on his phone.

I sit on the couch, biting my nails off one by one.

"So what if Becky isn't here? I'm am." He comes to a stop and squares his shoulders. "I'm her father!" he snaps. "Listen ..." he trails off, and I can hear my mother raise her voice, and I know she's won. She's been trying to get me to come to Texas ever since their divorce five years ago. My only leverage was that Becky was here. I hate her, but my mother felt she was responsible enough to help

my father raise me. Even though the truth is I've pretty much raised myself.

Our father isn't a bad guy. He's not an alcoholic, and he doesn't bring strange women in and out all hours of the night. In fact, he hardly ever dates at all. He's married to his work. That has always been his mistress. And that's what drove my mother to have an affair with her now husband. She left him, and he just buried himself deeper. But he's always been there for me when I needed him. Even if it was through a phone call.

He hangs up, and I look up at him, already feeling the tears threaten my eyes. He turns to face me and lets out a long breath.

"Please don't make me go," I beg. "I want to finish school here. With you. My friends."

He kneels in front of me and takes my hand. "Pumpkin ..."

"Don't," I shout, yanking it from his. "You always take her side. What about what I want?"

He stands, pocketing his cell phone. Any sympathy he showed me moments ago is now gone. She's made up her mind, and he's decided as well. He's not going to fight to keep me. And she just wants me there because of Becky. "I'm sorry, Demi, but your mom wants ..."

"Fine!" I run out of the living room and up the stairs to my room. As I pass Becky's room, her door swings open, and she steps out, blocking my way.

"Why are you crying?" she asks, looking me up and down.

"I hate you," I say, wanting to punch her in the face. She is a waste of air. All she does is take and take from me. And she does it just because. I've never done anything to her.

"And I hate you too." She shrugs. "Mom called me. Asked if you've been good." She looks down at her nails and smiles. "I told her that I've seen you with a boy." Her eyes meet mine. "An older one ..."

"You fucking bitch!" I scream and shove her into her room. She trips over a jacket lying on her messy floor, and I go down with her.

"He never wanted you!" she shouts, yanking on my hair.

"You took him from me!" I fist my shaking hands and hit her in the

face. She killed him!

"I'll take them all from you." She growls.

I go to hit her in the jaw, but I'm yanked back by my shirt. "What the hell are you two doing?" our father shouts.

"She attacked me." Becky begins to sob, placing her hands over her face.

Fucking fake bitch!

I try to kick her, but my father shoves me out of her room. "She ..." He slams the door in my face, closing himself in there with her to hear her side of the story and calm her down.

My world just got ripped out from underneath me. I have to move right before my senior year. I've got less than a month left of my junior year, and in just a few months, I'll be packed up and moved to Texas to live with my mother. The only thing I can hope for at this point is that Becky moves in with Deke because that's the only reason she plans on going there. For him and for her best friend, Austin. I overheard her saying that Austin is following Cole and his little sister, Lilly, to Texas. And I plan on making my sister's life a living hell just as she has done to mine.

"How was your weekend?" my friend Lauren asks as she enters the classroom and sits down next to me. We're not close like I was with my friends back in Collins. But I don't have to have friends. I'm just fine being alone.

I groan. "Shitty. Yours?" I ask.

She gives me a big smile. "Perfect. I got to see Billy."

"And how did that go?"

"Amazing." She sighs heavily. I want to puke. "He's having a bonfire party this weekend out on his parents' property. Wanna go with me?"

I stiffen. The last time I went to a bonfire was my sophomore year while I was still living in Collins. Back when things were somewhat normal.

I sit on my bed, flipping through the channels and looking for something to watch on TV. As usual, there's nothing. A knock on my door has me shutting it off. "What?" I ask.

My sister pops her head in. "Wanna go out tonight?"

I eye her skeptically. She wears a crimson long-sleeve shirt with black lips on it and matching black skinny jeans with a pair of black boots, and her blond hair hangs straight down her back. "No." She never asks me to hang out with her, so for her to do it now is sketchy as fuck.

"Come on." She pushes my door all the way open and steps into my room. "I just spoke to Deke, and the GWS are gonna be there."

My heart skips a beat at the mention of the sharks. I don't know why. He doesn't know I exist. And if he did, he would never like me the way I like him. "Pass." I turn my TV back on. Might as well save myself the embarrassment.

"This is your chance, Demi. Dad is out of town. And Mom keeps threatening to make you move to Texas."

I bite my bottom lip as I think that over. My mother doesn't mind that Becky lives here with our dad, but she's been telling me for four years now that she's going to make me move to Texas to live with her. The only reason she hasn't forced that on me yet is because she's gone more than my dad and she doesn't want me left home alone. I'll hate her if she makes me move. I've only got a couple of years left in high school, and then I'm off to college. And I'm going to choose the first place that accepts me that is far from my family. "Fine," I growl.

She gives me a big smile, and it throws up all kinds of red flags, but I ignore them because I do want to see him. *No matter how much I tell myself I shouldn't. "Get dressed. David will be here in fifteen to pick us up." Then she leaves, shutting my door.*

I jump out of bed. Fifteen minutes? I run to my closet and yank a T-shirt off a hanger and then snap another one from pulling on my jeans too hard.

"Shit. Shit. Shit." I have to hurry! I don't have time to shower.

I pull my jeans up, kicking them in the process to help slide the tight-fitting denim up my legs. I fasten the button and pull up the zipper. I don't even remove my sports bra. I just throw my black T-shirt on over it. Sliding my feet into a pair of black Converse, I pick up the lip gloss and quickly apply it, looking at myself in my vanity mirror. Then I grab the jacket hanging over the chair and run down the stairs.

"Demi, he's here early ..." Her voice trails off when she sees me. She gives me a smile that tells me the fucker was already here when she asked if I wanted to go.

God, I hate her.

"Let's go."

I follow her out of the house, and sure enough, David's leaning up against the hood of his car, and his best friend Maxwell stands next to him.

Fuck. I hate this guy. He likes me. At least I think he does. At this point, I'm not sure if he's just fucking with me or if he truly is interested in me, but I don't care because he's not the one I want to see tonight.

"Hey, Demi, glad you could join us." David smiles at me.

I'm not sure how she got him to date her. He's a nice guy, but she fucking cheats on him. And with Deke Biggs, no less. One of the biggest players in our school. I overheard her talking to him on the phone the other day when she thought I wasn't home. She plays it off as if they are just friends, but he doesn't have any girls who are friends. She was telling him about how much fun she had in the back seat of his Range Rover after one of his swim meets.

"Hey." Maxwell wraps his arms around me and pulls me in for a hug. I leave my hands down by my sides and try not to choke on his cologne. The guy is swimming in it tonight.

"Come on." David nods his head to the driver's side of his black Aston Martin.

"Thank you," I mumble, and he nods his head once at me.

I climb into what should be a back seat, but it's not really. It's cramped, and David is so tall that he has to have his seat shoved all the way back. But I'm not about to sit behind Maxwell. He's just as tall.

"Shit." I hiss.

"What?" Becky asks, getting in beside me.

"Nothing," I answer, looking away from her.

"What the fuck is it?" She snaps at me, showing her true colors.

"It's nothing," I growl.

She huffs.

"You sure, Demi?" David asks, his dark green eyes meeting mine in his rearview mirror.

I nod. I forgot my phone upstairs, but I don't need it. I know David won't leave me behind. It's my sister I'm worried about. And I doubt Maxwell will let me out of his sight.

The car purrs to life, and he puts it in gear before we tear out of my parents' driveway. Sitting in the back, I tune out their conversation and focus on the radio. "Invincible" by Adelitas Way plays.

David drives us to the outskirt of Collins where all the bonfire parties are thrown—on the beach. Kids bring in kegs and tables. They litter them with bottles and cups. They get fucked up. Most end up passing out on the sand or in the forest right off the beach. I've only been to a couple of them, and both times were because David told my sister to let me come. We'll get there, and my sister will ditch me, but David will make sure to keep an eye on me. I trust him.

We pull up and get out. I stretch my cramped legs as my sister walks around the front of the car. "Don't get fucking lost." She throws over her shoulder to me, heading over to the beach. "Keep an eye on her, Maxwell."

"I forgot my phone," I tell David, ignoring her. "Do you know how long we will be here?"

He digs into his pocket and holds out his. "Take mine."

"What?" I look up at him wide-eyed.

"Here. Take it." He offers it to me. A lazy smile on his face. "The code is 1234."

Well, no one ever said he was smart. Most of the rich kids of Collins aren't.

"In case we get separated. You can call your sister's," he offers.

"Thanks," I say softly, "but I doubt she'll answer."

He waves it off. "I've got hers in my other pocket."

I smile up at him before he, too, turns and walks off after her. To my surprise, Maxwell follows him, leaving me completely alone.

I put my jacket on and place his phone in the pocket, then I make my way down to the beach. Kids stand by the tables, filling their drinks. Another group has their jeans rolled up with their feet in the water as they get high. And others sit on big logs that surround the fire. I make my way over there because the breeze from the ocean has me shivering.

Sitting down, I look over to see all the Great White Sharks together. Becky was right; the man I wanted to see is present.

Deke, Bennett, Kellan, Eli, Maddox, and Landen each drink out of their own bottles. The only one who's missing is Cole. I don't see him anywhere. Deke has his arm around a redhead. She's got her legs across his lap. He looks over at me as I sit down. He looks me up and down in a way that tells me what I already know—I'm not wanted here. But then he surprises me when he asks, "Want a sip?" and holds the bottle out to me.

Everyone laughs. "Deke, she's too young," his date says. Her brown eyes look at me, but I don't think she really sees me. She's far too gone at this point.

My jaw tightens. These kids forget I'm not much younger than they are. I may be a sophomore, but they're only juniors. They've been running Collins High since they walked in the doors their freshman year, though.

Eli's eyes meet mine, and I feel a blush creep up my cheeks. He's by far my favorite out of the group, and the only one who ever seems to notice me. Like I'm not invisible. All the others treat me like Becky does—a nuisance.

"I bet you pass out before Demi does," Eli says to the girl on Deke's lap, giving me a wink. And my breath hitches as my body begins to heat up. Whew. The fire is hot all of a sudden.

"She looks to almost be there," I say, and everyone laughs. My shoulders relax a bit.

Deke still holds out the bottle to me, and I yank it from his grasp and down a gulp. I pull it away from my lips, gasping for air. My lungs burn, and I cough at the invasion of the liquid fire.

Again, they all laugh at me. I tilt my head back and bring it to my lips, *drinking some more. I'm prepared to show these fuckers I can hang with them, even if I have to fake it, when the bottle is yanked away. The vodka runs down my chin and onto my T-shirt.*

"Fuck's sake, slow down," Cole growls. He stands beside me, glaring down at me with the bottle in his hand. "None of us are gonna hold your hair later when you're puking everywhere."

"I'll hold your hair, Demi." Eli smirks at me again. "I'm a gentleman."

I bite my bottom lip, trying to hide a smile.

"Yeah, only because your favorite position is doggy style," Deke quips.

Everyone laughs, and my heart beats faster.

Cole just snorts, giving me his back as he walks off with the bottle in his hand. I reach up and wipe the alcohol off my chin and stand. I shouldn't have come. It was a bad idea. I just wanted to party and be around my sister, but she hates me. Not sure why. We've never been close, but it's been worse ever since she noticed I had a thing for Eli.

"You okay?"

I look up to see David walking over to me. A quick look, I see my sister is by one of the tables making a drink.

I nod, crossing my arms around my stomach. It's on fire from those two drinks I had. "I should go home." He frowns. "I'll find a ride."

"Nonsense."

"Yeah, I shouldn't have come."

He looks over my shoulder at the bonfire where I was sitting a moment ago. His jaw tightens. Everyone hates the GWS. They are their own group, and they don't allow anyone into their stupid club of dares and illegal activities. Pretty sure the only way you get in is if you beat the shit out of someone. But they no longer take new members.

"Come on." He throws his arm over my shoulder. "You can hang with us."

I groan. "It'll just make Becky mad."

He snorts. "She wanted you to come."

The question is why. She never wants to hang out with me. What would make this night any different?

We come up to the table, and David speaks. "Hey, babe, hand me that drink you just made."

She turns around. "Why?"

"Your sister needs one." He holds his hand out.

She eyes his hand and then the drink. She spins back around, giving us her back. "Babe ..."

"Here." She hands it to me, cutting him off, then smiles. "I topped it off for you. You're welcome."

I look down at it to see it's full of what looks to be water, but the strong odor tells me otherwise. "What is it?" I ask him.

He laughs, pulling me into his side and answers. "A good time."

Her blue eyes instantly narrow on me, and I pull out from under David's arm. "What is she doing?" she asks, not even bothering to say my name.

"She's gonna hang with us," he answers.

She rolls her eyes, giving me her back, and walks away. "Babe?" He calls after her.

I turn around to go wait for them by the car when I run into a body. "Shit. Sorry ..."

"It's okay."

I look up into a set of brown eyes, and I feel my breath catch. "Hey," I say lamely.

"Wanna get out of here?" Eli asks.

My heart begins to pound in my chest at his question, and my hands get sweaty. He's the only guy at our school who has ever made me feel this way. It's scary. "What?" I blink. I'm afraid he may be talking to someone who stands behind me, but I'm too nervous to turn around and check. This could be some kind of joke. And I hate the thought of it not being real.

He tilts his head as his brown eyes look me up and down in a way that tells me I should run. No one should look at you like that. The hunger in his eyes makes it clear what he wants. And I want to give it to him.

He reaches down and takes my drink from my hand. Bringing it to his nose, he smells it. "Mmm vodka. My kind of girl."

I bite my bottom lip and look at my shoes in the sand. Without a word, he grabs my right hand, and I allow him to lead me off the beach and over to his car, praying he doesn't feel how it shakes with nervousness.

"I'm not sure," I answer her, pulling myself out of that memory. That was almost two years ago. Right before things went to shit. I've tried to forget it, but it'll never go away. Not completely. It's just another reason I hate my sister.

"Come on. Invite Seth." She shrugs. "We'll sit around the fire, tell some ghost stories, and get trashed." Lauren wiggles her eyebrows. "It'll be fun."

I pull my cell out and send a quick text.

Me: Wanna go to a bonfire this weekend?

He messages me back immediately.

Seth: Of course.

I look over at her and smile, knowing that Seth will never hurt me. Not like others have tried. I trust him with my life. "We're in."

DEKE

I open my heavy eyes as I stare out my tinted driver's side window. Leaning against it, I enjoy the cool glass on my skin. Cole sits in the passenger seat with his back ramrod straight and stone-cold silent.

I sat outside for another twenty minutes this morning with him while he swam, but we didn't speak. After I had a couple of cigarettes and enough to drink, I left him and went to bed. When I finally woke up, Austin and Lilly were already gone, and he was in the kitchen. He didn't even look up at me; he just told me we were leaving in an hour to go pick up Bennett at the airport.

So we're playing hooky from classes today, and here we are, sitting in uncomfortable silence. I don't know what to say to him. Or what I can do for him. At this point, I'm afraid he's about to jump off the deep end. And I wish I could say I feel lighter now that he knows Becky was lying, but I don't. Instead, I feel worse. And I hate that bitch even more for putting us all in this situation.

"Why the fuck did he bring him?" Cole snaps.

I look out the windshield to see Bennett walking toward us and right beside him is Shane.

Well, fuck! I don't think Cole's seen or spoken to him since the night at the hospital when Kellan shot Austin.

Cole, Bennett, and I all sit in the waiting room. Becky cries, and I try to console her, running my hand through her hair, but there's not much I can do or say. Honestly, I'm surprised they haven't come out to tell Cole that she's dead.

Cole hangs up his phone with his nanny, making sure she can take care of Lilly. Seconds later, he jumps to his feet, and I look up to see Shane standing in the waiting room. I push Becky off me and do the same.

"What the fuck are you doing here?" Cole snaps.

Bennett snorts, waking himself up. He looks up aimlessly and wipes the drool that runs down his chin. He slowly rises to his feet. "What's going on?" he asks roughly before clearing his throat and trying to focus on his surroundings.

We all look at Bennett. "I don't know. You tell me," Cole demands, thinking that Bennett has informed Shane about what Kellan did to Austin.

He holds his hands up when he sees Shane standing there. "I haven't said anything—"

"I saw the news," Shane interrupts him and then looks at Cole. "Hours ago. I've been calling you guys. Why aren't you answering?"

I've been ignoring his ass. I'm here for Cole and Austin. Anything involving Shane could wait. And Cole hasn't had his phone. He handed it to me when he willingly got arrested because I didn't want them taking it away from him. I just gave it back to him ten minutes ago.

Shane's jaw clenches when no one answers him. He takes a quick look around the waiting area, and then asks, "Where's Kellan?" Shane steps up to Cole when silence follows, his eyes narrowing. "Where. Is. Kellan?"

Cole closes the small distance between them. "Why don't you ask—"

"Cole!" I interrupt him and yank him back by his arm. "I'll talk to him."

"It's none of his business," he snaps at me.

Shane lets out a rough laugh. "Did you make him disappear, Cole? Is that why his phones are off, and he's nowhere to be found?"

"He fucking shot her!" he yells.

Bennett walks over to Shane, grabs his shirt, and all but drags him out the double doors.

I go to stand before Cole. "You need to calm down, man," I whisper harshly. I search the room, and thankfully, it's not crowded this time of the night. But the few people who are in here with us are staring our way. "Cole?" I snap when he stares past me at the doors. Reaching up, I slap his face. Not hard enough to hurt but enough to get his attention. "Listen to me! If you make a scene and get kicked out of here, then that's it. You're done." I place my hands on his upper arms. "The police are just looking for a reason to lock you up, so keep your shit together just a little longer."

"What is going on?" Becky asks, confused about what just happened.

I ignore her.

Cole shoves me out of the way and storms out the sliding glass doors.

I throw my head back. "Fuck."

"What is going on, Deke?" She stands.

"Stay here." I growl and then spin around to run out after him. I walk out to see Cole shove Shane backward. "Cole, don't—"

"No," he interrupts me. "If he wants to be a part of this group, then he's going to fucking tell me."

"Group? What group?" Shane demands, throwing his arms out wide. "You guys have completely lost your fucking minds."

Cole fists his busted knuckles. "No! Kellan lost his mind the moment he decided to want what was mine!"

He throws his head back, letting out a loud laugh. When his eyes

125

meet Cole's again, his laughter dies. "She was never yours. His plan all along was to make her his."

Cole goes to jump him, but I wrap my arm around him and haul him back. "Cut it out!" I growl in his ear. "You're causing a scene!" I whisper, "He could be lying just to get you wound up." At this point, my friends have all taken sides. And Shane is obviously not on Cole's. Who knows what he is gonna say or do to push Cole to make a move? It won't take much. It never has when it comes to Cole.

He shakes me off, and I choose to let him go with every intention to jump him if he lunges for Shane again.

Bennett comes to stand beside Shane. "He remembered her," Shane spits out. "He wanted her! He was only fucking Celeste for his own revenge on Bruce!"

"What did Bruce do to him?" I ask and wonder why in the hell Shane knows this information but not us? One look at Bennett and I know he too knows that secret.

I turn my attention back to Shane. He laughs, shaking his head. "It doesn't fucking matter. None of it fucking matters anymore." Then he turns and walks away, and Cole allows it.

Cole jumps out of the passenger car door, bringing me out of that memory, and I get out as well, though much slower. I pop the hatch to my Range Rover when the guys near us.

Shane looks at me and then at Cole, narrowing his eyes, and I hold in a sigh. I don't even think they've spoken to one another since that day at the hospital five months ago.

"Why did you bring him?" Cole asks, not even bothering to hide his hatred for Shane.

Bennett opens his mouth to speak, but Shane is the one who answers. "I got a message too."

I scratch the back of my head. This can't be happening. "From—"

"Evan Scott," he interrupts me. "It was in a three-way chat with Bennett."

"You didn't mention he was in the chat." I look at Bennett.

"Yeah, well, my mind wasn't completely alert when I was woken up in the middle of the night." He glares at Cole. "After I was hung up on, I looked at it again and saw where Shane was also involved in the message, and I called him. Told him the same thing I was ordered to do, which was 'pack a bag and get his ass to the airport.'"

I grab their luggage and place them in the back and then slam it shut before we all crawl into the SUV. Silence fills the inside of the car, and I can't take it, so I turn up the radio. "Can't Go to Hell" by Sin Shake Sin plays.

"So, what …?" Shane begins to ask, but Cole reaches forward and turns it up louder to drown him out.

I take a quick look at Shane in the rearview mirror, and his eyes are glaring holes into the back of Cole's head.

This should be fun.

We walk into Cole and Austin's house. "You're at the end of the hall." Cole gestures to Bennett. "You're on the couch," he tells Shane, not bothering to look at him.

"Don't you have four bedrooms?" he asks.

"I'm in the other one upstairs," I answer him. It's been months since I've spoken to Shane. The last time was the night he got into it with Cole at the hospital.

He frowns. "You're living here?"

"Isn't that what he just said?" Cole snaps.

Shane drops his duffle bag to the tile floor in the entryway. The motion makes Austin's damn Halloween ghost go off.

Here we go.

"What is your problem?" he snaps at Cole.

Cole takes it as an invitation and doesn't waste a second. He's just waiting to beat the shit out of someone. "You are my problem!" He growls, getting in his face. They're nose to nose. "I don't trust you here! Around Austin."

Shane snorts. "That's rich. Out of the four of us in this room, you and Deke are the ones whose body count are the highest when it comes to our dead friends. And he's fucking living here!"

"I trust him." Cole growls.

"He'd kill Austin without a thought if you told him to."

Cole goes to punch him, but I push his chest, knocking him out of the way. "Okay!" I say, stepping between them. "Can we at least limit the bloodshed to outside? I don't want Austin killing me when she comes home to find blood everywhere," I joke.

No one laughs.

"Come on, Shane." Bennett slaps him on the back and pulls him out of the entryway, grabbing his bag up off the tile.

Cole goes to walk up the stairs, but I stop him. He looks at me over his shoulder. "It doesn't hurt to have numbers on our side," I tell him.

"It only helps if you know they're with you and not against you."

I feel a pain in my chest for him. "No one is gonna touch her, Cole. I promise." He says nothing. "You know I would protect her, right?" Austin is like the little sister I never had. Shelby was always the big sister, and we're close, but Austin is just different. She's just like us. Not afraid to get her hands dirty. Where Shelby would run and hide, Austin would jump to be out in the front. And I think that's what scares Cole the most. He can't hold her back if she decides to dive in.

He finally nods, and with that, he turns and walks up the stairs.

ELEVEN

Deke

LATER THAT EVENING, we find ourselves sitting in the Range Rover once again. I'm driving down the darkened road as Cole's cell rings through the silence. He picks it up out of the cupholder and lets out a long breath before he hits answer and places it to his ear.

"Hello?" There's a pause. "It'll be late." Another pause. "Don't wait up. Love you." Then he hangs up.

I slide my eyes over to him and see that he holds down the power button until it shuts off completely, and then he tosses it back into the cupholder. "Cole—"

"Drop it," he interrupts me coldly.

My hands tighten on the steering wheel, and I clamp my jaw to keep from telling him he's making a fucking mistake. Pushing away Austin is not the answer, but we all deal with our demons differently. And Cole is going to do whatever the fuck he wants.

My phone dings, and I take a quick glance at it. My eyes dart to Cole when I see it's from Austin. "I need to get gas," I say suddenly, needing to pull over so I can read it.

Cole waves his hand in the air, and the guys mumble an okay from the back seat as if I was asking permission. I wasn't. Pulling into the nearest gas station, I put it in park and get out, taking my phone with me. I begin to fill up my SUV when I open the message.

Austin: I don't know what's up with Cole, but you need to figure it out and tell me what I can do. It's getting worse.

I run a hand through my hair and let out a sigh.

Me: I'm working on it.

Austin: Are you with him right now? He's turned his phone off.

Me: Yes, I'm with him.

I top off my tank, and no one questions the fact that I only pumped ten dollars in gas. Or the fact that I just filled up this morning on the way home from the airport.

Twenty minutes later, we pull up to the cabin, and I shut the car off. My lights continue to shine on the little house that the address brought us to at Lake Travis.

"Sure this is it?" Shane asks.

Cole doesn't answer. He just opens the door and gets out. I make sure to grab my gun out of the center console and tuck it into the back of my jeans. Who knows what kind of situation we are walking into? I'm not going to go unarmed. And I know that Cole isn't either. Since the police kept his gun for evidence back in Collins, he's gotten a new one, and he never goes anywhere without it. I'm not sure about Shane or Bennett. I doubt they're armed, though, since they flew in today and wouldn't have been able to carry a gun on the plane with them.

Walking up the five steps, Cole picks up the small flowerpot and grabs the single key. The message we had received told us it would be there. Cole opens the door; it creaks as we step in.

I reach over and flip the single switch on the wall, and it lights up the room. It's not bad for a cabin. A brown leather couch sits in the middle of the room. It has various photos on the walls of the lake that it overlooks, and a TV hangs on the wall. It has a musty smell to it, letting us know it hasn't been lived in for a while.

Cole walks farther into the small house, and I shut the door behind me.

I follow him into the kitchen, and we all come to a stop. In the middle of the kitchen table sits a glass bowl, just like the one we used to draw our dares from. My heart starts to pound in my chest when I see a folded-up piece of paper inside it.

"Shit!" Bennett hisses softly.

Cole walks over to the table and removes the paper from the bowl. Unfolding it, he looks down at it for a few long seconds. Then he wads it up in his fisted hand and throws it to the floor. "Goddammit!"

"What does it say?" Bennett asks.

Shane just stands there, staring at it on the floor.

I pick it up and swallow when I see it's been typed. *Smart fucker.*

"First, there was eight. Then there was five. But you chose to add one more. Now you've killed one of your own. Putting you back to where you were before. What would you do if you lost any more?" I read it out loud.

Then our names are typed one by one, but Eli, Landen, Maddox, and Kellan have a black line through theirs. Then Austin is after that. Her name is also marked out but in red. And below hers, the last name is Demi. Typed black letters but with no line.

What the fuck ...?

"Cole ..."

He reaches up and grabs the glass bowl off the table and throws it into the nearest wall, shattering the glass.

We all stand silently, and Bennett grabs the crinkled-up paper from my hand and his shakes as he reads over it.

Cole places his fisted hands on the table and leans over. His shirt sleeves strain against his taut muscles, and he's breathing heavily.

Shane shakes his head, clearing his foggy mind, and takes the letter from Bennett. He swallows nervously as he too reads over it. "Cole ..." He starts.

But Cole doesn't allow him to finish. He spins around and shoves Shane's back into the closest wall. "Whoa!" Shane throws his hands up in the air. "What the fuck, man?"

Cole grips Shane's shirt. His eyes murderous, and I'm just waiting for him to punch him. Cole loves to handle his problems with his fists. But instead, he takes in a deep breath as though he's trying to calm himself. "If anything happens to her, you're the first one I'm going to kill. Do you understand me?"

Shane's eyes narrow on him. "I wouldn't …"

"Do you understand?" Cole yells in his face.

He gives Cole a curt nod. "Understood."

"Who the hell is Demi?" Bennett asks, looking over the paper again.

Cole lets go of Shane and answers. "Deke's new fuck buddy."

"I'm not screwing her." I sigh. I just dream about killing her. *No big deal.*

Shane brushes his hand down his shirt. "You're fucking Becky's little sister?" He obviously remembers her.

"No." I growl. "It's not like that. And she's with Seth."

Cole snorts.

The rest stare at me with hard jaws and narrowed eyes.

"What?" I snap, not in the mood to play some game with a new psychopath.

"What all does she know?" Shane asks.

"Noth …" My words stop when I realize that's a lie.

"Fuck!" Shane growls. Throwing his hands up in the air, he knows I've run my mouth.

"What does she know, Deke?" Bennett asks, stepping forward.

"Enough." I growl.

"How much is enough?" Bennett snaps.

Cole begins to pace with his head down. Shane drops into a seat at the table and places his head in his hands.

"She knows I've killed five people," I admit.

"Of course, she does," Shane mumbles to himself. I'm about to let Cole knock the shit out of him.

"Why the fuck does she know that?" Bennett shouts.

"After Cole told me that Becky was driving the car when the accident happened, I confronted her at her house and told Becky what I had done. I was pissed. My intentions were to scare her. Demi overheard us talking …" I pause when his eyes widen.

Cole has stopped pacing, and Shane is looking up at me from the table with the same look Bennett is giving me.

"What?" I ask again. "Quit looking at me like that and use your fucking words."

"Becky was driving?" Shane asks breathlessly and then looks at Cole. "Becky was driving the night our friends died?"

Fuck!

Cole says nothing, and Bennett takes a step back from me, running his hands through his hair. He looks stressed but not surprised. "You knew she was driving," I accuse him.

We all suspected that Cole wasn't driving. We thought he was covering for Eli, but he wasn't. Cole took the fall for Becky. I thought Austin and I were the only ones who knew that.

Silence fills the room. And his eyes drop to the floor. "Bennett?" Still, he looks down. His body rigid. My heavy breathing fills the small room, and I take a step closer to him. "Did you know she was fucking Eli too?" I demand.

Bennett says nothing, but I hear the small gasp from Shane. He obviously didn't know. Glad I wasn't the only one who didn't know that information. "Bennett?" I shout.

Lifting his head, his eyes finally meet mine. "I had my suspicions. But no, I didn't know for sure. And when I confronted Eli earlier that week, he denied it." He looks over at Cole, who stands leaning perfectly still against the wall with his arms crossed over his chest. "I saw her that night ... of the accident." He swallows nervously. "The girl I was hooking up with was hanging with Becky. I drove them to the party and she had me drop her off next to Cole's car. I thought she was sleeping with him." I run a hand through my hair. "But then I realized Cole was with Eli, and I knew. I just knew she was there for him." His eyes meet mine, and they soften. "Thirty minutes later, you called me."

I sit in my parents' living room. My father stands, glaring at me in his ten-thousand-dollar suit. His graying hair slicked back and hands in the pockets of his black dress pants. He stands at six foot four, two inches taller than me, but I'd take him in a fight any day. He's strong but slow. Sitting in an office with a girl on her knees sucking you off will do that to you.

I lean back, placing my arms along the back of the couch, and ask.

"Are we done here? I have plans tonight." Being the smartass kid he raised me to be.

His jaw clenches, and I bite back my smile. *"No, we are not done! And no, you are not going anywhere tonight."*

The guys and I had a swim meet earlier, and of course, he missed it. He was too busy to attend were his exact words, but the second I walked in the door, he decided he had time to spare for a chat.

Just then my phone rings, and I reach into my pocket to get it.

"Deke, don't you fucking ..."

"Hey, sis." I answer, looking up at him, and he shuts his mouth once he knows it's Shelby and not one of the guys wanting to know why I'm not at the party yet. *"What's up?"*

"Deke ..." She sniffs.

I lean forward. *"What's wrong? Are you okay?"*

"It's Cole ..." She begins to sob.

I jump to my feet. *"What is it?"* I demand. He and some of our friends went to a party tonight. I was supposed to meet them there, but my dad cornered me on the way out and said we needed to talk about my future. *"Shelby?"* I snap.

"He's here, Deke. At the hospital. They were in a wreck ..." She pauses. *"Maddox, Eli, and Landen ..."* She sobs. *"Didn't make it."*

I run out of my parents' house while my father yells my name. Jumping in my SUV, I fly to the hospital. But on my way, I call Bennett.

"Kinda busy, Deke," he answers breathlessly, on the third ring.

Tears burn my eyes, and I try to take a calming breath while I drive twenty over the speed limit. *"I'm headed to the hospital."* I swallow the lump in my throat. *"Shelby called me ... Cole and the guys were in a wreck."*

"What? A wreck? What are you talking about?" he asks in a rush, and then I hear movement from his end. Sounds like he's getting dressed. *"Is he? Are they ...?"*

"Cole is the only one ..." I blink, and a tear runs down my face. Fuck, I can't catch my breath. *"They're dead, Bennett,"* I say and choke on the words. *"They're all dead. And she didn't say Cole was in the clear."*

He's silent for a long moment. When he finally speaks, I can hear that he, too, is having problems getting his emotions under control. "What about her ... is she ...?" He pauses.

"Who?" I ask, and he doesn't answer. I pull into the hospital parking lot. "Shelby called me and said that Cole was brought in. But Eli, Landen, and Maddox didn't make it. She didn't mention a she." Cole didn't say anything about going out with a girl tonight, but that doesn't mean he didn't pick one up along the way.

"Deke ..."

"She didn't mention a girl," I shout, interrupting him. "I don't know who you're talking about, Bennett. But I just got to the hospital." I pull into a parking spot and shut off my Range Rover. "I'll see you when you get here." Then I hang up before he can go on about some fucking chick.

I rub the bridge of my nose. "The girl was Becky." I nod to myself. "Everyone seemed to know except me."

"I didn't know shit!" Shane snaps.

"I'm gonna tell you both what I told Deke, and that is none of it fucking matters." Cole finally speaks. He points at the paper in Shane's hand. "Someone is trying to fuck with us."

Shane lifts his chin. "What are we gonna do about it?"

"Whatever we need to," I answer.

"It doesn't make sense, though. Why is Demi's name on there?" Bennett sighs.

"She knows. Maybe she set this up, and that's why her name is on it," Shane offers.

Cole shakes his head. "That would be too obvious. She would be the first person we suspected."

"Does she know you're Evan Scott?" Bennett asks me.

I try to think back to what all I said to Becky when I stood in her bedroom three months ago.

I take the stairs two at a time and knock on her bedroom door. "I said not right now, Demi ..." She yanks the door open but stops when she sees it's me.

"Hey," I say gently.

135

She has her blond hair up in a high ponytail and is wearing my Hollywood Undead T-shirt from the concert I went to last summer with the guys, a pair of skinny jeans, and pink high heels. My cock instantly hardens. She knows what it does to me when she wears my clothes.

"What do you want, Deke?" she demands before looking out in the hallway to see if we are alone. Her arms cross over her chest, and those big blue eyes narrow on me—just like her sister. Both Holt women seem to hate me today. This house is like a motherfucking ice castle—cold. "Or should I call you Evan Scott?"

My jaw tightens at her sarcasm. "You know my name is Deke."

"I'm not sure what I know anymore." She shrugs.

"Becky ..."

A noise to my left has us both turning to look, and we see Demi coming up the stairs carrying a bottle of water. She looks at her sister and then at me before she walks right past us with her nose up in the air.

Becky grabs my arm and yanks me into her room, then slams the door shut behind us. I take that as an invitation and step into her. She stiffens. Placing my hands on her hips, I pull her to me. My hard cock straining against my jeans.

"Deke," she warns, feeling it.

I lower my head to her neck and inhale. Her scent of strawberries hits my nose, and I bite my tongue to keep from moaning. I love it when my clothes smell like her. My bed. My car. I love knowing she was there. With me. All mine.

"Well, let me remind you it's me, baby." My voice is rough, and my cock throbs. I wish we were alone. I've fucked her in this room so many times before, but since I know Demi is next door, I won't.

"No." She shoves me away, and I go willingly. I honestly didn't come here to get between her legs. Or her mouth. Although that would be a bonus. "Who the fuck is Evan Scott?"

I run a hand through my hair. "I had to create a fake profile for a dare."

"I don't know." I answer his previous question. "She could have,

136

but I can't say for sure." I don't know how long Demi had been standing on the stairs when Becky called me Evan Scott. But she could have heard Becky ask me about him once she and I were in her room.

"We take her out," Shane announces.

I throw my head back and laugh at that ludicrous idea. I wanted to threaten Demi, but *take her out*? Not happening. Make her life a living hell if she's behind this? Absolutely.

"We're not doing that." Cole shakes his head.

"I didn't get this far to let some little bitch get us thrown in jail. Who the hell knows what kind of information she has?" Shane fists his hands.

"We can't kill her." Cole growls. "We're not in Collins, you fucking idiot. She has a sister. Parents. She's a senior in high school. Not some old guy with no one who would look for her."

"You did whatever the fuck you wanted to do with Austin," Shane snaps.

Cole's eyes narrow on him. "Yes, but she had no one. This situation is not the same. And we're not in a place that we know well enough to start killing people and hiding bodies."

I hang my head and run my hand through my hair. "How about we just ask her what she knows?'

"Do you think she'll be truthful?" Bennett asks me. "Like if she knew her life was in danger?"

I shrug my shoulders. "I don't know."

"This is bullshit," Shane snaps.

"Watch it, Shane," Cole warns. "You're starting to sound like Kellan. And we all know how that worked out for him."

Shane ignores his threat and looks at Bennett. "Speaking of Kellan, how do we know you really killed him?"

"Excuse me?" Bennett quirks a brow at the accusation.

"*I* killed him," Cole corrects Shane.

"But how do we know he stayed dead?" Shane argues, pointing at Bennett. "This fucker could have …"

Shane doesn't get to finish that sentence because Bennett's fist connects with his jaw, knocking his ass into the table.

I grab Bennett by the shoulders and yank him back. "Cole? A little help," I snap, watching him leaning up against the wall.

He releases a huff and pushes off the wall, yanking Shane up off the floor by the collar of his shirt. Not exactly what I meant by helping, but it'll do.

"It makes total sense." Shane shoves Cole away with a growl. "His name is on there and marked off 'cause we believe he's dead, but what if he's still alive?"

"No." Cole speaks. "He. Is. Dead. I made sure that fucker was cold before I handed his ass over to Bennett."

Shane runs the back of his hand over his bloody chin as he glares at Cole. "You willing to bet Austin's life on that?" he asks.

Silence fills the small area. Bennett pulls away from me, and I cross my arms over my chest. Cole squares his shoulders and fists his hands. "I don't care if God himself wrote us this fucking riddle. I've already told you if something happens to her, you're the first one I'll kill."

Shane ignores him and turns to face me. "Did Kellan know Demi?"

"We all went to school together. Of course, he knew her," I answer.

"No, I mean really knew her." He growls. "She's the only one on the list who doesn't make sense." He licks his busted lips. "Did they fuck?"

"Who didn't Kellan fuck?" Bennett growls.

The thought of Kellan and Demi together makes my jaw tighten. I always saw Demi Holt as a good girl. A bitch, yes, but someone with very little experience in the bedroom. She never flaunted herself like her sister did. I figured she'd take a little more time to spread her legs open for a guy. And Kellan didn't have that kind of patience. But then again, I'd never have guessed she would allow me to finger-fuck her in a haunted house either. So, what the fuck do I know when it comes to her and what she will do?

I try to think back to anything that would give away the two of them even communicating in any way. "No," I say when I realize we already know the answer. "But I know how we can figure it out."

"How so?" Bennett asks.

"We have Kellan's phone …"

Bennett shakes his head. "We gave it to the police. Plus, other than the recording I wanted them to have, I wiped it clean."

"We still have his other one. Let's go through it." His phone never mattered before. Austin survived. Kellan was dead, and his body was never going to be found, so we never went through it, but that doesn't mean we didn't keep it.

Cole finally nods. "Grab the note and let's go."

We lock up the cabin and get back into my SUV. As I start my car, my phone dings. It's a new text from Austin. I open it up.

Austin: *Where are you guys? His phone is still off. I'm really worried, Deke.*

Me: *Headed home.*

I throw my car in reverse.

"Who was that?" Cole asks, staring down at my phone sitting in my lap.

"Demi." My stomach instantly knots at the lie. And, fuck, why did I have to say her? Becky would have been a better choice. More believable.

His eyes meet mine, and I know he knows I just lied. I wait for him to call me out on it or maybe punch me in the face. Nothing would surprise me at this point. At least I didn't think so. But then he nods his head once and looks away from me, not saying one word.

DEMI

I sit in my bath, the only light from the flickering candles lining the bathtub. I have bubbles in my water, and Austin's journal in my hand. I haven't been able to put this down. It's like a dark and mysterious maze. Even though I know they end up together, I'm still trying to figure out how Cole will win her over.

He treats her like shit. Blackmail and physical harm are just a couple of things he puts her through, but she dishes it back. In a way, she's my hero. I wish she was my sister and not Becky. Yeah, Austin gave in and had sex with Cole, but it was more than that.

She reminds me so much of myself. She feels this pull to Cole's darkness just as I do to Deke's. I want to see what he can do. How dark he can go. Push his limits like Austin did with Cole. And push him, she does.

She has just completed her first dare in this part. She pulled the fire alarm at school and stole Cole's car keys out of his locker. She needed a distraction to get Bennett out of the school so he could steal Jerrold's laptop. Eli's brother-in-law. The man who was married to his sister. The murderer who killed her just months after Eli died in the car wreck. Deke threw her a party to celebrate it on the beach. And it reminds me of when I went there with my sister and David. The night that changed everything.

I fall into Eli's passenger seat and inhale the scent of his car. It smells like his cologne, and I smile to myself, knowing it's going to be on my clothes long after he drops me off at home.

He gets into the driver's seat and starts it up. "Darkest Hour" by Memory of a Melody plays through the speakers.

A knock comes on his driver's side window, and it makes me jump. He rolls it down. "What's up?" he asks.

Cole leans over, poking his head in. He still holds the bottle of vodka he took from me by the bonfire. His cold eyes sweep over my body and then go to Eli. "Leaving so soon?"

"Just going for a ride," Eli tells him.

"Sure, you are." He slaps the hood of the car. "So am I."

I look over at his Porsche Cayenne parked a few cars down and watch a blonde climb into the passenger seat. She pulls down the visor and fixes her lipstick as if Cole gives a fuck if her lips are fresh.

When I look back at Cole, he gives Eli a smirk. "Make it worth it." Then he pushes off the door and strolls over to his car.

Eli pulls out onto the winding road, and I look down to see I'm still holding my drink. "Will you stop for a second?" I ask.

"Why?" he asks, sliding his eyes over to me for a quick glance.

"So I can pour this drink out."

He snorts. "It's fine."

"What if we get pulled over? I don't want to get you in trouble."

He just laughs. "Don't worry about me, D. It'll be fine."

Warmth runs up my spine at the way he called me D. I bite my lips to hide my grin and turn to look out the passenger window. "Where are we going?" I ask nervously.

"To my favorite place," he says.

My knees bounce with nervousness. This is the first time I've ever been alone with Eli. Or any boy. I've thought about it a hundred times, but none of those compare to him finally showing an interest in me. We talk here and there in the halls of the school, and I've caught him staring a few times. All he did was smile, but I was the first to look away.

I take a small sip of the drink. And hiss in a breath.

He laughs. "Is this the first time you've ever had a drink?"

Among other things. "No," I lie and take another one. The lie burns more than the alcohol. It makes me think of Becky. She lies to everyone about everything. I'm nothing like her. "Yes," I admit and take another.

He stays silent, but I watch a smile spread across his face that's lit up by the lights on his dash. He looks fucking gorgeous with a strong jawline and dark hair that looks like it needs a trim falling in his eyes and curling at the ends. He wears a black hoodie and ripped jeans with a pair of tennis shoes. His parents died when he was younger, but his sister is quite a bit older than him. They had Eli when they were older. Aimee met a good businessman and married him. They took Eli in to live with them when their parents passed.

I take another sip as my thighs tighten. I've wanted to kiss him for so long, and I pray that tonight is the night that happens.

He slows down the car and exits the road onto a gravel drive. I turn and look out the back window but can only see the red glow from the brakes behind us. "Where are we?" I ask.

"You'll see." He remains cryptic, and I take another sip.

He brings the car to a stop and turns it off. "Come on."

I push open the door and do a three-sixty, looking at our surroundings. "Eli, that's the Lowes house," I say, pointing over in the general direction of the only lights on at this time of night.

"I know." He walks around to the back of his car and pops the trunk.

I follow and watch him unzip a black duffel bag. Before I can see what's in it, he yanks out a flashlight and zips it back up. "Come on." He shuts his trunk and grabs my hand. My knees threaten to buckle at the contact. Then he begins to walk me up a hill.

We stay silent. The only sound is our shoes crunching on the ground beneath us. The weather hasn't been as crazy as usual. We haven't had any rain in a couple of weeks.

I shiver from the cool night air and take another small sip of the vodka. My chest heats from the burning alcohol, and I take another.

We walk in silence, and I turn to look back at the car, but nothing's there. Just the dark night surrounding us, hiding us. And I take another sip.

We come to the top of the hill, and my legs falter, bringing us both to a stop. "What are we doing here?" I ask, and my voice shakes.

He turns to face me, his light shining down on the ground. "I told you, this is my favorite place."

Is he joking? He's got to be fucking with me. "Eli, this is an abandoned cemetery."

He shrugs. "And?"

I swallow nervously. "It's creepy."

An evil smile lights up his face as bright as the flashlight he holds. "I know." Then he turns and starts to drag my heavy feet through the bodies laid to rest and never thought of again. I watch as names I've known for years in this town but never really knew pass by us. But then there's one I know all too well. Betty Reynolds—Cole's mother. She was always so nice to me. She'd go out of her way to say hello or check on you.

"Here we are." Eli gets my attention as he comes up to the cliff that overlooks the ocean. He releases my hand and sits down on the ledge. When I make no move to get any closer, he turns to look up at me. "Come on." He pats the spot next to him.

"I'm afraid of heights." I shake my head; my hand tightens on

the cup.

His face grows serious, brown eyes looking up at me. "I'd never let anything happen to you, D." He lifts his hand to mine. "Come on. I wanna show you something."

I take in a deep breath and then take another drink before I place my hand in his along with all my trust.

TWELVE

DEKE

WE ENTER COLE'S house to find Austin sitting at the kitchen table with a plate of untouched pasta in front of her, the fork in her hand just pushing it around. The moment we enter, she stands, and her green eyes widen. "Oh." She's surprised when she looks at Bennett and then Shane.

Did Cole not mention to her that they were coming?

"Hey, Austin." Bennett is the first one to greet her; he walks over and gives her a hug. She returns it. Shane stays where he is, settling for a nod. She gives him a smile, but it looks forced.

"I'm off to bed," I state. "I'm fucking tired."

Bennett slaps me on the back.

"I'm gonna go for a swim," Cole announces to no one in particular. He turns, exiting the kitchen, and heads up to their room to change into his board shorts.

"If any of you are hungry, there is spaghetti in the fridge." Austin mumbles, "Excuse me," and exits the kitchen after Cole.

I, too, make my way up the stairs, not bothering with dinner. I had a late lunch. Closing my door, I hear them talking through the wall.

"Cole, please talk to me," she begs him.

Silence.

"You can't keep doing this."

"Don't Austin," he warns.

"Cole … please …"

"I don't wanna have this conversation with you!" he snaps.

She lets out a huff. "Well, too fucking bad. We're gonna have it."

I rip my shirt up and over my head and unfasten my jeans before shoving them down my legs. I yank the covers back and crawl into the soft bed.

"Why didn't you tell me the guys were coming?" she continues.

"Slipped my mind," he lies.

I know why he didn't tell her. He doesn't want Austin to have the slightest clue of what is going on, but she's a smart girl. She'll figure it out. He should know that by now.

"Well, how long are they staying?" She huffs.

"Don't know." His response is flat.

"Do you know anything?" she snaps.

"I know I'm going for a swim." Their bedroom door opens and then slams shut.

I sigh, placing my hands behind my head and stare up at the white ceiling. I should go down to the pool and talk to him, but sometimes the best thing you can do for Cole is give him space.

I just close my eyes when my bedroom door bursts open, hitting the interior wall. They snap open. I hold in a sigh when Austin enters my room, hands on her hips and a sour look on her face. "What the fuck is going on, Deke?"

I sit up. "That's for Cole to tell you."

"He won't."

"Then I can't help you—"

"Bullshit!" she snaps.

I lie back down and close my eyes, dismissing her. When I hear my bedroom door slam shut, I smile in victory. My left hand reaches out to grab my phone. I need to set my alarm. I have a nine a.m. class tomorrow. My eyes spring open when I feel nothing but my nightstand.

I throw the covers off. "Shit!" My phone is missing. I just had it. I put it right there … "Austin?" I shout her name, running out of my room. I enter their bedroom without knocking and find it empty. But their adjoining bathroom door is shut. I run over and try to open it. It's locked! "Austin?" I pound on the door.

Silence.

Shit! I move back, about to shove my shoulder into the door to get my phone back, but then decide against it. This is Cole's problem. Not mine.

I make my way downstairs and out to the back patio. Cole has his head underwater, swimming laps. I reach over and grab the first thing I can find, which is a towel. I take it and throw it at him. His arm gets caught in it, pulling it underwater. He comes to a stop and lifts his head. "What?" he demands.

"Austin locked herself in your bathroom."

He just stares up at me from the pool.

"And she has my phone with her."

He frowns.

"I don't have a lock on it."

Recognition dawns on his face. Placing his hands on the edge of the pool, he pushes himself out of the water and makes a mad dash for the house.

I follow him but much slower.

"What's going on?" Bennett asks as I walk through the living room, my feet stepping in the puddles that Cole left behind. He and Shane are sitting on the couch.

"Nothing," I answer, not wanting to explain it. Making my way up to my bedroom, I enter and shut my door. I can hear them arguing once again.

"This is no joke, Cole." Austin growls. "This is Evan Scott!" she snaps. Maybe she doesn't know. "Becky told me a while back that Evan Scott was Deke." *Well, fuck!* "And I highly doubt he sent this to you and himself." He says nothing. "And all of a sudden Bennett and Shane show up? Obviously, someone is fucking with you guys. And you were gonna keep this from me?"

"Yes."

She gasps at his honesty. "Why?"

He sighs. "Why would I tell you? Sweetheart"—he softens his voice—"I pulled you into this game nine months ago, and it almost got you killed. I can't lose you …"

"Nothing is going to happen to me, Cole."

"You don't know that," he argues. "And I'm not willing to take that risk. Not again."

"Wouldn't you want me to be alert? I take Lilly to school. I pick her up. She has dance and ballet. I'm not with you a hundred percent of the time. Barely fifty percent now that you have classes and swimming. Wouldn't you rather me know to keep my eyes open for something off than be in the dark?"

He doesn't answer that because he knows she has a valid point.

"You're different," she whispers, and it's so low I almost didn't catch what she said. "And I can handle dark and moody, Cole, but not this one who keeps secrets. We're supposed to be a team."

"I know," he says with a rough voice.

"I'm going to be your wife."

"I know."

"Whatever you are getting into, I'm getting in too."

"No!" He growls.

"Yes! This isn't just about you anymore. You, me, Lilly, and the guys. You're all my family, Cole. I trust you all with my life. You need to trust me just as much."

"I trust you." He snorts.

"Then show me that."

A long silence follows before he speaks. "I love you, sweetheart."

"I love you too."

Then they're kissing. Her moaning follows shortly after. I roll over onto my side and grab the spare pillow on my bed and place it over my head, not wanting to hear them fucking. You would think as much as houses cost these days, the walls would be soundproof.

"Stop," she says.

"Excuse me?" Cole asks, sounding surprised. Pretty sure he's never heard that word from a woman before.

"We need to talk to the guys."

"It can wait …"

"No. It can't. This is important." She growls.

Seconds later, my door opens, and she pokes her head in. My phone sails through the air, almost hitting me in the head. "Get dressed and meet us downstairs."

I sigh and do as she says, wanting to get this over with. I already told them I'm fucking tired.

DEKE

We all gather in the living room. Austin sits on Cole's lap in the leather recliner. I'm perched on the couch next to Bennett, and Shane stands by the back door, refusing to sit.

"Do we have any idea who it is?" Austin asks. Her eyes scan the paper one more time. Cole gave it to her ten minutes ago, and we've all sat here while she silently went over it.

"No." I answer.

"Demi has to be behind it." Shane growls.

"I don't know," she says slowly. "Demi doesn't seem to be that type."

He pushes off the wall. "Deke is fucking her."

"What?" She gasps, her large green eyes meeting mine.

"I'm not." My jaw clenches. I'm only fucking her in my dreams. My dreams where she pretends to be Becky and tells me to hurt her. Too bad I end up killing her every time. I keep that to myself, though. Don't want to cause more worry than there already is.

Shane goes on. "She knows too much. And she needs to die."

I didn't think Austin's eyes could have gotten any bigger when she looks at him. "You can't be serious."

"You have a better option?" he asks.

She turns and looks at Cole. He's running his hand absentmindedly through her hair. "Please tell me you don't want to kill Demi?" I haven't heard that kind of fear in her voice in a long time.

His hand pauses, and he looks up at her. His eyes give nothing away, but his brows crease. "No."

She looks back down at the paper in her hands.

This would be a good time to tell them she threatened me the last time I saw her, but I keep my mouth shut. For some reason, I feel like I need to protect her from Shane. He's on a mission to kill someone, and Demi is his target. Do I think she's capable of this? Not really. But am I suspicious? Yes. If she's behind it, I'll handle her myself. It's not going to require all the GWS to take her down.

"We don't have a lot of options here." Shane growls. "She comes out of nowhere, and all of a sudden, she's on a piece of paper that has some cryptic riddle on it. And we've checked Kellan's phone. Of course, there was nothing on there. He must have deleted everything."

Yeah, that was a dead end. "What do you suggest we do?" I ask her.

Shane snorts as if asking Austin for advice is beneath him. I don't give a shit what he thinks.

She doesn't answer right away. Folding up the letter, she stares out the floor-to-ceiling windows that overlook their pool in the backyard. Regret and sadness flashes across her face, and I wonder what she's thinking about. I'm not sure how well she knows Demi. Becky never hung out with her much. Demi came to a few bonfires on the beach with Becky, David, and his friend, but that was the last time I knew of them ever hanging out together.

Finally, after what seems like forever, she looks at me. "How do you push a girl to think irrationally?"

None of us answer.

She chuckles at our clueless minds. "You make her jealous."

I frown. "Jealous?"

She nods. "A jealous woman is a scary one."

I think back to the time I saw Austin jealous over Cole.

I lean my shoulder up against the lockers as Cole digs through his. Austin walks down the senior hallway, not bothering to look his way, but he sees her, grabs her, and pulls her back to his front before she can pass him. "Miss me, sweetheart?"

She spins around in his arms, reaches up, and slaps him across the face. The sound bounces off the walls.

I take a step back from them. What the fuck ...?

"What the hell was that for?" Cole demands, now glaring down at her.

She throws me a look of disgust, and my brows rise. What did I do? She turns her attention back on Cole. "I'm sure you can figure it out." She turns around and walks toward the door, but he grabs her arm and yanks her back. "Cole!" she snaps.

"What the fuck was that for, Austin?" he demands. "Because I didn't tell you where I went? It was none of your fucking business!"

He spent the day in Texas meeting with his counselor at the University of Texas. He plans on taking Lilly with him, and he can't live in the dorm with a child. He needed to discuss housing, and he already had a few lined up to look at while he was there. He told me this morning before he boarded his plane that he's gonna ask Austin to go with him. He tried to make it sound like it was no big deal, but Cole wanting any woman to move in with him is huge. He loves her. I know it. He knows it. He just refuses to admit it. She had no clue where he went or what he has planned. I don't know why he won't just tell her.

Tears fill her green eyes. She tries to pull away from him, but she gets nowhere. "Just forget it." Her voice cracks.

And I watch in fascination at the way he melts for her. How can he not see it? Feel what she does to him? His eyes soften as he steps into her. "What's wrong?" he asks, cupping her face.

Her first tear falls. "I know where you went."

My eyes widen. How the fuck does she know? I'm the only one he told.

Cole's jaw sharpens. "How do you—"

"I heard it," she interrupts him.

He looks at me, and I throw my hands up, shaking my head. "I haven't said anything."

"What do you mean? You heard it? Who did you hear it from?" He turns his attention back to her.

"I'm not gonna spell it out for you, Cole."

She had overheard her stepmom calling out Cole's name the night before while she was fucking our friend Kellan. He tried to convince Austin that Cole was cheating on her. And she believed it for a day. That was long enough to drive her crazy. That was also the day I found out Kellan was fucking Celeste. We didn't need to know why. There was a reason behind it, but we just couldn't figure it out.

Austin nods, getting my attention. "You force her hand. If she is really Evan Scott, she'll get pissed and act without thinking it through. Make her jealous and see what Evan does next. We get another letter, message, or whatever, then you know it's from her. But ..." She pauses. "I'm just gonna give you my opinion now. It's not Demi."

"Who do you think it is?" Bennett speaks up for the first time.

"I don't know," she answers honestly, and he leans back on the couch, letting out a sigh. "I mean, how many enemies could you have left behind in Collins?" She shrugs. "I think it could be anyone at this point. And if for some reason, I'm wrong, and it's Demi pretending to be Evan Scott, she's not doing it alone. She'd have to have help, right?"

No one answers, but she makes a valid point.

I pull out my cell and send a quick message to Becky. She had messaged me the other day about wanting to meet up this weekend. I don't have time to wait that long.

Me: Wanna have dinner tomorrow night?

"I'm not sure this will work." Shane growls. "How are you gonna make Demi jealous?"

I look over at him. "I'll stay the night with Becky."

"Whoa ..." Austin starts. "I said to make Demi jealous, not hurt Becky. She loves—"

"Becky and I are never going to happen," I interrupt her.

Her mouth clamps shut at my words. Some things just can't be undone. And Becky and I reached that point months ago. But I don't mind using her.

My phone dings.

Becky: I'd love to.

"I'm on. Tomorrow night," I announce.

The room falls silent, and I place my phone down without responding.

"Do we need to tell you this stays between us?" Shane asks, narrowing his eyes on Austin. He doesn't want her running to Becky and telling her our plan.

Cole glares up at him, but Austin just sighs. *She's mad at me.* And a part of me hates that. I see her as a little sister, but no matter how much I love Austin, it's not going to make me love Becky.

"What?" Shane snaps. "She's best friends with Becky. One word could ruin it."

"I'll keep my mouth shut," she tells him. "But thanks for the reminder." Austin gets up and leaves the living room, making her way upstairs. Cole follows her without saying a word, knowing he's finally going to get his dick wet.

THIRTEEN

BECKY

Sᴛᴀɴᴅɪɴɢ ᴀᴛ ᴛʜᴇ foot of my bed, I look over the clothes I have thrown around my room.

I'm having dinner with Deke tonight. And I can't find a single thing to wear.

Every girl's worst nightmare.

The problem is this isn't a first date. I need something that screams love me. Take me back. I can't live without you.

And I have nothing.

All but running out of my room, I enter Demi's. She's out with Seth tonight. I overheard her telling him earlier when she came home to get ready and she would meet him at seven thirty at Lake Travis. His parents have a cabin over there.

I rummage through her closet. She normally doesn't dress like me. She prefers frumpy shirts and jeans with tennis shoes.

Not my style.

But that doesn't stop my mother from buying her expensive dresses. My mother has high hopes for Demi. She sees her representing her lingerie line one day even though my sister gives zero shits about it. I think that's why my mother pushes her. If Demi would just give in, then our mother would probably back off.

I come across a royal blue bandage dress. It wraps around the ribs, showing off a little midriff with a high skirt, connecting the two in the back. I hold it up to my body to measure the length. I'm taller than Demi and my boobs are bigger, but I can make it work. It would probably come to her knees so my upper thighs.

I remove my jeans and tank top right here in her closet and then step into it, thinking it would be easier to pull up than push down. After wiggling my hips and shaking my ass, I get it on. I run my hands down the form-fitting skirt and face the floor-length mirror in the corner of her room.

I smile at myself. It's a little tighter than I'd like, but it will work for dinner. If I play my cards right, he'll be taking it off me later. Just like old times. It reminds me of this one time when he took me on a date, but we had to keep it a secret because I was with David.

Junior year

"What are we doing here?" I ask Deke as he pulls into his sister's driveway.

He turns his Range Rover off. "Don't panic. Shelby's at work tonight." Getting out, he comes around the SUV and opens my door for me.

"Thank you," I say with a nod.

We enter the house, and I wait in the entryway for him to turn the lights on, but he doesn't. Instead, he grabs my hand and leads me down the hallway. "Deke, what are we doing?" I ask again with a soft laugh, but he doesn't answer.

Why did he bring me here? No one knows about us. Even if Shelby isn't home, it's too risky.

We turn the corner, entering the kitchen, and I gasp. A single red rose sits in a glass vase surrounded by four candles in the center of the round table. A white tablecloth covers it, and it's set for two. He lets go of my hand and walks over to the table. He picks up the lighter and lights them, giving the room a soft glow.

He places the lighter in a drawer and looks over at me with a sly smile on his handsome face. "I hope you're hungry."

"Starving," I lie. I had dinner earlier with David and his parents. I tried to get out of it, but he wouldn't let it go. And his mom offered me a glass of wine, so I couldn't turn that down. She's a lush and doesn't care if you're legal age or not.

He walks over to me and places his hands on my hips. His blue eyes look darker in the dim light. Sexier. "You did all this for me?"

His answer comes in a smirk.

I lean forward and place a chaste kiss on his lips. I go to pull away, but he places his hands in my hair and devours my lips with his. When he pulls away, I open my heavy eyes. He runs his knuckles down my cheek. "I'd do anything for you, Becky. All you have to do is ask."

I smile at that memory. Let's hope he still feels that way.

DEKE

I park Austin's Range Rover in Becky's mother's driveway. Her father had bought her a red BMW when she arrived in Collins last January, but she traded it in for an SUV like mine after we moved to Texas. She said it was a better choice and safer for Lilly. But where mine is black, Austin's is white. I drove it tonight because I don't want Demi spotting mine in the driveway when she arrives home. I want to surprise her. And then Angelica won't question why a guy's car is here all night either. She knows Austin's ride, and she'll think for some strange reason Austin stayed here. Not me.

I knock on the front door, and Mrs. Holt's housekeeper answers the door. "Hello, sir." She nods her head in greeting.

"Ma'am. I'm here to pick up Becky."

She smiles at me and gestures for me to enter. "She's upstairs getting ready."

"Thank you." I make my way up the left staircase, knowing that Demi's room is on the right. I come to a stop and lean up against the doorframe. Becky stands in her room, bent over looking at herself in her vanity mirror. She wears a dark blue dress that looks a little too small, but that's nothing new. She's always liked to show off every curve, not that she has many. Demi may be smaller than her sister, but Becky isn't big by any means. She has no hips and no ass, but she does have long, sexy legs. I'll give her that. I used to love having them wrapped around my hips. And her tits, they're a good handful. I always wanted to fuck them, but Becky wasn't into that sort of thing.

As I stand here looking her over, I can't understand why I fell for her. What was it that made me believe every lie? Made me fall in love with her? Was it because she chose me over David? I wasn't faithful to her, but she knew that. I didn't lie to her. She was very aware that I slept with other girls and she couldn't say shit to me about it. She fucked both David and me, and I fucked whoever I wanted. I mainly just did it to piss her off, though, and it worked.

Now I'm going to fuck her to piss her sister off. And I'm hoping that it works. When I find out that Demi is the one fucking us over, I will give her what she wants—me. A motherfucking shark. I'll destroy her.

Becky smacks her lips together and straightens. She pulls her blond curls over her shoulder and turns to face me. She jumps back, letting out a squeal of surprise. "Deke. How long have you been standing there?"

Even her voice makes my skin crawl. "Long enough."

She runs her hands down her dress nervously, and I give her a smile. *I'm not gonna hurt you.* Just going to use you.

"I'm ready when you are." She clears her throat and reaches for a clutch that sits on her dresser. Her eyes move to her bed for a brief second, but I don't miss the longing in her eyes. There was a time when I would have already had her dress off and her lying on her back with my head between her legs.

Not tonight.

I'm in no rush to fuck you. I'm going to take my time. I've got all night, after all.

She makes her way over to me, and I reach my hand out for her. We make our way down the stairs, and just as we reach the door, I hear a set of heels clapping on the tile floor behind us. "You kids have fun tonight."

I turn around to see Angelica walking toward us. I remember her from when we were younger—back before the divorce—and she has always been a bitch. Angelica has her bleach blond hair up in a tight bun. She wears a skintight black skirt that reaches her bony knees and a white silk blouse tucked into the high waist with a black blazer. A string of pearls rests along her thin neck. She looks every bit of the powerhouse woman she is. A self-made billionaire. Becky looks identical to her. She has Becky's height, but I'm pretty sure she weighs less than Demi. I don't think the woman ever eats. The buzz going around town was she used to be addicted to diet pills back when we were in middle school. My mother chatted about it for months because she was jealous of Mrs. Holt. I think because she wasn't afraid to go after what she wanted. She wanted to be skinny, and she was willing to do whatever it took to achieve that. My mother wouldn't know commitment if it bit her in her silicone ass.

She comes to a stop and frowns. "Becky, isn't that Demi's dress?"

Becky smiles but rolls her eyes. "Yes, but it's not like she's ever gonna wear it."

Her mother sighs. I know Becky is her favorite because she never hid that from anyone. Becky was her mini-me in every way. Demi may look like them, but she never had that desire. She was forced. But that doesn't stop her from wanting Demi to give in to their ways.

"Just be careful with it." She places her hands on her nonexistent hips. "And put it back where you found it afterward."

FOURTEEN

BECKY

He TOOK ME to Austin Stonelake. I've never been here before, but I've heard of it. It's just as fancy as they say. Dim lighting with white tablecloths and folded black napkins. There's a vase at every table with a single rose in it. It immediately reminded me of our dinner at his sister's house that night. It must be a good omen.

We've already had our appetizers and are currently finishing our main course. It's been awkward. We've been quiet, but I'm not sure what to say. And I don't think he has much to talk about.

I lick my lips and take a deep breath. "I was in Collins last weekend."

"Oh, yeah?" he asks, not bothering to take his eyes off his plate.

"I saw your father." That gets his attention.

He drops his fork and looks up at me. Slowly, he lifts his black napkin and rubs the corners of his mouth. "And?" His voice has gone cold.

I knew it would. His father is the last thing I want to talk about, but if it gets his attention … "He misses you."

He snorts at that. "Doubtful."

I lower my eyes to my plate. "He said he's been calling you."

"And I've been ignoring him."

"Why?"

He takes a drink of his water and sets it down. "Since when do you care about my father? You never have before."

Honestly? I hate that man. He always tried to use Deke. He had Deke's life mapped out for him from the moment he was born, but Deke didn't care. That was the problem Langston had. His only son wanted nothing to do with him or his plans to take over the world. Deke always had that ability on his own. Deke and Langston both know it.

I shrug. "I don't. I just thought you should know."

"Thanks," he says dryly before picking up his fork and getting back to his meal.

The rest of dinner went by slow and silently. We didn't speak, and I hated it.

Things aren't going how I wanted them to. He was supposed to see me in my dress, take it off, and make love to me. I can work with that, but this? I don't know what to do. Things used to run smoothly between us, but now nothing but secrets and lies hang in the air, choking us with every breath.

We pull up to my house, and I pause when he brings the car to a stop. I haven't asked him why he's driving Austin's Range Rover. I'll ask her tomorrow. She won't lie to me. Not like Deke will. I lick my lips nervously, trying to think of an excuse to get him to come inside, but he turns the car off.

We make our way inside silently. All the lights are off, and I know my mother is already in bed. She goes to sleep early because she starts her day before the sun ever rises. I make my way up the stairs slowly, and he's right on my ass.

We enter my room, and I flip the light on. He makes his way to the end of my four-post bed and sits down on the peach satin comforter. I watch him unbutton his cuff links and roll up his sleeves. He wore a black button-down and black slacks, making him look so much older than I know he is. This moment feels as if we're a married couple coming home from an anniversary dinner. Our kids at the sitter. And an endless night of me and him rolling around in our bed.

My mouth goes dry at the thought of him touching me. It's been too long. Deke has always had this hold on me. No matter how many lies I told him, I loved him. And I know he loves me just as much. It's just going to take a little push on my end.

"Would you like anything to—"

"No," he interrupts me, standing.

I swallow the knot that forms in my throat when he reaches up and undoes the first button on his button-down.

Why am I so nervous? Maybe because he knows the real me. No matter what I tell him now, he'll see right through me. And that's terrifying.

"Stop," he orders.

"What?" I blink.

He comes to stand in front of me. His hands go to the hem of my dress. He grips it in his fingers and slowly pulls it up my thighs. "Thinking."

"Deke."

"Shh," he whispers, bringing the dress up and over my hips to expose the black lace thong that I wore just for him. He used to love it when I wore lace. It's a pair from my mother's line.

"Undo my pants," he commands.

My hands go to his black belt, and I undo it quickly. I pop the button on his slacks and then the zipper. His right hand slides into my hair, and I whimper when he tilts my head back. I stiffen, afraid he may rip my throat open with his teeth. Just because I want him to love me again doesn't mean I trust him.

"Tell me," he whispers before peppering my neck with feather-like kisses.

"I miss you," I say, knowing exactly what he wants to hear. It's the same thing he told me the night he kissed me in Cole's kitchen before we went to Silence.

"How much?" His left hand slides between my legs, and he rubs my pussy over the thin material. I'm already wet. Have been all night.

"So much," I pant.

"Tell me to fuck you."

My heart beats quicker at his words. He knows I don't like the word *fuck* when used in reference to us. I know Deke has a dark side, but he can be the gentlest lover. He can make you feel loved and not used, but clearly, tonight is about him. I should have suspected it would go down this way. He's still mad at me, and he's going to make me grovel before he gives me what I want.

"Fuck me." I choke on the words, but I feel him smile against my neck.

He's going to win this round because I need him to think he has me right where he wants me. *Enjoy it, Deke. It won't stay this way for long.*

DEMI

I pull up to my mother's house and get out of my car. I frown when I spot Austin's Range Rover parked in the driveway. What is she doing here this early? It's a little after eight a.m. Doesn't she have to take Lilly to school? Maybe she's already dropped her off and came over here to pick up Becky to hang out for the day.

I enter the house, not caring about going unnoticed. My mother is already at work, and by the five texts she has sent me, she knows I didn't come home last night and that I'm running late to school. I just haven't cared to open them up to read them. I make my way up the right staircase but slow my pace when I hear Becky's door creak open. What's she doing up this early anyway? She stays up late and sleeps in, which makes me question why Austin is here even more.

I get my answer the very next second. She leans up against the doorframe, and Deke stands in front of her, his massive size filling the doorway. He has his right hand on her hip and his left in her hair. She smiles up at him like a fucking schoolgirl. I reach the landing and quit walking completely, but I don't release the railing. I grip it so tight my knuckles are white.

"I had a great time," she purrs.

He smirks down at her. His black dress shirt is unbuttoned and untucked. It's wrinkled so I know it spent all night on her floor. She wears an oversized T-shirt, and that's it. It barely covers her pussy.

He doesn't say anything to her. Instead, he tells her how much fun he had by placing his lips on hers. He wraps both arms around her and pulls her away from the door. He spins her in a half circle, placing her back to me. Letting go of her waist, he places both of his hands on her face. She moans, and I stand watching like a deer in headlights.

What the hell is he doing? Does she truly believe he wants her? He hates her. I saw it in his eyes when he spoke of her in his room. When he compared me to her. This must be some kind of joke.

He pulls his lips from hers, tilts her head to the side, and lowers his lips to her exposed neck. He opens his eyes, and they land right on me, across the balcony. He knew I was here. "Fuck, *Becky!*"

My heart pounds at the way he moans her name while he stares at me, but it makes total sense. Why he's here. Me. He wants to fuck with me. He's making it very clear that no matter what kind of lying whore she is, she's better than I am, and I'll never live up to her. He doesn't have to say the words. I can read it in his cold crystal blue eyes. And the fact he's not the least bit surprised to see me.

"Deke," she pants, falling for his shit.

His eyes remain on mine as he licks his way up her neck to the shell of her ear.

I want to run over and rip her off him. I want kiss him, to show her that he was touching me the same way just two nights ago, but I can't. I've become immobile at the sight of him taunting me. Playing with me as if I'm some fucking amateur.

He pulls away, and the smirk on his face tells me all I need to know.

Fuck you, Demi!

He finally looks away from me and leans down, giving her a peck on the cheek. "I'll call you later." Without another word, he walks down the staircase and exits the house.

I look at my sister, and I watch a smile grace her face. It's that Becky Holt smile she hides from everyone but herself. The I-fucked-you-over smile.

They're both playing their own games on one another. *But why?*

As if she just realizes that he's gone and no longer has to pretend, the smile drops off her face. Taking a step back into her room, she slams her door shut.

I stand there still trying to wrap my head around what I just saw and why I'm so pissed off about it when her door opens, and she tosses a wad of clothes into the hall by her door, then shuts it again. I notice a dark blue dress that looks familiar and find myself walking over to it. Our housekeeper hates when Becky does this, but she doesn't care.

I pick up the blue dress and clench it in my hand. *She wore my dress.* Not that I would, but I hate the idea of her being in my room and snooping through my shit. This is exactly why I make sure to have Austin's journal on me at all times. I turn the dress over and frown when I see a white spot that looks like a dried substance. I run my thumb over it, and it hits me. It's come. She wore my dress last night while he fucked her. And didn't even bother to remove it.

Motherfucker!

I enter my room. Plopping down on the end of my bed, I pull out my phone and send a text to Seth. My fingers moving so quickly, my mind can't keep up with them.

Me: Party at my house Halloween. Spread the word.
Seth: You sure you wanna do that?
Me: Yes.
Seth: What about your sister?
Me: She won't be here. She's going back to Collins for the weekend to spend it with my dad.

I smile as I lean back onto my bed and stare up at my ceiling. I have a plan already. One that will knock them off their game. They won't know what hit them.

FIFTEEN

Deke

I'M IN ENGLISH Lit. Cole sits to my right, holding his pencil like a fucking weapon. He's still on edge. Austin's been able to calm him down in the evenings, but he's still on high alert most of the time. It's been five days since we went to the cabin, and three since I fucked Becky.

Nothing has happened.

No new messages or threats.

I can't decide if that's a good or bad thing. Bennett and Shane went back to Collins last night. They had missed enough classes and decided that since nothing was happening, it was time for them to return. I couldn't agree more. Bennett was always texting away on his phone, and Shane was constantly looking at Austin as though he was plotting her murder, and Cole noticed. It was hard for us all not to see it.

I haven't heard from Becky. She put the ball in my court on purpose after our night together. I told her I'd call, and I haven't. At this point, I have nothing to say to her. She played her part. And I played mine.

"Tell me to fuck you," I whisper.

"Fuck me." She chokes on the word, and I refrain from smiling. She knows what I want, and although she doesn't want to give it up,

she's going to take one for the team.

She's so fucking transparent.

I reach down and push her underwear down her long legs, and she steps out of them. Then I grab her hips and pick her up. She gasps, wrapping her legs around my waist. I toss her onto her bed and run my finger over her pussy. She's not soaked, but she's also not dry. It'll work. I'm not in the mood for foreplay, and she never was one who liked it. She may be a slut, but she's not up for playing around. She normally spreads her legs and lies there like a fucking doll, but that won't be the case tonight.

I lift up and flip her over. Spreading her legs with mine, I grip her hair in one hand while I push inside her in one quick motion. She cries out, but I don't slow down. I fuck her hard and rough. My hand maintains a hold of her hair while my other hand shoves her chest into the comforter, making her back arch at an uncomfortable angle. And once I'm done, I pull out and come all over her dress that I didn't remove on purpose. I left it bunched up around her waist. And I'm leaving Demi a little surprise that I hope she'll find. It's her dress, after all, and I know if Becky gets the chance, she'll throw it in Demi's face. Literally.

"Hey, man?"

I look over at Seth as he's putting away his books.

"What are you guys doing for Halloween this weekend?" he asks.

"We're taking Lilly trick-or-treating," I answer.

"We're having a party on Saturday." The day after Halloween. "You guys should come."

"Who is?" Cole asks, Seth getting his attention.

"Demi is. At her parents'."

I smile. "Really?"

He nods. "Her parents are gonna be away for business, and Becky will be in Collins. She's gonna have the house to herself." He smiles, leaning back in his seat. "Thought I'd let you guys know. You're more than welcome to come, and you don't have to dress up if you don't want to."

I turn to look at Cole, and he nods to Seth. "We'll be there."

"Awesome." He grabs his books. "I'm guessing you don't need the address?"

"Nope," I answer, and he laughs, getting up and walking out of the classroom.

Cole looks at me. "Think that's what she's waiting for? A party at her house?"

"No." I shake my head. That's not how Demi would do it, if it's her. "She wouldn't do anything in front of a crowd. Otherwise, she wouldn't have sent us to some old cabin to read a fucking letter."

He snorts in agreement.

We make our way out of the classroom, and I see Seth leaning up against the wall talking to a brunette. She looks up at him with big brown eyes, totally transfixed by his words. I knock my arm into Cole's to get his attention.

We come to a stop and watch them openly. She nods a few times, and he smiles down at her with what could only be described as love. I recognize it because I've looked at Becky that way before.

"Interesting," Cole mumbles next to me, seeing the look on Seth's face.

They're unfaithful. Just as Becky was to David. No wonder Demi allowed me to touch her so easily and begged me to prove she was better than her sister.

They're exactly the fucking same.

It pisses me off. Not sure why. I've known that Demi is with Seth. Every time I touched her, every dream I've had of her, I've known she's taken. But when has that ever stopped me before? Why would it now?

She leans up on her tiptoes and gives him a soft kiss on the cheek, then turns and walks off. He pulls his ringing cell out of his pocket and puts it to his ear. "Hey, babe." He greets who I can only guess is Demi. Or hell, maybe he's got more on the side. "Yeah, I'll come over after you're done with class." He smiles to himself. "Wear the black one," he says and then turns and walks off.

We stay standing, my mind wondering what *black one* he's referring to. And wishing I could see it as well.

DEMI

Sophomore year

I take Eli's hand, and he helps me sit down beside him on the cliff. My legs dangle off the ledge, and I take another drink. My body shakes, and my breathing is labored. Why do girls do things they don't like to impress a boy? I'm not sure anyone will ever be able to answer that question.

"Hey." I jump when Eli places his arm around me and pulls to his side. "I got you."

I look over at his brown eyes and soft smile playing on his pretty face. "Why are we here?" I ask.

The smile drops off his face, and he looks out over the dark ocean. The moonlight shines down on it, making it look beautiful but deadly. "I come here a lot with Cole and Deke." He swallows. "After Betty died, there were times he wouldn't answer our phone calls or texts. He'd miss school and swim practice. We always worried about him." He sighs. "But one day, Deke convinced me to skip school and go look for him. We found him here, sitting at his mother's grave."

My chest tightens for Cole and the loss of his mother, and tears sting my eyes. I can't imagine what it would be like to lose a parent. Even if I don't like mine most of the time, I'd hate to have to live without them.

"We sat here with him in silence until the sun went down. And then without saying a word, he turned and walked down to the Lowes estate."

"Why?" I ask curiously.

"That's where Lilly was. Celeste always watches her for him."

I don't like her. There's just something about Celeste and Bruce Lowes that I don't trust.

"Deke turned and left as well, but I walked over here and sat down." He smiles, looking out over the calm water. "And that's when I heard them."

"Heard what?" I whisper.

He turns to look at me, his left hand coming up to cup my face. "Just listen."

I stop breathing. My heart pounds wildly at his warm hand on my cheek. I feel a blush creep up my face, and I'm thankful it's not daytime. "Kiss me," I say without thought.

His eyes drop to my lips, and he licks his. "Demi, I can't ..."

"Please," I beg him.

He sighs heavily. "Listen to me, Demi." His other hand comes up to hold my face as well.

The world starts to spin.

"You're too good to be someone's secret. And we both know that's exactly what you would have to be if we got together."

I know he's right. He's the oldest of the GWS. He'll be turning eighteen this coming summer, and I'll still be sixteen. "I don't care," I whisper. My mouth going dry suddenly.

He frowns. "You deserve to be someone's fucking world, Demi Holt. Don't ever think anything less of yourself."

"I wanna be your world," I say, feeling dizzy. I blink a few times, but it doesn't stop. I fall backward, and he catches me.

"Whoa." He gets to his feet and helps me move away from the edge of the cliff. He tries to get me to stand, but I stumble over my feet. "How much did you drink?" he asks.

"I ..." I blink. "Not much."

He grabs the drink from my hand and looks down at it.

"I think ... I'm gonna get sick ..."

He brings the cup to his lips and takes a sip. Then he's spitting it out. "What the fuck? Who gave you this drink?"

I try to think back. Who was it? My mind is foggy and ... "Becky." I slur.

"You sure?"

I nod and almost lose my balance again. "Yeeeaaahhh."

He pours the drink out and shoves the now empty cup into the pocket of his hoodie.

"I ... I don't feel well," I slur, leaning over and placing my hands *on my knees.*

"I know." He places an arm under my legs and the other across my back to pick me up.

Looking up at him, I blink as he carries me through the cemetery and down the hill. I watch his sharp jaw and a muscle tic in his neck. He's angry with me.

"I'm sorry. I don't ..." My eyes close. "Drink."

Then everything goes dark. When I open my eyes next, he's placing me in the passenger seat of his car. He reaches across me and buckles my seat belt. My arms feel heavy, my mind sluggish. Then his hand cups my face. I lean into him.

"This isn't your fault, Demi." His narrowed eyes search mine before he growls. "Your sister drugged you."

Present

"Ready To Die," by TheUnder pumps through the speakers of my mother's house. I stand in the kitchen sipping away on a rum and Coke. It's my third one. I've come a long way since I had my first drink out of Deke's bottle that night on the beach. I learned several important lessons that night that I'll never forget.

"What are you thinking?" Lauren asks, coming to stand beside me.

She's the only friend I have here. But I'm not like Becky; I choose to have a very small circle. Most people don't like my sister, but it's the opposite with me. I don't like most of them. They lie. You can't trust anyone.

She pours herself a drink. She's pretty much the only one here from our high school. Most of the people have been invited by Seth from the University of Texas. And hardly anyone dressed up in costume. They're all too old for that shit. There are a few girls who remind me of my sister and are half-dressed begging for attention from the men, but for the most part, the partygoers are just here to get drunk and have a good time. I didn't even put up any decorations. And my mother doesn't bother herself with such pointless shit. Her words.

"Nothing."

"Liar." She giggles. "Where's Seth?" She looks around the packed kitchen. The guy to female ratio is laughable. There are probably five guys to every one girl. Seth plays football for UT, so he's popular with all the athletes at the college. He spread the word well.

"Somewhere."

"What is up with you?" She shoves my shoulder.

When I don't respond, her eyes follow my line of sight across the open kitchen to see Deke and Cole standing in the formal dining room, leaning up against the forest green wall. *They came.* Just as I knew they would. Deke can't pass up a party. They're talking to a couple of guys who Seth knows from UT. I watched them walk in an hour ago. Neither one of them has said a word to me. Cole hasn't even looked my way, but I've caught Deke staring several times.

"Damn. Who the fuck are they?" she asks.

"Taken," I say.

She snorts. "As in married?"

"The one on the right is engaged." Cole might as well be married.

I finally finished Austin's journal. And to say I was surprised to read about their love story is an understatement. They went through so much. He tortured her in such a way that it made me rethink what I'm going to do tonight. He is pure evil in the prettiest form, and I bet Deke could match him on any given day.

I'm going to find out either way.

"Then he's available." She winks over at me.

I turn to face her fully. She's just like my sister. When she sees a pretty face, she wants to spread her legs, even if that means cheating on Billy. "He will eat you up and spit you out. And if he doesn't kill you, his fiancée will." Her green eyes widen at my words. I lean in and whisper, "Then she'll burn your body and take a hammer to what's left. Stay the hell away from him," I warn.

She swallows nervously but chuckles.

I aspire to be a mini Austin—badass and untouchable. That's why I decided to continue with my plan for tonight. *It has to be done.* It's time. I've been holding onto something for too long that means so very little. Not to me. My sister tried to take it before, and now I'm going to throw it away.

For revenge. And it's going to be so fucking sweet.

I pour two shots of vodka and hand her one. "Drink up," I order. She clinks her glass to mine, and I look over the rim, throwing it back to see Deke's blue eyes on me. I smile to myself.

The song changes to "Left Alone" by Zero just as Seth enters the room. I give him a smile when his eyes lock on mine. "Hey, babe," He grips my upper arm and yanks me from the counter, causing my drink to fall over. "Ow …"

"You did not do what I think you did!" he snaps so loudly that it causes people to look our way.

My eyes widen. "I don't know what—"

"Don't fucking lie to me, Demi," he shouts.

I look around nervously, and I don't miss seeing Cole and Deke looking right at us now. I quickly look away and back at Seth. "Can we talk about this somewhere else?"

"Fine!"

SIXTEEN

DEKE

I PUSH OFF the wall the same time that Cole does, and we make our way out of the formal dining room, through the kitchen, and to the grand foyer. I watch Seth drag Demi up the stairs like a rag doll. My fists clench when I see how hard his fingers are digging into her upper arm.

"You're hurting me." Her small voice travels down the stairs.

"And you're being a slut! Just like your sister," he snaps.

"Seth?" I call out, already taking the stairs two at a time.

He looks down at me, then at Cole who I notice is following close. "Walk away, guys, this doesn't concern you."

"Actually, it does." Cole crosses his arms over his chest as we hit the landing. "Let her go."

The upper floor of the house is quiet because it's off-limits to guests tonight. And I know that's why he brought her up here. To be alone with her. The only sound is the song playing through the speakers.

He releases her, and she immediately cradles her arm to her chest.

"Fine." He looks down at her with disgust. "You can have her." He turns and storms back down the stairs, shoving a guy into a wall.

"Demi …" I reach down to look at her arm, but she pulls away and turns, running over to her bedroom door.

"Go," Cole says, but I'm already moving.

"Demi?" I call out, but she ignores me.

I reach her before she can open the door and spin her around. She looks up at me with tears in her beautiful eyes. "You okay?" I ask, clearing my throat. I've had quite a bit to drink tonight, knowing that Cole was going to be my DD. He doesn't drink much anymore after the night of the car wreck. And if he does, it's at his house.

She sniffs and looks away from me. I step into her, grip her chin, and force her to look up at me. "I asked if you're okay."

Her wet lips part, and she takes in a deep breath. "Fine." She gives a clipped answer.

"Let me see your arm," I order. Surprisingly, she holds it out for me.

Bruises are already forming, and I clench my teeth at the thought of him hurting her. "Does he do this often?"

She drops her eyes to the floor again.

"Demi?"

"No," she whispers. "He's never done that before."

I run a hand through my hair. "What happened?" Not that whatever happened excuses what he did. I'm just being nosy.

She sniffs. "He found out about us."

"Us?" I frown.

She nods. "I was texting my best friend about what we did at Silence ... and he read it."

"Fuck," I hiss.

She looks up at me, and the first tear runs down her cheek. "He thinks we had sex."

I have. Fuck, I have fucked her in so many different ways in my head. Each one more sinful than the last. She cried, she screamed, and she came so fucking hard. But I know the real thing could never live up to my imagination.

Stepping into her, I reach up and run my knuckles through the single tear, smearing it across her cheek.

Her hands come up and grip my shirt. "Deke." She whispers my name, and it goes straight to my dick.

The alcohol swirling around in my head tells me to kiss her, but another part says back away and leave. I've watched her since the moment I walked through her mother's front door. I attempted to follow pointless conversations with kids from school, but nothing kept my interest. Nothing but her. No matter how hard I've tried, she is there. In my mind, she's naked and begging me to fuck her. "You're with Seth." I find myself saying out loud as if I'm trying to talk myself out of it.

Don't touch her!

Her bright blue eyes meet mine. "He already thinks I've betrayed him." She licks her lips. "Might as well give him a reason to put his hands on me."

"Don't say that." I growl, stepping into her. I know there's a darker side to Demi. I watched her the first night I snuck into her mother's house. She sat on her bed watching that fucking documentary on YouTube about the serial killer. She's curious, and that isn't a good thing. She can push the wrong man to do something very bad to her. And my anger rises at that thought. If any man is going to put his hands on her, it'll be me.

She tilts her head back, licking her plump nude-colored lips. "It'll be worth it."

I slide my right hand into her hair, and her eyes close as she lets out a moan. Her hands go to my jeans, and she pulls my hips into hers. My hard cock aches as it rubs against the fabric of my boxers. Fuck, this can't be happening. Someone needs to interrupt us …

"Kiss me, Deke."

"I won't stop," I admit. I want to hurt you, Demi. I want to show you what I can do as much as you want to see it. It won't end well for her. But she may like it …

Don't do it. Walk away, Deke.

Her lashes flutter open, showing me those gorgeous blue eyes once again, and I'm fucking done. I'm about to do something I'll regret, and she knows it. She reaches back, turns the knob on the door, and pulls me inside the dark bedroom.

I rip her shirt up and over her head, and I allow her to remove mine. She is fumbling with my jeans, and I've already got her jeans down to her ankles. "Light …"

"Leave it off."

I yank her to a stop with my hands on her hips. I dig my fingers into them, holding her in place. "Are you shy, Demi?"

I can hear her panting, and I want nothing more than to see her bare chest. "Kinda."

I smirk. "There's nothing to be shy of, baby. I've already had my fingers inside you."

She whimpers. "Please," she begs, and it does things to me that I can't quite explain.

She reaches inside my unbuttoned jeans and grabs my dick. I jump when her soft hand makes contact. "Fuck." I groan, pumping my hips into her hand.

"Yes, please …"

My lips find hers in the dark, and we stumble backward. I dig into my back pocket and grab my wallet; I remove the condom and then shove my jeans down my legs along with my boxers. Somehow, we find the bed, or she leads me to it. I don't know.

"I Don't Even Care About You" by MISSIO blares through the speakers as I crawl on top of her and slide my cock into her. No time for foreplay. No need for it. She's soaking wet, and I'm fucking hard and have been waiting for it for what feels like forever. My teeth clench, and my breath catches at how tight she is. "Fuck, Demi!" I groan in pleasure. "God, you feel …" I push my hips forward, going in deeper, feeling her squeeze me to the point it's almost painful. In the best fucking way.

"Deke ..." She gasps, her nails digging into my back.

"Incredible."

Things begin to get blurry. In the darkness, all I can do is feel her. And I do. Every fucking inch of her tight cunt. She's screaming my name. My hands are in her hair. My lips on her warm skin. The room is hot, almost suffocating. She's coming once, then a second time. And I throw her legs over my shoulders as I fuck her with so much force, I can taste the salty tears that run down her cheeks when I kiss her.

I don't know how long I'm inside her; all I know is that it's not long enough. And then I'm coming.

Her body shakes uncontrollably. We're both covered in sweat and trying to catch our breath. We lie silently next to one another as what we just did hits us with full force. And I fist my hands at the weakness I showed.

I just fucked Demi Holt!

Fuck!

The sad thing? I'm ready for round two. I wrap my arms around her small body and pull her back into my chest. I'll do her from behind this time. But I pause because she's shaking uncontrollably. "You okay?" I ask. Kissing her shoulder, I feel pieces of her hair stick to my lips.

"Just go, Deke," she whispers.

"What?" I ask, pulling away from her.

"I'm tired. Go."

I get out of the bed and begin to feel around the floor for my clothes. I find my jeans and shirt but can't find my boxers. Fuck 'em! Once dressed, I stand in the darkness and just listen. A softer song plays in the house so it's easy for me to make out her even breaths. She's passed out.

I exit the room and come face to face with Cole standing on the balcony leaning up against the railing. His eyes meet mine, and he frowns. They dart across the balcony to the other door and then back to the one I just exited.

"What?" I snap. I'm fucking pissed at myself, on one hand for doing what I did and on the other for wanting to go back in there and do it again.

"Nothing." He shakes his head. "Ready to go?"

I don't answer. Instead, I turn and run down the stairs and out of the fucking house. Once outside, the cool air hits my sweaty skin, making me shiver. I inhale the fresh air and close my eyes.

What the fuck did I do?

You just fucked Demi, and she was right. It was better than Becky.

DEMI

Sophomore year

"You're okay." I hear Eli's soothing voice as he rubs my back.

I'm on my knees hugging his toilet, puking my guts up. I can't stop my body from shaking, and my eyes are so heavy. I've lost count of how many times I pass out and come to.

"Here." He hands me the cup of water, and I wash my mouth out with it and spit it into the toilet.

I push myself off and lie down on the tile. The cool floor feels good on my warm face.

"Come on, baby," he says, bending down and picking me up off his bathroom floor. Then he's laying me on his bed.

"Where is your phone?" he asks.

"Pocket," I barely manage to mumble. "David's ... 1234 ..." My eyes close.

Seconds tick by, and then I feel the bed dip next to me. I open my heavy eyes to see him lying next to me. "Eli ..."

"I'm not gonna do anything, Demi. I promise." His jaw clenches. "But I am gonna sleep next to you in case you get sick again." He reaches out and pushes some hair behind my ear. "I'm sorry," he whispers.

And before I can ask why he's sorry, my heavy eyes betray me once again and close.

Present

I stand in the kitchen, getting ready to leave for school Monday morning. It's been two days since my Halloween party. I threw it on Saturday night, knowing that Halloween was on Friday night. I knew that Austin had plans to take Lilly trick-or-treating, and that if Cole didn't come to my party, Deke might not either. So I had to plan my party accordingly. I was a tad worried that Cole would bring Austin, but I was hoping she would stay home with Lilly. Thank God, I was right.

I hear the front door open and close, and then seconds later, my mother's housekeeper walks in. "Good morning, Demi." She greets me with a nod of her head.

"Isabella." I smile at her warmly. "I spoke to my mother last night, and she said to give you the day off today."

She frowns, looking at the scattered cups and liquor bottles that litter the kitchen. I haven't touched that shit. "The day off, ma'am?"

I nod and slide the white envelope over to her. "Here. Take a day for yourself. Go shopping and get you something nice for Mr. Rodriguez."

Her chubby face lights up, and her brown eyes widen. The leftover trash from my party long forgotten. "Thank you. Thank you so much. Tell your mother thank you." She nods quickly.

I wave at her as she all but runs out of the kitchen and then the front door.

That was easy.

I hear the door open and close again, and I smile behind the rim of my coffee cup. That would be my sister. She walks in, pulling a rolling suitcase behind her. "God, I just saw Isabella leaving. Where the hell is she going? She needs to get in here and do her job. This place is disgusting." She huffs as her blue eyes roam around the kitchen.

"How was Collins?" I ask, ignoring her.

Her lips pull back in disgust. "The same hellhole."

"Then why did you go?"

She doesn't answer. I think she's seeing someone in Collins. Why else would she go back and forth so much? And it's never for a week at a time. She only spends a day or two there.

This time, she chooses to avoid answering my question and goes to walk out. "Oh, wait. Who is Evan Scott?"

She comes to a stop and spins around to face me. "Why?" she asks slowly with narrowed eyes.

"Because I got a friend request from him Saturday night. I have you as a mutual friend." She snaps the phone from my hands. "Okay, then," I say, taking a drink of my coffee.

She begins to type on my phone.

"What are you doing?" I ask her.

"I'm sending this fucker a message." She growls.

"What? Why?" I reach for it, but she spins around, giving me her back. "Message him back from your own phone," I snap, setting down the mug.

"This motherfucker ... talking to my sister." She rambles to herself. I don't correct her that he didn't message me. He just sent me a friend request. "I'll kick his fucking ass."

"Is he like an ex of yours?"

She gives a rough laugh. "He's an ex all right."

She turns to face me and holds out my phone.

I look down and see she still has messenger open. "I'll kill you, fucker." I nod in approval. "Nice. I bet he's scared to death."

"He should be." She tosses my phone onto the countertop.

"Thanks," I say as it bounces a couple of times before stopping right before it falls off the edge. "Not like I have important shit on that or anything."

"Let me know if he says anything else to you." She growls. "And by the way, tell Seth to lighten the fuck up." She glares at my neck. "He's a man, not a vampire." She looks over my hickeys and bite marks.

"Oh, you noticed them?" I ask, pressing my fingers to the sensitive skin. I've heard of a few tricks to get rid of them, but I chose to wear them with pride. I didn't even bother caking on the makeup.

"Of course," she spits out. "Cover that shit up."

"Have a nice day," I singsong as she walks out of the kitchen.

I smile, picking up my keys and walk out the front door. The moment I sit down in my car, my cell begins to ring. "Hello, darling." I greet Seth.

He snorts at my pet name for him. "So, did it work?"

I smile to myself as I pull through the open gate, waving to the guard who sits in the guard shack. "A woman never kisses and tells."

"Deke wanted to kick my ass." He growls.

"He still might."

"Cole too. I might be able to take one of them, but not both."

I hide my laughter at that. Either one of them would knock his ass out with one hit. And I didn't need to read Austin's journal to know that.

Sighing, he adds, "I hope it was worth it."

"It will be." I hang up without telling him goodbye.

Twenty minutes later, I pull into the high school parking lot and park my car. I'm going through my locker looking for my books when my cell dings.

Smiling to myself, I pull it out of my back pocket knowing exactly who it is. And she doesn't disappoint.

Becky: YOU MOTHERFUCKER!!!

"What has you in such a great mood today?" Lauren asks, coming up to me.

"It's Friday," I answer.

"No." She frowns. "It's actually Monday. Are you high?"

I shrug. "Same thing."

My phone dings again, and I look down at it.

Becky: I SWEAR TO FUCKING GOD, DEMI! YOU WILL PAY FOR THIS! YOU FUCKING BITCH!

My sister hates being ignored, so that's exactly what I do. Instead of responding, I exit out of her message and look up Deke in my phone. The night he and Cole had broken into my house and he tied my hands behind my back, Cole had taken pics of me and Deke. I'm not sure why and haven't asked, but Cole had sent them to an unknown number in my phone. It didn't take a rocket scientist to figure out it was Deke's number. I pull it up and send him a message.

Me: My sister knows.

I stand in the hallway holding books in one hand and my phone in the other waiting for a response. He doesn't make me wait long.

Deke: What exactly does she know?

I smile and type out my reply.

Me: That you took my virginity. In her bed.

Then I turn the bitch on silent and throw it into my locker with a smile on my face.

SEVENTEEN

DEMI

I STAND BEFORE Deke with my head down, biting my lip to hide my smile. Did he really think I'd let Seth hurt me? Put his hands on me? I forget that he doesn't know me all that well.

"What happened?" Deke asks.

I sniff for effect. "He found out about us."

"Us?"

It's a long shot because we both know there is no damn us, but I'm going to work it. I nod. "I was texting my best friend about what we did at Silence …. and he read it." I haven't told a soul what happened at Silence or at my mother's house. The only person who knows what is going on is Cole, and I'm not even sure how much Deke has told him. But I'm not one of those girls who runs to their friends and blabs about boys.

"Fuck." He hisses.

I look up at him, a tear runs down my cheek, and he watches it. "He thinks we had sex."

Have you thought about it, Deke? I have. Over and over. And every time, you get better and better.

Stepping into me, he reaches up and runs his knuckles through the single tear.

I place my hands on his shirt and grip it tightly. "Deke." I whisper his name, and I pray that it's enough to get what I want. We stood here days ago, and I watched him make out with my sister after he stayed the night, and I decided right then what I needed to do. I was going to win him over. Becky can have him but not until I'm done with him.

"You're with Seth," he says, and I know I've won. He's thinking about it.

I lift my eyes to meet his. He looks ready to throw me to the floor and fuck me right here. Caveman style. "He already thinks I've betrayed him." I lick my lips. "Might as well give him a reason to put his hands on me."

"Don't say that," he growls, stepping into me.

I tilt my head back. "It'll be worth it."

He slides his hand into my hair, and I close my eyes, letting out a moan, and for once, since he followed us out of the kitchen, something I do is real. The butterflies in my stomach, the trembling in my knees—he does this to me. The last time I felt like this for a man was with Eli. And this time, the tears are real. The thought of him hurts my soul. I need Deke to cleanse it with his evil. Betrayal. Eli was as good as they came even though no one knows that but me. "Kiss me, Deke."

"I won't stop," he admits.

I won't let you even if you try.

I look up at him, and I see it in his eyes. From the way his lips part and his breathing picks up, I know I've won. I reach back and turn the knob to the bedroom and pull him inside.

He rips my shirt up and over my head, and I grab at his. He leans forward, and I pull it off. I'm trying to get his jeans undone when he speaks.

"Light ..."

"Leave it off."

He yanks me to a stop with his hands on my hips, and my heart pounds in my chest. Keep them off, Deke. It'll ruin everything. I know he's been drinking. He's not wasted, but he's also not sober. If he was, this would never work. "Are you shy, Demi?"

"Kinda." I lie.

"There's nothing to be shy of, baby. I've already had my fingers inside you."

I whimper at his words. And there's nothing fake about it. "Please," I beg. The lights must stay off. One, he'll notice it's not my room. And two, he'll know I'm a virgin once I start bleeding. Hell, there is still a risk he might feel a difference once that starts. I don't know anything about it since this is my first time. I just have to pray he doesn't notice.

When he doesn't say anything, I undo the button to his jeans and reach inside, grabbing his cock.

Distract him.

Fuck me! It feels huge. I've never seen one in person before, let alone felt one. My heart races in my chest as I wonder if I can pull this off. How painful it's going to be. I've heard horror stories about it from girls at school. I may have had a few drinks, but I'm not drunk enough to numb the pain.

"Fuck." He groans, pushing his hips forward, and all nervousness disappears.

I can do this. I take in a deep breath to slow my racing heart. "Yes, please …"

His lips capture mine, and we stumble backward. I hear his jeans hit the floor when the back of my knees hit Becky's bed. "I Don't Even Care About You" by MISSIO plays in the house as he crawls on top of me. I've already shoved my underwear down my legs to make things easier for him. I feel his finger between my legs. He shoves one into me, and I arch my back. I'm already so wet for him. Just like I was at Silence and when he snuck into my house. Just like I am every single time he enters my mind.

I hear what sounds like a wrapper of some kind, and I take a deep breath, guessing it's a condom. This is about to happen. I'm going to have sex with Deke Biggs in my sister's bed. Boy, that'll piss her off.

He positions himself between my shaking legs and spreads them wide. I feel his head push against my entrance. I take in a deep breath, and he pushes forward. I cry out as a hot, quick pain shoots through *me, taking my breath away.*

"Fuck, Demi!" He gives a deep groan. "God, you feel ..." His hips press forward, going deeper, and I feel pressure.

"Deke ..." I gasp, closing my eyes, and dig my nails into his back, clinging to him for life.

"Incredible." He finishes.

I'm trembling and can't stop. Tears sting my eyes. He pulls out, and I whimper before he enters me again. My breath gets caught in my throat. He places his arms behind my legs and spreads me open even further, and I scream as he leans forward, pressing his chest into mine.

"Fuck, yeah, baby. Open up for me." His hands grip my hair, and he yanks my head back to expose my neck to him. For a second, I can't breathe. All I feel is a burning sensation between my legs until he moves. Really begins to move. And then a feeling that I've never felt before replaces the pain. Tears of pain and unexpected pleasure run down my face as I lie there and let him have his way with me.

Deke did exactly what I needed him to do. I was hoping that he wasn't going to ask me to take control because then I'd be fucked. He'd have known then that I lacked experience. I was banking on the fact that he's a take-charge kind of guy in the bedroom and, thank God, I wasn't wrong.

I came twice. I had never come so hard. It felt like getting caught under a tidal wave. You try to come up for air just as another one hits you. He was drowning me in pleasure, and I would have died happily.

Then after he was done, I lay in my sister's bed pretending to be asleep so he would leave me alone. Again, I prayed he would. I didn't need him to cuddle me or profess his love to me. It was just sex. And I needed him to leave the moment he got his.

After he exited the room, I got up and turned on the light to inspect the damage. I hadn't bled all that bad. I was worried about that because I didn't want him to notice it. I was afraid the blood would make it feel different to him, but maybe he didn't notice due to the condom.

I lock her door, just to make sure no one comes in here, and survey the room. He left his boxers on the floor along with the condom.

I walk over to the desk that sits in the corner and rip open a drawer to grab a black Sharpie. Then I go back over to her bed and look down at the sheets. They're mainly just wet from sweat and my come. I grab the sheet and rub it between my legs, trying to be gentle since I'm sore as fuck. I smile when it shows a little more blood on it. I throw his boxers along with the used condom on the now wet and bloody sheets and climb onto the bed. Placing the end of the Sharpie in my mouth, I bite on the lid to remove it and write.

Dear Sis,

I gave him something you never could—innocence.

DEMI

Sophomore year

I wake up with a pounding headache. Rolling over onto my side, a moan escapes my cracked lips.

"Just what the fuck did you think you were doing?" I hear Eli snap. Did he take me home?

I blink, trying to take in my surroundings. I'm in a boy's room. The clothes thrown on the floor and lack of anything remotely girly give me the first clue. The second is his black hoodie and black bag both sitting on a chair. My memory is a little foggy. How did I get here?

"Oh, come on—"

"No!" He interrupts the girl's voice. "She could have died."

I shove off the covers and make my way across the room on shaky legs. My mouth is dry and my head pounds. Cracking the door open, I look at Eli standing by the front door. My sister stands before him on the front porch.

She rolls her eyes. "We were just having some fun."

"We? David knew what you did?" He growls.

"No. It was Maxwell."

"Jesus." He hisses.

She pushes her right hip out. "They like each other, and she needed to let loose and have some fun."

Liar. She knows I don't like him.

"So you chose to drug her? Fuck, Becky! What if he had wanted to have sex with her? She wouldn't have been able to give him consent. Or what if he wouldn't have cared?"

She looks down, inspecting her nails, confirming what he's already thinking with her silence. That was their plan.

"God, you are such a fucking bitch." He sighs.

She looks up at him, glaring. "I'm not here to listen to this. Where is she?"

"She's not leaving with you," he answers flatly.

"Eli ..."

He slams the door in her face and locks it.

"Eli." She pounds on it with her fists.

"Go home, Becky!" he shouts before punching the door.

He stands there waiting for her to say something else, but seconds later, her car starts.

He runs his hand down his face, releasing a long sigh.

I make my way back to his bed and crawl under his sheets. They're nice and cold and feel amazing against my heated skin.

His door slowly opens, and he peeks in to see me now awake. He's changed his clothes from last night. I remember him sitting at the bonfire and Deke giving me the bottle of vodka. Me walking away and finding David. Then my sister giving me a drink before Eli and I got in his car. Everything else is kind of fuzzy. He wears a white T-shirt that has a band I've never heard of and a pair of black shorts. His dark hair damp as if he just took a shower.

"How do you feel?" he asks, coming to sit beside me.

"Lightheaded," I admit. The room still spins but not as bad as last night. "I have a pounding headache."

"Here." He grabs a bottle of water off his nightstand and a couple of aspirin. "Take these."

"I heard you," I say, staring at his dark comforter. Tears sting my eyes. "Why would she ...?" I can't finish the question because I know *the answer. She hates me. Always has.*

He reaches out, grabbing my chin and forcing me to look up at him. "You're okay, Demi. I'm not gonna let anything happen to you. You're safe here." Then he leans forward and places a soft kiss on my forehead.

Present

Becky didn't give two shits about me. We weren't close, but I never gave her a reason to drug me. I still wonder what would have happened had Eli not been the one to take me home that night. He took care of me. Protected me. I passed out thinking I loved him, but I woke up sure of it. But like anything else in my life, if I wanted it, Becky had this need to take it from me.

That's why I willingly spread my legs for Deke. A part of her sick and twisted mind still loves him, and I wanted to take something from her that she'll never forget. And Deke will hate me. Now more than he did before.

I was never a slut like my sister, but this one act made me one. I used him. And for what? To piss off my sister. To show them both I'm not to be fucked with? I had never had someone touch me the way Deke did at Silence. And so, after I allowed him to touch me, it just went downhill. My mind. My decisions. Now my fucking life. Becky will think of something to do to me, but it'll be so worth it. My entire body hurts. Will it be like this every time I have sex? God, I hope so.

"What happened the other night?" Lauren asks, sitting down in her seat next to me. "I've been calling you all weekend. Did you and Seth break up?"

"No," I answer.

"What was that fight about?"

"He thinks I'm cheating on him." I shrug.

Her dark brows pull together. Lauren and I never talk about my sex life or lack thereof. She just assumes Seth and I fuck like rabbits.

He's a college student, after all. A boy with needs. I'm just not the one who fulfills them.

"Are you?"

I give her a big smile. "Well, I wasn't when we started fighting."

EIGHTEEN

DEKE

I STAND IN the kitchen staring down at my phone as it rings in my hand. **Becky** lights up the screen. I press ignore. And what I now see isn't any better. It's Demi's message.

Demi: *That you took my virginity. In her bed.*

I blink and read it again.

No!

She was a virgin? That can't be … but I know it's the truth. I felt it. She was too tight. It had been a long time since I'd slept with a virgin, but you never forget what it's like. It was too good. She felt too unbelievable. I almost had myself convinced yesterday that it was the alcohol. I was drunk and the liquor had enhanced what we did. What I felt.

I should have known!

"What's up with you?" Cole asks, entering the kitchen.

"I fucked Demi," I say more to myself than him.

He nods. "I was there." He takes a drink of his coffee.

"In Becky's bed." He spits out said coffee. It dribbles down his chin and onto his shirt. I feel it land on my arm, but I ignore it. "And she was a virgin."

"What the fuck?" I hear from behind me.

I turn to see Austin now standing with us. Her eyes are wide, and her hands on her narrow hips.

"I … I didn't know …" I stumble over my words. Almost fucking speechless. My thoughts a mess. She was a virgin. I took her virginity. I shouldn't feel proud about that because she tricked me, but I do. I fucked her first, before any other man. Why? Why would she give that to me? She hates me.

"You didn't know?" she asks me skeptically.

I just shake my head. That's usually the first thing a girl tells you when she's throwing herself at you. Hell, I've had girls tell me they're virgins when I knew they weren't. They never lie about not being one. That's just another thing about Demi that I'm starting to like. She's unpredictable.

She runs her hand through her dark hair. "Does Becky know?"

I nod.

Her lips thin, and she steps into me. "Was this part of your game?"

Was it? I wanted her, yes. Would knowing she was a virgin have stopped me? Probably not. But I would have done it differently had I known.

"No." Cole answers her question when I don't.

"Did you know this?" she snaps at him.

He nods. "I thought it was odd that he was in Becky's room, though."

That's why he looked at me strangely when I exited the bedroom. He knew I was on the wrong side of the balcony. I was too wrapped up in Demi and my dick to think about it. I would have fucked her in the laundry room if that was where she had taken me.

"I can't believe this." She growls. "This is beyond fucked up, Deke."

"I didn't know," I repeat.

My phone rings again, and I hit ignore, not wanting to talk to Becky. I don't have to explain myself. I'm single and can do whoever I want.

Seconds later, another cell rings, and Austin pulls hers out of her pocket. She sighs and hits answer. "Hello?" Her eyes narrow on me. "I'm so sorry." She spins around, walking out of the kitchen. Letting me know that Becky has given up and called her best friend.

"She set you up." Cole speaks my thoughts.

I nod. "Seems so." She planned on me fucking her in her sister's bed. She wanted to rub it in her face. But how did Becky find out? Did she text her, and Becky just believed it? I'm not sure, but I'm not going to ask Becky how she found out.

"Again," he adds.

I grind my teeth and glare at him. "Why do you feel the need to state the obvious?"

He shrugs. "Surprised is all."

"And what shall I do about that?" I ask, arching a brow.

He chuckles. "Whatever the fuck you want."

DEMI

I lie on my bed doing homework and listening to music. "Nightmare" by Halsey plays softly in my room. My phone vibrates, and I ignore it. That's what I've done all day. Deke and Becky could have messaged me a hundred times, and I wouldn't know.

A knock comes on my door. "Go away," I call out. If it was my sister, she'd just charge right in, so it's either my mother or Isabella, and I don't want to speak to either of them.

The door opens, and I sit up when I see it's Austin.

This can't be good.

"Hope you don't mind. Your housekeeper said you were up here. May I come in?" she asks, standing in the doorway.

I wasn't able to get rid of Isabella for long. After my sister found out what I had done, she called our mother and told her that I trashed the house over the weekend. So my mother called Isabella and told her to get back to our house and clean it. Thankfully, Isabella didn't rat me out and tell my mother that I paid her to stay away. She kept the cash I gave her and her mouth shut.

I cross my arms over my chest. "Depends. Are you here on behalf of Becky or Deke?" Neither one matters.

She sighs heavily. "I'm here for you, Demi."

"I'm not sure what that means."

Without asking again or waiting for permission, she enters my room and closes the door behind her. She sits down on the edge of my bed and tilts her head while she looks me over. She frowns when her eyes run over the faint marks left by Deke. They're fading, but I don't wear much makeup, so you can still very much make them out.

"I'm not in the mood for a lecture," I tell her. I'm not sure which one told her what I did with Deke, but it doesn't matter. It's done.

"I'm just worried—"

I laugh, cutting off her words. "About Becky? She's a big girl. She can handle herself. Trust me."

"No." She reaches out and pats my leg gently. "About you."

Austin has always been nice to me. I didn't get to see her much back in Collins. She didn't come around my father's house very often, but when she was there, she would go out of her way to say hello to me or ask how my day was going, but she never invited me out with them. At the time, I thought it was because Becky filled her head full of lies and made her hate me. Now I know it was because Austin was dealing with her own demons—the GWS.

"Why would you be worried about me?"

She runs a hand through her dark hair. "I don't know what kind of game Deke is playing with you, but I've been a part of a game before, and it would have been nice to have someone on my side."

I look down at my hands sitting on my lap, unable to meet her eyes. I already know what she went through. And I hate that my sister wasn't there to help her. She was too wrapped up in Deke to see what was really going on. Or maybe she did and just didn't care.

"I'm nothing like her," I find myself saying.

"I didn't say you were."

My eyes meet hers, and she gives me a soft smile. I highly doubt she knows what Becky is really like. No one does. No one among the living anyway.

"I'm not here to judge you, Demi. I only came here in case you needed to talk to someone."

I snort. "And to go tell my sister."

"No." She shakes her head quickly. "I want to be your friend. And to me that means something. I would never betray your trust."

I fist my hands. "Then you're here for Deke."

"No, Demi—"

"I don't believe you, Austin," I shout, interrupting her.

Silence follows my outburst, and she nods her head once before standing. She turns to leave, and I look down at my backpack next to my bed. It's open, and the top of her journal peeks out.

"Wait," I call out.

She comes to a stop and turns to face me. I reach down, pick it up, and walk over to her. "I told you I'm nothing like her, and I mean that." I hold out her journal. "This belongs to you. You should be the one to have it."

Her green eyes widen when she looks down at it. Slowly, she takes it from my hand like it's a grenade that can blow up any minute. "Where did you get this?" she asks clearing her throat.

"I found it."

Her eyes snap up to mine. "What do you mean you found it?"

"I went looking in Becky's closet for something to use against her, and it was in a box she brought with her from Collins."

Her eyes drop back down to it, and she grips it tightly.

"I read it," I admit.

When she just stares at it with terror in her eyes, I feel bad for giving it to her. I should have just thrown it away. I'm sure she wants to forget many events in there. Cole may have fallen in love with her in the end, but there's more than just him and the sharks in there. There's a lot of Phillip—her mom's boyfriend. He touched her. Hit her. And I have no doubt he would have done much harsher things if she hadn't moved to her dad's when she did.

I'm not going to apologize for reading it because I'm glad I did. It taught me a lot about Austin and helped me understand her more. Not only is the girl beautiful, but she's fierce. No wonder Cole fell for her. What guy wouldn't? I believe her when she says friendship means something to her. And that she is loyal, but I'm just not sure she considers me a friend.

"I …"

The opening of my bedroom door cuts her off. She spins around to face it, and I look up to see my sister barge into my room. "You fucking bitch—"

"What the fuck were you doing with this?" Austin interrupts her. And the look on my sister's face tells me all I need to know.

She's fucked!

NINETEEN

BECKY

I STAND IN Demi's room. My plan was to come in here and beat the shit out of her, but that is clearly not going to happen for two reasons.

One, because I'll have a witness, and two, because my best friend looks like she will be the one beating some ass.

I swallow nervously, looking at her journal in her hand. *How did she find that?* "Where did that come from?"

"Why did you fucking have this?" Austin demands, taking a step toward me.

I take a step back out of the bedroom. Austin and I have never had a falling out; she's always been nice to me, but I've read her journal. And you don't want to be on her bad side. "You asked me to take it."

"No. I told you to fucking burn it!"

Five months ago

I walk over to her hospital bed and sit down. We weren't even sure Austin would survive the shooting, and now here she is, wide awake and asking for a favor three days later. She just asked me to go back to her father's house with Cole. By myself. Not sure what the hell she wants me to do for her, but no was on the tip of my tongue when she asked the guys to leave the room so she could talk to me alone.

"I need you to grab something for me."

"Can't Cole get it?" I ask, not wanting to be left alone with him. The last time I was alone with him, his hand was wrapped around my throat, and he told me that I'd owe him a favor. Then Austin showed up. And being her friend was my favor. What started out as payment for my sins ended up becoming my best friend. Although I have a bad way of showing it.

"No." She sits up better in her bed and flinches from the pain. "I have a journal." I frown. "I need you to get it. He can't see it."

"You want me to bring it to you?"

She shakes her head. "Burn it."

"Burn it?" I repeat.

She nods. "Yes. It's in my nightstand." She grabs my hands and squeezes them. "One more thing. Don't read it."

"Okay ..."

"Promise me you won't read it and will destroy it. Immediately."

I nod slowly, wondering why in the fuck she wants me to burn a journal. What could possibly be in there that she doesn't want us to see? Him especially. "I promise."

"You promised me." She growls.

"I didn't get the chance." I lie.

She doesn't believe it. "How in the hell did you not get the chance? It's been five months."

I don't answer.

"Did you read it?" she demands.

"No." Another lie. Of course, I did. And I haven't looked at her the same since. I always knew Cole was a fucked-up kid, and her journal just proved I wasn't wrong. And honestly, she's not far off from him. That's probably why they are so good together.

"Demi?" she snaps. "Did you read it?"

"Yes." She answers without hesitation, but I have a feeling that Demi already divulged that information.

The more important question is how the fuck did she find it? What was Austin doing in my room? I had it hidden in a box. I knew I should have left it in Collins.

"You know what, Becky? I thought we were friends, but I guess I was wrong." She shoulders past me.

I'm already in a pretty shitty mood. Your sister fucking the man you love in your own bed and leaving your sheets stained with her blood and her words written in black Sharpie will make you irrational. That's why I'm not proud of the next thing that comes out of my mouth. "Cole read it too." That fucker outed me that I was the one driving the car. Why the fuck should I keep his secrets?

I turn to face her, giving my sister my back.

Austin stands at the top of the stairs and spins around to glare at me. "What?" she snaps.

"Back at your father's house. I left him alone in your room to get some trash bags. I was gonna be a nice *friend* and pack up some of your belongings, and when I returned, he was sitting on your bed reading it." I was going to have to grab it without Cole questioning me. I figured if I threw some shit in a trash bag, he wouldn't notice me trying to sneak a journal out.

"Why didn't you tell me this?" she grinds out.

I cross my arms over my chest. "I think the real question is why hasn't he told you?"

"Don't turn this around on him, Becky. I asked you to do one thing for me, and you couldn't even do it." She looks down at the journal and then back at me. "I will never forgive you for this."

The words hurt more than knowing my sister fucked Deke. I can win Deke over. I cheated on him; he paid me back. He got to have a little fun, and now we can move on. But her? Austin was all I had left. "Why is it you forgave him?" I glare down at her journal. "Huh? He can hurt you, fucking blackmail you, and you forgive him so goddamn easily?"

"He never lied to me!" she yells. "He never pretended to be someone he's not."

I snort at that sorry excuse for an answer. "Be honest, Austin, it's just us. It's because of the money. You let him treat you like shit because he has money?" Her nostrils flare. "You saw a way out and took it. I get it ..."

"I couldn't care less about his fucking money!" she shouts.

I believe her. I do, but I can't stop. I have to hurt her. She hurt me. She is abandoning me. "So, it's the fact that he's the first guy to ever show you any kind of love then? Your mother hated you 'cause her boyfriend wanted to fuck you. Your father didn't want you, and then Cole Reynolds comes along." I give her a smile. Our friendship is over, so I might as well go out with a bang. "The devil as you called him in your journal. Girls like you disgust me. A man shows a broken girl a little bit of attention, and you fall in love with them. He can never love you." I lie. The truth is, he's beyond in love with her. That man has killed for her. He'd do anything for her, and I'm jealous of that. I want that with Deke. "He'll only use you. You'll become a frumpy housewife, and he'll get bored of you …"

She slaps me across the face, knocking me into the railing of the balcony. The force was so hard it takes my breath away. My hand comes up to touch my tender cheek when she steps into me, pressing my back into the railing. "You bitch …"

"I'd rather be the girl who fell in love with the devil, than the whore who jumps from man to man because she can't stay faithful." She growls in my face. "I don't care if Deke comes to me tonight and tells me that he is taking your sorry ass back and plans on marrying you tomorrow. You are never welcome in my house again."

My teeth grind at her words and the tears sting my eyes. But I manage to say, "The truth hurts."

I think she's going to slap me again, but instead, she laughs in my face. "The truth? The truth is that I've always been a fighter. And I would have fought for you, no matter what, but you lied to me and you betrayed me. So you no longer have my loyalty." Then she turns, and storms down the stairs and exits the house, slamming the door behind her. The sound echoes up the stairs, and it makes me flinch. My chest aches, and my stomach sinks at the loss of my best friend.

"Sucks, doesn't it? Losing everyone who you thought cared about you?"

I turn to look at my sister leaning up against the doorway to her bedroom. She has a smile on her face and not a care in the world. My eyes go straight to the hickeys on her neck. Deke never gave me any because I wouldn't let him. I couldn't chance David seeing them. I told him not to give them to me so many times that even after we were out in the open together, he still didn't leave any.

I fist my hands and push away from the railing. "You did this …"

"No, you did." The smile drops off her face. "You fucked everyone over. And now you're completely alone." Then she steps back and slams her bedroom door. I hear it lock, and I let out a scream of frustration because I know she's telling the truth. I just lost Austin and any chance I have of getting Deke back. And it all started with fucking Demi!

She'll pay. No matter what I have to do or who I have to fuck, I'll get my revenge. I always do.

I enter my room, slam my door, and run over to my desk. Yanking open the drawer, I pull out a pair of scissors and crawl onto my bed. I scream as I slice the sharp edges through her hurtful words. Through her innocence. I fucking stab it over and over, imagining it's her face.

She will pay! Even if I have to have someone else do it for me.

DEKE

"So, what are you gonna do?" Cole asks as we sit at the kitchen table.

Demi: That you took my virginity. In her bed.

I read over the text Demi sent me earlier this morning for the hundredth time. The more time that has gone by, the more pissed I've gotten. "I'm not sure," I say honestly. I wasn't able to concentrate in my classes today or during swim practice. My mind was completely consumed with everything Demi. And it's literally gotten me nowhere. I'm like a dog chasing my own tail.

"What do you wanna do?"

"Strangle her," I grind out. "She fucking played me." I sit back in my seat. *But how did she do it?*

"Have you heard from Becky?"

"I did earlier." She stopped calling when she realized I wasn't going to pick up.

"And what does she have to say about it?"

I glare at him. "Since when did you become a nosy little bitch?"

He chuckles. The bastard has been in a good mood today for some reason. And I know it's not because he got laid last night. They do that every night, and he's still always a moody fucker. "Just wondering what you're gonna do to pay Demi back. I could use some excitement."

"I've been thinking the same thing. I can't kill the bitch, and I can't physically torture her." I mean, I could, but then what? I'd have to get rid of the body somewhere. And I'd look suspicious. Too many people know I've slept with her now. I doubt Becky would mind if I offed her sister, though. Hell, she'd probably help me.

"You could make her fall in love with you," Cole states.

I throw my head back, laughing at that. "Funny."

He levels me with that blank stare he does so well.

"You've got to be joking?" I ask when he says nothing.

"Why not?" He leans forward, placing his forearms on the table. "Isn't that the best kind of payback? Make her fall in love with you and then leave her for Becky?"

My brows pull together. "You make it sound like you have experience in this department? We both know you've only ever loved one girl." Austin. And he's marrying her.

He looks away from me, and his jaw clenches as though he's thinking of a similar situation. When he looks back at me, that blank stare is back in place. "Austin said it the other night. A jealous woman is irritational."

"How in the fuck would I get Demi to fall in love with me? She hates me." And why would I want her to love me? The girl is fucking crazy.

He snorts. "Obviously not. She just gave you her virginity."

My teeth grind. "It was clearly to piss off Becky. Not for her benefit." *Fucking bitch.*

"She's young. Naïve. A rich little girl who has been sheltered all her life." He smirks. "You're Deke Biggs."

"You say that like it means something." I growl.

He arches a brow. "Doesn't it?"

I let out a long breath and lean back in my seat. "There's only one flaw in your plan. It'll never work because I will never get back with Becky."

We hear the front door open seconds later. "Cole?" Austin shouts his name.

We both jump up at the same time as she enters, all but running in. "What's wrong?" he asks her, already rounding the table.

Breathing heavily, she slams down a black and white notebook on the table. He looks at it and then at her. "Did you read this?" she demands, pointing at it.

"Yes," he answers, crossing his arms over his chest, and I know this isn't going to be good.

She picks it back up, waving it in his face. "All of it?"

"No, just a few pages ..."

She storms over to our junk drawer and yanks it open. I frown when she pulls out a lighter. Is she going to smoke? Austin doesn't smoke cigarettes. But instead of pulling a pack out, she walks over to the sink and lights the corner of the book on fire.

"What the hell are you doing?" Cole demands.

"What I should have done a long time ago," she answers, still holding the lighter to it even though it's already up in flames.

"What the fuck, Austin?" He snatches it from her hands and turns on the faucet, putting it out.

"I told her to burn it." She reaches for it, but he holds her back with his other arm. "And she didn't. And she lied to me. Told me she didn't read it. Fucking bitch." She's shouting, and her fists shake. I don't think I've ever seen Austin this pissed. And we've put her through some very sketchy situations in the past.

"Who?" I ask, confused by what the hell is in that notebook and why she wants to burn it.

She looks at me as if she's just realized I'm also in the room. "Becky."

I frown. "What's in it?"

She opens her mouth, but her phone begins to ring. She pulls it out of her pocket, looks at it, and then silences it. "Fuck!" she shouts.

Cole turns off the water and drops the now soaked notebook into the sink. He places his hands on her shoulders and looks down at her with concern in his eyes. "Sweetheart, what's going on?" he asks softly as though he's talking to a child.

She takes a deep breath, trying to calm herself. "I went to go see Demi, to tell her that she could talk to me, and she had my journal. When I was in the hospital, I asked Becky to burn it. I didn't want you finding it," she tells him. "But she kept it. She read it. She told me that you read it." She pokes him in the chest. "And neither one of you ever told me. Then she tried to tell me that I'm with you for money." She pushes Cole away with disgust. "Like I give a fuck about that shit." She starts pacing the kitchen. "Then she began to tell me that the only reason I fell in love with you was pretty much because I was broken and enjoyed abuse."

Oh, shit. I can't believe Becky would say that to her.

He runs a hand through his hair nervously. "Austin—"

"I slapped her," she interrupts Cole.

My eyes widen. "What?"

She looks back at me. "And I told her that she is not welcome here."

"Austin ..."

She ignores Cole and walks over to me. Her green eyes have tears in them, but I can't tell if they're from sadness or anger. She licks her lips and the look on her pretty face makes me think she's about to break down and sob. "I'm sorry, Deke, but I cannot forgive this. I will never tell you who you can and can't date, but she's not allowed back in my house."

"Sweetheart?" Cole steps up behind her.

She spins around and looks up at him. He opens his mouth to speak, but whatever he sees written on her face makes him pause. He reaches out to cup her face, and she shoves him away. "How could you?" she asks, and her voice breaks.

"I—"

"No," she interrupts him. "That was private. You had no right."

Then she turns and storms back out of the kitchen just as fast as she entered, but I don't miss the tears running down her face.

"What the hell is in that damn thing?" I ask.

Cole runs his hand down his face, releasing a sigh. "Things her stepdad did to her. And everything we did to her. From the point she saw us on New Year's night committing murder in the cemetery up until the night before Kellan shot her."

Fuck! No wonder she's mad. "You told her you only read a few pages." *Had he been lying?*

"I read enough," he says through gritted teeth, knowing none of it was pretty. "I gotta go talk to her."

"Good luck," I offer, thinking he may be the thing she sets on fire.

He slaps me on the back as he exits. "Austin will forgive me. You're the one who needs luck. Two women equally hate you at the moment."

TWENTY

DEMI

SETH BRINGS HIS car to a stop in front of my mother's house. "You okay?" he asks.

I nod my heavy head. "Yep."

He chuckles. "Need me to carry you upstairs and put you to bed?"

I snort. "I didn't drink that much."

"I know, but you also haven't eaten anything."

I open the door and look over at him. "I'm fine."

"Okay. I'll talk to you tomorrow." I crawl out and turn to shut the door, but he speaks. "Don't let her get to you," he tells me.

"I won't …"

"She's pissed. Just lost her best friend and her boyfriend."

I snort. "You don't know them like I do." After what went down with my sister and Austin, my sister left. I'm sure she went running to Deke. Begging him to love her from her knees. I'm sure he promised her the world since he owes her for fucking up and sleeping with me. He probably told her we were drunk. Or he thought I was her. Who knows what he said and what she'll believe?

"I know your sister is a bitch." He growls. "And that you should sleep with your bedroom door locked and one eye open."

I nod. "Thanks for the ride home." I slam the door shut and make my way up to the front door.

It's a little after midnight. I left a few hours after Becky and Austin did. I called Seth, and we went to hang out with a friend of his. We had some drinks and played video games. I needed to celebrate. I fucked over my sister, and she fucked over her best friend.

It was a great Monday!

I hated the look on Austin's face when she realized she had been betrayed, because I've been there with Becky, and it hurts. I'll go see her tomorrow after school and apologize for how things went down. And let her know that I'm here for her too. I can be her friend.

I make my way into the house and up the stairs. I enter my room and gently close my door. Flipping on my bedroom light, I squeal like a pig when I see a man sitting on the end of my bed.

"What the fuck?" I breathe. It's midnight.

How the hell does he keep getting into my house?

Deke looks up at me. "A little late to be out on a school night, isn't it?"

My eyes catch sight of a black bag at his feet. It reminds me of the same one Eli kept close to him. And Austin had mentioned in her journal that the GWS gave her one when they forced her to join their group.

Any other time, I would be afraid of him being in my room at midnight after I tricked him into sleeping with me, but I'm not sober at the moment. He's come to play. To piss me off. I know how he works. I do something to him, and he comes and threatens me. But he has yet to hurt me. I haven't seen that side of Deke that Austin wrote about in her journal or the one I heard when he threatened to kill my sister. I want to poke the shark. See how much he can endure before he gets deadly.

I push off the door and walk slowly over to the foot of the bed, crossing my feet as I walk. I've seen enough of my mother's models grace the stage to know how to walk like them. I come to a stop before him, and he tilts his head back to look up at me. Placing both hands on either side of him, I lean over, making sure my tits are in his face. "Is that why you came here, Deke?" I lick my lips. "You want me to play Becky while you play my daddy?"

His jaw sharpens and eyes narrow as my words piss him off. I laugh. Pushing off the bed this time, I stumble more than anything as I make my way back to my door. And I'm not even in heels. I dressed comfortable for my evening celebration. I swing it open and lean against it. "We both know you're only here to tell me that you love her." I roll my eyes dramatically, and it almost knocks me off balance. Maybe I had a few more drinks than I thought. "And that you made a mistake. So go ahead and walk over to her room and be with her." Somehow, Becky has talked him into rubbing it in my face. That even though he fucked me, he still loves her. I'm not surprised. But it does piss me off. Again, she's so goddamn perfect, and I'm insignificant.

He stands, squaring his broad shoulders. He looks taller, scarier for some reason in a pair of black jeans and matching long-sleeve shirt. He's got the sleeves pushed up, showing off his tan, muscular forearms. Walking over to me, he takes hold of the door and shuts it.

My eyes go to the door and then to his. He reaches up and runs the back of his knuckles up and down my neck. I swallow nervously as my heart rate picks up. I close my eyes at the feel of his hands on me, but they spring open the moment his hand grips my throat, and he pins me against the door.

"I'm here for you, Demi." He whispers my name, and even though the hairs on the back of my neck stand up in warning, my pussy throbs.

I swallow. "Is that supposed to scare me?"

His right leg forces its way between my knees. I tighten mine, refusing to let him through, but he's stronger. He smiles when he's pressed fully against me. His muscular thigh now wedged between mine.

"I'm not afraid of you," I state, moving to my tiptoes. His hand keeps getting tighter, and my knees threaten to buckle.

"That's your first mistake." He gives me a cruel smirk that makes him look like the beautiful bastard he is.

My hands grip his wrist that holds me in place. "The … second?" He's almost cutting my air off.

"Playing me." His free hand comes up and palms my breast over my shirt.

I moan, and my eyes fall closed. He pushes his hips into mine, and he's hard. I'm wet. Fuck, why does he do this to me? Why, out of all the boys in the world, does Deke Biggs manage to make me want to spread my legs and slap him at the same time?

"Feel how hard I am for you, princess?" he asks, running his lips along my jawline.

Pulling all the self-control I can manage, I rasp. "You think I'll give in that easily?"

He gives a rough laugh before taking my earlobe between his lips while his hand tightens on my neck, taking away my air before he whispers, "I don't need permission to take what I already own."

And his cockiness brings me out of my drunken and lust fog. I'm not in the mood to play his stupid games tonight. I'm tried, drunk, and need a shower. I push him off me. He takes a step back with a smug smile on his face.

I rub my sore neck and swallow roughly. "I can't tell you how much I hate your unannounced visits, but it's time for you to go." I walk over to my adjoining bathroom, trying to stay upright, and flip on the light.

I go to slam the door shut, but his black boot stops it, and it flies open. "Deke ... What ...?"

He reaches out, wrapping his arm around my waist and pulling my back to his front. He stares at me in my bathroom mirror. "Where do you think you're going?" he asks, bringing his right hand up and wrapping it around my neck again, forcing my chin up.

"I need a shower," I say, trying to fight him off, but he's not allowing it this time. He's too strong.

He leans down, whispering in my ear, "It's cute that you think I give a fuck what you need."

"I'm dirty," I protest. I smell of weed and alcohol. I don't smoke the shit and neither does Seth, but his friend was. Pretty sure I have a contact high at the moment.

He leans down, inhaling my ponytail. "Baby, I'm about to make you filthy."

My breath hitches when he releases my stomach and lowers his hand to the button of my jeans. "Deke?" What is he doing? We're done. The back and forth game is over.

"Yeah, princess?" His ocean blue eyes stay on mine. The sound of my zipper being lowered is barely heard over my heavy breathing. A smirk graces his handsome face when his hand slides into my jeans. "All you gotta do is tell me to stop."

I don't.

My heart pounds, my body physically shakes, and my mind screams *fucking stop!* But I can't make my lips move. My hands lie heavy at my sides completely useless against this man.

He lowers his lips to my ear, and whispers, "Tell me to stop, *Becky*!"

And just like before, that knocks me out of this trance. I shove him off, and he doesn't even resist. Spinning around, I glare up at him, and it makes me even more pissed to look at his smug smile. "I hate you, Deke!" I seethe.

He throws his head back and laughs as if I just told him a joke. It makes his entire body shake, and I let out a scream of frustration. *I think I'm losing my mind.*

"Say it like you mean it, princess." He looks me up and down while licking his perfect lips.

I ignore the way it makes my heart race. I shove him. "I FUCKING HATE …"

He grips my hands, pins them behind my back, and slams his lips to mine. "I fucking hate you too." He growls.

My hands fight him, and he lets them go, but instead of shoving him away this time, they wrap around his neck. His large hands grip my ass, and he picks my feet up off the floor. My legs wrap around his hips, and he walks me back to the bedroom. Then he's tossing me onto the bed. His blue eyes stay trained on mine as he stands by the edge. He removes my shoes, socks, and then yanks my jeans down my legs. I find myself kicking them a little to help the guy out. My heart pounds like a drum in my chest—loud and viciously. I'm trying to catch my breath, but I'm afraid I may pass out before he undresses me. Without taking his heated eyes from mine, he grips the white lace fabric of my thong, and in a much slower pace, he slides them down my shaking legs.

"Are you still bleeding, princess?"

If I wasn't so drunk, I'd blush at that question. "No."

He drops them to the floor and reaches up, gripping the back of his black shirt and pulls it up over his head. His abs flex, showcasing a six-pack that looks carved out of stone. Then he pushes his jeans down his muscular thighs along with his boxers.

My eyes slowly travel down over the V that you only see on the cover of magazines. I bite my bottom lip when I get to his hard dick. It stands to attention and makes my thighs tighten. When we had sex, I had the lights off, so I never got to see it. My mouth goes dry at his impressive size. *No wonder it was so painful.*

"Is this the first time you've ever seen a cock, Demi?" he asks, wrapping his hand around the thick base.

My wide eyes shoot up to meet his, and this time I do blush, telling him what he already knew.

He gives me that smug smile that I fucking hate. The one that makes his blue eyes dance with mischief and my belly flop. "Spread your legs," he orders.

My bended knees begin to shake. I should have had another drink.

He lets go of his dick and steps up to the bed. Placing his hands on my knees, he slowly pushes them apart.

I fall onto my back, and my hands come up to cover my face. My entire body is shaking uncontrollably. Even the alcohol can't help mask my fear and embarrassment of what is to come.

His hands leave my knees and travel up my thighs. They firmly spread them farther until I'm completely exposed to him.

This is where I'm nothing like Becky. I lack experience and confidence. I have never felt more vulnerable and turned on at the same time. I'm ashamed because I'm completely wet for him. And the lights are on, allowing him to see every inch of me.

His thumb slides over my pussy, and I moan loudly.

"Such a pretty pussy," he says softly.

I swallow, my mouth suddenly going dry. I wish I would have known this was going to happen. I would have put some music on so he wouldn't have to hear my heavy breathing.

"Has a man ever eaten your pussy, Demi?"

Dear Lord! I'm going to come at the sound of my name and pussy being mentioned in the same sentence. "No," I mumble my answer.

His hands grip my hips, and he yanks me toward him. I remove my hands from my face and cry out in surprise as my ass now hangs off the edge of the bed. "Deke …"

"Unless you're telling me to stop, I don't wanna hear it." He growls.

I watch his eyes trail down over my chest; the only thing I wear is a black bra. And it's not even pretty or flattering in any way. He didn't get the chance to remove it. Not like I have much to show, though. They continue their assault, raking over my stomach and pussy. When he drops to his knees, my breath gets stuck in my lungs.

He places my shaking knees over his shoulders. My wide eyes go to my bedroom door. I didn't lock it. "What if someone comes in?" I ask in a panic.

"Let them watch me eat you out, baby," he says, not sharing my concern.

"Deke …" I protest, but he leans forward, and my words die as I feel his mouth touch where no man has before.

"Oh, God." My hands grip the comforter.

His fingers dig into my hips, and I buck them when I feel his tongue enter me.

He grips me tighter, pulling me closer to his face, and I close my eyes at the pure pleasure of his tongue touching me in the most intimate way.

My legs tighten on his head, my back arches, and I start to pant as a fire runs up my back. Then I feel a pulsing between my legs, and it travels up through my body. I'm screaming his name as what can only be described as an energy rush reaches my head and explodes.

DEKE

I stand and lick what's left of her from my lips. She lies before me, shaking uncontrollably with her back arched and her eyes closed. Her lips are parted, and she is panting.

Fuck, she looks beautiful.

I had planned to come and hurt her, to remind her who the fuck she's dealing with, but I couldn't do it. I had brought my bag since I wasn't sure how I was going to do it. Make her bleed? Leave her restrained again? Carve my fucking name in her ass? I didn't know which plan of action was the best one.

But the moment she entered her room, all I could think was to get her naked and underneath me. I saw how turned on she was. How much she still wanted me. Last time I was drunk and a fucking idiot, so I didn't ease into it. I just fucked her like she was the same whore her sister is.

Demi deserved better for her first time.

I reach out, grab her hand, and yank her to a sitting position. As she looks up at me with heavy eyes, I remove her bra. Her hands go to my stomach, and they roam my body, exploring every inch of what I work hard to achieve. Being a swimmer keeps me in shape, but even at eighteen, I have to spend a lot of time in the gym due to my bad eating habits and alcohol consumption. But I have no problem working as hard as I play.

I remove her loose ponytail, and her long blond hair falls over her shoulders. I push it back, exposing her chest to me. Her pretty pink nipples harden as I run my thumbs over them.

"Scoot back and lie down," I order, dropping my hand to stroke my cock. It's been hard since the moment she entered her room with an attitude that I wanted to fuck out of her.

She does as I say, and her still shaking legs fall open without me having to say a word. I smile. *She's already learning.*

I crawl onto the bed.

"Is this why you came here?" She licks her lips. "To fuck me?"

"Why else would I be here?" I arch a brow, centering myself between her parted legs.

"To hurt me," she answers breathlessly.

I place my hands on either side of her head and lower my lips to her ear. "Oh, I have every intention of hurting you."

Lie. If I wanted to do her any harm, I would have done it the moment she stepped foot into her room. Caught her off guard and taken advantage of a situation I knew I could win. I never act without knowing the outcome.

"Good." She wraps her arms around my neck. "I thought you were going soft."

My eyes roam her face, and I watch as her soft features harden just a bit. Her orgasm is wearing off—fading away. The only reminder that I'm not a fucking douche quickly diminishes. And that urge to hurt her returns. I rack my brain, trying to think of what I could do to her. How I could make her remember that what she did was wrong. She crossed me. I wanted her, and she only used me. Was any of it real? I doubt it. And I hate that I fell for it so easily again.

"You look like you're trying to decide if you want to choke me to death or fuck me." She taunts me as if I'm not onto her.

I can read her like a book. One that I want to rip the pages out of and burn to ashes. A story left to never be told again. It'd be a tragedy, but one she earned with too many pages filled with lies.

I slide my right hand into her hair and jerk her head back to force her to look up at the ceiling. I lean down, lowering my voice to a dark whisper. "What if I said I want to do both?"

It's what I do to her in my dreams. When she tells me to pretend she's Becky, and she'll pretend to love me. It's so fucked up, but nothing about this is sane. Ever since I touched her at Silence, we've been hiding who we really are.

A beautiful mess and a demon.

I have killed, and she has lied. We are exactly what we should stay away from, yet here we are.

"Are you going to fight me?" I ask, inhaling the scent of her hair. It smells of vanilla, and it makes my mouth water. Becky's always smelled of strawberries.

"That depends on which option you choose," she answers breathlessly.

I smile against her neck. "Well, princess, I already have you naked underneath me, legs spread wide, and my lips still taste of your cunt. But …" I pull away and run my free hand up her chest to wrap around her neck. "If I sit here and choke the life out of your pretty eyes, you'll fight?" I'm not sure which one sounds more appealing.

Becky never allowed me to be rough. She always told me she wanted me to be my best self. And I believed that fucking bullshit. She didn't change for me; I should have never tried to pretend with her.

She looks up at me the best she can since my right hand is still holding her head back by her hair. "You think I have pretty eyes?"

I can't help but chuckle. Of course, that's what she takes from what I said. "You know I think you're gorgeous," I say honestly.

There's nothing wrong with admitting that to her or myself. Over the past week, I've noticed the difference between Demi and Becky in their looks. Demi is more of a natural beauty while Becky is just all-out fake. Demi's blue eyes hold more truth and anger. She carries herself differently. She doesn't need to dress like a slut to get attention, and she doesn't need the world to bow at her feet. No, Demi doesn't need anyone, and that's what draws me to her. To need someone is a weakness, and I want to see her need me desperately. Like her life depends on it.

Her lips part, and I feel her pulse race against my hand.

"But don't think that will stop me from hurting you," I warn, my hand tightening on her throat as a warning. She can still breathe, though. I don't want the fun to start too soon.

"Maybe I want you to hurt me."

My eyes narrow as I press my hard cock to her dripping pussy in warning. I was so rough with her two nights ago in Becky's bed. She has to still be sore. "Did I hurt you the other night?" I ask. She had cried. At the time it didn't register until she sent me the message that I took her virginity.

"Yes." She licks her lips.

"And?" I ask, not liking her simple answer. I'm sure as shit not going to apologize because she should have told me.

Swallowing against my hand, she whispers, "I liked it."

"Demi." I growl. *She's playing with me.* This is another one of her fucking tricks. This is where she's just like her sister.

She places her hands on my chest. "Is that what you want, Deke? To hurt me?"

"Yes." No. *Fuck!* Do I want to hurt her? I'm not sure what I want right now. So much has happened over the past couple of days that I can't even think straight.

Her hands drop to her sides, and she whispers, "Then do it."

"Is this why you're with Seth?" The thought of him makes me want to punch him in the goddamn face and choke her out. "You piss him off, so he'll hurt you?"

She lets out a laugh, so pure that her body shakes underneath me. "I found another thing I like about you."

I release her hair and neck, placing my fisted hands on either side of her face, then I ask, "What's that?"

"Your jealousy," she answers, licking her lips.

"I'm not—"

"Liar." She cuts me off. "But Seth isn't here, Deke. It's just you and me. So there's only one thing you need to ask."

I'm afraid to ask her anything. Demi has this way of pushing me. I always seem to be off my game around her. *I don't like it.*

"Are you gonna fuck me or not?" She finally asks when I don't.

The words piss me off more than they should because she's right. I am jealous. Demi doesn't belong to me. She belongs to Seth. Just like Becky never belonged to me. And I refuse to go down that road again with another Holt Ice Princess.

I lift my right hand and run my knuckles down her soft cheek and lie just like she does to me. "You may be gorgeous, baby, but your sister is the one I plan on fucking tonight."

I enter the dark house and drop my bag at the front door. Thankfully, Austin put that damn Halloween decoration up in the attic, so I no longer have to hear it go off when I walk by. I grab a pack of cigarettes and a lighter out of the junk drawer in the kitchen and make my way to the back patio.

"What are you doing out here?" I ask, seeing Cole in the pool doing laps. No surprise there.

He pushes the wet hair from his face. "Needed to relieve some stress."

"Austin still mad at you?"

He nods his head. "She locked herself in Lilly's room for the evening."

I snort and light my cigarette. Guess that talk earlier didn't go so well for him. "I'm surprised that stopped you." A locked door isn't going to keep him away from her.

"Oh, her ass is gonna be in our bed when she wakes up in the morning," he says matter-of-factly.

"I'll make sure to leave early." I take a drag and lean back in the lounge chair.

"How did things go with Demi?"

I grunt. "Well, I left her in her bed naked and wet." After I got her off.

"Sounds like we both have some groveling to do."

"I can go get pussy anywhere." I give him a smug smile. "You're the one who is limited."

"But you want Demi's."

The smile drops off my face, and I take another drag. "I'm not going to touch her. Again." I've made up my mind. We've both overstepped a line, and I'm drawing a new one. *It's over.*

I change the subject. "Heard anything from Bennett?"

"I spoke to him a couple of hours ago, and he hasn't got any leads on Evan Scott."

"He once said that when Austin stole Jerrold's laptop, there was shit there that he missed." I growl.

Austin had dared Shane to steal Jerrold's laptop and that also gave us access to all the bank accounts to JJ's Properties—Jeff and Jerrold's businesses. Bennett syphoned all the millions combined from those accounts, and we split it equally between us. But what Bennett almost missed was that it also held details revealing that his brother Jeff—the guy we were killing the night Austin found us in the cemetery—had been paid by Bruce, Austin's dad, to tamper with the brakes on Cole's car, which ultimately led to the accident that killed three of our friends.

"Do you believe him?" he asks.

I take a drag of the cigarette and slowly blow the smoke out. "I think that whoever is behind it is smart. And they have help." He frowns. "It's gotta be more than one person."

"What makes you say that?"

"A hunch," I answer. "And Austin had mentioned us having enemies in Collins. She wasn't wrong. It's the only thing that makes sense. Someone back in Collins is helping someone here 'cause no one here knows what all we've done in the past."

"Except for us, Demi, and Becky. The girls admitted that they read Austin's journal."

"Yeah, but we don't know what all was written in there. And she hasn't had it since she was shot. And they knew that we killed Kellan." His name was marked out in red.

"But that was all over the news." He shrugs. "People thought I killed him. They just couldn't prove it."

Five months ago

I called the cops on our way to Bruce's from the clubhouse. But I didn't disclose that Kellan was involved. I gave an anonymous tip that there was a homicide at the Lowes' residence, then hung up. When we arrived, Austin was lying in a pool of blood in the kitchen, and Kellan was leaning against the countertop. Cole told me to remove him from the scene because he didn't want the cops getting to him first. So, I brought him up to the abandoned cemetery behind the Lowes estate, making sure I didn't leave a trail of blood. Kellan doesn't deserve to be behind bars. What little life he has left is up to Cole.

Cole reaches down and grabs Kellan's ankle, dragging him across the uneven ground. Even though we are too far from the Lowes' residence and no one can hear him, Cole drops his ankle and then straddles him, placing his hand over Kellan's mouth to quiet him.

"I'm not even going to ask you why." His bloodied chest rises and falls quickly as he sucks in breaths through clenched teeth. "Because it doesn't fucking matter." Then he punches him in the face. Kellan opens his mouth to cry, but Cole does it again. And again.

I don't stop him. Or offer him any help. When Cole is in this kind of mood, you just stand back and thank God you're not the guy he plans on destroying. He used to do this for sport, but ever since Jeff, things have escalated to murder. And I don't hold him back. If anything, I encourage him.

He comes to a stop and falls off Kellan as though he was functioning solely on adrenaline, and it just ran out. Cole sits on a patch of dead grass next to him, breathing heavily with his eyes closed. Pulling his knees up, he places his elbows on them and drops his forehead into his open, bloody hands. They're shaking. His entire body is.

I take a step toward him to make sure he's okay but then stop myself. This isn't like all the other times. No matter how much Kellan has betrayed us, he was still one of our best friends at one time. But now he has tried to kill the love of Cole's life. And by the amount of Austin's blood covering him, I would say Kellan succeeded, causing my chest to tighten for him. For Becky. I'm gonna have to break my girlfriend's heart and tell her that her best friend is dead.

"She was ..." Cough. "Always going to die," Kellan chokes out. "The game ..."

Cole lifts his head slowly, blood now covering his face, and he opens his eyes. He stares at Kellan for a long moment, and I see the fire raging in them. I've seen it so many times, and I know how explosive they can get. Then he kicks him in the face.

"Fuck the game!" he roars.

Kellan's head snaps back, and I hear bones breaking. For a moment, I think Cole broke his neck. But then Kellan releases a strangled moan, and I realize it was just his jaw. His bloody hands come up to cover his busted face. He sobs into them like the little bitch he is.

"You're the only one who is dying tonight," Cole snaps. "She's alive. And she's gonna stay that way."

"Naaa ... Pwe ... ase ..."

It's hard to understand his words with a broken jaw.

Cole finally looks up at me. His chest rising and falling fast. "Call Shelby."

I scramble to remove my phone from my pocket. When she answers, I place it on speaker. "Are you at the hospital?" I ask in greeting.

"Deke? What are you ...?"

"Are you at the fucking hospital?" I bark out. Austin's alive for now. But how long will she stay that way?

"Yes," she snaps.

"Austin is on her way. She's been shot."

"What?" She gasps. "What the hell, Deke? Cole shot her?"

"I don't have time to go through this with you again!" She always thinks the worst when it comes to him. "I'm calling you 'cause Cole isn't family, and he's gonna need updates. So fucking update me!" Then I hang up before she can say anything else.

Kellan coughs before turning onto his left side. Blood runs from his mouth and nose. His face is busted. "I'm ... sowwwy," he cries out.

"You will be," Cole tells him. Then he looks at me. "Call Bennett. Tell him to get his ass here."

"No ... no ... no," Kellan cries frantically.

I dial Bennett's number. He answers on the third ring. "Hey, Deke ...."

"I don't have time to explain. Get your ass up to the cemetery behind the Lowes' Estate."

"Everything okay?" he asks quickly.

I look down at Cole as he straddles Kellan again. He wraps his hand around the butt of the knife that sticks out of his side. "Fuck you, Kellan." He yanks the knife from his side, tosses it away, and then begins to punch Kellan in the face again with fists still covered in Austin's blood. Kellan tries to fight him, but it's no use. He's lost too much blood, and Cole is a killer. When you become his target, he doesn't stop until the job is complete.

Kellan knew this would only end one way. Even if Cole had to track him down, the outcome would have been the same.

Death.

And I was going to help my best friend achieve that goal. No matter what I had to do to make it happen. Because we're sharks. And what do sharks do? They kill.

"Deke ...?"

"No, Bennett, it's not."

"The town did call off the search." I shrug. They were never going to find his body. Bennett arrived and dropped him off in the ocean—attached to some dive tanks. He was never going to resurface. I'm sure the sea creatures took care of what was left of him. "With no body recovered, that leaves a lot of questions."

He sighs. "I'll call Bennett in the morning and see if he's got anything new."

"Has he found any information on who owns the cabin?"

He shakes his head again.

"So we're just supposed to wait around for the fucker to throw something our way?" I growl.

"I'm just as pissed about it as you are, but until we know who it is, there's nothing we can do."

A silence falls over us, and I finish the cigarette. I stand to walk inside when he steps out of the pool, and asks me, "What if it's not her?"

I turn to face him but don't answer.

He picks up his towel off the ground and wraps it around his neck. "Her name was on the list. So she's either behind it or about to be thrown into it."

"Your point?" I quirk a brow, wondering where he's headed with that statement.

He runs his hands through his hair, shaking off the excess water. "My point is what are you going to do if she's not behind it?"

"We have never killed someone for the hell of it. If she's innocent, then I'll protect her."

TWENTY-ONE

DEMI

I PULL UP to Austin's house and knock on the door. Rocking back and forth on my heels, I wait for someone to answer. There wasn't a car in the driveway, but I'm sure her Range Rover is in the garage. The guys aren't here. I only came over because they have practice. I haven't even gone home. I came straight from school because I wanted to get this over with before they returned home.

Just when I'm about to give up and turn away, the door swings open. Austin stands before me in a pair of dark jeans, a white T-shirt, and her hair up in a messy bun. And she doesn't look very happy.

"I'm sorry," I say immediately. I never meant to hurt her.

She lets out a long sigh and steps to the side, allowing me to enter. "It's not your fault," she says, shutting the door.

"I should have never read it. I should have told you …"

She waves me off and walks to the kitchen. I follow her. She goes straight to the fridge and pulls out a bottle of wine. "Do you drink?"

"Yes."

She pops the cork on the bottle, then she pours two drinks. "I prefer Fireball, but since it's not five yet, I'll keep it to a glass of Merlot." I take the offered glass, and she raises hers. Knocking them together, she says, "To the friends we lose, and the lessons we learn." Then she takes a big gulp of hers.

I sip on mine. "Have you heard from her?"

She nods. "She's called me. I've ignored them."

I look down at my drink. "I hate that she hurt you, but I can't say I'm surprised."

"I'm not mad about the journal. I mean, I am, but it's what she said to me." She sets the glass down, and her eyes meet mine. "I'm not with him because—"

"I know." I interrupt her. "You don't have to defend yourself to me, Austin."

My sister read her journal, and anyone who knows Cole and Austin knows that their love is real. Becky just wanted to hurt her and knew exactly what to say in order to accomplish that.

She gives another nod and throws back her wine.

I take another sip of mine.

"So enough about me and onto you," she says, faking a smile.

I sigh. "There's nothing about me to be said."

She quirks a brow. "Deke Biggs," she says, and this time when I lift the glass of wine to my lips, I take more than just a sip. "You love him."

I choke on it. "Hell no."

She tilts her head to the side. "Then why did you sleep with him?"

"Did you love Cole the first time you slept with him?" I counter. I know she didn't. Their first time was in a bathroom at a party. Deke stood outside the door and recorded it. Then someone uploaded it to social media the next day. I hate to say that I tried to find it, but it must have been taken down because it's nowhere to be found now. I'm sure Cole made it disappear once he realized he loved her.

"No, but he also wasn't previously in love with my sister. And I wasn't a virgin." She eyes me skeptically. "You slept with him for a reason, Demi. He may not know that, but I do."

I fall onto the barstool and place my elbows on the marble island. "Would revenge make it any better?"

"I told you I'm not going to judge you." She shrugs. "Everyone does something for a reason. I'm just trying to figure out why you did what you did." She refills her drink. "I know why he slept with you."

"Because he wanted to make my sister mad."

She shakes her head. "It had nothing to do with her and everything to do with you." I frown. Taking another drink, she smiles at me over the rim of her glass. "So I'll ask you again. Do you love him?"

DEKE

I stand at my locker with a towel at my bare feet and my jeans pulled up to my hips but still undone. My shirt lies on the bench behind me.

Cole walks up next to me, also fresh out of the shower, and all he's wearing is a towel draped around his neck. He yanks his locker open and picks up his phone. "Bennett called me."

"And?" I ask.

He throws his phone back into the locker. "And I missed it. He left me a voicemail. I'll call him back on the way home."

I sit down on the bench and put my socks and tennis shoes on as Cole throws his towel down to the floor. He's still pissy. This morning, Austin wouldn't even look at him. As I suspected, she woke up pissed when she realized he had broken into Lilly's room and carried her up to theirs. If I didn't know she loved him, I'd half expect his clothes to be on fire in the front yard when we get back to the house.

The guys walk around the locker room after swim practice. We've just finished our showers. I'm ready to get the hell home and go to bed. I'm tired. I can't survive on no sleep like Cole does.

"What did you do last night?" a guy by the name of Peter asks his friend Braden.

Cole and I aren't close to the guys on the swim team like we were back in Collins. We keep our distance. They don't try to be our friends, and we don't go out of our way to be theirs.

"Seth came over," he answers, sitting down on the bench a few spots down from me. "He brought his hot little girlfriend with him."

Cole looks over his shoulder at me. I ignore him and keep listening to the guys.

"Damn, the high school bitch he's fucking?" the guy asks.

He nods.

"Fuck, I'd be all over that every chance I got."

He laughs. "Yeah, it was weird, though. She just sat there and drank while playing video games. They didn't even talk much."

Cole throws his towel into his locker and steps into his jeans without even bothering with his boxers.

"You should have jumped on that. I bet he would have shared her with you. I hear they have an open relationship."

My hands fist. *Is that what you call it?* Then why did he get so pissed when he heard she was sleeping with me? I've seen him in class since then, but he's sat down on the front row. He's the last to show up to class and the first one to run out once the professor releases us. He thinks he can run from me, but he can't.

"Maybe that's what he was waiting on," the guy jokes.

"I know I'd share if she was mine. I'll take that sweet ass while you take her mouth."

And I've heard all I need to know. What the fuck has Seth been telling his friends? She was a fucking virgin, so I know they haven't done much. Hell, he's never even eaten her out. And I saw the way she looked at my cock. She'd never seen one before. What makes these guys think that he would share her?

I stand and turn to face him, but Cole grabs my upper arm. "Don't."

I look over at him and growl. "What if it was Austin?"

He lets go of my arm and nods. "I got your back."

"Fuck that mouth, I want her pussy …"

I step forward, gripping the guy's hair, and I rip him from where he sits on the bench and shove him headfirst into the lockers.

———————————

"What the hell happened?" Coach snaps as we all gather in his office.

I only got a few punches in before he came running into the locker room and broke it up. The bastards got off lucky.

"They jumped us," Peter barks.

I snort. Fucking rats. I place my bloody hands behind my back and step forward. "They were discussing in much detail how they planned to, for lack of a better word, fuck a girl. At the same time. A girl who I know, Coach. And I didn't feel comfortable listening to their derogatory comments. Especially since she is underage."

Coach's face instantly goes red. Our fathers taught us to do our research so before I took the scholarship at the University of Texas, I did some on Coach here. He has three sons and once had a daughter. She was an all-star athlete. Head cheerleader, played soccer, softball and ran track. One Saturday morning, she left her parents' house for a run. They called the police three hours later when she didn't return. Two days later, they found her body twenty feet off the running path. She was completely naked. The man had sexually assaulted her and strangled her with a shoelace. He pulled it so tight that it was still embedded in her neck. She was only a junior in high school. The report went on to say that her boyfriend told the police to look at Rodger Simmons, a swimmer at UT, because he had been calling and harassing her. I knew I wanted to come here when I read that he left town and never returned. Never to be heard from again. Of course, Coach was a suspect in his disappearance, but it's all about what you can prove, not what you think. That's why he's here with us, and Rodger's rotting corpse was never found.

"Coach …" Braden begins.

"Shut the fuck up!" he orders, placing his fisted hands on his desk and leaning over. "If you want to keep your scholarships, you will not breathe a word of it to anyone. Do you understand?"

"Yes, Coach," we all answer in unison.

"Get the hell out," he snaps.

We all turn to exit, but he stops us. "Except for Mr. Reynolds and Mr. Biggs."

Cole and I turn back around, and he points at the two seats in front of his desk. "Sit."

We do as we're told.

He walks behind his desk and picks up two manila envelopes. "I've read your files, boys. And I didn't like what I saw." He looks at Cole. "You were arrested back in Collins for shooting your girlfriend and killing her stepmother."

I watch Cole's body go rigid out of the corner of my eye, and he grips the armrest on his chair. He still only wears his jeans. He didn't have time to put a shirt on when I started throwing punches, and he jumped in.

"I was taken in for questioning, Coach. And released after proof of my innocence was found."

"Ah, yes. And the friend of yours who committed the crime has never been seen again." If I'm not mistaken, I would say Coach looks at him with pride. It takes a lot of planning and patience these days to kill a man and not get caught. If only he knew we did it by the seat of our pants and within minutes after we found him with Austin's body. Sometimes you just have to work with what you got. Then he looks at me. "I have no doubt you helped him." He quirks a brow.

I just cross my arms over my chest, and he nods once as if he understands that my loyalty lies with Cole.

He goes on. "Your father shipped you off to boarding school at the age of ten." My teeth grind. "Wanna tell me why they kicked you out after three months?"

"They said I was unteachable," I answer honestly. "And they believed I was possessed."

Cole chuckles, and I smile. It's the truth. My father sent me to an all-boys boarding school in Switzerland. I found him in the kitchen with his hand around my mother's throat, and I ran at him with a knife. After he beat the shit out of me, he shipped me away. The man was afraid I was going to kill him in his sleep. My mom begged me not to. It wasn't until years later, once I was older, that I understood why she was with him and put up with his shit—money. Bitch loves money as much as he loves having his options of pussy.

They had it out for me the moment I arrived at the boarding school, so I had to live up to my reputation, of course. I played a few pranks here and there, which all landed me in deep water. But the final straw was when I beat the shit out of three boys at once in the boys' bathroom. It didn't matter that they jumped me, and I kicked their ass. They kicked my ass out. Even my father's money couldn't keep me there. They had a no tolerance rule and told him I was the spawn of Satan. If they only knew how true that was.

He gives us his back and looks out his floor-to-ceiling windows that overlooks the courtyard of the university. "Your accolades spoke higher than your behaviors." He spins back around and stares at both of us. "Don't make me regret giving you both this chance."

"Yes, Coach," we both say.

He nods and sits down in his chair. "Go home, boys, and come back tomorrow ready to swim until your muscles ache to the point you'll have to crawl out of the pool."

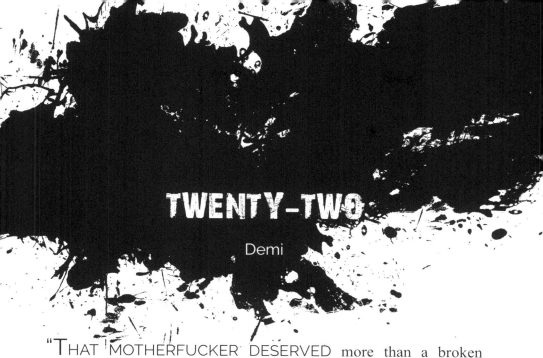

TWENTY-TWO

Demi

"THAT MOTHERFUCKER DESERVED more than a broken nose."

I sit on the couch next to Austin sipping on a new bottle of wine when we hear Deke's voice.

"Then let's go pay him a visit tonight," Cole offers.

"I should go," I say. Standing, I grab my phone to get an Uber. I wasn't thinking about how I was going to get home after I finished my second glass. I've been here for over three hours. I colored some pictures with Lilly before Austin put her to bed, and then we sat down to talk, and time just got away from us.

"You can go if you want, but this is my house too, and you're more than welcome here," she states before walking out of the living room. "What the hell happened?" I hear Austin gasp.

I make my way into the kitchen to see Cole standing at the fridge and Deke in front of an open drawer.

"Some guys were talking shit about Demi," Deke answers. "Me and Cole broke some shit."

"What?" I ask, taking a step into the kitchen.

Everyone turns to face me. Deke's jaw sharpens, and Cole runs a hand through his hair. Deke looks at Austin as though he expects her to explain my presence. As if I'm not welcome here. She doesn't.

"What?" I ask again. "Who was talking about me?"

Deke ignores me as he reaches into the open drawer and pulls out a pack of cigarettes. Slamming it shut, he stomps out of the kitchen.

"Cole?" Austin demands.

He arches a brow. "Oh, now you're talking to me?" He realizes his fuckup the moment the words are out of his mouth and looks away from her.

"Fuck you, Cole," she growls and goes to leave as well, but he grabs her by the upper arm, preventing her escape.

"A guy on the swim team was talking about him and another fucking Demi." He looks at me. "At the same time."

I frown. Who the hell at the University of Texas would know me? "Do I know them?" Maybe they meant another Demi.

He lets go of her and shrugs. "They didn't seem to know you very well. One mentioned that you were over at his house last night with Seth."

"Ahh," I say, remembering that Seth did tell me that when he introduced us last night. I didn't pay much attention. "Seth knows him through his sister. Last night was my first time to meet him."

"Well, I wouldn't go back there if I was you," he warns.

"Noted." I nod.

"Did you get suspended?" Austin asks through gritted teeth.

He snorts. "Hell no. Coach yelled at us and then told us to go home. He can't afford to lose us." He looks at me after answering her. "You need to figure out whatever the fuck you and Deke have going on."

"It's nothing." I just needed to use him one time.

"I've known Deke all of my life, and he wouldn't have jeopardized his scholarship for a girl he didn't give two fucks about." Then he looks down at his future wife. I can see the regret flash across his face for just a short second before it disappears. "May I talk to you?" When she doesn't answer, he adds, "Upstairs." Then he too exits the kitchen, not waiting for a response or giving her any room to protest, leaving me and Austin alone.

"I'm gonna go—"

"No," she interrupts me and turns to the fridge. Opening the door, she pulls out a half-full bottle of wine. We finished off the first one earlier. "Here." She holds it out to me. "Cole is right. You and Deke need to talk this out. And you are more than welcome to spend the night in the spare bedroom."

I arch a brow. "And you and Cole?"

She sighs heavily. "I'm going to go upstairs and talk it out too."

I walk out of the sliding glass door to find him sitting in a lounge chair. His head back, eyes closed, and a cigarette between his lips. He lifts his right hand and removes it before letting out a puff of smoke. My eyes catch sight of his busted knuckles. There's dried blood on them.

"Gonna tell me why you hit a guy because of me?" I ask.

His eyes spring open and meet mine. He doesn't say anything, but I choose to stay instead of letting him intimidate me. I walk around his chair and fall into the one beside him. His eyes follow my movements before landing on the pool.

I remove the cork and take a big sip of the wine, trying to fight the shiver that runs through me. It's cold out here.

We sit in silence, and I wrap my arms around my chest. "Austin thinks I love you," I say, trying to get some kind of response out of him. *Maybe shock him.* I want to see the Deke I saw that night at Silence. Confused and hot as fuck.

He just laughs and takes another drag. "Austin doesn't know you."

I smile at myself.

"Not like I do," he adds like the smartass he is.

The smile drops off my face. "What does that mean?"

He looks over at me. "You don't love anyone but yourself."

His words feel like a knife to my chest. He couldn't be more wrong. I take another drink from the bottle and say the one thing I've never said out loud. Not even to the boy I wanted. "I loved Eli."

DEKE

I laugh, shaking my head in disbelief. *Of course, she did.* "And you're pissed off because he didn't love you back."

"You know nothing." She growls.

"He was my best friend. I know enough."

"You didn't know he was fucking your girlfriend."

My entire body stiffens, and I look over at her. She has a smug smile on her face. A look of total satisfaction. Becky wasn't my girlfriend at the time. She was my secret. She was not only fucking me, but also David and Eli. I knew she got around, but I didn't know she was that big of a whore. How could I have? It's not like I followed her around everywhere or went through her phone. I believed her when she said she loved me and that I was the one she wanted to be with, but it was complicated, and we needed to wait. I hate that I believed her, but more importantly, I hate that everyone seemed to know but me.

"Guess he still picked her over you in the end," I say to hurt her, not really knowing what she and Eli had. It obviously wasn't sexual. I knew he liked Demi because I always saw him looking at her and secretly talking to her, but being the girl Becky is, she won.

She jumps to her feet and comes to stand before me. I look up at her and take a drag from my cigarette. She knocks it out of my mouth and to the ground before stepping on it. Then she leans forward, placing her face in front of mine.

"And if he wouldn't have died, she would have picked him over you," she states. "You were second best, Deke. To David. To Eli. To every other guy she's ever spread her legs for. How does that feel?"

I want to throw her into the pool and drown her mouthy fucking ass. But what will that solve? I'm with Cole. I'm tired of having to hide bodies. I left Collins to forget the terrors and run from my demons. I backed his need for revenge one hundred percent because Eli was my friend too, and he and his dead sister deserved revenge, but look where it left me. I lost Becky. The girl I thought I was going to spend the rest of my life with. I lost a friendship I thought could never be broken. And I hate it that Eli's dead. I want to call him up. Scream at him. Punch him. And then tell him he can have her. If that's what he wanted, I wouldn't have fought him. You don't fight your friends over trash.

"It must sting to know that she never loved you the way you loved her," she continues.

And I've had enough. Reaching out, I grab her shirt and yank her toward me so hard that she falls onto my lap. She gasps, placing her hands on my chest to push her stiff body from mine. "How do *you* feel about being second best, princess?" I ask, wrapping one hand around the back of her neck and the other around her waist, not giving her the chance to get away from me. Leaning in, I whisper, "I'm sure it hurt when you found out you'll never be her."

I pull back and see angry tears in her blue eyes. Moving my hand around her neck, I trail my fingers softly down over her collarbone and push her blond hair back from her shoulder, noticing that her hickeys are gone. I have an urge to lean in and give her more just because I can.

She bares her perfectly straight teeth at me. I remember when she had braces during her freshman year. I thought it was strange. Her teeth were already straight, but her mother made her get them anyway. You can never be perfect enough for Angelica Holt. "I don't want to be her, Deke."

I bite back a snarky comment at her words and look over her pouty lips and sad blue eyes. I think it's the first real thing she's ever said to me. "Then what is it you want?"

She closes her eyes and lets out a long breath. The fruity smell of her wine hits my face. "It doesn't matter what I want. It never has."

I don't like her answer. It makes me want to give her everything. And that's a rabbit hole I can't go down. "Why are you with Seth?" I change the subject.

"Why did you defend me tonight?" she counters.

I sigh, and she arches a brow. We're at a standstill. Neither one of us wants to answer.

Her body relaxes on top of mine, and her hands come up to my chest. I've got a direct line of sight to hers, and I move my hands to her narrow hips. My fingers dig into her jeans, and it takes everything in me not to move them against mine. To feel her grind against me. Just the thought makes my cock start to harden.

She licks her pouty, nude painted lips. "If I asked you to forget who I am for one night, could you do it?"

"Why would I wanna forget who you are?" I ask confused by her question.

"I don't wanna be Becky. But I also don't wanna be Demi," she answers honestly.

"Who do you wanna be?"

"Someone who matters," she whispers, dropping her head to stare at my shirt.

Letting go of her hips, I grip her chin and lift her head, so she must look at me. "Demi Holt matters to me," I say, and I hate that the words are true. I thought she was a Becky mini-me, but she's nothing like her. Demi pushes me. She wakes up a part of me that I didn't think I wanted again.

"What if she's not behind it?" Cole had asked me.

"Then I'll protect her." It's not even a question. I'd do whatever I have to do to protect her from whoever thinks they can go toe to toe with us. But if she's behind it … I'll also do what has to be done.

"Forget it." She goes to push away from me, but I hold my grip on her.

"Demi …"

"I don't need your lies," she snaps.

I cradle her face in my hands and pull her lips to mine. She doesn't hesitate before opening for me. Her tongue enters my mouth, and mine meets hers. Exploring her mouth as if it's never been there before. Wanting to know her sweet taste. Savoring it. Knowing that I may have to hurt her eventually. I want to drink her in. Swallow her whole.

Her hips begin to grind, rubbing her jeans on my hard dick, and I moan, tilting her head to the side to allow me to deepen the kiss. She moans, opening up for me as if she belongs to me. And I take from her.

I pull away, and she pants. "Does that feel like a fucking lie?" I demand.

Her heavy eyes open, and they search mine; for what, I don't know. Licking her wet lips, she replies roughly, "It doesn't feel like the truth."

TWENTY-THREE

DEMI

I LIED TO him. Again. He has no clue what Eli and Becky were doing, but I do. I'm the only person who knows what was really going on, but I can't tell him. Not now. I won't allow her to ruin another day of my life. I don't want to have to think of her, or Eli, or his death. I want Deke.

Austin thinks I love him, and honestly, I'm not sure she's a hundred percent wrong. What is love anyway? All the movies tell you that it's sweet and romantic, but it's such bullshit. Cole and Austin are proof of that. You don't always need hearts and flowers to prove you love someone. Sometimes you need each other's names carved in blood.

I push away from him, and he allows it. I stand on shaky legs. I'm not drunk, but I'm not sober either. He sits there looking up at me. Is he waiting for me to leave? For me to shout at him? Beg him? I want to fall to my knees and tell him that it's me he wants. That it's me he sees. Not her. But that's just the wine talking, so instead, I go for plan B.

I remove my shirt and kick off my shoes. I'm shoving my jeans down my legs when he sits up straighter in his lounge chair. "Demi …"

"Shh," I say, straddling him again. But only now I'm naked. I place my hands on his handsome face and look at his pretty blue eyes. "I want you to fuck me, Deke. It's just you and me. No lies. No pretending. Can you do that?"

His large hands slide up my bare back, making my body break out in goose bumps. I shiver and it has nothing to do with the cool night. "I was never the one faking it, Demi."

I lean in and capture his lips with mine, done talking for the night.

DEKE

I wake up with an arm draped over my chest and a soft leg over my thigh. Demi's blond hair covers most of her face, and I push it back to give me a clear view of her. After we had sex last night out on the patio, we took a shower together where I took her again up against the wall. She didn't hold anything back from me. I think Demi is confused on who she really is, but she didn't hide.

I lean in and kiss her cheek, and her eyes flutter open. "Good morning, princess."

"Good morning," she whispers.

I go to pull away from her, but she tightens her hold on me. "Five more minutes," she whispers.

I move to my side and wrap my arms around her, pulling her small frame into me. "Five more minutes." She closes her eyes. "How do you feel this morning?" I ask. She had quite a bit to drink last night. And I tried to be gentle with her since I know she's still getting used to sex, but it was hard to restrain myself.

"Like I knew I would," she mumbles into my chest.

"Want me to get you some ibuprofen?"

She shakes her head. "I just want five more minutes."

When I open my eyes some time later, I'm alone. Sitting up, I look around to see her clothes that were lying on the floor are now gone. I throw off the covers, get up, and pull on a pair of jeans. As I make my way down the stairs, I hear voices in the kitchen.

Demi stands at the kitchen island with her hand in a plastic container full of brownies. She places one in her mouth and moans, closing her eyes. "This is by far the best thing I've ever put in my mouth."

I lean down, and whisper, "That'll all change once I fuck that mouth with my cock."

She begins to choke on the chocolate at my words and pieces are flying out onto the counter. She grabs for the bottle of water and gulps it down. Slamming the bottle down, she sucks in a long breath.

"See, it's already choking you." I smile.

She stares up at me with watery eyes from her near-death experience by her favorite snack.

Placing my hand on her face, I say, "Cheeks flushed. Lips swollen and tears running down your pretty face." I kiss her cheek and taste the saltiness. "You'll be a beautiful mess, Demi."

Her lips part, and she licks them.

"Good morning," Cole announces, entering the kitchen.

He's a cheerful fucker. He and Austin must have made up last night. For once, I didn't hear them fucking because I was too busy doing it myself. I've brought girls home but never slept with them in my room unless Lilly was staying at a friend's house. I don't like the idea of having them around her. She sees Austin and Cole kiss and love on one another even though Austin tries to stay discreet. She's never asked about it, and as far as I know, they haven't sat her down to tell her anything. She's only six. What could they possibly tell her that she could understand?

"Morning," I tell him.

Austin enters a second later with Lilly on her hip. "We're gonna be late," she mumbles, setting her on the counter and going to the fridge to grab Lilly's lunch.

"Did you and Austin have a sleepover?" Lilly asks Demi.

She chokes on another piece of the chocolate, but nods. I chuckle.

"I wanna have a sleepover." She starts bouncing on the counter. "Can we have one this weekend?"

"You already have one with Mrs. River," Austin tells her.

She nods her little head, blond curls bouncing. "She's my dance teacher," she tells Demi. "It's her daughter's birthday."

Demi swallows a piece of chocolate. "Is she in your dance class?"

"Yep. She's not very good, though."

"Lilly," Austin scolds her. 'That's not very nice to say."

"That's what she says."

"Come on," Austin throws her backpack over her shoulder and scoops Lilly off the counter. "We gotta go."

Cole comes over to kiss them both goodbye, and then he walks them to the garage, leaving me and Demi alone.

She stares down at the now empty box. I step into her, and she looks up at me. "Let me take you out this weekend," I offer. I haven't spent time with just her. I've known her all my life, but what do I really know about her? Besides she's gorgeous with a fucked-up mind.

"Wanna get me alone?" She arches a brow.

I smile at her. "Maybe."

"Where you wanna take me?" she asks but doesn't let me answer. "I'm guessing the woods. Somewhere quiet and secluded so you can kill me."

I'm not sure if she's joking or being serious. "The only reason I would take you out to the woods would be to bury your body." I step into her, reach out, and grab a piece of bleach blond hair. "If I wanted to kill you, you'd already be dead." She swallows. "I would have done it while you laid on your bed with your hands tied behind your back. I could have wrapped my hands around your neck and squeezed while you gasped for breath. I could have made it quick and snapped your neck, or I could have held a pillow over your face and suffocated you," I whisper. "Murder doesn't have to be messy, princess. It can be sensual, or it can be brutal, depending on my mood."

Her eyes search mine, clearly understanding my sincerity. "You've thought about it."

"That wasn't the only thing on my mind that night." My eyes drop to her thighs, letting her know exactly what I mean.

"Okay." Cole enters, rubbing his hands together. He spots us and exits the kitchen just as quickly.

"I can't," she finally answers, pulling away from me.

"Have plans already?" I tease, not in the least bit worried that she just turned me down. Demi Holt has gotten my attention, and I won't let her walk away easily.

"Yes. With Seth."

TWENTY-FOUR

DEMI

FINALLY, FRIDAY ROLLED around. I've been able to avoid Deke since I spent the night at his house and slept with him. Again. Things were starting to get weird. The sex was too soft. He was too nice. I didn't need him to coddle me or pretend I'm Becky. Maybe he just can't help it, but I wasn't going to stick around to find out. And then the whole thing about going on a date. At least that's what I think *let me take you out* means. Hell, to a murderer, it might mean something completely different. And then he told me how he would do it. I hate that it turned me on. Fuck, I need therapy. I'm going to tell my mom to call her friend that she's been trying to get me to see for years now. I didn't lie about my plans with Seth this weekend, but I could tell Deke was pissed about it. He clearly forgot that I have a fake boyfriend. I didn't stay after that.

I exit the bathroom and enter my walk-in closet. As soon as I got home from school, I showered, ready to get the hell out of here for the weekend. Seth had messaged me earlier about going to the cabin for the evening. We were supposed to go see a movie, but the idea of getting away sounded better. I didn't realize how much I needed to get away and clear the fog of Deke Biggs until I read his message with our change of plans.

I pull on a pair of underwear and holey jeans along with a white

T-shirt that has some donut holes on it that says *eat my hole*. I grab my Louis Vuitton bag from the top shelf and start throwing clothes in it as I hear my door open. I storm out of my closet to see if it's my sister. She's been MIA ever since her argument with Austin on Monday. I'm guessing she went back to Collins, but who knows when she'll return. I come to a stop when I see it's my mother.

"How was school today?" she asks.

"Fine." *Like she cares.*

She nods her head once, and asks, "Are you making friends?"

Really? It's November. I'm three months into my senior year, and she wants to know now if I'm making friends. She knows the only one I bring around is Lauren. And Seth. "Yep." If she only knew I've friended Deke, Austin, and Cole. She never liked Cole. Said he was evil. She thinks he killed his mother. She never cared much for Deke, but when she found out Becky was dating him, she began to come around to the idea of them together because the Biggs have money. A lot of it. I'm talking millions. And she'd rather a man support her daughter than her.

"Good. How are things with Seth?"

What is with all the questions? "Good. He's busy with football." Not a total lie. They have a bye weekend this weekend. That's why he wanted to hang out tonight.

"Going somewhere?" she asks, looking at my bag.

"Yeah. Lauren asked me to stay the night with her tonight."

She reaches up and grabs her pearls that hang around her neck, usually a clear sign that she's going to turn me down. I used Lauren as my excuse when I passed out at Deke's Tuesday night. She didn't like it, but she didn't ground me over it.

"She had a bad day," I add. "You know? With her parents and all …"

"Ahh. I see." She glances around the room. It's spotless. I have a thing about tidiness when it comes to my personal space. The rest of the house I couldn't care less about. "Is your homework done?"

I hold in a sigh. "Yes." From a young age, my mother drilled into me that education is important—make good grades and make

242

something of yourself—but she never once said that to Becky. It was like Becky was destined to marry royalty, and if I didn't get into college, I'd be scrubbing toilets. And I find nothing wrong with that profession.

"May I go?" I ask, trying not to show my anger. I hate that Becky gets to come and go as she pleases, yet I have to ask. I still have three months before I turn eighteen, but that won't matter. As long as I'm in school, I'll have to do what she says.

"I suppose." She sighs before leaving the next second. No goodbye. No I love you. Nothing. And I'm totally fine with it. I'm used to not being shown any kind of affection.

An hour later, I'm pulling up to the cabin and see his Jeep is already here. I grab my bag and get out.

Walking in, I find him sitting on the brown leather couch. He looks away from the TV, noticing me, but doesn't smile, which is unusual. Seth is always in a good mood.

"What are you doing here tonight?" I ask him. He hates this place. Says it's too low class. It belonged to his grandmother or some shit, so his parents kept it but never use it. His mom and stepdad are filthy rich. They've got a house on the lake and several homes all over the world. They even have a yacht in the marina where they sometimes stay.

"Felt like getting away," he answers, looking back at the TV.

I can understand that. I plop down beside him and cross my legs, trying to put Deke out of my mind. I haven't heard one word from him, but why would I? He got what he wanted. Sex. I hate that I crave it again. It hurt just as much this past Tuesday as it did the first time, but it was still amazing. The way he held me and kissed me. My skin tingled for days after. And last night, I craved it so much, I took care of myself thinking of him. "What are we watching?" I try to focus on Seth.

"Friends."

Of course. Pretty sure he's seen every episode more than twice.

He leans forward, picking up a green cup, and hands it to me. "I made you your drink." I don't take it, and he sighs. "Demi …"

"You know I can't drink that," I say softly. Ever since Becky drugged me, I have this thing about drinking from a cup that I didn't make. My father warned us about it back in middle school, but I never thought my own sister would betray me in that way.

"Fine." He places it back on the coffee table.

"You can have it," I offer.

"I'm not in the mood to drink." He gives a clipped answer.

I frown. Seth is always up to party. "Is something going on with Hayden?"

He doesn't respond, but I notice the tic in his jaw, so I drop it.

"What movie are we gonna watch?"

Again, he doesn't answer, and it sends up red flags. I sit back and watch him. His right knee bounces up and down nervously. He pulls his bottom lip in and chews on it. His breathing has picked up.

"Seth …" I place my hand on his shoulder, and he jumps. "What's going on?" I demand, starting to get worried. He's never like this.

He picks up the remote and holds it out in front of him as a long silence fills the room. When he finally speaks, his voice wavers. "You let Deke fuck you, right?"

I stiffen. Why does he care? And more importantly, why is he asking a question he already knows the answer to. He knew what my plan was the night of my Halloween party because he helped set it up. But he only knows about that first night. I haven't filled him in on the fact that Deke was in my bedroom Monday night when he dropped me off at home, or that he fucked me three times Tuesday night. "Yes," I respond slowly.

Another silence falls between us before he presses the button on the remote to turn up the volume. Ross's laughter rises to the point it hurts my ears.

"Seth, what are you …?"

He turns to face me. Brown eyes full of regret. I push myself farther into the couch.

"Demi, I'm sorry." I barely hear him whisper over the blaring TV.

"For what?" I look around the empty cabin. It sits on three acres, backed up to the lake with a small dock, there's not another close by. You would only turn a TV up if you didn't want someone to hear what you are about to do. "What's going on?" He doesn't answer. Instead, he places the remote back down on the coffee table.

I stand on shaky legs, picking up my bag. "I'm gonna go." And begin to walk toward the door.

But he jumps to his feet and walks up behind me. He grabs my arm, spinning me around, and slams my back into the front door. "Demi." He sighs my name, staring down at me.

"Stop, Seth." I try to shove him away, but he doesn't budge.

He pushes his body into mine instead, holding me captive against the door. Seth has played football all his life and got a scholarship to the University of Texas for his ball skills. He's not a little guy by any means.

"Seth," I snap. "Stop."

His brown eyes narrow on mine. "I would if I could."

"What the fuck …?" He grips my hair, cutting off my words, and yanks me from the door before slamming me face-first onto the hardwood floor.

BECKY

I drive down the gravel road with my windshield wipers on. I hate Collins, Oregon. It's always cloudy and rainy, and I prefer sunny days and warm weather. I need to move to a beach where I can sunbathe all year round. Taking a deep breath, I get out of my father's car and enter the clubhouse. I'm here to see Bennett.

"Hello?" I call out, the sound bouncing off the walls and high ceilings. Looking at the table that sits to my right, I smile when a black duffle bag catches my eyes. I remember all the things the GWS always keep on them from Austin's journal.

"What are you doing here?" I watch a man step out of the bathroom at the top of the stairs. He stands there, drying off his hands with a white towel before he begins to descend the stairs.

I roll my eyes. "Cut the shit, Shane. Is Bennett here?" I need to talk to that fucker. He's been ignoring my texts and calls. He doesn't want to piss me off.

He shakes his head. "Just you and me."

"Well, I'm not staying." I turn to leave.

"Why are you here?" he presses.

"None of your business," I call out.

"How's your sister?" he asks.

I stop and turn back to face him as he hits the bottom step. "Taken care of."

"Doubtful."

"Why do you care?" That bitch will die after what she did to me. I haven't decided what I'm going to do with Deke just yet, but Demi will suffer before I end her miserable life.

"I tried to get them to kill her." He shrugs. "But he wanted to protect her for some fucking reason. They all did. From me. Ever since Kellan shot Austin ..." He waves a careless hand in the air. "No one trusts me anymore."

"No one should trust a shark," I snap.

He laughs. "Deke will fall in love with Demi, you know. If he hasn't already."

"He's supposed to love me." I feel like if I say it enough, it will happen.

His lips curl up slightly, and he rubs his chin while looking me up and down. "No one can love a slut, Becky."

I slap him across the face.

He slaps me back and growls. "Don't confuse me with Deke."

I want to laugh it off, but tears fill my eyes at the sting that lingers. "Austin hits harder than you."

He chuckles. "Any girl Cole falls in love with would have to be strong." He leans in close to my face. "A lesser woman would be dead by now. He would have torn her apart. She was made for it."

"Whatever." I roll my eyes, holding my hand over my throbbing cheek. "Fuck her." I've now put her in the same category as my sister.

They'll both get what they deserve.

"Would you be saying that if she knew everything you've done?"

My heart begins to pound in my chest. "I don't know what you're talking about."

"No need to play dumb, Becky. It looks ugly on you," he whispers. "You know …" His hand comes up, and he runs his knuckles over my sensitive cheek. "Kellan and I were the closest. He told me everything."

My breathing picks up. Fucking Kellan, I knew he'd fuck me over. That's what these guys do. Their loyalty is only to one another, and even that weakened over the years as they grew older. "They'll never believe you." I decide on.

"Oh, they will. Especially when I show them proof." My breath gets caught in my lungs. "What do you think Austin will do to you when she finds out what you've done?" I don't answer. "What do you think Cole will do to you?" I stiffen. "Or Deke? He loves her like a fucking sister."

I slap him again. "Fuck you."

He slaps me, and this time, it has me stumbling back. He grabs me and throws me against a wall. My heart races, and I cry out from his force.

"What do you wanna do, babe?" His voice drops to a whisper, and he leans his body into mine, pinning me to the wall. "How about I just take care of you right here? Right now? I can tell the boys what you've done and then show them your body lying in a shallow grave. I'll be their hero."

I try to shove him away, but it doesn't work. His lips find my earlobe, and he sucks on it. Bile begins to rise. "Shane, please …"

His free hand grips my right thigh and lifts it, wrapping it around his hip. "Do you remember? Me and you?"

"I try to forget." I sniff.

"I was the first one to touch, lick, and fuck that pussy. Before you went and passed it around like a joint at a party." His hand slides up my thigh to cup my ass, and he grinds his hips into mine.

I whimper, hating the fact that I gave my virginity to Shane. I was fifteen, and he was gorgeous with a car. He had just turned sixteen, and Cole threw him a party at his father's house. I had snuck out to go. After countless drinks, I ran into him in the backyard. He wanted to go to the beach and get some fresh air. Even though I knew it was bullshit, I left with him. I had spread my legs for him in the back seat of his car that night at the beach. Then he took me home, and he never looked at me again. I knew it was going to be that way. That's how all the sharks were. Months later, Deke kissed me by the football field. A short time after that, I got with David. Somehow, my numbers just kept climbing. I hate how much criticism I get for doing what they do without a second thought. A guy can fuck four girls in one night, but a girl can't fuck two guys in the same month without being tainted.

Such bullshit!

"I always kept that fun fact a secret from Deke, knowing he'd be pissed at me, but I don't think he'd give a fuck now."

I close my eyes, hating how much that thought hurts. How he betrayed me more than I ever could him. I could sleep with every fucking GWS, and it wouldn't even come close to the fact he fucked my sister. "Shane ..."

He pulls away from me with a smirk on his face as though he just won some fucking bet. Honestly, I wouldn't be surprised if he did. They dare each other to do all kinds of shit, and nothing is off-limits. Not even women. "Don't worry, Becky. I just fucked you then 'cause I knew it'd be easy. I sure as hell don't want you now."

My chest tightens. That's all I ever am—a fuck! No one ever wants to love me. "Fuck you, Shane ..." I shove him away.

He just smiles at me. "Did you know you were a dare?"

"What?"

"Eli dared Deke ..."

"No." I shake my head. "You're lying." I had asked Deke this very question four months ago when he stood in my bedroom at my father's house.

"Was I a bet that night at the party? Did Cole bet you to take me home?" We were finally able to be with one another. Cole was

claiming Austin for all to see. It was our time. After all the secret hookups and quiet whispers, we were able to be together. But was it true?

"You can't be serious. That night was not our first night together, or have you forgotten?" He growls.

I jab my finger into his chest, and he takes a step back. "So? And I'm dead serious. Did you record us that night too?" *I went home with him and stayed in his pool house.*

"Fuck, no!" he snaps. "I would never do that to us."

"How am I supposed to know that?" I shout. I bow my head and sigh. I've lied to him for so long, maybe I missed his lies. "The bottom line, Deke, is I don't trust you. And I can't be with someone I don't trust. I've done it before, and I won't do it again."

"You can trust me. I would never cheat on you. Or film you. Fuck, I love you."

"You're lying," I repeat. "He was not dared to take me home the night of the party."

"Party?" He laughs. "No, I'm talking about the day he kissed you at Collins High by the football field."

"What?" I gasp.

"I won't lie. Somewhere along the way, Deke managed to fall in love with you, but you've fucked him over too many times. See, Becky, you always were nothing more than a game to us." He tilts his head to the side. "A game that has come to an end." Then he turns and walks over to the small kitchen.

Without another word, I walk out of the clubhouse, fall into my father's car, and start it up. "The Best You Had" by Nina Nesbitt plays through the speakers. Removing my cell from my pocket, I pull up Deke's number, and fresh tears begin to fall. I need to make it right with him. He's the only one who can save me at this point.

TWENTY-FIVE

DEKE

I SIT BY the pool in the cool night air, and I'm on my third cigarette while Cole does his laps. Now that it's November, he's turned the heater on in the pool.

My phone dings, and I pick it up off the table next to me to see it's a text from Becky. It's like all the others she's sent me. She's relentless.

Becky: Why her?
Becky: Did you think she was me?
Becky: Why didn't you tell me?
Becky: Do you not love me anymore?

Same ole, same ole.

I ignore them and drop the phone onto my lap. Cole pops his head out of the water, sucking in a deep breath, but says nothing.

My phone begins to ring, but I don't even bother looking at it. I have nothing to say to Becky. I didn't sleep with Demi for any other reason than I wanted her. Simple as that. And I was single. Am single. I don't have to explain myself, especially to her. She'd kill me if she knew I did it for a second time. Third time. Fourth time. They were all better than the first, if that's even possible. And it's all I've thought about. I've been hard for the last three days.

It stops for a second and then starts up again.

"You gonna answer that?" Cole asks.

"Nope." I take another drag. It stops after the second ring this time, and I sit back in the lounge chair.

"Wanna talk about it?" he asks.

I almost laugh. "Not much to say." At this point, I'm not sure who fucked me over more. Demi or Becky. One cheated on me, and the other used me.

Fuck, I'm starting to sound like a bitch whining to her girlfriends about a guy she expected to love her.

I hear the sliding glass door open, and a moment later, Austin comes to stand beside me. "Get your ass out of the pool," she tells Cole in a rush.

"Austin, what …?"

"Get the fuck up." She ignores him, smacking my arm so hard I drop my cigarette in my lap.

"What the hell?" I bark, trying to shove it off before it burns my fucking dick through my jeans.

"What's going on?" Cole demands, jumping out of the pool.

"Demi is here."

My teeth grind at the mention of her name. I can't do this again. I don't see it ending well. I hated that I felt the slightest bit sorry for her when she confessed she wanted to be anyone but herself. It's just another trick. Now that I haven't seen her in days, I've been able to think clearly. She picked Seth over me. And I refuse to do this again. I've already done it with Becky.

"And?" Cole growls.

"And she needs our help."

I snort. "Tell the bitch to go to hell."

Austin shocks the shit out of me when she slaps me across the face. And fucking hard, I might add. I jump to my feet.

"Get the fuck over it," she yells. "This is serious."

Cole grabs her arm, forcing her to face him. "What is going on?"

She takes in a deep breath. "It's about Seth."

"That doesn't help her case." I growl.

She pulls away from Cole and places her hands on her hips. "Every time I forget how big of dicks you guys can be, you remind me." Then she spins around and enters the house, slamming the sliding glass door shut.

Cole grabs his towel and dries off with a hard look on his face. I step on my cigarette, making sure it's out before I go inside to face whatever bullshit is going on.

Cole and I enter the house and find Demi sitting on the couch with her head down between her hands. Austin sits beside her, rubbing her back and speaking softly.

"Why the fuck are you here?" I demand, coming to stand in front of them.

Austin's head snaps up, and she glares at me. "Deke …"

"No, he's right. I shouldn't have come," Demi whispers.

"This is my house, and you are welcome here anytime you want. This is a safe place."

What the fuck is Austin talking about? Safe place? Is she trying to say I hurt her last time she was here? Because Demi never told me no or to stop. She was very willing. "Get the fuck out."

"Deke!" Austin shouts my name, jumping to her feet. "Don't fucking talk to her that way!" She steps into me, but Cole pulls her back. She spins around on him. "Cole …"

"Austin." He growls her name in warning, but what Cole doesn't understand is that he no longer holds any kind of power over Austin Lowes. "This doesn't concern us."

"It does," she argues.

"It doesn't …"

"He tried to rape her!" she shouts, yanking free of him.

Silence fills the large living room at her words. I look down at Demi, and she still sits with her head down, but I now see the trembling in her small body.

Austin lets out a long breath and sits down next to her again. When she reaches out to touch Demi's back, she jumps slightly. "It's okay," she whispers to her.

I run a hand through my hair. "What happened?" I ask through gritted teeth. This better not be another damn trick! Her sister pretended to be pregnant so who knows what Demi is capable of?

That silence continues, and it makes my jaw tighten. If it's true, it doesn't make any sense. First, he hurt her at the Halloween party, and now he tried to rape her? What the fuck is his deal? And why the hell is she with him?

"Demi?" I snap her name.

She stands, keeping her head down. "I'm leaving," she says in a soft voice, and she turns to exit the living room.

I reach out, grab her arm, and spin her around to face us, about to scream at her, demanding to know what the fuck happened, but the words die on my tongue when I see her beautiful face streaked with tears. And my heart begins to beat faster as I look her over. Her T-shirt has been stretched out; it hangs off her right shoulder, showing the strap of her nude-colored bra. She has a rug burn on her elbow, and her hair is tangled. Her cheek has a small cut on it. But it's her eyes that make my chest tighten. They look like the saddest fucking thing I've ever seen.

I step into her, placing my hands on her face. "What happened?"

She licks her trembling lips. "He was gonna rape me."

DEMI

I expect him to push me away. To throw me out. I didn't come here for him. I came here for Austin. I read her journal, so I know what she went through with her mom's boyfriend. Not only would he slap her, but he also touched her inappropriately, and I wanted to talk to her. Not explain to Deke how my fake boyfriend decided he wanted to fuck me and wasn't going to take no for an answer. At least that's what he told me his plan was.

"What makes you think that?" Cole is the one who breaks the silence.

I reach up and push Deke's hands from my face. Thankfully, he doesn't fight me. "He …" I swallow. "I went to go see him, and he was acting weird." I drop my head to the floor. "When I tried to leave, he grabbed me. I told him to stop, and he said he wished he could.

Then he threw me face down onto the floor. I started screaming, and he kept saying sorry, over and over. I felt him undo his jeans, and he flipped me over. That's when I lost it." A tear runs down my cheek. "I clawed at his face, bit his arm, and managed to kick him off. Then I just ran." My body shakes. "I left … and … I didn't know where else to go." I choke out the words. I can't tell my mother this. She thinks I was with Lauren. And I can't tell Lauren because she thinks we are already sexually active. I had nowhere else to go.

Strong arms wrap around me, and I bury my face into Deke's shirt. "You're safe now, princess," he says, kissing my hair.

And I sniff. "I shouldn't have come here …"

He pulls back and places his hands on my face, forcing me to look up at him. "You're exactly where you need to be, Demi." His clouded blue eyes search mine before they look at Cole's. He nods at Deke once.

"Where was he?" Cole asks me.

I'm not sure what they plan on doing, but Seth deserves it. After everything I've done for him … "At his parents' cabin on Lake Travis."

Deke's body stiffens against mine, and Cole's eyes narrow on me.

"Lake Travis?" Cole yanks Austin back from me and Deke, cutting her off, placing himself between her and us.

"What were you doing there?" Deke demands.

I pull away from him, wiping my face, confused to what is happening. "I told you. He messaged me to come over."

"Bullshit!" Cole snaps, taking a step closer to me.

Deke reaches out, placing a hand on Cole's bare chest, bringing him to a stop. But his next words say he doesn't believe me either. "Can you prove that?"

I'm starting to get pissed off. I've had one hell of a fucking night. I cross my arms over my chest. "Why does it matter? I just told you that he confessed he was gonna rape me. Why do I need to prove that?" I snap.

"'Cause I don't believe you," Cole answers.

I snort in disbelief at these guys.

"Cole, stop!" Austin tells him.

"No." He turns to face her. "The guys and I get a message from Evan Scott and possibly go to the very same cabin that Demi's boyfriend owns, and you don't think that's a coincidence."

She opens her mouth, but I speak first. "Evan Scott? You got a message from him?"

This time, it's Deke who steps into me. "You mean the message you sent us?"

My eyes widen. *What the fuck?*

"And it's game over for you, Demi."

TWENTY-SIX

DEKE

MY BLOOD IS pumping, my fists are clenched, and my mind is screaming that this bitch played us better than anyone else ever has. I reach out for her, and she takes a step back from me. Her eyes are wide, and her face drained of any color. Finally, she shows true fucking fear. Good for her to realize that I can and will hurt her.

"There has to be an explanation." Austin speaks.

"That was why your name was on the list," I say more to myself than anyone else. "You put it there to throw us off." *Fuck, Shane was right.*

"List? What list?" Demi asks.

Her eyes going from mine to Cole's. He wants to murder her. I can feel it. Anything that threatens his *sweetheart*, he would destroy without thought. But I won't let him have Demi. I'll handle her myself. She's had it coming since she pretended to be her sister at Silence.

Austin steps out from behind Cole. He tries to grab her, but she manages to get away from him. "Demi, you have to explain why you wrote that note. Did Seth make you do it? Was he the one who sent out the messages?" She rattles off questions, the next one sounding even more desperate than the first.

"The one from Evan Scott?" Demi asks still putting on her best fucking show of confusion. Like a little lost girl in a forest that is about to swallow her up.

She reaches into her back pocket and pulls out her cell. "I got a friend request from him the night of my Halloween party. I have yet to accept it, but I showed it to Becky a couple of days later and she got pissed. Sent him a message. He responded earlier this week, but I blew it off."

I yank her phone from her hands and look at it. She has her messenger pulled up, and sure enough it has a message to him a few days ago.

"She said it was an ex of hers." Demi adds.

Her: I will fucking kill you.

"Becky sent this to him?" I ask, still skeptical.

"Yes. I don't know the guy. We only had one mutual friend, and it was her. Why?"

I look over at Cole and hand him the phone so he can read it. "He responded to you."

She nods frantically. And Cole reads it out loud. "Not if I kill you first."

"It didn't make any sense, so I ignored it," she whispers. "Is Seth Evan Scott?"

"Fuck!" Cole hisses. "This explains why Becky was so pissed to begin with. Demi slept with you the night of the Halloween party and then shows this to Becky two days later. She knows you're Evan Scott …"

"You're Evan Scott?" Demi interrupts him.

We all ignore her. "She probably thinks you both set her up," Cole finishes.

A cell begins to ring, and Cole looks down at the one he holds in his hands. "It's Seth," he announces.

I rip Demi's cell out of his hands and hit answer. He begins to ramble instantly.

"I'm so sorry, Demi. You have to understand. I had no choice. I tried to think of a way around it. I even offered them money. You know I'm good for it. I would never hurt you, not like that, if I didn't have to. If you would have just taken the drink, I wouldn't have had to force you. You probably wouldn't have even remembered it."

He tried to drug her? *What the actual fuck?* And he actually thought he was doing her a favor. I stare into Demi's blue eyes while I listen to this guy who is supposed to be her boyfriend, and I can't figure out what I'm missing.

"Please say something," he begs. When my silence lingers, he breaks down like a fucking chick. "I'm sorry," He sobs. "They have a video of me and Hayden … you know that can't get out, Demi. It can't …" He sniffs. "Please tell me that you forgive me."

"If you're afraid of a video getting out, wait until I'm done with you."

He gasps. "Wait … What? Deke, is that you?"

I don't answer.

"I didn't …"

"But you tried," I shout, interrupting him, knowing where he is going. I can literally see the evidence on her body as she stands in front of me. He tried to drug her!

"She has to understand," He growls, no longer begging for forgiveness since he knows I'm not Demi on the phone. "I helped her out when she wanted to fuck you. Putting on that fake fight for you to sweep in and feel like a fucking man trying to save her. The least she could have done was let me do what I needed to do to save my ass. It's not like she was still a virgin anymore."

My eyes swing to Demi's at his confession, and I take a step toward her. "You're dead."

DEMI

You're dead?

He still holds the phone to his ear, but his eyes are on mine. I'm not sure if he meant that for me or for Seth, but my heart pounds in my chest, nonetheless.

He pulls the phone from his ear, holds down the button to turn it off, and then throws it across the room. I hear it slide on the tile hallway that leads out of the living room. His eyes never leave mine. "Cole, take Austin—"

"No." She interrupts him, coming to stand beside me.

My eyes shoot to Cole. He looks like he's debating on staying. As if he wants to have a hand in whatever Deke plans on doing to me. Why do they think I've somehow betrayed them? I haven't done shit to Cole.

"Now!" Deke shouts, making me jump.

Cole steps up to us, grabs Austin by the arm, and pulls her away from me. "Don't you fucking hurt her, Deke!" she screams at Deke as Cole drags her out of the room. The front door slams shut moments later.

We stand in silence, facing one another with only a few feet separating us. He stands, shoulders pulled back, and he's breathing heavily. He looks like a storm about to drown me before carrying me out to sea to never be found.

I swallow nervously. "I don't know what he said …"

"Enough," he says in a clipped voice.

"Deke, let me explain," I growl, tired of this shit.

"How you played me?" He quirks a brow.

My jaw tightens. "This has nothing to do with you."

"Bullshit!" he shouts.

I step into him. If I'm going to go out, I'm going to go out with some fucking balls. Men aren't the only ones who can have them. "I did what …"

"Needed to be done." He nods. "You said that before. And Seth obviously feels the same."

I slam my fist in his hard chest. He doesn't budge, but he grabs my wrist, and I whimper when he squeezes it tightly. "I never did anything to you against your will," I shout, feeling the tears begin to burn my eyes. Once again, my sister wins. She fucked me over. I tried to do something to piss her off, and it burned me. I should have never let Deke touch me.

I hit him with my other fist, and he grabs that one too. I cry out when he holds them both captive. His long and strong fingers digging into my bony wrists.

He leans down, placing his face in front of mine, and whispers, "Two can play that game."

"Deke ... what ...?"

"Seth told me that he helped you set me up. That first night I fucked you."

My eyes widen. That sorry little bastard. I will out him. I will no longer keep his fucking secret.

"I'm guessing this is just another game you two are playing." He spins around, drops my wrists and grips my neck, slamming my back into the wall by the TV. My vision blurs for a second from his force. When it clears, I see his murderous eyes stare into mine. "You asked me before if I wanted to hurt you." He growls, tightening his hand.

I try to shove it away, but he's too strong.

"The answer is that I want to fucking kill you, Demi. You're a fucking pain in my ass. Your sister may be a fucking slut, but you are nothing to me. Do you understand that?" He shakes me and dots take over my vision. "Nothing."

Panic sits in my bones as my body screams for a breath. To survive. I kick my feet, but all I hit is air. I slap at his face, but I don't think he even feels it. My already bruised cheek throbs, and my head pounds. When that gets me nowhere, I scratch at his arm and try to shove his wrist away, but he's just too strong. Tears run down my face, and he watches them as if fascinated. I've heard of the sharks and how ruthless they can be, but I've never seen one firsthand. Until now. He doesn't care about me or my life. I'm a problem for him, and he's going to make me go away. My lips move, but nothing comes out. I try to beg him to stop, but it's pointless. My head pounds so hard it feels like it's about to explode. I'm losing mobility, my body becomes heavy.

I reach out to the mantel below the TV and wrap my fingers around the first thing I feel, swinging it into the side of his head with as much force as I can manage.

"Fuck!" He lets go, stepping away from me, and I crumple to the floor.

I gasp for breath. My chest is tight, throat burns, and tears run down my face.

He stands before me, reaching up and wiping his fingers through the trail of blood that runs down the side of his gorgeous face.

I stay on my knees with my head bowed for a few seconds, trying to catch my breath. I don't have much time before he comes at me again. I can't swallow without it hurting and gasping for air. When I look up at him, I blink, allowing fresh tears to run down my face.

His blue eyes tell me he's not done with me. That was just the beginning. I'm a toy he wants to play with. There's a promise there that I will die, but not yet. Maybe he'll make me beg first. Men prefer a girl on her knees.

He kneels in front of me, and I push back away from him, falling to my ass. I had dropped the object I had hit him with, so nothing is in my reach now. My back hits the wall again, and I whimper when he reaches out, pushing my hair behind my ear. His bloody fingers graze the bruise on my cheek from Seth, and I swallow a sob. My body shakes, and my heart pounds.

"It's a shame, Demi." He sighs as if he hates to do what he is about to do. As though he doesn't have a choice to kill me or not. "You are very beautiful." Then his soft blue eyes harden, and his pouty lips thin. "But …"

"I set you up." My voice is rough, and the pain makes me flinch, but I need to explain it to him. My life depends on it. "We set you up," I say honestly. It's time to fill him in because there's obviously bigger shit going on right now. And I need to know what it is. "I wanted you to fuck me to piss off Becky."

He pulls away from me and stands. I look up at him through watery eyes, placing my shaking hands on my thighs. "But you already knew that. What you don't know is that Seth is gay, and I'm his cover. We pretend to be a couple because he is fucking his professor. And if it got out, he'd get kicked out of school and lose his scholarship. Not to mention, Hayden would lose his job." I'm panting, trying to catch my breath.

He stays looking down at me for a few seconds before spinning around and giving me his back. Running a hand through his dark hair, he lets out a growl. "There's a video. That's what he doesn't want to get out," he mumbles to himself.

I pull myself up on my shaky legs, having to use the wall for help. I can finally breathe a little better, and I suck in a long breath. He turns to face me, and I square my shoulders. "Decide right now," I demand.

His baby blue eyes glare at me. His jaw sharp and nostrils flared. I think he's debating on whether to let me live or just finish me off. I deserve all his anger, but I've had enough tonight. I've reached my breaking point. "Decide!" I shout, but my voice cracks. Obviously, I'm not back to myself just yet.

"On what?" He growls.

"Whether you're going to kill me or not," I answer with a huff. "I'm tired of this fucking game, Deke. Make up your fucking mind. Either you want me dead or not." I'm not dumb. Deke will be harder to fight, especially considering I'm still a little lightheaded from his hand being around my throat, but I'm fucking done.

He takes a step toward me. I glare up at him, muscles tight and ready to pounce on him with everything I got. Shit will get broken in this house, but I will fight until my last breath.

Reaching out, he runs his knuckles softly down my sensitive neck. I tense, expecting him to pull on my hair and throw me to the floor like Seth did. "What have I told you before?" he asks, and I don't say a word, not sure what he's talking about. "If that were the case, then you would already be dead."

I shove him away from me. I have a feeling if I hadn't hit him, I'd be lying dead on his floor right now. "Then stay the hell away from me, Deke."

"You came to me."

"I came for Austin," I snap. "I don't need you!" I look him up and down, noticing the way his jeans hug his narrow hips and muscular thighs. How his shirt shows me his pecs and bulging biceps. I hate how attractive he is with everything that I am. The fucker just tried to kill me, but the twisted part inside me likes it. I've challenged him before, and he didn't give me the Deke Biggs I wanted to see until today. And fuck, he's powerful. Fucking ruthless. I like that. When my eyes meet his again, I say, "You served your purpose."

His hands clench, and I realize I struck a nerve. *Good.*

He steps into me just as we hear the front door open followed by Austin's voice call out frantically. "Demi?"

"Here." I try to holler, but my voice cracks.

She enters the living room and runs to me, throwing her arms around my shoulders, shoving me away from Deke. Her green eyes look me up and down to make sure I'm not missing any body parts. "Oh my God!" She gasps when she sees my neck. "Deke, what the fuck did you—"

"She's alive," he interrupts her.

Cole enters much slower and looks over at me. The way he fists his hands, I can tell he's not as pleased as Austin is that I'm still breathing.

The guys exchange a look before Cole gestures to the sliding glass door with his head, and Deke follows him out back.

"Are you sure you're okay?" Austin asks me.

I sniff but nod my head.

Sighing, she pulls me in for another hug. And I cling to her, wishing she had been my sister. I always wanted to be close with Becky, but it was just never an option. I know it wasn't just me; she's that way with everyone—a coldhearted bitch.

"Come on." She pulls away from me and takes my hand.

"Where are we going?" I ask her.

"Out."

I look over my shoulder to the backyard and see the guys standing by the pool. Deke's head is down, and Cole stands with his arms crossed over his chest. "But Cole—"

"Fuck Cole." She interrupts me. "Fuck them both." On the way out, she bends down and picks up my phone off the floor.

She took me to a bar. Well, I guess that's what some call it. To me, it looks like a run-down shack.

"He'll find you," I tell her.

"Most likely," she agrees. "I've heard Deke talk about this place on several occasions. If he can get in, so can we."

We enter the old wooden door and look over the small dance floor. Now I understand why the parking lot was so dead for a Friday night. Most of their customers are over sixty. An old man with silver hair is hunched over on the dance floor dancing with a woman who can't quite get the steps right. He's got a smile on his face, and she is laughing.

I follow Austin over to the bar and sit down. The bartender lifts a brow at us.

"Two shots of Fireball," she orders.

"IDs?" he asks.

I bite my bottom lip nervously, but she pulls her wallet out and shows him one. He looks at it for a long second and then back at her.

"Problem?" she asks.

He sets it down and slides it over to her. "Your friend?"

"Got her purse stolen. That's why we're here. Drink away the shitty fucking day."

After looking over my face as well, his eyes drop to my neck. I'm sure my bruises match her lie perfectly. I look like a girl who was beaten before robbed. He nods and turns his back to us and begins to make us our shots. I wonder how in the hell her ID is going to get us drinks but then remember the guys giving her a fake ID when they made her join the GWS back in Collins. I read it in her journal.

"Here you go, ladies."

She tosses her debit card on the bar. "Open a tab."

She grabs her shot and hands me mine. Without wasting another second, she throws hers back and hisses in a breath. "It's been a long time since I've had anything to drink. Besides that wine the other night. And I didn't get to have much since Lilly was home."

I swallow mine and try to keep it down when it wants to come back up. *I hate this shit.*

"He's gay, isn't he?" she asks.

"Yes," I answer honestly, knowing who she's talking about.

"I figured. I saw the way he was checking out the guys at Silence. And you guys weren't very affectionate with one another."

I never paid attention to who and what he was looking at. I wasn't jealous, and Seth isn't out in the open. He plays straight very well because he's been doing it all his life. He once told me his dad would disown him if he ever found out, and he feels he has to hide it from his team members. I once thought it was very sad and depressing, but after what he tried to do to me tonight, I no longer care what he's going through.

"There were things he did here and there. Very subtle, but I picked up on them. How did you guys hook up?" She lifts her hand to signal for two more.

"His mother was my mother's real estate broker. I first met him when she got the house five years ago, and we became friends. My mom has made me spend a few weeks with her here in Texas every summer, and I always hung out with him 'cause our mothers were friends. So when she made me move here for my senior year, he asked me for a favor, and I said yes. Wasn't like I planned on getting a real boyfriend." I shrug.

She nods her head, and her cell rings. She shuts it off.

"Cole?" I ask.

"Yep. Let him feel what it's like when you're worried about someone, but they ignore you."

I frown, not knowing what she is talking about. The bartender sets two more shots down.

"Make it four next time," she tells him.

I drop my head to stare at my shot; she's already downed hers. "I'm sorry you guys are fighting because of me."

She looks over at me. "It's not your fault, Demi."

"Wanna talk about it?" I ask.

She runs her hand through her dark hair and lets out a sigh. "I ... I couldn't stand by and let Deke hurt you. I understand they have this unwavering loyalty, but Cole shouldn't have let him hurt you. He dragged me out of the house and put me in his car. I was screaming at him. He was just gonna leave you there with him, knowing he was going to do something to you. But I opened up the door and ran back inside before he could get out of the driveway. I had to make sure you were okay." The bartender sets four shots on the bar now, and she throws back one. "I used to be scared of them. The sharks. But now, they're like fucking flies that I just wanna swat with my bare hand on most days."

I laugh at that. She looks over at me and laughs as well. Then I pick up my shot, and we clink them together.

She slams her glass down as I try to swallow mine. "She wasn't wrong," she whispers.

I don't say anything, confused by what she means.

"I think about it too," she admits softly.

I begin to understand. "Austin, don't …"

"What if he gets bored with me?" she whispers.

"Cole is madly in love with you," I say, placing my hand on hers.

She looks over at me. "We can't fight forever. We both can't be this stubborn. One of us is going to have to give, or it will end."

"Cole would never leave you. Ever."

She closes her eyes and takes a deep breath. "He's here."

"Who?" I take a quick look around the bar. *Did Seth follow me?* My heart pounds at the thought. The odds of me fighting him off twice are not good. I'm already weak and tired.

"Cole," she answers, opening her eyes.

"How do you know?" I ask.

She lets go of my hand and takes another shot. "I can feel him watching me." She throws back the shot and a smile appears on her face before she whispers, "I dare you."

Just then, a man walks up behind her and places his hands on her hips. I watch Cole lean down and whisper in her ear. "Hello, sweetheart." He's no longer the pissed-off guy he was thirty minutes ago, but I can't tell if it's a front or real. He's put a shirt on and now wears jeans instead of his board shorts and has his hair spiked.

She wipes the smile off her face and stands, turning around to face him. "I didn't want to be around you."

He tucks her hair behind her ear. "And I didn't care."

She huffs. "Cole …"

He cuts her off with a kiss. One hand cups her cheek while the other goes to her ass, and he kisses her. It's passionate. Slow and sexy. I watch his tongue enter her mouth as he pushes her back into the bar. I've never spent much time with them, but I've read about their passion, anger, and sex life in her journal. And the words she wrote don't even compare to the real thing. To what he feels for her.

He pulls away, and she licks her lips, her eyes slowly opening. "I'm not leaving," she states.

"I didn't expect you would." He lets go of her, grabs her hand, and says, "Dance with me," before pulling her away from the bar.

I sit on my stool and watch them take their place on the mini dance floor. There's no grinding. Nothing to show that he once used her for his own sick game. He makes love to her out there. Slow and sweet. He holds her to him and kisses her while they dance to their own song. It's beautiful.

I realize I want that. The fighting. The passion. The love. I want someone to love me so much that I make them crazy. Anything less would be boring. Lifting my hand to my throat, I flinch when I realize that's exactly what Deke and I have. I wanted him to fuck me, and now I want him to love me.

Spinning around, I hold up two fingers to the bartender. "Vodka," I state. I've had enough of that cinnamon shit.

"Here you are." He sets them down.

"Thanks," I mumble as a man slides onto Austin's seat. I look over to see a new set of blue eyes. Ones that make my breath quicken and my thighs tighten.

Fuck!

"If you're here to force me to leave, I'll make a scene." Not a good idea on my part since I'm underage, but he doesn't want to push me on this.

Deke shakes his head. "We'll go when you're ready."

"We?"

He nods once.

"Waiting for me to get drunk before you try to kill me this time?" I ask. He doesn't answer.

I reach out for the shots and throw one back. Tears sting my eyes, and I hold up two fingers for more. I'm going to do exactly what Austin said—drink this fucking day away.

I hear him release a sigh. "Demi …"

"Don't." I choke on the single word.

I swallow the knot that has formed in my throat. My fake boyfriend tried to rape me because he said he had to. Cole and Deke mentioned that I'm on some list. And Deke has taken it upon himself to babysit me. But just thirty minutes ago, he wanted to kill me. Hell, maybe he still does. Why not drink myself into a coma tonight?

TWENTY-SEVEN

DEKE

"HEY, WE'RE GONNA head home," Cole announces, coming up to me.

I look over at Austin, and she sways even though he has an arm over her shoulders. The girls probably got quite a few shots before we got here, and that was over an hour ago.

"Okay. We'll see you guys back at the house."

Austin steps up to me. "Don't you dare—"

"I'm not going to hurt her," I interrupt her. "I promise."

She looks like she wants to argue, but Cole doesn't give her the chance. He pulls her away and out the front door.

"What's the damage?" I ask William, the bartender.

"The brunette had a tab open. The guy already covered it, Deke." The guy knows me by name. I come here when I want to drink alone. The music isn't too loud, so you can actually hear yourself think. No one bothers you.

I let out a sigh and look over at Demi sitting next to me, staring down at an empty shot glass. She hasn't spoken to me since I arrived. Not that I blame her. I throw down a hundred anyway. "Let's go, princess."

She doesn't argue as I help her to her feet and out to my Range Rover. Cole and I drove together so he could drive Austin's car back.

I buckle her into the passenger seat. Getting in, I start it. I avoid the highway and take the backroads.

She's notices. "You're going the wrong way."

"We're just taking the long way." I'm giving Cole and Austin time alone to dish out whatever issues they've got going on right now. And I know they'll do that in their bed.

He acted like he wasn't mad at her when we arrived at the bar, but when we entered the house to find them gone, he was furious. He tried calling, and she ignored it. I instantly knew she was paying him back for the night we went to the cabin, and he turned his phone off. He was not happy. But no surprise, he has a tracker on her car. She has no clue. After she bought her Range Rover, he took it to have her windows tinted and had them add a tracker. He's so paranoid of something happening to her. Of losing her. It just happened to come in handy tonight.

"Giving Austin and Cole some time together," I tell her.

"Can you keep a secret?" she asks.

She has no idea. "Yes."

"She's worried he'll get bored with her."

I snort. "That'll never happen."

"You and I know that, but Becky got in her head." She sighs. "That bitch gets in everyone's head."

Can't argue that. But I say, "That's just the alcohol talking." Referring to Austin.

"What's that saying? A drunk man's thoughts are a sober man's words. Wait ..." She pauses, her drunk self having to think about it. "A drunk man's words ... are a sober man's thoughts."

I smile. "Oh yeah? What are your drunk words?" I've never been around her drunk before. She was tipsy at her Halloween party and the other night, but nowhere near gone like this. I watched her have six shots on top of what she had before we got there.

"I've got all kinds of secrets."

I arch a brow. "The ones you say you know about me?" Which I now know came from Austin's journal.

"No. Everyone else," she whispers.

I frown. "Like what?"

Her head falls to the side, and she looks at me. "I know more than you think."

"Whatcha got?" I ask. She can't know much.

"I know that Becky lost her virginity to Shane."

"What?"

She closes her eyes and nods. "Yep. She was acting weird for a couple of days, and I was in her closet looking for a shirt of mine that went missing. I heard her enter her room on the phone. She was crying. Told Shane that she had been bleeding for two days and it wouldn't stop. He asked what the fuck was he supposed to do about it?" She laughs. "That was when I realized a girl's virginity didn't mean anything. Which is crazy, right? We're told it's supposed to be special. You're supposed to give it to someone you love." Her drunk laughter grows. "Such bullshit."

I shift in my seat because I didn't make anything about her first time special. "What was the second?" I ask, fully taking advantage of her intoxicated state.

"When my sister drugged me and didn't care if I got raped."

What? "When the fuck did this happen?" I growl.

"You were there." She gives me a smile, and that's how I know she drank too much. Because nothing about what she is about to tell me could be anything worth smiling about. Her eyes are still closed. "The beach party. You handed me a bottle of vodka. That was actually my first drink. Anyway, Cole took it from me, and I wanted to leave. So I went over to tell David I was going to wait in the car, but he told Becky to make me a drink. After that, I ran into Eli, and I left with him. He took me to the cemetery. But then I started feeling weird, and I couldn't open my eyes. He tasted my drink and said I had been drugged." My hands tighten on the steering wheel. "How was I supposed to know it didn't taste right? I hadn't had a drink before that night. Anyway, he had to carry me to his car. Then he took me to his house where I got sick. The next morning, my sister showed up to get me, and when he confronted her about it, she said she and Maxwell did it. He called her a bitch and said that he could have raped me. That's when we learned that was their plan all along. That bitch knew I was a virgin. She didn't fucking care."

I come to a red light and clear my throat. "Demi …"

"That's one of the reasons I slept with you."

I look over at her, and her head falls toward me, and her pretty blue eyes look up into mine. The same ones I watched the life slowly drain out of while I choked her earlier. I hate that I hurt her. Now that I know the truth of how much shit she has been through. It seems someone is always wanting to hurt her.

"I know I lied to you. Tricked you. We set you up. But …" She licks her lips. "I wanted you to take it, Deke. Don't think for one second that I didn't want you."

I hate how much I like the sound of that. But I find myself saying, "I'm sorry."

"For what?"

I reach out and cup her face. For wanting to kill you. For fucking you? My list just seems to keep growing, but I pick. "Your first time should have been different …"

She snorts. "I didn't want different. And I don't regret it." She closes her eyes.

I watch her lips part slightly and her chest rise and fall slowly. She's so drunk, she won't be with me much longer. But I still have questions. "If Eli knew what she did to you, then why did he fuck her?"

"I lied about that too the other night. On the back porch."

"What?"

"He never slept with her." She yawns, and I know I'm losing her. "Demi?"

"Hmm?"

"What do you mean he never slept with her?" Cole told me that they were sleeping together. He wouldn't lie to me.

"He faked it."

"How do you fake fucking someone?" I growl.

"He set her up. For you … just like I set you up." She's beginning to mumble her words.

"You're not making any sense, princess."

She digs into the pocket of her jeans and produces her cell phone. She goes to hand it to me but drops it to the floor. "It's all on our FB chat," she manages to say before she passes out on me.

DEMI

Sophomore year

"This is a horrible idea," I say, grabbing Eli's arm.

"It'll be fine."

"Please don't go," I beg him.

He runs a hand down his face and lets out a sigh. He's clearly getting pissy with me. His phone dings, and he looks down at it. "It's Deke."

"What did he say?"

"His father wants to talk to him, so he won't be at the party, but he'll meet up with us afterward."

"See, this may not even work."

He cups my face with both of his warm hands. Brown eyes staring into mine. "It will. I promise you."

I don't understand how he thinks my sister will fall for this shit. She'll see right through him. She won't risk her secret relationship with Deke. She keeps saying that she and David are on a break right now, but I'm not sure how much I believe that since her phone seems to go off a hundred times a day, and I know it's David.

*His cell rings this time, and I get a quick look to see it reads **Cole**. Eli answers it. "Hey, man. I'm about to leave." He nods to himself. "Okay, I'll meet you there. Then we can all ride with you." He hangs up and gives me his attention once again. "I'll see you in a few hours." He kisses my forehead and then walks out of his front door.*

TWENTY-EIGHT

DEKE

I PULL UP to the house and carry a passed-out Demi inside. It's quiet, letting me know that Austin and Cole are already asleep. Opening my door, I lie her on my bed and undo her jeans before sliding them down her legs. Then I'm removing her shirt. I leave her in her bra and underwear and make my way back out to my SUV. I open the passenger side door and pick up her phone off the floormat.

Going back inside the house, I grab the pack of cigarettes out of the drawer and make my way out back. Cole is in the pool.

"Thought you'd be asleep," I say, sitting down.

Standing in the shallow end, he gives me a clear view of his bare chest and all the red scratch marks along his stomach and sides. I bet his back matches. That is why I took the long way home. No telling what Austin looks like at the moment.

"I just got out here," he tells me.

I lean forward. "So, I found out some interesting stuff tonight."

"I think that's an understatement."

He's talking about the Demi situation and Evan Scott. I sigh. "Other stuff."

He arches a brow. "Like what?"

She asked me if I could keep a secret, and I will keep what she said about Austin to myself. But the other stuff I need to talk to Cole about. "Demi filled me in on all kinds of information."

"Do you believe her?"

I nod. "I do."

"Does it have to do with anything regarding Seth and Evan Scott?"

My jaw tightens, but I shake my head. "No. But some of it has to do with Eli."

"What about him?" He frowns.

I sit back in my seat. "She claims he was not sleeping with Becky."

"Well, I didn't see him physically fuck her, but I did see them all over each other," he states. "And he acted like he had been when I confronted him about it."

I hold up her phone. "She said everything I need to know is on here."

He gets out of the pool and dries off before sitting down in the seat beside me. I open her Facebook app and search his name. None of us ever deactivated it after he passed. It was like erasing too many good memories when we were a team. When there were eight sharks and not five. And it wasn't much time after that that his sister was killed. There was no one else to take it down besides her.

I click on his page and go to message him. Their conversation pops up.

"Scroll up," Cole orders.

I do as he says and then stop when I see the date of the night of the car wreck. It didn't take long since this was the last conversation they had. Cole begins to read it out loud.

Eli: I might have oversold it.

Demi: What does that mean?

Eli: Cole is pissed at me. I thought he was gonna knock me out right then and there. He's probably already messaged Deke.

Demi: What did you do?

Eli: I kissed her. A lot. Acted like I was already fucking her.

Cole lets out a sigh from beside me. I continue.

Eli: Demi?

She doesn't respond.

Eli: I had to do it.

Again, nothing from her.

Eli: I'm sorry, baby.

Baby? Just how much were they seeing each other? He never mentioned her to us. I knew he had a thing for her, but I didn't think it was anything serious.

Ten minutes later, she texts him back.

Demi: I hate this.

Eli: Me too.

Demi: I don't understand why you couldn't have just told him what kind of person she is. What she did to me.

Eli: Sometimes words aren't enough. I know him, and he'd confront her. Her being the vindictive bitch she is will cry and lie her way out of it. He'll fall for it. Not because he's stupid, but because he is in love with her.

Demi: Are you going to sleep with her?

Eli: Fuck no! Cole, Landen, and Maddox now know. That's enough.

Demi: Why is she doing it? Why would she jeopardize what she and Deke have for you?

Eli: She's pissed at him. I overheard Cole telling Maddox at the party earlier that Deke hooked up with Kaitlin last weekend. Becky hates her. So, she's willing to spread her legs for his best friend. In her eyes, it's retaliation.

Demi: Your friends are gonna hate you. Think you backstabbed him.

Eli: Yeah. But maybe eventually, he'll understand.

Demi: Will I see you tonight?

Eli: Yes. Cole is going to go fuck some girl. Not sure what Maddox and Landen have going on. Once I figure out what I'm doing, I'll call you, baby.

Then there's a thirty-minute gap before all messages turn one-sided. And they're all pretty much the same thing.

Demi: How did it go?

Demi: I keep calling.

Demi: It's going straight to voicemail.

I exit out of it and shut down the screen. Leaning back, I run a hand over my face.

"I should have never said a fucking word to you about it." Cole growls.

"I'm glad you did," I tell him, trying to reassure him that he did the right thing.

"Why the fuck didn't he tell me the truth?"

I could ask the same thing. Why did he choose to parade Becky around, knowing that I would be pissed at him? He knows I would have broken his nose over her. I can't say if he was wrong or right about me believing him if he had just told me what kind of girl she was. Would I have believed him? I was in love with her. Or so I thought. Definitely obsessed. I guess in a way I do understand because I would have cut her off right then and there for fucking my best friend. That was a line I wouldn't allow her to come back from. "We'll never know." I sigh.

"Fuck, what else do we not know?" he asks.

That's a loaded question that I don't even want to get into right now. Too much shit has happened to dig any further tonight. I look at the cigarettes and no longer want one.

"Do you think it's a coincidence that we got in a fight with Peter and his friend over Demi about how they would share her and then Seth tries to rape her? Saying he had no choice?" he asks.

I've thought about it. "How would they know about what we've done? How would they know Evan Scott is me?"

"Becky," he answers and shrugs "She's pissed at Demi. I don't think that any of us should underestimate what she's capable of doing."

Isn't that the truth. "Maybe we should pay them a visit?"

"I think so." He nods. "And Seth?"

I just give him a smile, and he chuckles.

Standing up, I go to walk inside when I hear a phone beep. I turn back to look at Cole, and he shakes his head. "Wasn't mine. It's upstairs."

I look down at mine. Nothing. Then I open Demi's, thankful she doesn't have a passcode on hers. "It's from Evan Scott." I growl.

Cole comes over to me, and I open the PM.

Evan Scott: You should have let him fuck you. It would have been far less painful than what's to come.

"Fuck!" Cole hisses. "Guess whoever it is knows that Seth didn't succeed tonight."

"What the fuck?" I bark out.

I type back.

Demi: Try to touch her … If you dare.

Cole runs his hands over his wet hair, and I fist mine. "This fucker …" I screenshot the message and then back out of it. I go to my old spam page and block it. Then I go to our GWS PM and drop the screenshot.

Bennett reads it immediately. Seconds later, my cell rings. I place it on speakerphone. "Hello?"

"What the fuck is going on?" he demands. "And what does he mean by let him fuck her? Who?"

"Seth." I growl.

"Her boyfriend?" he asks.

"He's not her boyfriend," Cole answers. "He's gay. She's his cover."

"Oh, well that changes things."

"There's more." I sigh.

"What is it?" he asks, sounding irritated. Aren't we all?

"The cabin on Lake Travis …" I start.

"Yeah?"

"His parents own it."

A long silence follows my words.

When he finally speaks, he sighs. "Hang on. I'm gonna call and wake up Shane. We all need to be in on this conversation."

DEMI

Sophomore year

I pace my bedroom at my father's house. I've called Eli a hundred times by now, but it keeps going straight to voicemail. And I don't know why he would turn his phone off. His Facebook says he hasn't been active in over thirty minutes. I dial it again.

"Come on ... pick up. Pick up."

"Hey, you've reached Eli. Leave me a message ..."

I yank the phone from my ear and scream out of frustration. I told him not to do it. That it was fucking stupid! He should have listened to me. I hope Deke didn't catch them ...

My bedroom door flies open, and I spin around to see my sister running in. Her blond hair is a tangled mess. Her crop top and shorts are covered in dirt and blood. Her makeup is streaked from tears.

"Becky? What the hell?" I ask.

She's sobbing. Her bottom lip trembling. I stay where I am, not sure what the hell is going on. "Where's Eli?" I ask, looking behind her. Is this some trick she talked him into? It can't be. He wouldn't do that to me. He may be ignoring my phone calls, but at least I know she's here and no longer with him.

"Help me." She sobs, falling to her knees in the middle of my room.

"What the hell happened to you?" I ask, watching the blood and dirt get on my white rug.

"There was an accident." She swallows. "The car flipped. Cole ..."

I fall to my knees before her. "What?" I grip her tear-streaked face and force her to look up at me. "What do you mean an accident?"

"I ... I think I killed them." She begins to rock back and forth. "He told me to run."

"Who told you to run?" My hands begin to shake.

"Cole." She bends over, cradling her stomach. "I told him I was pregnant, and he told me to run."

I know she's not pregnant. She was in my bathroom just last weekend borrowing tampons. My eyes look over her body, and I see scratch marks on her thighs and arms. I blink, running a hand through my hair. "Who do you think you killed, Becky?"

"Landen." She sobs. "Maddox and Eli." My heart stops. "Cole

kept hollering for them, but none of them answered."

I fall back onto my ass, trying to comprehend what she just said.

"I went back." She nods to herself. "Cole was sitting in the ditch with Eli in his arms ... He wasn't breathing." Her shaking hands grip her cell. The screen is shattered. "I called the cops." Dropping the phone to my floor, she buries her busted face in her hands.

It begins to ring, and I pick it up to see David light up the busted screen. "Why is David calling you ...?"

She snatches it from my hands.

Present

I open my eyes and roll out of bed. I trip over a pair of shoes but manage to make it to the bathroom door. Turning on the light, I blink rapidly and then decide to just pee in the dark. Once done, I wash my hands and pick up the mouthwash to try to get rid of this god-awful taste in my mouth. And it's not the vodka. It's cinnamon. That damn Fireball Austin had me drinking.

I exit the bathroom and make my way back to Deke's bed. It's still dark out; the clock on his nightstand says a little after three a.m. He lies on the right side, closest to the door. The covers sit low on his hips, showing me his smooth chest and impressive six-pack. His right hand lies on his chest while his other is behind his head.

I come to a stop and just watch him sleep. I told him too much last night. I remember running my mouth while in his SUV on our way back here. A part of me wanted to get it out. To purge everything that is Collins, Oregon. There were so many lies and so much deceit in that town. No one was who they said they were. Not even Deke.

I blamed my sister for killing Eli. I still blame her. And I blame Eli for thinking of that stupid plan. If she hadn't gone, maybe the timing would have been different. Maybe he would have survived.

Did I love him?

I thought I did. But I didn't really know him. He said that I didn't deserve to be someone's secret, but that's exactly what I was. No one knew about us. Or what I thought we were.

I went to his funeral, and I watched the town mourn a kid who was loved by some and hated by most. I saw him differently, but he was still a GWS to everyone else, and the town didn't like the sharks. Parents and most of the city wanted Cole's head on a fucking stake for what happened. His father threw a lot of money at the city to make sure the law didn't touch his son, but he too was more than what the town thought. They thought Cole was driving a car drunk after leaving a party with his friends. He took the blame for the accident and covered for my sister. You know how many times I wanted to out her sorry ass? She had lied to him about being pregnant. What kind of woman does that? She begged me to stay quiet. I did, knowing I'd be able to use it against her, but then Deke came along and threatened her when he also realized she had lied to Cole. Cole might not have known that Becky lied about being pregnant, but Deke did. And he was far scarier than I was capable of being.

You know what they say—all secrets come out eventually.

Deke shifts and turns onto his side. I crawl into the bed and cuddle up against him. He reaches out and pulls me into him. I inhale his scent and close my eyes. His hand glides up my back, and I kiss his chest.

"You better stop that," he mumbles.

I smile and do it again.

"Demi …"

"I don't want to," I whisper.

His hand comes up to my hair, and he grips it in his fingers. Then he dips his face to the crook of my neck. "How do you feel?"

"Horny," I answer. And still a little drunk.

He lets out a growl that makes his chest vibrate against mine.

I shove the covers off us and push on his chest. He rolls onto his back, and I get up to straddle him. His hands go to my hips, and he tugs on the lace of my thong. "What are you doing, Demi?"

"You," I answer, biting my lip.

His hands slide up my sides and to my chest. I arch my back and throw my head back, closing my eyes and just soak in the feel of his hands. It's nice to have someone touch you. Want you. Even if he wants to kill you. It makes things much more exciting. I should have pursued Deke a long time ago.

"Not with your underwear on, you're not." He growls.

"Then take them off me," I tease.

I squeal as he tosses me down beside him and positions himself between my legs. His hands grip my panties, and he pulls them down my thighs before tossing them to the floor.

He leans down, his lips close to mine, and he runs his fingers over the cut on my cheek. "I'm gonna kill him."

My heart begins to pound at his words. "Why?" I can't help but ask.

His blue eyes move from the cut to my eyes. His jaw sharpens when he says. "Because he touched you. And I am the only man allowed to touch you."

I hate that my chest tightens at his words. That someone actually cares for me. But I say, "You mean hurt me?"

His face grows serious, and he lets out a long breath. "I'm sorry," he whispers.

"Are you?" I challenge him. That's not the answer I wanted.

"Of course. I shouldn't have …"

"It's okay," I wrap my legs around his hips.

"It's not."

"I wanted to push you the other night." *Shut up drunk, Demi.*

He frowns.

I don't fucking listen to myself. "When I lied to you on the back porch, I wanted to push you to see what you could do."

His hard and smooth chest rises and falls as he sucks in a long breath. "Why?"

I run my hands up his chiseled abs, ready to lay it all out. Deke loved the lie that was Becky. I keep saying I'm not her. So if he is going to like me, he's going to fall for the real me. "Because your darkness turns me on." I watch to see if his expression changes, but it doesn't. "She wanted to tame you. I want to see what you can do. I wanna see the real you. All of you. I know I could never win against you, Deke, but I don't want you to hide. Not from me."

He sits there between my legs not saying a word, and my heart begins to race. Bringing up my sister while we're lying in bed naked together probably wasn't the best idea I've ever had, but I feel like she's always lingering around us anyway. Like a dark cloud just waiting to pour down on us.

"You've seen the real me," he finally says, and his eyes drop to my neck.

"And I'm still here." I give him a drunken smile.

His jaw sharpens. "I could have killed you …" He pauses and sighs. "I can't promise that I won't hurt you again."

I almost laugh at that. "Good." I pull his face down to mine and whisper against his lips, "Now show me how hard you can fuck me."

"Demi." He growls my name, his chest vibrating against mine, making my legs tighten around him. His lips trail down my jaw to my neck. I arch it to give him better access. Then I feel him sliding his hand between our bodies. I smile when he grips the base of his already hard dick and pushes into me, making me cry out at the feel of him stretching me. I don't think I'll ever get used to him.

His hand slaps over my mouth, and I take a deep breath through my nose. He whispers, "Gotta be quiet, princess. Don't want them hearing you scream my name."

I want to roll my eyes at his cockiness, but he begins to move, and my eyes roll back for a different reason.

TWENTY-NINE

DEKE

Cole and I exit my car and walk up to the small cabin. Cole unlocks it, and we step inside. I stop and look around the living room and entryway. There was a small square table that sat next to the door. It has been knocked over, and the glass covers the hardwood floor. But other than that, there is no sign of a struggle.

I walk over to the coffee table and pick up the cup. It's full to the brim with what looks like a clear liquid of some sort.

"He left in a hurry," Cole observes. "He didn't even bother disposing of the evidence." Then he walks down the hallway.

I fist my hands and look down at the side of the couch. A Louis Vuitton bag sits on the floor. I reach down and pick it up. Grabbing the drink with my other hand, I walk it into the kitchen and pour it down the sink.

"Hey," Cole enters the kitchen. "Look what I found in the bathroom?" He holds up a small clear bottle with a blue lid. A piece of tape is on the side of the bottle and written in black Sharpie is GHB.

My jaw tightens. "It's almost fucking empty."

He nods and places it in his pocket. "I'm guessing he wanted to make sure she had enough so she wouldn't fight him. Or wouldn't remember a single thing."

I throw the cup into the sink and drop her bag. Gripping the counter, I growl. "He could have killed her." Who knows how much he would have had her drink? Demi is fucking small. Too much and she could have had seizures. Could have fallen into a coma. Not to mention he mixed it with alcohol.

His phone rings, and he answers, placing it on speakerphone. "Hello?"

"You guys there?" Bennett asks.

"Yes." I growl and push off the countertop.

"Find anything?"

"A bottle of GHB." Cole speaks.

"Fuck." He hisses, then sighs. "Hang on, I'm adding Shane to the call." Seconds later, he's back. "Okay. We're all here."

"Did you guys get your tickets?" Cole asks him.

"Yes. We fly out tonight," Bennett answers.

"I'm confused as to why we have to come back to Austin." Shane speaks.

"Don't," I snap, not in the mood for his bullshit today. "Stay the fuck up there."

Bennett sighs. "We're both coming. This involves more than just Demi. Whoever it is hasn't physically touched us, but we've been threatened and that's enough to worry. If we can get a hold of Seth, maybe his phone can tell us what we need to know."

I hang my head and run my hands through my hair aggressively. I'm starting to lose my shit. I kept it together for Demi's sake this morning when she woke me up horny. I wanted her, needed to feel her, but I was rough. I took my anger out on her, and she liked it. She passed out immediately afterward. I didn't get to tell her about the message she got from Evan Scott or the fact that I blocked whoever the fucker was. Cole and I snuck out this morning before the girls had even woken up. It's a Saturday. They both got wasted last night, and Lilly was sleeping over at her dance teacher's house, so the odds of them sleeping in pretty late are on our side.

"What I can't figure out is why he was going to do it." Bennett speaks. "He's gay. Why would he fuck her …?"

"Hate to be the dick in this situation," Shane interrupts him. "But he could have been planning on fucking her ass. That is what they prefer."

My head snaps up, and I snatch the phone from Cole's hand, but he speaks before I can bark at him more. "Or maybe he didn't care where he had to fuck her. I mean, to some men, a hole is a hole."

"Shut the fuck up …"

Cole takes his phone back from me. "He was forced. He told Deke there was a video of him fucking his professor."

"Who all knew he was gay?" Bennett asks.

I run a hand down my face. "I'm guessing not many. Demi said she was his cover. And his friends who are on the swim team at UT think they have an open relationship."

"Hmm …" Bennett sighs. "What about the professor?"

"I … I don't know." I growl and close my eyes. I try to put what few pieces we have so far together. "It can't be him. Demi got a message last night from Evan Scott. You guys saw it. It stated she should have let him fuck her. How could the professor be Evan Scott? They wouldn't know my information to get into it."

"True," Bennett says. "Listen, I know it's gonna be hard, but just lay low. We'll be there later on tonight, and we'll do whatever we gotta do to get the information we need to figure this out. Okay?"

———————————

I enter my room and remove my hoodie. Demi's still in my bed passed out cold. It's not even ten a.m. yet. And by how quiet the house was when we entered, I'd say Austin is still asleep as well.

The guys and I have a plan. But I'm not going to lie to her like Cole did Austin. I'm going to be honest with Demi. She deserves that. She may not like it, and she may hate me, but I'm not going to allow Evan Scott to fuck with us. Or her. I'm going to protect her, and in order to do that, she needs to know just what we're up against.

Undoing my jeans, I kick off my shoes and then push them down my legs before removing my shirt and then climb in beside her. My knuckles run over her busted cheek and down over her jaw to her neck. The bruises from my hands remain. They're worse today than they were last night.

I wanted to kill her. If she hadn't hit me with that stupid swimming trophy of Cole's that Austin put out, she would be dead right now. And it makes me sick to my stomach.

I've killed people but not for sport. The men and woman I killed deserved it. Demi would have been innocent. She played me, yes, but I was just jealous that, for once, I met someone who knew how to play the game better than I did.

She releases a little moan and shifts, causing the comforter to pull down and expose her chest to me. My fingers make their way over her chest bone and then her breast. She shifts again and my hand lowers over her stomach and between her legs. She's naked. "Deke." She sighs my name when I run a finger over her pussy.

"Yes, princess?" I ask, leaning down and kissing her neck as my finger slides into her.

"Oh, God, Deke." She pants, her hips lifting off the bed.

I shove off the covers and position myself between her legs. She looks up at me with heavy eyes. I remove my finger and slide two in this time. She arches her back and whimpers. "Does that hurt?" I ask as my thumb starts to rub her clit.

"Yes." Her hands grip the sheets.

"Good," I say and remove them before gripping my hard cock. She likes it when it hurts. And I hate to admit that she can take the pain. Becky hated it. Demi craves it. I like that I don't have to pretend with her.

DEMI

I sit on Deke's lap in the living room with my second cup of coffee in my hand. Austin sits beside me, glaring at Cole who lounges in the recliner across from us. I haven't heard them say one word to each other all day. She's pissed, and he seems indifferent about it. Like this is something that happens often. Not sure what went down after they left the bar last night, but she obviously isn't over it.

"I don't understand how this is gonna work?" I finally say.

"We're gonna ask him," Bennett says simply.

He and Shane arrived an hour ago. That could be another reason the tension is high in this house. "He won't tell you anything."

"Oh, he'll talk." Deke snorts.

"You don't know him," I argue.

"I don't need to know him. There's something he loves, and if he doesn't tell us what we want, we take it from him."

Austin finally speaks. "You're gonna kill the professor? That's not smart. You're all gonna end up in jail."

Cole smiles at her. "I'm glad to see you still care about me, sweetheart, but no. No one is gonna die tonight."

"That we know of. But plans change," Deke says cryptically.

I sigh. "Then what are you gonna take?"

"His legs. His arms." Cole shrugs carelessly. "Hands. Whatever body part the man needs to play football."

"You're gonna break his bones?" I ask.

Deke chuckles behind me. "No, princess. Bones can heal."

I swallow at the amusement in his voice, but I feel butterflies in my stomach. This is the part of Deke I wanted to see. The ruthless evil that swims inside him.

Cole leans forward, placing his elbows on his knees. "I've got a question, though. There was a woman. She was at UT. Before we knew he was gay, we saw him talking to her outside the classroom. And we thought he was cheating on you with her. Do you know who she is?"

I frown. Seth has a lot of girls who are friends. He gets along with everyone. "What did she look like?"

"Pretty," he says with a smirk and I know he said that just to piss Austin off. "She had brown hair and brown eyes—"

"That's his twin sister." I interrupt Cole, knowing who they are talking about. "She is dating Peter. The guy who you guys beat up the other day after swim practice."

A slow smile spreads across Shane's face and it has me sitting back more into Deke. I don't know much about him. Less than the others. He was closest with Kellan. Who knows what Shane is thinking now?

"Are you going to hurt her?" Austin asks.

Cole sits back and runs his hand over his chin. "We'll do whatever needs to be done."

"Our concern is Seth," Bennett says, looking at Austin. Clearly trying to smooth over what Cole just said. "He's our main priority. I doubt she knows much."

Austin gets up and walks out of the room. Cole watches her from his seat but makes no move to go after her. Seconds later, you hear their bedroom door slam shut.

Shane laughs. "Don't you worry she'll kill you in your sleep?"

Cole just smiles. He'd probably get off on that.

THIRTY

DEKE

I MAKE MY way through the crowd of kids who clutter the living room. "Boneshaker" by Redlight King blasts through the large speakers that are placed in the corners.

I take a drink from my Solo cup as a blonde pushes her way past me. She steps up onto the coffee table and removes her shirt, showing everyone her pink bra with white polka dots on it. She tosses the shirt to another girl who stands beside me. Guys and girls holler over the song. I keep walking, not seeing who I'm looking for. I exit the living room and head down a long hallway. I catch sight of Cole standing in the kitchen talking to a girl who sits next to us in one of our classes at UT. His eyes meet mine briefly, but he doesn't acknowledge me in any way. I pass the kitchen and keep going until I'm in the back of the house.

The lights are dimmed back here, and the song changes to "Legend" by The Score. I take another drink and spot who I'm looking for.

She stands back in the corner, leaning up against the wall. She has a cup in her hand and a smile on her face while talking to another girl. And I recognize her. She doesn't look the same, but I would never forget her face.

What are the odds?

I walk over to them. "Excuse me?"

They both turn to look at me. "I know you." I point at the brunette that I'm not here for.

She bites her bottom lip and looks me up and down. "I don't know you."

I chuckle. "Well, not officially." I hold out my right hand. "I'm Deke."

"Brynn." She introduces herself.

"You work at Silence."

She nods her head quickly and shakes my hand. "Yes, I do. You've been there?"

"I have," I say to the girl who had asked me to help her. Brynn was strapped in a straitjacket and sitting in a tub full of black water.

"She's been doing that job for two years now," the other girl says, rolling her eyes. "I don't know why she does it."

"What can I say?" Brynn smiles. "I like being restrained and held under water."

"Dear lord." Her friend sighs. "You need to fire your therapist. He is not doing you any favors."

Brynn laughs. "Oh, he gives me favors all right."

"Did I hear something about restraints and water?" An arm drapes over my shoulders, and I look over to see Shane now standing with us. His eyes start at her red heels and work up her white skinny jeans and black V-neck tank top that shows off her impressive cleavage. She wears a black choker and a smile on her pretty face. "I'm sad I missed it."

She takes a drink from her straw. "Well, we get to keep our props."

Shane chuckles and takes her hand. "Let me get you another drink while you tell me all about it," he says, pulling her away.

I turn to the girl who I came here for. "Melissa." She holds out her hand. She tilts her head to the side. "I've seen you around campus."

"Really?" I ask. "Do we have classes together?"

She shakes her head. "No, but I've seen you with my brother."

"Oh, who is your brother?" I play dumb.

"Seth. Seth Wilson."

I nod my head. "Yeah. Yeah. He's friends with some of my

teammates."

Her face lights up. "You play football?"

"No. I'm on the swim team at UT."

"That's awesome." She smiles up at me. "My boyfriend is too. Maybe you know him? Peter."

Yes, unfortunately, I know that fucker. I feel my phone vibrate in my back pocket and pull it out. I drop it on purpose. "Shit." I hiss.

"I'll get it." She leans over and picks it up for me.

"Thank you." I laugh. "Had a little too much to drink."

"It happens." She lifts her cup to her lips and takes a sip.

I look down at my phone and open my messenger.

Cole: *Are you almost done? I can't talk shit with this girl anymore. Fuck, this is why I never hung out with people at parties.*

I chuckle but respond.

Me: *It's done. Get ready.*

"I know him," I say, getting back to our conversation. "How long have you guys been dating?"

"It's new," she answers with a laugh.

"Is he here tonight?" I ask, looking over my shoulder to see if people are watching us. But nope, everyone is too busy doing their own thing. I don't even see Shane and Brynn.

"No. He went out of town this weekend to see his grandmother."

I want to laugh. The bastard is probably shacked up with some bitch. The way he spoke of Demi didn't sound like a man in a committed relationship. I guarantee this chick isn't the only one he's fucking.

"Whoa," she says.

I pocket my phone. "You okay?" I ask, placing my hand on her arm.

She closes her eyes and sways on her feet. I take her drink from her other hand and see that she had finished it off. "Good girl," I whisper.

"Huh?" She asks with heavy eyes.

"Nothing. Here let me help you."

"I … what …?" she slurs.

I walk her out the back door where there are less people, and she stumbles over her own feet. I lean down and pick her up, carrying her in my arms to the SUV parked a few houses down so the partygoers don't see us. Cole is opening the hatch to my Range Rover for me. I place the passed-out girl in the back. After removing her phone from the back pocket of her jeans, I jump in the passenger seat. Cole gets in the driver seat since he hasn't been drinking. Bennett already sits in the back.

"Where the fuck is Shane?" I growl.

Bennett pulls out his cell and calls him. "Where are you? We're ready," he snaps. "Get your ass out here." He hangs up. "He's coming. Pretty sure he was fucking."

I roll my eyes. "Should have left his ass in Collins," I mumble.

Seconds later, I see him running down the street, and he jumps into the back seat barely in enough time before Cole takes off.

I smile as I slide her screen and see that she didn't have a lock on it and go to Seth's name. I type out a message.

Me: Meet me at the cabin. ASAP. It's important.

Then I shut her phone off so he can't contact her.

I sit on the couch at the cabin, and Cole sits next to me. Shane sits at the kitchen table texting away on his phone. Pretty sure it's to the girl from the party who works at Silence. Bennett stepped out back five minutes ago, saying he needed to make a call.

"How long has it been?" Cole asks.

I look down at the clock on my phone. "Thirty minutes. He should be here any minute."

The back door opens, and Bennett steps inside.

"How long do you think this will take?" Shane asks. "I've got plans later."

I roll my eyes. "Would these plans consist of a girl and a straitjacket?"

"Yep," he answers. "All I need is a tub. Or a pool would do."

Bennett shakes his head. "I don't wanna know anymore. Drugging and kidnapping one girl is enough for one night."

Headlights shine through the front window, and seconds later, they shut off followed by a door shutting.

"Showtime," Shane says excitedly.

The front door bursts open, and Seth runs inside. He comes to a quick stop when he sees all of us taking up the small area. He swallows as his eyes go to each of us. He looks at the floor and at the chair next to me. He realizes instantly that it wasn't his sister who messaged him. "Where is she?" he demands.

"Safe. For now." I stand.

He takes a step toward me. "If you …"

"What?" I ask. "Rape her? Take advantage of her? Like you were going to do to Demi?"

He swallows, making his Adam's apple bob up and down. "I didn't have a choice."

"Funny," Cole says, coming to stand next to me. "Neither did we."

His jaw sharpens. "I'll tell you anything you need to know." I expected it to be that easy. Too bad it had to be this way.

I reach out my hand. "Give me your phone."

"No." He shakes his head, taking a step back. "Anything but that."

"Shane," I call out, not taking my eyes off Seth.

I hear the chair he's sitting in slide across the tile and then his shoes on the floor as he exits and goes to the only bedroom in this small cabin. Seconds later, he comes back into the living room, and this time, he has a woman in his arms. She lies across them, still passed out.

"Melissa!" Seth snaps and goes to take a step toward them, but Cole places a hand on his chest, stopping him.

I walk over to the kitchen area as Shane sits her in a chair. She slumps forward, and I walk behind her, gripping her dark hair in my hand, I pull her head back. With my free hand, I gently push her brown hair off her face, neck, and chest. I slide my knuckles down over her exposed neck, making him think the worst, but really, I'm just checking her pulse. When satisfied, I pull my hand away and look back at him.

"Melissa?" he shouts.

"She can't hear you," I tell him. "See, I gave her what GHB you had left."

Cole holds up the now empty bottle that he found here earlier this morning. "You know, what you didn't use on Demi."

"You son of a bitch!" he shouts and goes to walk toward me, but Cole slams his fist into Seth's face, knocking him back.

"But there wasn't much left," I add. "I say we've got maybe thirty minutes before she starts to come around."

"If you hurt her …"

"What?" I ask. "What are you going to do? There's four of us and one of you." This guy has no clue what we are capable of.

"And unlike you, none of us are gay." Shane says, stepping up next to her. "And in case you were wondering, brunettes are my favorite," he adds, pulling a long piece of rope out of my black duffle bag.

Blood runs from Seth's nose as he watches Shane somewhat speechless and wide-eyed.

Shane moves behind the chair and pulls the girl's arms behind it. He begins to wrap the rope around her small wrists, binding them together before tying the rope to the chair. Making it impossible for her to move if she wakes.

"Stop," Seth chokes out, finding his voice. "I'll give it to you."

I stay where I'm at, holding the girl's head back by her hair, and Cole takes the phone from him. He brings it over to me. Pulling up his Facebook app, he then goes to his PMs. He scrolls down until he gets to Evan Scott and opens it up.

Evan Scott: Want to keep your secret a secret? Fuck Demi Holt.
Seth: What? Who the fuck is this?
Evan Scott: Someone who knows everything about you.
Seth: Fuck off, man.

Then Evan sends a video to him. Cole pushes play. Sounds of grunts fill the silent room as we watch Seth and our English Lit professor fuck under the sheets of a bed. It's clear who it is and what they are doing. Cole exits out of it.

Seth: What the fuck? How did you get that?

"Where was this recorded at?" I demand, not bothering to look up at him.

"Here," he answers roughly.

Evan Scott: Fuck Demi Holt at the cabin in the bedroom, and I'll keep your secret. You've got twenty-four hours.

Cole exits out of the app. I look at Seth. "When were you here with him?"

Blood still drips from his nose and onto his white T-shirt. He won't look us in the eyes. Instead, he stares at the floor. He's embarrassed. I don't give two shits who he fucks as long as it isn't Demi against her will. "Last time was earlier this week. This is where we always meet."

"Go check the bedroom," I order to Shane. "There has to be a camera set up."

"Evan didn't tell you to drug her. What made you think to do it?"

"I thought it would be easier …" He swallows. "I overheard Peter talking about it. He sold it to me."

"You bought GHB from your sister's boyfriend?" I demand.

He flinches but doesn't answer.

"Who all knows you're gay?" Cole asks him.

"No one did. No one other than Demi."

"And Professor?"

He shakes his head. "He wouldn't do this."

"What makes you so sure?" I ask. Now that I know he bought the GHB from Peter, and Peter had been the one openly bragging about how he would fuck Demi. I'm thinking that maybe they weren't as careful as they thought. And the professor needed to cover his tracks.

He runs his hand over his dark hair. "'Cause we've been hooking up for over a year. There's no reason to do it now."

Shane enters again and shakes his head. "Nothing."

My jaw clenches. "It doesn't make any sense. Someone had to know. And they are connected to both you and Demi." And us. They had us come to this very cabin to give us that fucking letter.

"Becky."

We all turn to look at Shane. He leans up against the wall with his arms crossed over his chest. "I accused the wrong sister. She's the only one who connects them both and the four of us. She came here to Texas with you. You fuck her over for her sister." He shrugs. "She was around him." He points at Seth. "Who knows what she heard or saw. She's crazy enough to do it."

"But not smart enough to pull it off." Cole growls.

"She did have Austin's journal. She knew a lot more than we knew she did," I add.

"What?" Shane asks. "Austin had a journal? What all was in it?"

"Everything," I answer.

"Fuck." He sighs, leaning back and hitting his head against the wall. "I swear, every time I'm around your asses, I find out more shit that I should have already known."

"Bennett." I turn to face him. He sits at the kitchen table, typing away on his phone. "Bennett?" I snap.

"Oh." He drops it to the table and joins our conversation. "It could be her. All she'd have to do was see you log in one time. It's not hard to change an email address and login info." He shrugs.

That's all the confirmation I needed. We've spent too much time on this already. If Becky did it, Cole's right, she won't be smart enough to cover her tracks. And it'll be easy to prove.

I release her hair and lean down to untie the passed-out girl's wrists and throw the rope to Bennett who is already back to texting on his phone. "Shane," I say, and he pushes off the wall. He walks over to us. "Go load her up in the back of my SUV. Take her back into town."

"No!" Seth shouts.

"He's just gonna take her home," I tell him. We did some research earlier before we went out to the party. Their parents are out of town for the night on their yacht. They're throwing a party for a co-worker of his father's. Showing off their wealth is the best way to do that.

"I'll take her home," he growls.

"You'll be staying with us," I inform him.

He swallows nervously, and Shane smiles at him. "Don't worry, man. I'm not into fucking chicks who are unconscious. I like it when they fight." He winks at him as he lifts Melissa into his arms.

"I don't believe you." Seth fists his hands.

I was never going to hurt her. I slipped some GHB into her cup when she bent down to pick up my phone, but I never had any plans to do her any harm beyond that. I didn't even give her much. I just needed enough for her to sleep while I interrogated her brother.

"You have my word," I tell him. "I don't hurt the innocent."

"You've drugged her."

I take a step toward him. "And you slammed Demi's face into the floor while you held her down and unzipped your pants. If she hadn't gotten away, you would have raped her!" I scream the last part. "Your sister will wake up tomorrow with a headache and no memory of tonight, but she won't think her friend betrayed her."

He hangs his head, and I look at Cole. "Help Shane get her in the car."

Bennett brings the chair to the center of the room that Melissa just occupied and hands me the rope. "Have a seat, Seth," I order.

DEMI

I chew on my nails as Austin drives us down the dark highway. The clock on her dash reads a little after midnight. Deke sent me a message a half hour ago to head their way. They didn't tell Austin and me much about their plans for tonight, and I'm not sure I even wanted to know them. The less we know, probably the better.

Austin slows down and turns onto the gravel road parallel to Lake Travis. She comes to a stop in front of the cabin, and my heart begins to pound when I see Seth's Jeep parked out front. Shutting off her car, she exits, and I follow. We make our way up the stairs, and I enter behind her.

I come to a stop as I look down at the hardwood floor in the entryway.

"Seth! Please stop!" I cry as he lies on top of me. I reach out in front of me, trying to grab something, but there's nothing there. My

cheek throbs, and it's hard to breathe with all his weight on me.

I hear his zipper lower, and then his hands are on my hips. He lifts up enough to flip me over onto my back. And I slap at his face.

"I have to." He growls.

What is he talking about? "No." Tears run down the sides of my face. "You don't." I slap at him again, and he jumps up off me.

I get to my shaky legs and reach for the door, but he grips my hair with his fists and starts dragging me across the floor. "Stop!" I cry, trying to twist in his grip. "Please," I beg.

He kicks the bedroom door open and shoves me inside. "It's just sex, Demi. Not like you're not already a fucking slut."

He reaches out for me, but I dart to the left. He gets a hold of my shirt and yanks on it, stretching it out before shoving me onto the bed. I kick and scream, knowing I won't be loud enough. No one will hear me.

He takes a second to shove his jeans off his hips, and I ram my head into his face, smashing it into his nose.

"Fuck!" He growls, rolling off me.

I jump to my feet and run for the front door. I don't look back. I don't even stop to grab my bag. Nothing is more important than getting the fuck out of here.

"Demi?" I hear him scream my name as I run outside and to my car. "Demi!"

I yank open my car door, start it up, and throw it in reverse, not even bothering to look behind me.

"Demi?"

I blink to see Deke standing in front of me. "You okay?" he asks softly. His blue eyes searching mine.

"Yeah," I lie. "Fine. Why are we here?" I look around to see a chair sitting in the middle of the living room. It's empty, but a rope sits next to it on the floor along with a black duffle bag. Cole stands behind it, wiping his bloody knuckles off with a dish rag. And Bennett sits at the kitchen table with his phone in his hands.

I look at Deke and notice that he too has blood on his knuckles and shirt. "Are you okay?" I ask, placing my hands on his chest. His heart beats slowly, and his breathing is even. Whatever he did, didn't even work him up.

"It's not mine," he says.

I swallow, immediately knowing who it belongs to. "Where is he?"

"He's in the bedroom." Cole is the one who answers.

I go to walk that way, but Deke places his hand on my shoulder and pulls me to a stop. I look up at him, and his blue eyes soften. "I'd rather you not."

"But …"

"Can you trust me that I took care of it?"

"Did you kill him?" He had told me while in bed that he was going to kill him.

"People don't have to stop breathing to stop living," he says, and I understand. They took something from him, but it wasn't his life.

I drop my eyes back to the chair and take a step back, letting him know I won't go back there. No matter how badly I want to see what they did to him, he's trying to protect me from something that he thinks I can't handle. I like that he's trying. That he actually cares to keep me innocent in their world filled with blood and chaos.

"Let's go," Deke orders.

Cole reaches out and snatches Austin's car keys from her hands. Deke places his hands on my shoulders, spins me around, and ushers me out the front door. He opens up the back door of Austin's SUV, and I crawl in with him. He pulls me into his side as Bennett gets in on the other side of me. Cole throws his dish rag and a black duffel bag into the back before he gets in and starts up the SUV as Austin gets in the passenger seat.

I snuggle up to Deke, and he kisses my hair. I close my eyes and release a sigh. It feels good for someone to stick up for me. I used to hate the GWS, but it seems they all came together to help me tonight.

"Where is Shane?" Austin asks no one in particular.

"He's got my car," Deke answers. "He had to run an errand but will meet us back at the house."

THIRTY-ONE

DEKE

I PACE THE gravel road, holding my phone to my ear, but I'm met with silence. The drizzle slowly soaks my shirt, making it cling to my body. The Collins night air is cold, but I don't feel it. I'm too wound up. My free hand is shoved into my jeans pocket, and I kick a loose rock around.

"I miss you," she finally says. Her voice so soft, I barely hear it.

I smile and admit, "I miss you too, princess." Coming to a stop, I turn and look at the clubhouse where the sharks and I spent most of our time over the past year and a half. "What are you doing right now?" I ask her while watching Cole pack his black duffle bag into the back of Bennett's car.

"Lying on your bed," she answers. "Naked."

I moan at the visual. "You better be that way when I return tomorrow."

The guys and I decided last night to make a quick trip back to Collins. Well, Bennett and Shane were coming home, but after Shane suggested Becky was Evan Scott, Cole and I decided it was time to find out once and for all. And if she is, we're ending it.

We weren't putting anyone else in danger. Evan had threatened Demi when Seth didn't do as he ordered, so the clock was ticking. I wasn't taking that chance again. I won't gamble with Demi's fate.

Especially if her sister is the one calling the shots. She's already hurt her enough. I was going to end it for her. That's the least I can do after trying to kill her myself.

"We'll see," she teases me. "Depends on what time you get back." She's fishing.

The guys and I didn't tell the girls much. Just that we were taking a quick trip to Collins to take care of something. They knew. They exchanged a look. Austin turned and left the room. She's still not talking to Cole. And Demi just nodded, leaving it at that.

They both knew they weren't going to change our minds. It's not like we're going to kill Becky. We're just going to make sure this shit ends once and for all.

"You ready?" I hear Austin's voice on the other end of the phone.

"Yeah, give me one minute," Demi answers her.

"What are you girls doing?" I ask. It's a little after seven here. That makes it past nine there.

"Austin and I picked up Lilly earlier, and she asked if we could have a girl's sleepover tonight since you guys are gone. So we're gonna make a pallet in the living room, pop some popcorn, and eat our weight in chocolate while we get drunk off cherry Kool-Aid."

I laugh.

"What's so funny?"

"Just remembering when we were at Silence standing in line to get popcorn and you told me that you admired my lack of empathy," I recall. She stays silent, and the smile drops off my face.

"I still do, Deke." she says in a soft voice. "I never once wanted you to be or pretend to be someone other than who you are."

I hate how much I needed to hear her say that. Deke Biggs doesn't need permission to do anything. I always kept Becky in the dark regarding what I did with the sharks. She would have hated it, bitched about it, and made me out to be the bad guy. Which I am, don't get me wrong. I know where I stand in the world of good versus evil. The one drowning in blood and full of hate. But look what she did. Look how far she went to hurt Demi. Or what she did to her back when they were younger. She's tried to have her raped twice now.

She deserves to pay for that. And that's what the sharks do. They make you pay. In blood.

"I gotta go," she says.

But how would she feel if I said those words to her? Her imagination isn't nearly as dark as our actions are. "Demi—"

"I'll be here when you get back tomorrow." She interrupts me. "Waiting on you." Then she hangs up.

I drop the phone from my ear and walk over to the door of the clubhouse. Cole stands over at the table, leaning up against it. Shane sits on the couch typing away on his phone, and Bennett is standing in the small kitchen area looking down at a piece of paper in his hands.

"What's that?" I ask him.

He looks up at me and lets out a long sigh. "There's something I need to tell you guys."

"What is it?" Cole asks, pushing off the table.

"I received this right after you guys moved to Texas." He hands me the paper.

"This glass can break as easily as your promises. What would you do to keep them both intact?" I read the typed letter out loud.

"What the fuck is that shit?" Shane asks, jumping up from the couch.

"I don't know." Bennett shrugs. "Another cryptic letter."

"And you've had this the entire time?" Cole growls.

"I didn't say anything because it didn't have my name on it. It could have been to any of us or all of us." He sighs. "I honestly thought it was for you, Cole, since you own the place. I figured it was someone who knew what you did to Kellan."

"It was just sitting in here. Waiting on you?" I question.

He nods. "It was in the glass bowl. On the table."

"Fuck!" Cole growls.

"So why tell us about it now?" I rip the fucker to pieces and throw them in the trash.

"Well, 'cause now I think it was Becky who gave it to me," he answers.

Cole shakes his head. "She didn't know anything. And why leave it in the bowl? People knew we did dares but not specifics."

"That's not true," I argue. "He said he received it after we left for Texas. Becky got Austin's journal while Austin was still in the hospital. We waited three months after she was shot before we moved."

Cole nods once and growls. "So the bitch has been playing us for six months now? And none of us saw it?"

"The letter has to be for me." Shane speaks.

We all turn to face him. "What makes you think that?" Cole asks him.

He squares his shoulders and takes a deep breath. "Because ... I know some secrets. Some that would totally change how this night is going to go. And that letter was threatening me to keep my mouth shut."

I frown. "I don't understand, Shane."

"We all have secrets," Cole grunts. "Why you specifically?"

"I know something that you guys don't. And if I told on the person who I'm guessing sent me that letter, I would also be implicating myself." His eyes go to Cole, and I stiffen at the challenge in his eyes.

What the fuck does he know? And why hasn't he told us?

Cole takes a step forward, closing the distance between them. "Just what in the fuck do you know, Shane?"

And with that, he informs us of something he should have told us a long time ago. With each word, the room grows smaller. Colder. I watch Cole's body tighten, his fists clench, and his breathing picks up. I cuss, Bennett kicks the table. Shane was right. Tonight is going to go differently than we had planned, but I have no problem adjusting it accordingly.

BECKY

I sit at my father's kitchen table eating a piece of pie. He's out of town for the week so I have the house to myself. It's actually nice to be alone. I've always had to share. My school. My space. My car. My father made me take Demi everywhere. I was so fucking happy once she turned sixteen and could drive herself to school. I should have told my mom to let her stay here while I moved to Texas by myself.

Finishing off the pie, I place the plate in the sink and make my way upstairs. The thunder shakes the walls, and I hear the rain pick up. Typical Collins. This place is such a downer.

I enter my room and fall onto my bed. I close my eyes and let out a sigh. But they snap open when I hear a noise. "Hello?" I call out, looking outside my room but see nothing.

I remove my shirt. Tossing it onto the bed, I undo my jeans and push them down my legs. Standing in a black bra and matching thong, I enter my bathroom to take a bath. I need to relax. My entire body has been tight for days. I've been in a bad mood. Nothing has been going right, and I don't like that.

I hear another sound and walk back into my bedroom. "Hello?" I ask again. Silence follows. My clock on my nightstand shows it's a little after midnight. The thunder rattles the walls again and lightning flashes, lighting up my room. I shrug it off, knowing it must be a tree branch hitting my window or something.

My phone rings on my bed, and I look down to see **Deke** written across the screen. My heart begins to race with excitement.

"Hey?" I try to say calmly, but my high pitch gives me away. I turn, placing my back to the door and bounce toward the windows. The falling rain making visibility nonexistent. "What are you …?"

"Do you miss me, Becky?" he asks in greeting.

A cold chill runs up my spine at his tone. There was nothing affectionate about it. Just cold. Detached. "Of course, … I …"

"What if I said I wanted to see you?"

I swallow, and the hairs on my neck rise. "Deke." I give a nervous laugh. "What do you mean? I, uh, I'd love to see you, but you're too far away." Thank God. He sounds like a serial killer calling his next victim. He's probably drunk and playing some sick game with me.

"What if I told you I'm here?"

I whip around to face my bedroom door, my chest rising and falling quickly. "In Collins?" My voice shakes.

He gives a dark chuckle, and my stomach drops as I watch a man dressed in black jeans and a black hoodie move to stand in the doorway of my bedroom. His blue eyes look me up and down, taking in my half-naked body, but he shows no sign of interest. When they reach mine, I hear him whisper in my ear. "Your bedroom."

I drop the phone and run into my en suite bathroom. I slam the door shut and lock it. He begins to pound on it from the outside. "Stop," I cry as I press my hands up against it, knowing he's fucking with me. If he wanted in, that lock wouldn't stop him. "Deke, please …"

The banging stops, and I flip on the light before taking a step back from the door. Tears sting my eyes and my body shakes. What the fuck is he doing here? In Collins? My bedroom?

Other than my heavy breathing, silence now fills the room. I still hold my hands out in front of me as I take another step back and bump into a hard surface. I gasp, spinning around only to come face-to-face with Cole Reynolds.

They tricked me.

The phone call was to distract me, allowing Cole into my bathroom. Where Deke knew I'd run. He had been covering the door, there was no other escape option for me. His emotionless blue eyes stare down at me. Cole has this way of making you feel cold deep down in your bones. Like death coming to collect your soul. He's come to drag me to hell. To make me pay for my sins. My breath hitches and my heart hammers in my chest. "Cole …"

He grips my hair and shoves my face into my bathroom mirror. Pain explodes behind my eyes. The impact takes my breath away. He yanks me back and shoves me away from him so hard that I slide across the countertop, knocking off my beauty supplies in the process. I hit the tile floor on my side as my shaking hands come up to shield my bloody and busted face. I sob into them, and it just intensifies the pounding in my face.

Cole opens the door, and I get up on my hands and knees, crawling away from them. "Fucking bastard," I cry. He's a fucking psycho.

Deke enters followed by Shane and then Bennett. I begin to shake.

They're gonna kill me. Right here. In my bathroom. "Fuck you guys! All of you!" I shout.

"You like to play, Becky? So do we." Deke speaks, dropping a black duffel bag to his feet.

Shane gives me a cruel smile and kneels by the bag. Slowly, he unzips it. "Sorry, Becky. I ratted you out."

My chest tightens. "I don't know what you're talking about …"

"But you do." He nods. "Kellan had told me ..."

"No, no, no, no," I chant.

"And you knew that I knew … How long did you expect me to keep that secret?"

Now it all makes sense. That's why Cole slammed my face into the mirror. Because that's exactly what Kellan did to Austin. The night I helped him break into the Lowes house.

Eight months ago

Austin walks into the kitchen and grabs the Fireball off the counter and takes a sip from the bottle. Her birthday party has been in full swing for over an hour now. She's already pretty drunk. I'm sober as shit.

"What the hell was that?" I demand, running up next to her. I just stood in her father's game room where she told the sharks that she has insurance on them. Whatever the fuck that means.

"Me putting them in their place," she says and tips it back again.

I sigh. "What do you have on them?"

"Enough."

I roll my eyes. "That's not what I asked, Austin."

She takes another drink as Deke walks into the kitchen, and I tense. What the fuck have they been up to? I know Cole is playing a game with Austin, but I didn't know they were all playing with her. Now I know everyone is involved.

He comes over to us, his eyes on mine. "We're leaving, babe," he says, and I watch Cole storm past the kitchen and out the front door.

She takes another drink.

"I'm staying again tonight," I tell him. I stayed last night as well to bring in her birthday.

He nods, already knowing that. Then he looks at Austin. He opens his mouth to speak and then closes it.

"What?" she snaps.

He just shakes his head. "Nothing." Then gives me a kiss before he turns and leaves.

"You can go with him if you want," she offers.

I shake my head. "Absolutely not. I'm your only friend, remember?" I give her a smile before taking the bottle from her hand. All the girls hate her 'cause of Cole and all the boys want her 'cause of him as well. She's fucked either way. "Someone has to watch over you."

She rolls her eyes and sighs in disappointment. I can tell he's ruined her birthday. Things have been tense since we stood at the clubhouse and he confessed that her father raped his mother and she has a half-sister.

I place my hand on hers and give her a reassuring smile. "You should give him a chance."

"Some people don't deserve a chance,"

"Austin—"

"I don't wanna talk about it," she interrupts me. "Can we just get drunk?"

I chuckle, handing her back the bottle. "Drink up, birthday girl." She tosses it back, and I look over in time to see Kellan walk by. He stops, then looks at me and jerks his head. "I'll be right back," I tell her.

She waves me off.

Exiting the kitchen, I walk down the hallway to a half bath. Kellan shuts the door behind us. "What do you want?" I ask; he and I aren't friends. I put him in the same category as Cole. Fucking evil.

He takes the phone from my hand and begins to mess with the keys. "I want you to text me later after the party is over."

I snort. "Why would I do that?"

He hands me back my phone to see he entered his number into it. "Because if you don't." He steps into me. "I'll tell Deke what you're really doing with him."

My eyes narrow up at him. "I don't know ..."

"I'm not stupid, Becky. I see everything." I swallow. "I know everything."

"It's not what you think."

He gives me a slow smile, his brown eyes looking me up and down. He reaches up and pushes some hair behind my ear, and my heart hammers in my chest. "It's exactly what I think. Now are you going to let me in, or am I going to go to Deke?"

This can't be happening. He can't go to Deke. Deke can't find out what I've been doing. He'll destroy me. He'll make school a living hell for me. "What are you gonna do?"

"I just want her phone."

"I'll get it for you," I offer.

"No." He shakes his head. "I want to get it."

"But why?"

"Because I wanna know if Austin is full of shit, or if she really does have insurance on that phone."

"What was she talking about?" I ask. "What kind of trouble could she get you guys in?"

"The kind that will get all of us sharks thrown in jail." He leans in, and whispers, "For life."

I swallow nervously. "She wouldn't. Cole ..."

"She is pissed at Cole right now. Believe me when I say she'll turn his ass in without a second thought after everything he's done to her."

"But ..."

"Becky?" A hand pounds on the bathroom door, and I jump at Austin's voice. "What are you doing in there?'

"I'll ... I'll be right out." I holler.

He quirks his brow at me, and I take in a deep breath and nod. He just wants her phone. I can handle that. Then I exit out of the bathroom, closing the door behind me. She holds her bottle of Fireball in one hand and her other sits on her hip. "Let's get fucked."

THIRTY-TWO

DEKE

"AFTER COLE KNOCKED out Kellan's car window with a bat and found Austin's phone the day after her birthday party, I called and asked him what the fuck he was doing. And how the hell he got into the house. He told me Becky helped him ..."

"What the fuck, man?" I bark. She was supposed to be her best friend.

"Why would she help him?" Cole snaps.

"I don't know." Shane throws up his hands. "That's all I know. He never went into detail, and I didn't get the chance to ask. Just that he needed whatever insurance she had on her phone, and Becky was willing to help him. And he was pissed that you caught him."

I remember what Shane told us just hours ago at the clubhouse. He stands and hands me two bundles of rope from the bag.

"Please," she sobs. "I'm sorry."

"Not yet."

I walk over to her, and she begins to scream. She kicks her legs out and starts flinging her arms. I grip her ankle, yank her across the tile on her side and flip her on to her stomach. I fall to the floor and straddle her hips. I yank her hands behind her back and wrap the first bundle of rope around her wrists, tying them tightly together.

"Deke! Please ... please don't do this ..."

"Someone shut her up," I order.

Shane drops in front of her with the bag and pulls out a roll of duct tape. He yanks a washcloth off the side of the counter.

"Please …"

He shoves it in her mouth and then tears off a piece of tape and slaps it over her face. Once I'm happy with her wrists, I move off her and grab both her legs. I secure them with the second rope and then connect the remaining rope, hog-tying her in the middle of her bathroom floor.

I stand and turn to face Cole and Bennett. They are looking down at her phone that they got from her room. "Well?" I ask.

Moment of truth, Becky. Let's see what's in store for you tonight.

Cole holds up her phone, and sure enough, he's found where she had two Facebook apps and one was signed in as Evan Scott. And she sent a message to Seth this morning. I read it out loud.

Evan Scott: *I'll give you one more chance. Either you fuck the bitch, or you're fucked.*

Shane laughs. "The problem with that, Becky, is that we have Seth's phone. We took if after we were done having fun with him last night."

"I didn't think you had it in you, Becky. Good for you for proving me wrong."

Shane pushes her over onto her side and slides a towel underneath her. She struggles in her restraints and sobs behind the tape over her mouth. Once he's done and places her back on her stomach, I straddle her upper back, almost sitting on her shoulders so I don't break her restrained arms. Taking a hand full of her blond hair, I grip it and yank her head back and place her phone in front of her face. "You wanna be a shark, baby?" She sobs while her body shakes uncontrollably. I lean down, whispering in her ear, "Well, welcome to the group."

I hold out my right hand, and Cole places the knife in it. I gather up all her hair in my fist and hold it out to Shane who still kneels in front of me at her head. "Hold it," I order.

He pushes her forehead to the tile, holding her head down for me at an odd angle to expose the back of her neck. Then he places her head between his knees, making escape impossible. I take the knife and carve a tally mark along the soft skin right below her hairline. About an inch long. She screams into the gag as her body shakes and her skin breaks. The blood runs down the side of her neck onto the towel beneath her.

Then I hold it out, and Cole takes it. He carves another tally mark next to mine. Shane goes, and then Bennett does his. One by one, we each make our mark on her. A reminder that we fucking own her. That no matter what she does, or who she fucks, she belongs to us.

I reach my left hand out, and Bennett places the can of hair spray in it. I take the end of the towel and wipe it across the back of her neck. She whimpers as I smear the blood to see the four cuts and then spray the hair spray over them to help with the bleeding. I don't want her to bleed to death. Just experience the excruciating pain that she deserves. I toss the can to the side once satisfied.

Cole takes the lighter that Shane pulls out of the bag and runs the knife through the flame, heating it before passing it back to me. I lay it across the lines to cauterize them. And her body fights mine while her muffled screams fill the bathroom.

Then Shane hands me the powder, and I dump it on there to seal what the knife didn't get.

Getting up off her, she immediately rolls onto her side. Her eyes are closed as snot, tears, and blood cover her face. She lies at our feet with nothing but a bra and thong on. Her chest heaves, and she sobs behind her gag.

I kneel beside her and rip it off before shoving my fingers in her mouth to remove the washcloth.

"I will murder you," she sneers. "Fucking murder you for this! All of you sorry bastards. Austin and my sister ..."

I grip her chin. "No. You won't. Because if you try anything, and I mean anything, I will hurt you."

Tears run down her face, smearing her once perfect makeup along with snot and drool. Her blue eyes narrow on me. "You ... can't kill me." She sucks in a breath. "I'm not one of those fucking bastards

Austin wrote about in her journal." She sniffs. "You won't get away with this ..."

I smile at her. "You're right. You're not." I can't kill her. Too many questions will be left unanswered. "But I can make you mine, Becky. I can make you wish you were dead. Every second of every day. From the outside, everyone will think we are in love and happy. No one will know what I do to you behind closed doors. When we're all alone." I run my free hand down her bloody neck and feel her pulse race. "How I'll fuck you. How I'll beat you. Starve you. Don't underestimate how fucking evil I can be. And how little you mean to me." I stand.

"I ... hate ... you ..." She sobs.

I nod to Shane, and he begins to untie her.

"Here." Bennett hands me her cell. "Everything is gone. I changed all emails and passwords for anything related to Evan Scott and then deactivated his page."

I drop her phone on the tile and step on it for good measure. Shane picks up the towel and wads it up before placing it in the duffle bag. It's going with us. Once it dries out, we'll burn it.

Cole starts dumping peroxide on the tile floor to clean up the blood.

She crawls over to the corner of her bathroom and pulls her legs up to her chest. Her blond hair wild and bloody. She looks so fucking broken. And I give no fucks that I did that to her. This bitch has fucked us over way too many times. She's the reason Austin was hurt. I consider her my little sister. And she's tried to hurt Demi, a woman who is quickly becoming my everything.

"Do you love her?" she asks as if she can read my mind.

"Does it matter?"

"Is that why you're doing this?" she demands. "Because Demi got a little scared? Nothing ever fucking happened to her!" she shouts "She always managed to get away. Unharmed. Untouched."

I just stare at her.

"Do? You? Love? Her?" She screams so loud, my ears ring.

I walk over to her, and she presses herself further into the wall as

I lean over and push some blond strands off her slick face. "I love her more than I could ever love you," I say truthfully. "Does that make you feel better?"

Her tear-filled eyes narrow up at me, and she sucks in a heavy breath.

"I mean it, Becky. Stay away. I won't be so kind next time." Then I give her my back and walk out.

I step out into the dark and cold night as Shane speaks. "I'm sorry, man. I didn't know Kellan …"

Cole punches him in the face.

That was the first thing Shane has said to him since he informed us of the secret he knew.

"I'm sorry." He stumbles backward, holding up his hands. "Hit me again. I deserve it."

Cole doesn't need to be told twice. He hits him so hard this time it throws Shane into the side of Bennett's car. Blood pours from his nose and a busted lip.

"You knew all this time …" Cole growls and looks him up and down. "I should have beat you to death that night as well. And had Bennett drop your sorry ass to the bottom of the ocean to rot with him." With that, Cole opens the passenger side door and falls into the car.

DEMI

It's been a week since the GWS took care of Seth and then made a quick trip to Collins. Austin and I didn't need to ask what they did there, but we knew. They were going down a list of people who needed to pay for hurting me or threatening them. No one was going to stop them from doing what they do best. I can't say I feel sorry for any of them.

I lick my lips as I look in the bathroom mirror. My hair is down in big waves. Placing my hands in it, I bend over and fluff it, giving it some volume. Standing, I run my hands down the front of my holey jeans.

We're having dinner tonight with my mother.

I asked her if I could have some friends over for dinner, and she looked at me like I was someone she's never met. I know it's not a good idea, but at this point, I don't care. I want her to see that Seth is long gone. And that her lovely plan she had for my life is crumbling. Because Deke sure as hell isn't what she wants for my future.

I hear the doorbell ring, and I run out of my bathroom and down the stairs, yelling, "I'll get it."

Opening the door, I smile up at the prettiest man I've ever seen. I hate how he makes me feel, yet I can't push him away. I can't deny that Deke has gotten under my skin in the worst way.

"Hey, princess." He steps into the house and wraps his arms around me, picking me up off my feet. His lips crash down on mine, and I wrap my arms around his neck, kissing him like I'm desperate for him. I just saw him last night for a couple of hours, but it doesn't feel like enough.

I don't know how my sister ever thought he wasn't enough for her. He would have given her the world, but he's going to destroy mine.

I'm just waiting for that other shoe to drop. For everything to come crashing down and kill whatever this is that we have.

"Oh, get a room," I hear Cole grumble.

I pull away from Deke's lips and giggle. That's another thing I do lately. I used to be disgusted with the girls at school who went all happily stupid over boys. And now I'm there.

I see Austin enter the house, and she holds a dish in her hands. "You didn't have to bring anything."

"I figured I could at least bring dessert." She shrugs, and Cole pulls her into his side, kissing her head. I don't know what all happened last week, but whatever it was, it's like they're finally breathing fresh air. They both seem very happy. And I can't be more thrilled for them.

"Thank you," I say, taking it from her, and then ask, "Where's Lilly?"

"She's at home with Misty," Cole answers.

"Deke?"

We all turn to see my mother standing in the foyer. She's wearing a pair of black slacks with a red silk top. She has her blond hair up in a tight bun and her black rimmed glasses hanging from her neck.

"Becky isn't here," she tells him.

I swallow the anger at her words, and say, "Deke is here to have dinner with us tonight, Mom."

She tilts her head to the side as if she doesn't understand my meaning. So I reach out, grab his hand, and place it in mine. Looking up at him, I give him a big smile. "We're dating," I say in case my show of affection wasn't enough. I'm not sure what the hell we are exactly, and I don't care. I'm not one of those girls who has to put a label on things. I just want to piss her off.

I hear Cole cover a small laugh with a cough. He fails.

"I see." She grabs her pearls and then turns, giving us her back and walking toward the formal dining room.

"This'll be fun," Cole mumbles. "Like that one time I had dinner with your father," he tells Austin, and she sighs.

THIRTY-THREE

DEKE

"THIS LOOKS AMAZING," Austin says, looking over the table covered with food.

Angelica had her chefs make a variety from escargot to a kale salad and blackened salmon. Just to name a few things. It's like they couldn't decide exactly what they were in the mood for.

"So." Her mother starts before I can even get a piece of bread on my plate. "When did you two start dating? You were just here a few weeks ago to take out my other daughter."

"Does it matter?" Demi challenges her mother.

She arches a brow. "I'm guessing this has to do with the reason your sister ran back to Collins."

I'm not sure why in the hell Demi wanted us to come over here for dinner tonight, but when she asked me the other day, I wasn't going to tell her no. She had a smile on her face, which I seem to see a lot of lately, and was lying underneath me completely naked. I would have said yes to anything. And I've decided that's a very dangerous thing. But one I'm not going to question.

"I'm not sure, why don't you ask her?" Demi offers.

Her mother's already sharp jaw tightens. She opens her mouth when Austin speaks. "I love the new color you chose for the formal dining room, Mrs. Lawrence."

Cole smirks at her trying to divert the conversation in such a bad way. Austin ignores him.

Angelica looks over at her, and her eyes drop to the red ruby engagement ring. "How do your parents feel about you being engaged at such a young age, Austin?" she asks.

She wipes the corner of her mouth with her napkin, looking unaffected by Demi's mother. "Well, I'm pretty sure my mother is dead." Cole stiffens beside her, and Demi's eyes shoot to mine. "And my father is in prison for life. So I don't think they care."

Silence falls over the table, and I take a sip of my water. She couldn't be more correct. Her mother is dead all right. Cole and I killed her and her stepdad.

I lie in Becky's bed at her father's house watching a movie when my cell alerts me of a message.

"Who is it?" Becky asks.

"It's from Cole." I open it up.

Cole: You busy?

Me: I'm with Becky. What's up?

Cole: I have something that needs to be taken care of.

Me: I can be ready whenever.

Cole: Give me five.

"I gotta go," I say, getting out of her bed.

"What?" She jumps up. "You just got here."

I grab my black leather jacket off the back of her chair. "Cole needs me."

She comes over to me, and I refrain from sighing because I can tell she's pissed. "Cole always needs you."

"Don't," I warn, walking over to her door.

"Deke." She grabs my hand. "What does he need?"

I don't answer. "I'll come back."

"When?" she demands.

"When I'm done," I say and exit her room. I walk down the stairs and out the front door. As I jump into my Range Rover, I see her sister pull up. She comes to an abrupt stop and jumps out. She all but runs to the front door and shoves it open before storming inside. Maybe I

got out just in time.

I pull out my cell and try calling him, but it rings several times before his voicemail finally picks up. I put the SUV in gear and pull out of their driveway as my phone rings. It's Cole calling me back.

"Hey, man. What's up?" I answer.

I hear his tires squealing, letting me know he's left wherever he was. Probably with Austin. "Austin's mother is in town. With her new husband."

"Okay," I say slowly.

He takes in a deep breath. I know absolutely nothing about her mother or stepdad, or anything about her life before she moved here to Collins three months ago. "They were waiting for Austin when we walked into Bruce's house."

"And?"

"And they need to be taken care of," he answers.

"Where do you want me to meet you?" I ask without hesitation, knowing he has a plan. Cole always has one. And I'll help him take care of whoever has fucked him over. Or in this case, it sounds like they have fucked over Austin.

We found them hiding out at the cheapest hotel in Collins. But it was in the middle of the day, so we decided on a plan, then he spent the afternoon with Austin and Lilly at the zoo. I went to the docks where our fathers once kept their yachts. There was an abandoned warehouse back there where they used to load and unload the shipping containers. They built a new one on the other side of town but hadn't demolished this one yet, so no one was ever here.

I laid down a blue tarp in the office to get it ready.

Later that evening, after they left the zoo, I went over to the clubhouse and picked up Cole, and we sat outside the hotel room and waited.

We had our duffel bags with us. We rarely left home without them. Cole knocked on the door like they were expecting us, and a man answered. Cole shoved the door into his face, knocking him into the room. I entered and slammed it shut. Cole was already on the man, so I grabbed the woman and had her face down on the bed before she could even scream. I placed duct tape over her mouth and then tied her hands and feet together with it as well before I threw a hood over her head. Cole did the same to the man. We took them back to the docks I had been at earlier in the day and carried them into the office.

We didn't play with them for very long. Cole fucked up the man pretty good with his fists, then took his knife and cut off the guy's dick while he was still alive. I didn't know what these people had done, but it was clear they had pissed him the fuck off. They were both druggies. I had grabbed their bathroom bag from their hotel and found a syringe and some crack in it. After I heated it up into liquid, I shot it into her. I'm not sure if she died from the drugs I gave her or the fact that I never removed the tape from her mouth and she choked on her own vomit. It didn't matter. They both died. We killed them.

After they were both dead, we stood there in that office. Cole had told me that Austin's stepdad had touched her. Sexually. The first time she was ten. It was then that I realized just how much he loved her. And how far I would go to protect his girl for him. She was one of us—a shark—and we protect our own. No matter what.

"Well." Demi's mother clears her throat. "I hope you wait a while before you get married. Finish school—"

"We're thinking January," Austin interrupts her.

Two months from now.

"That's awesome," Demi says with a big smile on her face. "I've always wondered why couples have long-drawn-out engagements. If you love each other, why not do it sooner?"

Angelica does not share her daughter's excitement. You would think this is me and Demi wanting to tie the knot.

"Have you found a venue already?" Angelica asks. Now she's just being nosy. "Not sure you will have much luck on availability with such short notice."

"Oh, we already know." Austin smiles, looking over at Cole. "An abandoned cemetery."

Demi's mother chokes on her fucking slimy snail.

"It's where we first met," she adds.

Cole reaches out and takes her hand. He brings her knuckles to his lips and kisses them softly. "Whatever you want, sweetheart."

Demi has her elbows on the table, her chin in her hands, and she looks at them wistfully. And I realize that I will do anything to keep that look on her face. It's crazy how pissed off she used to always look. She hated the world. Now she's always smiling at me. And laughing. Fuck, that laugh. I tickle her just to hear it. I toss her over my shoulder to hear her squeal my name. And I lie awake at night to watch her sleep. I wonder what it would have been like if I would have picked her instead of Becky. I never even looked at Demi. She was once nonexistent to me. Just like she was to everyone else. But I see her now. And she's the most beautiful thing I've ever seen.

DEMI

"That didn't go too bad." Austin laughs as we enter their house.

I told my mother after dinner that I was staying with Austin tonight. I didn't think that she knew Deke lived with them, and when she didn't tell me no, then I was positive she didn't know.

"It could have gone worse." I agree.

I'll have to listen to it tomorrow. About how much of her life she is throwing away to marry a man who can leave her at any given moment. My mother believes a woman should pay her own way, unless you're Becky. Well, then a career doesn't matter.

I make my way upstairs to Deke's room. I'm removing my shirt when he enters. He walks into his bathroom, and I quickly finish getting undressed before crawling underneath his cool covers. Seconds later, he walks out and does the same, but he leaves his black boxers on.

I frown over at him as he turns the light off. I wouldn't say I'm addicted to sex, but that is definitely a bonus when it comes to him.

He shifts onto his side and pulls me into him. "Ride home with me for Thanksgiving."

Not the conversation I thought we were going to have, but I say, "Okay."

We all decided last weekend to go home for Thanksgiving. He

wants to spend it with Shelby, and I want to see my father. Cole and Austin are also going back. Shelby told them they could stay at her house with Lilly since Cole doesn't speak to his dad and Austin's father's house isn't in any condition to live in at the moment. She told me the other day that after she was shot, and her stepmother was killed there, no one has cleaned up the house. Her father went to prison, and it was just abandoned.

He kisses my forehead, and I hear his phone ring. It's been going off nonstop the last few days. "Who keeps calling you?" I ask.

"Shane."

I pull away from him and sit up. "Why are you ignoring him?"

He reaches up and pulls me down to lie next to him. "It's nothing. I'll call him tomorrow."

He's lying, but I don't question it.

"Have you heard from my sister?"

I feel his body stiffen against mine. "No. Why?"

"My mother probably called her after we left her house."

"Hey." He pushes my hair from my face. "Who cares?"

"I do. My mother wants you with her." I growl.

He gives me a smile. "I'm with you, Demi."

We haven't had the we're exclusive talk. I just figured it's a given at this point. I haven't seen anyone else, and he spends every free second he has with me.

"Yeah, but ..."

"Shh," he says, pressing his lips gently to mine. "You're mine, and I'm yours. Neither Becky nor your mother are going to change that."

"Promise?" I ask, biting my bottom lip. My mother can be very persuasive. And relentless. That's where my sister gets it from.

His phone rings again. He sighs, rolling over, and shuts it off. He turns back to face me. "Promise."

THIRTY-FOUR

BECKY

I SIT ON the kitchen counter at a kid's parent's house in Collins. My legs swing back and forth, hitting the cabinets. People crowd around drinking, smoking, and high on whatever drugs they've ingested to get through the night. I understand it. Wish I could do it. Feel numb. But no matter what I do, it won't fix how I feel.

"Deke came over tonight. He, Austin, and Cole had dinner with us. He's dating your sister." My mother had told me during a phone call last week.

I tried to brush it off by telling her that I was done with him. I laughed it off that they belonged together. But after I hung up, I cried. I laid in my bed and sobbed. Mainly because of what he did to me. But also because he's with her. They've made it official. They wanted it to get back to me.

After he and the sharks cut me, I sat on my bedroom floor with a bottle of vodka, and I drank the entire thing until the pain subsided and the skin was numb. It hurt like fucking hell. I eventually passed out.

I woke up, knowing I needed a plan. I can't win him back. That's long gone. Now I want to kill them both. All the GWS.

"What are you doing here?" Shane demands, coming to stand in front of me.

I don't answer. He'll die slow and painfully. He betrayed me! Why didn't they carve his neck up? Because he has a dick? Or maybe it's because he has murdered with them. He knows too much about them for them to turn on him.

A brunette I've never seen before clings to his side.

"Hi," she says with a tilt of her head, her high ponytail pulling her hair back tightly. "I'm Brynn." She introduces herself like I give a fuck.

Her gray eyes twinkle at me. She's too bubbly. Too fucking annoying. She's dressed in a pair of skinny jeans with a pair of black heels, and a black and white shirt that hugs her small frame.

I instantly hate her.

She reminds me of myself. Back before the sharks ruined everything I had.

He whispers something in her ear, and she bites her lip before nodding like the good little slave she is. They all have one. Each of them feeds off a helpless, willing victim. Fulfilling their need for sex and blood. He pulls away from her, and she turns, all but bouncing away.

He reaches up and pushes my blond hair behind my ear. I slap his hand away. He lost the right to touch me when he told one of my secrets. I wonder if he knows the other.

What would he do if I told them what I know? What would Deke do if he knew about Bennett? That's why I went to the clubhouse the other day. To blackmail Bennett. Boy, did that plan backfire on me. They always seem to.

"Becky, you gotta get over it," he says.

I place my hand on his chest and push him away from me. He backs up, and I jump off the counter, almost tripping over my own heels.

"Whoa." He reaches out for me, but I shove him away.

"Leave me alone."

He doesn't know what it's like to love someone who you don't really know. To have that one person betray you in the worst possible way.

None of them do—the GWS. They're all just a group of spoiled-ass rich boys who have always been allowed to do whatever the fuck they want. In a town of people who either fear them or take payment from their parents to look the other way.

I always thought they were harmless.

Stupid girl.

I, of all people, should know that nothing is what it seems.

I fake a lot of shit. I learned it from my mother. Angelica Lawrence is the perfect model for a broken soul under flawless makeup and a fake-as-shit smile. *People will only see what you show them* is her motto.

I know I'm a hypocrite.

A liar.

A slut.

I'm what everyone whispers behind my back. I've never had any real friends. Not until Austin Lowes came along, and I was even forced into that friendship. But I managed to fuck that one up too.

I thought I could outsmart all of them. Thought I could play them at their own game. Told myself I could keep up with the lies and wouldn't get caught.

Turns out, I was wrong.

The worst part? Deke has always had a part of me, since the first time he kissed me on a hot and sunny day by the football field of Collins High. After he took my breath away, he gave me his back and walked away. I let him go. Even then, I knew I couldn't keep him. Not much later, he was standing in front of me again. It didn't matter that I was unavailable at the time. No one tells Deke Biggs no. He wanted me, and I swore I could use him for popularity. To get into a crowd that could make me more than the spineless bitch I was. I would use him the way he and his friends used others. But I promised myself I would not fall for him like all the dick-whipped girls in our school.

Fuck, I fell to my knees so fast. Like I was a sinner in church who was shown the light and needed to repent.

But instead of forgiveness, I got burned alive at the stake.

It was bound to happen. No one lies and gets away with it like the GWS. There was a frenzy of them and only one of me. I was never a shark. It was a loan. I played nice with Cole's girlfriend, Austin, while fucking his best friend—I was supposed to get a pass.

Instead, I got fucked without the benefits of the actual orgasm. Well, I guess I can't say that. Deke knows his way around a woman's body. But it's not like the bastard hadn't had any practice. I may not have been innocent, but I didn't have half the experience he did. He flashed his pretty blue eyes and panty-dropping smile at me, and I was gone. Just like all the others before me. And the ones to come after me.

I never had a fucking chance. Just like everyone else who goes up against any of them, failure was my only option. They come together and rip you to shreds before you can even blink. Then they step back and watch you bleed to your death. They find a sick pleasure in watching you wither in pain. They thrive on it. Feed off it.

They've always liked to play a little game of dare. They may have called it quits, but I'm about to call their bluff. And what's a game if not everyone plays?

I'm going to show them that Becky Holt can play just as ruthlessly. Deke Biggs is my target, and he'll never see me coming. I'm going to put on my makeup and my mother's smile. I don't care who you are—no man can resist a painted face and scandalous dress with a pair of heels as tall as the sky.

He may be a shark, but I'm about to show him that the bait can be just as threatening.

"Becky?" A hand grips my upper arm and spins me around.

"Get the fuck off me, Shane," I snap.

He grips the back of my neck, and I cry out as he shoves me through a door into a room. He lets go and I bend over, my hand flying to the back of my neck over the cuts he just grabbed. Tears fill my eyes, and my breathing has hitched.

"Listen." He grips my hair and yanks my head back. "You belong to us, Becky. Do you understand that?"

"Fuck you," I hiss.

He lets go of my hair and cups my face with both of his hands. I bare my teeth, ready to bite him if need be. "You think I want you?" he asks, arching his dark brows in amusement.

"Are you saying you don't?" I growl.

"If you're doing this to piss off Deke, it won't work. He doesn't care about you anymore, Becky." He leans and whispers. "Those cuts were a warning, baby, to always watch your back. You never know when we'll be there." He lets go of me. "You're lucky to still be alive. So, enjoy your life and go fuck someone who doesn't know what kind of whore you really are." With that, he pulls away and walks out the room. I exit behind him and see him find the brunette standing by the wall with two drinks in her hands. She hands him one and sips from the other.

I fist my hands and turn, storming out the back door of the house, but I run into a hard body. "Sorry ..." I look up and gasp.

A hand slaps over my mouth, and I'm pushed up to the side of the house. He takes his free hand and places a finger over his lips, silently telling me to be quiet. Then removes his hand.

"What are you doing here?" I whisper, looking around to make sure no one is looking our way. "No one can see you."

He gives me a soft smile as his hand grips the hem of my shirt before sliding underneath it. "I needed to see you, baby." Then his lips land on mine.

DEKE

It's officially Thanksgiving, and we are back at Collins for the week. We had planned on flying but then decided we wanted to have access to vehicles. My father has plenty to go around, but I'm still not talking to that fucker. And same thing goes with Cole's father. It took us two days to make the thirty-hour drive. We had to stop and stay the night in Utah and watched Lilly swim in the indoor pool with the girls. Things seem to be going pretty good lately. Cole is on edge again, though. He hasn't told Austin what all he knows. That wouldn't bother the old Cole, but it's eating the new one alive. I think he's afraid to tell her just how deep her friend's betrayal ran. And I think the fact that we're back here in Collins adds to that.

"Are you glad to be back?" Demi asks from the passenger seat.

"Yes," I answer, pulling up to my sister's house. I haven't spoken to her in a few hours. We're a little ahead of our scheduled time to arrive.

I frown when I see a white SUV parked in the driveway that I know all too well. I exit my Range Rover and walk inside with Demi right behind me. "Sis?" I call out.

I walk down the hallway and turn to enter the kitchen, thinking I'll find her at the table, but she's not there. "Shelby?" I yell this time.

"Deke?" She answers from behind me.

I turn to see her standing in the hallway with a dark gray towel wrapped around herself. Her blond hair, wet and sticking to her bare shoulders. She still has some soap on her face. "What are you doing?" I ask.

"I was in the shower." She smooths her hand down the towel and looks over to Demi who comes to stand next to me. She swallows nervously. "You guys are early."

I narrow my eyes on her neck. She has a couple of marks that resemble hickeys. What the fuck? I've never seen hickeys on my sister before. "Is that a problem?"

"No," She laughs like I told a joke and changes the subject. "Are you hungry? Want me to make you something ..."

"Babe, what's taking you so long?" A man interrupts her, coming into the hallway. "Deke?" His wide eyes meet mine.

I fist my hands down by my sides. "What the fuck are you doing here?" I demand, looking him over. He too wears a towel low on his hips. And soap still covers his chest and arms. *No fucking way!* "At my sister's? Also dressed in a towel?" I snap.

He runs a hand over his wet hair and squares his shoulders. "We were going to tell you."

"When?" I snap and look at my sister. This motherfucker ... "How long?" I demand.

She drops her blue eyes to the floor.

"How fucking long?" I shout.

"Hey." Bennett pushes her out of the way and steps up to me. "Don't yell at her. I was the one who wanted to keep this a secret from you."

I reach out, gripping the back of his neck and yank him to me. "I'm not gonna ask you again."

He gives me a smile, and says, "A year."

I punch him in the face, knocking him into a wall.

"Deke!" my sister and Demi both shriek.

"You fucking bastard …" I slam my fist into his face again. He doesn't fight me back, and I take full advantage of it.

I take him to the floor right here in the hallway. The force making a few pictures fall as well.

"What the fuck?" I hear Cole growl, and then I feel his hands on my shoulders. He yanks me off him, pulling me to my feet.

I stand, hands fisted and breathing heavily.

"What the hell is going on here?" he demands.

"What's it look like?" I shout. "He's fucking my sister."

Cole looks from Bennett to Shelby. But looks away quickly when he realizes she's only dressed in a towel. He throws his hands up and takes a step back. "By all means."

"Cole!" Austin growls his name as she pushes Lilly behind her legs. "Not here," she tells him.

He nods and tells Bennett. "Get dressed. Deke can beat your ass in the backyard."

Without a second thought, I turn and exit the house. Rolling my shoulders, I get ready to kick my best friend's ass when Demi walks out back behind me.

"Deke …"

"Don't," I growl, interrupting her. I'm in no mood to hear it. Whatever she has to say, she can save it.

"But …"

"Drop it, Demi!" I snap. He's been fucking her for a year. He deserves at least a broken nose for that.

She lets out a growl and turns, running back into the house just as

Cole and Bennett exit.

I lift my fisted hands ready to start punching his face.

"Can I explain?" he asks, lifting his hands in surrender.

"Nope." I slam my fist into him, knocking him back a few steps.

"Goddammit, Deke." He growls, covering his face. "Cole …"

"I can't help you out, man. I'm with Deke. We all knew she was off-limits."

I step into him ready to throw another punch.

"Just listen for two …"

This time, my fist connects with his jaw, sending him onto his ass.

"Motherfucker!" he shouts, jumping to his feet.

"Is she who you messaged nonstop while you were down in Texas?" I snap. The fucker barely ever looked up from his phone, but I never questioned it because I didn't give a shit who he was talking to. Obviously, I should have.

"Yes!" he snaps.

Cole falls down into a chair and takes a bite of an apple. The fucker is enjoying this too much. "And the girl you ushered out of the clubhouse the night I called you …? That was her, wasn't it?"

My hands drop to my sides as my mouth falls open. *No fucking way …*

"Yes!" he answers Cole.

I let out a growl and run at him. My shoulder hits him in the chest, and I lift him up off the ground before slamming his ass to the snow-covered grass. "I'm gonna kill …"

"I love her!" he shouts.

I pause, one hand fisted in his shirt and the other about to hit him in the face again. "What?" I pant.

He lets out a long sigh and licks the blood off his lip. "I fucking love her, Deke." He shoves me off, and I go willingly. Sitting up, he runs his hands through his hair. "You think I would risk losing you as a friend for a fuck or a fling?" I don't answer. "I've been in love with her for a long time, and a year ago, I got my chance to show her just how much." He looks over at Cole who continues to eat his apple with a smirk on his face. "I'm sorry we didn't tell you. She wanted to, but I didn't. I knew you wouldn't understand. I was selfish and wanted as much time with her as possible before you found out." He hangs his head. "She broke up with me after Cole killed Kellan. She thought I helped, which I did, but she said she wanted nothing to do with our lives." He glares up at me. "It took a lot of groveling to get her back and show her that I can be different for her." He huffs. "And I'll be damned if I'm gonna allow you to come in and fuck that up for me."

I stand staring down at my friend sitting in the snow with blood running down his nose. I should be mad, but all I can think about is how my sister can't accept him for who he really is. I'm not surprised. She never really did me either. But she doesn't understand our need for revenge. Demi understands it. She's lived it with her sister for years.

I walk over to him and reach out my hand. He looks at it and then up at me before taking it. I pull him into me and slap his back. "I already consider you a brother, Bennett. But if you hurt her, I'll have no problem killing you."

He chuckles pulling away. "That's not gonna happen."

The three of us enter the house to find my sister sitting at her kitchen table. She jumps up the moment she sees us and gasps. "What the hell, Deke?" She runs to him, placing her hands on his bloody face.

"He's fine." I wave her off. "Just a scratch."

"Where are the girls?" Cole asks, looking around for Austin.

"They left to go take Lilly to see Blanche for the day. They'll be back later."

THIRTY-FIVE

DEMI

I SIT IN the spare bedroom scrolling through my Facebook when I hear a knock on the door. "Come in."

Austin pops her head in. "Hey, I'm gonna go pick up Lilly from Blanche's. Wanna ride with me? I thought we could grab dinner on the way back for everyone."

"Yeah," I say, getting up and grabbing my jacket. "Sounds good."

She backs out of the driveway, and I send Deke a quick message. I haven't spoken to him much today. Austin and I left earlier while he was outside beating the shit out of his friend. We had dropped Lilly off at Blanche's and then met Shelby at the mall for some girl time. She explained the guys made up and how they were going to meet Shane at the clubhouse later to go over some things. Whatever that meant.

Me: Gonna pick up Lilly and grab dinner. Ask the guys what sounds good.

Locking my phone, I put it down in my lap and look out the windshield. When we arrived in Collins earlier today, it had been snowing. It's stopped for the time being but looks like it could start again at any minute.

We're on a two-lane road heading back to Blanche's. She lives on the outskirts of Collins. The road is curvy with lots of hills so we're going slower than normal due to the weather. We make a curve, and Austin slams on the brakes. Her hand comes out, shooting across to my chest to hold my back to the seat.

"What the hell is going on here?" she asks as we come to an abrupt stop.

"Maybe they wrecked," I say, looking over the tire tracks of a car that sits in the middle of the road. You can tell that they were heading in the same direction as us and then spun around, doing a one-eighty. When it finally stopped, it's now facing us head on but still across both lanes.

Austin opens her door and gets out, so I do the same. "Hello?" she calls out.

I look over at the ditch, and my heart begins to pound in my chest when I see the three, white wooden crosses that Deke and Cole placed here after their friends were killed in the car wreck. I remember being at Eli's funeral and hearing people whisper that Cole and Deke didn't show. They had been here, setting these.

Right where we stand.

"Austin?" I turn to face her, and she's got her hands on the window of the car, trying to look through the blacked-out windows. "I think we should leave," I say, getting a bad feeling about this.

"I don't see anyone …" The door opens, hitting her in the face, knocking her off her feet and onto her ass.

"Austin?" I shout, running over to her, but an arm wraps around me from behind, and I'm yanked off my feet. *Oh, no. God, no!*

She rolls over onto her hands and gets up on her knees. A guy steps out of the car, and my breath hitches. No, no, no. "Austin … run."

He walks over and kicks her in the side, and she cries out, grabbing it.

"Stop!" I scream, trying to fight the hands that hold me.

The passenger door opens, and I watch my sister walk around the back of the car. My teeth clench at the sight of her smiling at me. "You fucking bitch!" I scream.

The guy holding me tightens his hold, pinning my arms down to my side. "Nice to see you too, sis." She gives me a smile that I want to cut off her fucking face.

"Let her go," I order. I can't let Austin get hurt. Not because of me. Not because I stole my sister's boyfriend.

She laughs. "Not a chance."

"Your fight is with me." My eyes go to Austin, and she's now on her knees with her head in her hands. The car door hit her pretty hard, and I'm surprised it didn't knock her unconscious. She's definitely confused as to what is going on. "You hate me. I took him from you."

She steps into me, pressing her chest into mine. Her blue eyes narrowed. "I no longer give a fuck that he picked you."

She spits in my face. Then she gathers her blond hair to the top of her head and spins around, giving me her back. I see four tally marks across the back of her neck just below her hair and then one across it. *Fuck, Deke, what did you guys do to her?* They had to know she wouldn't quit. Not after that.

She spins back around. "The sharks did that to me. Because of you. Because of her ..."

"You deserved it." I growl. They should have just killed her.

She slaps me across the face, and I taste blood, but I refuse to make a fucking sound or let her think she hurt me. Instead, I spit it on her.

She laughs, and says, "Do it."

Before I even get the chance to comprehend what she says, I feel a sting in my arm. "What ...?"

"You're done, Demi. Once and for all."

I panic as I look over at Austin. She's getting to her feet, her hands up and fisted because she's more alert now. Just as the guy goes to swing, she ducks and punches him in the dick.

Good for her. Maybe one of us will survive this.

"Don't worry. It'll only hurt a lot," Becky taunts.

The guy shoves me forward, and I fall to my knees in the middle of the street. I watch Becky walk over to Austin, and I take the chance to pull my phone out of my back pocket and go to Deke's number.

"I'll take that." She yanks it from my hands and throws it out into the woods behind me.

"I hope he fucking kills you," I growl up at her from my knees.

"He already has," she states with a smile.

The guy who was holding me walks around and picks her up. She kisses him while he spins her around, and I blink, making sure I'm seeing what I think I see. What did she give me? Am I hallucinating? "No …"

He drops her back down to her feet. "Can't … be." My eyes are getting heavy, and my lips won't work.

She kneels in front of me. "Nothing is ever what it seems." That's the last thing I hear her say before my arms give out, and I fall to the snow-covered street.

BECKY

"Put her in the back of the Range Rover," I order David.

He bends down to pick up my sister and carries her over to Austin's SUV. I turn to face the bitch who was supposed to be my best friend.

"What's your plan, Becky?" she asks with a sarcastic laugh, wiping the blood off her bottom lip. Then she sticks her finger in her mouth and sucks it off. I never realized how psycho she is until just now. I had quite a few *what the fuck* moments when I read her journal, but I thought maybe she was overexaggerating. "Gonna kill us?"

"Yes," I say simply.

"It's gonna take more than this." She holds her hands out wide, gesturing to me and the two guys I brought. I knew she'd be harder to catch than Demi. Austin Lowes grew up having to fight to survive. My sister has always been handed everything.

I also knew I wouldn't be able to get them both on my own. I needed help. They've been helping me all along. "Oh, I've got an entire night planned for you." Her green eyes narrow on me. "And you know what?" I chuckle. "This isn't the first time I've ever fucked you over."

Six months ago

"I need a ride," Kellan says, leaning up against the locker beside mine in the senior hallway.

"Go away," I order.

He gives me a charming smile that makes him look like he's a nice guy. If I didn't know he was so evil, I would give him a chance. I hear he's a good fuck. "Come on, Becky. Help me out."

"No." I slam my locker and turn my back on him.

He grabs my upper arm and yanks me into the women's bathroom. "Kellan, what the fuck?" What is it with me and him always being in a bathroom?

"I'm not asking, Becky. I'm telling you that I need a ride." His brown eyes bore into mine. That smile no longer present. The charming act over.

"You have a car," I snap. "I'm pissed off at you, Kellan." He wasn't supposed to touch her. Hurt her that night of her birthday. Of course, Cole was pissed, and I was fucking terrified. He could have killed her.

"Like I give a fuck." He shrugs. I want to knock his head off with my books, but it wouldn't kill a shark. "Give me a ride, or I'll make sure that Cole finds out you were the one who allowed me entrance to the Lowes house on Austin's birthday."

My heart begins to pound, and I look around the women's bathroom to make sure no one overheard him. "Don't you dare ... "

He grips my chin, forcing me to look at him. "I think it's funny that no one has questioned you as to why I shoved Austin's face into a mirror, knocking her out and taking her phone, yet you stayed the night with her and never heard me."

I try to shove him away as panic crawls up my spine. "Fuck you—"

"Cole will kill you." He interrupts me, gripping me tighter, and I whimper. "If Austin doesn't get to you first."

"What do you want with Celeste?" I ask, trying to forget the betrayal of my best friend. I failed her, and she can't know that. Deke can't know it, and Cole sure as fuck can't know it. I've faked it this long, so I'm not going to allow Kellan to bring me down now.

Letting go of me, he takes a step back, giving me some space. "She fucked with the wrong person." He gives me a cryptic answer.

I let out a sigh. "Austin—"

"Has a date with Myers tonight." He interrupts me. "She won't be home."

"How do you know that?" I haven't got to spend much time with her since she and Cole broke up again. They got back together last time the morning after her birthday party. But the night after prom, they called it off. Well, I think she did because he's acting like a sad little bitch. I'm always with Deke, and he's always by Cole. Austin steers clear of him.

"I overheard Myers fucking running his mouth about it. They're going to a movie."

I bite my bottom lip. "I can't stay ..."

"Just drop me off and go."

"Who is gonna pick you up?" I ask, confused with his half-assed plans.

"That ..." He steps back into me, running his finger along my jawline, and whispers, "Is none of your business."

"I felt awful when the news broke that you had been shot. Especially since I was the one who drove Kellan to your house." I smile.

She gasps.

"He couldn't get the job done, but I will."

She lunges for me, knocking me onto my back in the middle of the road. "Fuck you, you fucking bitch ..." she shouts before punching me in the face.

Instead of hitting her back, I cover up my face, not wanting anymore marks on my damn body from these crazy fucking sharks. "Get her off me!" I shout, trying to dodge her hits.

She's dragged off me a second later. I get up and dust the snow off my clothes. The snow seeping into my jeans makes me shiver. She's like a feral cat in his arms, kicking, screaming and trying to head-butt him. "Throw her ass in the SUV and let's get the hell out of here before someone sees us," I snap. We had this planned. We've been watching Shelby's house, knowing they were coming in for Thanksgiving.

Thanks, Mother, for that bit of info.

Then today, they appeared. We weren't going to waste any time since we didn't know how long they were staying. So we followed them to Blanche's house and then the mall. We knew they'd have to go back to get Lilly, so we waited. They didn't disappoint me.

"Turn her phone off and tie her up," I add. I'm not going to drug her. Not yet. I've got some payback to give her and Cole. She betrayed me by walking away from me, and he fucking rammed my face into a mirror before cutting me. She'll pay.

Blood for blood.

He'll never want her after I'm done with her. That is if I decide to let her live.

THIRTY-SIX

DEKE

I SIT WITH the guys at the clubhouse. Cole is next to me on the couch. Bennett stands to our right, typing away on his phone. "Can you stop that?" I snap.

"What?" he asks.

"Sexting. My sister." I grip the beer bottle and take a swig. It's all I think about. And it's fucking disgusting. I know he loves her, but that doesn't mean I'm a hundred percent okay with it just yet. It's going to take time.

He sighs. "I told you it's not like that."

"So you guys haven't fucked?" I quirk a brow, knowing damn well that they have.

He shoves a hand through his hair. "Of course, we have ..."

"That's what I thought."

"But I love her," he admits.

I snort, but don't say anything because I believe the bastard.

"Where the fuck is Shane?" Cole growls, changing the subject.

I don't want to be here any more than he does, but we have shit to go over. Secrets just keep coming out like fucking vomit. One of my best friends is fucking my sister. Our other friend was keeping secrets about my ex. Like what else do we not know? At this point, I'm not sure what could surprise me.

Cole's phone rings, and he shifts on the couch to dig it out of his pocket to answer it. "Hello? When?" He stands after a second. "Okay. I'll call her." He hangs up.

"What's up?" I ask.

"That was Blanche. She said Austin was supposed to pick up Lilly thirty minutes ago but never showed. She's tried calling her, but she won't answer."

I sit back on the couch and take a drink of my beer. "It was snowing earlier. Maybe they got caught in it, and it slowed her down." Come to think of it, Demi had messaged me a little bit ago about dinner, but she hasn't read my response.

He places the phone to his ear and then pulls it away immediately. "Straight to voicemail."

I frown and sit up straighter. He tries again. And again. The worry and anger quickly taking over his features. "I'll try Demi's."

I pull up her name on my phone and push call. It rings five times before going to voicemail. I look up at him and just shake my head as I dial it again. "Nothing," I say when it does the same.

"It's not like Austin to have her phone off." He growls.

"Maybe it died," Bennett suggests.

Just then, the door flies open, and Shane walks in.

"You're driving," Cole orders, not wasting a second.

"Where to?" he asks, spinning around to watch Cole storm out of the clubhouse. "What's going on?" He turns to ask me.

"The girls aren't answering their phones," I answer.

"They're probably busy."

"And they never showed up to pick up Lilly," I add.

Cole and I jump into the back of Shane's car while he gets in the driver seat, and Bennett falls into the passenger seat. "Where are we going?" Shane asks

"Give me a second." Cole snaps, his fingers typing quickly on his phone. "I've got a tracker on her car. I'm looking it up now."

"Dear Lord, dude. Paranoid?" Shane chuckles.

I expect Cole to have a snarky comeback or punch him in the back of the head, but he does neither.

"I'm sure they're fine …"

"What the fuck?" Cole barks, interrupting Shane.

"What?" I ask, starting to worry myself.

He drops his phone in his lap and looks over at me. "They're at Austin's dad's house."

BECKY

I pull in the circle drive of the Lowes estate. The house looks the same as it always has. From the outside, it looks like the million-dollar mansion her father had built for his young wife ten years ago. It's over the top, but what house in Collins isn't? The bigger, the better is their way of life. Three stories, twelve fireplaces, and a six-car garage are more than any family needs. But I understand it. I don't want to live in a shack when I get older.

The last time I was here was back in May. The day that shit went very sideways.

"Get out," I say to Kellan as I come to a stop in front of the Lowes estate.

He laughs. "What? Don't wanna come in for a cup of tea?"

I roll my eyes. My phone starts to vibrate while sitting in my cupholder. I see that it's Deke and pick it up, placing it on silent. Then I put it in the side door pocket so Kellan can't grab it and answer the call. He's a dick like that.

"Thanks for the ride, baby." He opens the door.

I lean over and look up at him. "You're gonna keep your mouth shut, right? About me letting you in on her birthday?" He can't tell on me. Who knows what the fuck Cole would do to me if he found out.

He laughs. "Don't worry, Becky. Your secret is safe with me." He slams my door shut and walks toward the house.

Obviously, he informed Shane that I let him into the Lowes house the night of Austin's birthday. I'm just not sure why he chose now to tell them. What changed to make him do that?

Getting out of Austin's SUV, I slam the door shut and watch David get out of his car. He and Maxwell come around the back of it where

I stand. "We'll get the girls. Just get the front door for us."

I run up the steps and push the heavy door open, knowing it was unlocked. No one has been here since Kellan killed Celeste and shot Austin. I cover my nose when I open the door because the stench is overwhelming. The blood still covers the black and white checkered marble floor of the grand foyer. It's a shame they didn't have anyone come and clean it up after Bruce was arrested for paying off Jeff to cause the car wreck. He got life for three counts of manslaughter. For each of the guys who died in the wreck he caused.

Maxwell carries my unconscious sister over his shoulder while David drags a very pissed off Austin through the front door with his hand fisted in her dark hair. "Fuck, she's a handful." He grunts.

I slam the door shut. "Her room is upstairs."

"Let go of me!" she snaps as he shoves her up the stairs. "You won't get away with this."

We both ignore her. He comes to the landing, and I kick her bedroom door open. It looks the same as it did when she lived here. After she was shot, Cole and Deke came over and packed up all her clothes for their move to Texas, so she wouldn't have to come back here and do it herself. They left everything else.

He throws her onto her bed, and she grunts from landing on her back, her restrained hands underneath her.

There's not an ounce of fear in her green eyes, just pure hatred. She wants to kill me. Well, she'll have to get in line. We have a plan, and once we're done, we're going to run like hell. "Why are you doing this?"

"Because the sharks think they are the only things to be scared of."

She snorts. "You think this is gonna make them fear you?" She shakes her head. "You're more stupid than I gave you credit for." Her nostrils flare, and a small line of blood runs down from her forehead where the car door hit her. Her green eyes slide to David, then back to me.

"You guys haven't officially met. This is David," I announce, and her eyes widen.

"Your ex?" she demands.

"Who said we ever broke up?"

He walks up to the bed and looks down at her. "Pretty." He chuckles, and I narrow my eyes on him. "Hello, Austin, I've heard a lot about you." Reaching out, he runs his knuckles through the blood on her face, smearing it.

She yanks away from him.

I slap her, knocking her head to the side, the sound bouncing off the walls in her room. I go to do it again, but David grabs my arm and spins me to face him. "We've got all night with her, babe."

"You better fucking kill me," she sneers.

"I'm gonna kill her first. Then I'll get around to you," I say honestly. We walk out, slamming her door behind us.

We make our way down the stairs and to the living room.

Maxwell has my sister sitting in a high back barstool that he must have taken from the kitchen in the middle of the room and her head hangs back, eyes closed. She's still drugged and will be for a while. I gave her more than her body needed. Possibly too much. She may die from that alone. We'll just have to wait and see.

"Here you go, babe." David hands me a knife, and I look at it in my hand. It resembles the one that the fucking sharks used to cut the back of my neck with. A black handle with a black rubber grip. I press the button and the blade pops out. Silver with a black center.

"Is she already dead?" I ask.

Maxwell places his fingers to her neck and then shakes his head. "She's still alive. Just out." Then he looks over at the hallway. "What about the other one?"

"Alive and awake," David answers. "Why don't you go keep an eye on her?"

Maxwell gives him a smile, telling us that's not the only thing he plans on keeping on her. I don't even care. They've all betrayed me. She's a shark, just like the rest of them. They never wanted me or accepted me.

"Just don't kill her," I call out as he walks out of the living room.

"I'm not a murderer." His chuckle carries down the hall. "I just wanna play."

THIRTY-SEVEN

DEKE

SHANE PULLS INTO the drive of the Lowes estate. Once we clear the trees, I order, "Cut the lights." It's not dark yet, but it will be soon. The snow has started coming down again.

Austin's SUV sits parked out front by the five-tier water fountain, but it's not alone. A black Maserati is parked next to it.

"Who the fuck is that?" Bennett asks.

"Fuck if I know," I answer.

"Go around to the side," Cole snaps. "I don't want anyone to see us coming."

Shane puts the car in reverse to back out of the long driveway and then throws it in gear, turning on his lights and punching the gas to pass the house, then takes the next right. There used to be a road that ran parallel to the house leading up to the abandoned cemetery.

He comes to a stop, and we jump out. The house is set to be demolished. You can see they've already brought the equipment out to start soon.

Popping his trunk, I grab my black duffle bag. We brought everything we could think of. Throwing it over my shoulder, I look up at the side of the house.

"What the fuck is she doing?" Cole growls. Fisting his hands, he tries her cell again, praying she answers to explain this crazy situation.

Any excuse she could have would be better than our imagination. In my mind, they're both already dead.

"How we gonna get in?" Bennett asks. "I don't think we should just go through the front."

"The back door," Cole answers. "I knocked the glass out to get in when Becky and I came back here while Austin was in the hospital to get the USB drive."

"Then that's where we enter," I order. "Everyone, turn your cells on silent. I don't want anyone calling us and giving away our location." I'm not taking that chance. We have no clue what we are about to walk into, but I know the girls aren't here to take a trip down memory lane.

We make our way around the house, walking alongside the pool and step onto the terrace and go to open it, but I place my hand on Cole's chest stopping him. "Becky!" I hiss. I watch her through the broken glass. She stands in front of a barstool where another blonde sits slumped over. It's Demi. David stands next to them.

Motherfucker!

"What the fuck?" Shane barks. "Why the fuck is he with her?"

I shove my phone into Bennett's chest. "Call my sister. Tell her to get her ass over here right now," I demand.

"What ... Why?"

"Because Demi looks like she's gonna need medical attention, and I'm not leaving this house until I've killed him." I growl. No way in hell will he walk away from this. Even if he manages to kill me, the guys will get him.

"Where the fuck is Austin?" Cole demands. "I don't see her."

"Let's go find out," I say. Turning the knob, I enter with Cole and Shane. Bennett stays behind to make the call.

"God, I've hated her for so long," Becky says, gripping the handle of a knife in her hand.

"Well, I've always known that, babe."

"She ruins everything." She takes a step toward her.

"You've got her all to yourself. What do you want to do to her?" he asks, crossing his arms over his chest. The fucking bastard is just going to stand there and let her have her way with Demi.

"Hurt her. Kill her. I want her out of my life for good. I want to hurt her for Deke ever touching her." She lifts the knife like she's going to stab her, and I step out of the darkness.

He laughs like it's funny. Like her jealousy turns him on. *What the fuck is going on?*

"Hello, Becky," I say, calmly, holding my anger back. I want her to think I'm sane at the moment when I'm really far from it. She's not the only one who can act.

"Deke," she squeals, jumping back.

David shoves her away from him as if he can save her. "Deke." He growls my name.

I lift my gun. "Get on your knees."

"You don't fucking scare me." He snorts. "None of you fucking sharks ever did."

"Last chance," I say, aiming the gun right between his eyes. I don't see Cole or Shane, but I know they've got my back.

"Or what …?"

Cole comes up behind him and wraps his arm around David's neck, proceeding to choke him out. I run to Demi and pick her up off the barstool. I lay her on the couch, and her head falls to the side. I check her pulse, and it's strong. "What did you give her?" I bark out.

"Fuck you," Becky shouts as Shane grabs her. He drags her over to me and forces her to her knees next to the couch.

I point the gun at her head, pressing it to her temple. "What did you give her?" I ask again, breathing heavily. Whatever moment of calmness I had is now long gone.

"David got some Valium from a friend. He made it into an injectable …" she cries.

Bennett enters the room and comes over to us just as I hear David hit the floor from Cole getting the job done. "Where is Austin?" I demand.

Demi isn't going to be waking up anytime soon, and I know my sister is on her way to help her. I need to know what the situation is with Austin.

She closes her eyes, and her lips thin, refusing to answer me. "Where the fuck is she?" I shout, gripping her face in my hand.

She shakes but answers. "Upstairs in her room … with Maxwell."

"Fuck!" Cole runs out of the living room.

I jump to my feet to follow him. He may need help. He'd willingly die to protect Austin from harm, but I hesitate, not wanting to leave Demi.

"Go," Bennett orders. "Shelby is on her way."

"I've got Becky," Shane assures me.

I run out of the living room, down the long hallway, and come into the still blood-covered marble floor foyer. I grip the banister and spin around to run up the stairs. I enter Austin's room to see Cole cutting Austin's wrists free from the rope. But I don't see anyone else in here.

"Where is he?" I growl.

She points at her closed bathroom door while Cole pulls her to him. He runs his hands up and down her body to check for anything they might have done to her.

I walk over to it and crack it open. He stands at the toilet, whistling as he pisses. I place my gun into the waist of my jeans and push up my sleeves. Walking in behind him, I kick the back of his knees in.

"What the …?"

I grip the back of his head and shove him headfirst into the toilet. I straddle his legs as he kneels on the floor and hold him face down in his piss and water while he struggles against me. Cole enters the bathroom and stands there watching me with Austin by his side.

Maxwell's hands hit the toilet, his feet kick the back of my legs while I stand over him, but he's not going to win. There's no way any of us will let him walk out of this house. And what better way than to kill a man in his own urine? His body shudders one last time, and then he slumps against the toilet. I release him and take a step back.

"You okay?" I ask her, walking over to the sink. She has a cut on her forehead and a trail of smeared blood runs down her cheek along with a cut on her lip.

Lifting her chin, she nods. "I'll be fine. Is Demi okay?"

I don't answer because I'm not sure what to say at this point. I remove my shirt and tuck what little I can fit into the back of my jeans pocket, letting the rest hang out since it now has piss on it from him struggling. I go to turn her faucet on to wash my hands, but there's no water. "Fuck." I hiss.

"Maybe there are some bottles of water …"

"Fuck! Fuck" I shout, slamming my fists into the countertop, losing my fucking cool and interrupting her.

Cole turns to Austin. "Go downstairs."

"I'm staying with …"

"Go downstairs, Austin," he orders, interrupting her. Then he lowers his voice. "Shane and Bennett are down there with Demi. Shelby should be here by now. Check and see if she needs anything or if you can find any water."

With that, she pulls away and exits the bathroom.

I turn around and look at the guy I just killed. Fucking Maxwell. He was a year older than us and David's best friend. He's on his knees, head in the toilet and arms out to his side. His shirt is missing and so are his jeans. All he's wearing is his boxers.

He was gonna rape her! If he hadn't already.

"Did he touch her?" I ask.

"She said no." He growls, shoving his hands through his hair.

"Do you believe her?" Austin isn't the kind of girl to tell you everything. She thinks she's strong enough to deal with shit herself.

"Her shirt was still on, and her jeans weren't undone. Doesn't mean he didn't touch her over them. But I'm gonna make her go to the hospital and have a full workup done," he grinds out.

I'm not going to argue that she may not allow that because Cole will find a way to make it happen. Instead, I say, "Help me get him downstairs."

I take Maxwell's arms, and he takes his feet. We carry the heavy bastard down the stairs and through the house to the living room, dropping him on the rug.

My sister is sitting next to Demi with her wrist in her hand and another at her neck. Becky still kneels on the floor while Shane holds the gun to her head. Austin is nowhere to be seen and neither is Bennett.

"Where is Austin?" Cole demands, looking around frantically.

"She and Bennett went to the kitchen to look for water."

"Is she gonna be okay?" I ask my sister as she stands.

"Yes. She needs to be admitted, but she's gonna be fine."

I look around to see David still unconscious, now lying on his stomach with his hands cuffed behind his back. We've got to finish this. "I can't go just yet."

She nods understanding. "Help me get her to my car. I'll take her in and stay with her."

"Watch her," I order Shane, referring to Becky.

"She's not going anywhere," he promises.

I lean down and pick up Demi in my arms and carry her out of the house to my sister's car. "I'll be up there as soon as I can."

When I go to walk back inside, she grips my upper arm. "Deke?"

I turn to face her. "Don't, Shelby." I don't have time to listen to her tell me not to hurt them. Not to kill them after what they were going to do. When will it end? When will this all stop? I have to make sure Demi is never in this situation again. And Austin too. We may be sharks, but we protect the people we love.

"Don't get caught," she says, surprising me. Then she turns and gets in her car, driving off.

I enter the house and make my way to the kitchen. Cole, Austin, and Bennett are all standing by the fridge. "You guys ready?" I ask.

Cole nods along with Bennett.

"What are we gonna do?" Austin asks with her arms crossed over her chest. She's pissed and has every right to be. This was her best friend at one time.

Cole looks over at her, and I wait for him to tell her there is no *we*, but instead, he surprises me by telling her. "End it."

DEKE

The five of us stand on top of the hill at the back of the cemetery behind the Lowes estate. The sun has officially set, making the night cold, but it's stopped snowing once again. My shirt is still in my back pocket, but thankfully, Austin found cases of bottled water in the garage, so I was able to wash the piss off me.

Maxwell's body lies in a shallow grave that Cole and Bennett dug for him. David eventually woke up, but Cole placed tape over his mouth so we haven't had to listen to him cuss us or beg for his life. At this point, it doesn't matter.

Becky kneels on the ground next to Shane. He has his hand fisted in her hair so she can't get up and run away. She hasn't said one word. She sobs to herself. I'm pretty sure she's officially broken. She has tried so many times to hurt the ones she loves that she's just given up.

But she has always been good at pretending. So he holds a gun to her head with his free hand just in case.

Cole rips the tape off David's face. He sucks in a deep breath. "You motherfuckers …"

"Why did you do it?" I ask. He never liked us, but the feeling was mutual.

His eyes go to Becky, and she bows her head in shame.

"Don't tell me this was because I fucked her while you guys were dating." Why else would he want to hurt Demi? He was always nice to her from what I remember. Becky talked about it all the time. How he would make her bring her around to hang out with them. She loved that I never forced us to be around her. Why would I? I didn't like her then.

He snorts. "Like I gave a shit that you fucked her."

Becky flinches at his words.

"Then why?" Cole demands, gripping his hair and yanking his head back.

He lets out a rough laugh. "You guys really don't know, do you?"

None of us answer him.

"Tell him, baby."

She sobs with her head down.

"Tell him all the times you let him touch you and then came

crawling to me about how awful they were."

I tilt my head to the side.

"Or how we laughed when you told Cole you were pregnant, and he fucking believed you." His laughter grows. "That he let you go …"

"What? You lied about being pregnant?" Austin snaps and turns to Cole. "Did you know this?"

"Doesn't matter," he answers.

"It does too fucking matter," she snaps and walks over to Becky. She slaps her across the face so hard, it knocks her over into the snow. "You fucking bitch …" She jumps on top of her.

Cole wraps an arm around her waist and yanks her off her. She kicks her feet out before he sets her down. She's breathing heavy and trying to push him away. "It doesn't matter, sweetheart."

Her mouth falls open. "How can you say that?" Her eyes fill with tears. "She lied to you. Everything you went through—"

"Nothing regarding her matters," he interrupts her softly. Pulling her into him, he pushes her wild brown hair behind her ear.

"You guys are sicker than I thought." David speaks. "Becky let me read your journal, Austin. Gotta say, Cole, I was jealous at how much she let you abuse her and still fuck her."

"Stop," Becky cries.

"And that video …" He whistles, looking her up and down.

This time, it's Cole who throws a punch. Right into his face.

"Well, well, well, he's telling us all of your secrets." I smile.

"I know she wanted to pay you all back for how you used her in your own sick games," David shouts, getting angry before spitting blood into the snow from Cole's punch.

"Game?" I ask. I loved her. I never used her. Cole did when Austin came into the picture, but that didn't happen until after the car wreck …

"Why were you even with them that night?" Austin demands. Her thoughts mimicking mine. "Why were you with Eli?"

Becky doesn't answer, and neither does David. I arch a brow at him. He's willing to throw her under the bus but doesn't want to implicate himself as well.

I look at Cole and nod. He steps away from Austin, grabs his knife from his pocket, and flips it open. He steps behind David and places the knife to his neck. Cole doesn't say a word as he drags the blade down the side of his neck. David screams, and Becky tries to crawl to him, but Shane prevents her with his hand in her hair. "Stop! Stop! I'll tell you!" she cries. "Please, just stop."

Cole brings the blade to a stop but doesn't remove it from his neck. David is panting as blood runs down his neck to cover his shirt.

"We took Demi to a party at the beach. I ... drugged her for Maxwell. But she ended up leaving with Eli, and when I went to pick her up the next morning, he wouldn't let her leave with me 'cause he found out what we had done." She sniffs.

Demi had told me this story when she was drunk the night Cole and I found the girls at the bar. But I don't think she told me everything. This is my chance to find out.

"How?" I demand.

"David had given her his phone to use 'cause she left hers back at the house. When she passed out with Eli, he went through it and found our chats about our plans ..." she cries, shaking her head. "Eli threatened him ... David and I staged a separation, and I met up with them later on that night. He thought I was just trying to piss you off for sleeping with Kaitlin."

That's why Eli told me I could do better. He knew exactly what kind of woman she was. I wish he would have just told me. I'm not sure I would have listened, but I wish he would have tried. Instead, I thought the worst and have hated him when I should be thanking him. He saved Demi. He stood up for her. I'm glad she had someone in her life to do that, and I'm proud to say that he was one of my best friends.

"Becky!" David yells at her. Cole digs the knife into his throat again, silencing him.

Becky sucks in a long breath as fresh tears run down her face. "David thought that Eli was gonna go to the cops. Or send the sharks after him for what we did to her. He told me to seduce him. The night of the party, I was to get Eli away from the sharks and bring him to a secluded location where David and Maxwell were going to make sure he couldn't speak."

Cole steps away from David, and he growls at her. "Fuck! You bitch! I never heard you tell me no! You wanted him silenced just as much as I did."

"Then the wreck happened, and I panicked …" she cries. "After I went home to Demi, I met up with David, and his father stitched up my wound …"

His father is a doctor at the hospital where Shelby works. Now it all makes sense. Becky had told me that she cut it while at the lake. I never second-guessed her.

"They fucking deserved it! You all deserved to be in that car!" David shouts.

"We all get what we deserve." I nod my head and pull the matches out of my back pocket. Done with all of this. I don't have the time for this shit.

Cole reaches down and grabs the can of gasoline sitting next to him that we found in the garage of the Lowes house.

"What the fuck?" David barks.

Cole throws the gasoline onto him.

I nod my head to Shane, and he grips the back of Becky's neck where we cut her. Yanking her head up, forcing her to watch. "Do you love him?" he asks her.

It's the same thing she had asked me regarding Demi. I know what he's getting at.

"Yes." She sobs. "Please just let us go. I won't talk … He won't talk …"

"We're not afraid of you talking, baby." He smiles down at her, and her body wracks with a sob. "This is what happens to those who fuck with the sharks." She whimpers. "You can't beat us, Becky. No one can."

"Deke—" She cries my name, about to beg me.

I interrupt her, no longer caring. "I've heard that burning to death is a painful way to die." I strike the match on the side of the box. "I hope it's true." Then I toss it on him.

He screams out as the flames lick his body. Falling to his side, he rolls, and Cole grabs Austin to pull her farther away from the flames.

Becky leans forward, screaming out into the cold night as she watches the only guy she ever truly loved burn to death. And I feel nothing for her. For him.

There are times I wonder how we got here.

Evil.

Ruthless.

But then I remember that we started playing the game a long time ago and that turned into real life. And life is a fucking mess. It's bloody. If you want to survive, you fight. And just because I'm not afraid to die doesn't mean I'm ready to give up living. I've finally found a girl who I know will accept me for me. Love me for me. And I'm not ready to give her up yet.

DEKE

The guys and I stand around Austin as she kneels on the snow-covered ground, pounding away on the guys' smoldering bodies with a hammer. She has a lot of pent-up aggression after everything they have done. The cold air smells like burnt flesh, and Cole stands next to me, watching her with pride and lust. I'm pretty sure if me and the rest of guys weren't here with Becky, he would fuck her right here and now.

She wipes the sweat off her still blood-covered forehead and stands. "Done," she states.

"Now what?" Shane asks.

"Scoop up the remaining ashes and throw them over the cliff." She lifts her chin over to the right where the ocean hits the rocks at the bottom of the cliff. "Get rid of everything. The grass will show where the fire was, but by the time winter is over, it shouldn't be that noticeable." Then she looks at me. "Where are their phones?"

"I have them," Cole answers, removing them from his pockets.

She takes them from him before throwing them to the ground.

Then she walks over to Shane who still has Becky on her knees. "Where is your phone?" Austin demands.

Becky sobs, and Shane pushes her forward by the back of her neck, leaning down and ripping it from her back pocket. He hands it to Austin.

"What are you doing?" Shane asks her.

"Gotta get rid of everything." She looks up at Cole and snaps her fingers, ordering, "Knife." Once it's in her hands, she continues. "Who knows how much they shared through texts? Messenger?" Then starts pushing buttons on the phone. "I'm going to uninstall the messenger and Facebook app." We all stand silently as she does all three.

Then she begins to beat the shit out of them with her hammer.

Once she's done, she picks up a fishing net that she also found in the garage of her father's house and begins to cut it in three sperate pieces. "Hand me a few pieces from that broken headstone," she orders Bennett.

He does so without hesitation, then looks at Cole, and he just shrugs. He's just as much in the dark as the rest of us.

She lays the three pieces of fishing net down on the ground and then places a phone and a part of the headstone in each one. Then she ties them all off. Standing up, she walks over to the cliff and throws them over. Turning back to us, she places her hands on her hips. "If the police go looking for the guys, they will be able to pin their last location using their phones. But without the evidence, they don't have shit. And even if for some insane reason they manage to find one of their phones, they won't be able to get anything off it after it's been sitting at the bottom of the ocean. After I took a hammer to them."

We all just stand there staring at her in shock that she thought of that. She's one hell of a shark, and I'm glad she's on our side. I'm not sure how many of us could have beat her had she not fallen in love with Cole and joined us.

Shane chuckles to himself. "I knew you'd do well at a challenge."

"I love you," Cole says, pulling her into him and giving her a long kiss.

I turn away from them and pull my cell out of my pocket to call my sister. "Hello?" she answers.

"How is she?" I ask immediately.

"She's doing well. She's awake …"

"I wanna talk to her."

"One second."

"Hey?"

I let out a long breath at the sound of her soft voice. "Hey, princess. How do you feel?"

"I'm okay. Just tired."

I run a hand down my face, feeling my shoulders loosen. "Listen … I want to come see you, but …"

"It's okay, Deke. Is Austin okay?"

"Yeah."

I look up at my friends and watch them toss the ashes of the sorry bastards who hurt my girls over the cliff, and my chest tightens for what they've been through. And how it could have ended if not for Cole and that damn tracker. How long would they have been missing before we realized it? Would we have thought to check the Lowes house? I hate that the answers are no. "I'll be there as soon as I can," I promise her.

After we found Austin shot, Cole didn't get to go to the hospital right away either. He had stuff he had to take care of first, and that's exactly what I have to do now.

"I'll be here. Shelby said she's gonna stay with me. And she's called my dad. He's here as well. Just stepped out for some coffee."

"What does he know?" I ask, wanting to know what we're up against. I didn't kill Becky because it would be too hard to explain why she hasn't been seen or phoned home. But the sharks will see to it that she pays. Plus, I once told Demi that people don't have to die to stop living.

"That I passed out and hit my head on the way down."

I frown. "And he believed that?"

"He looked skeptical until Shelby showed him my chart."

I let out a sigh. "Let me talk to her again. I'll see you soon."

We say our goodbyes, and then my sister is back on the line. "Thank you," I tell her.

"No need to thank me. Just do what you gotta do, and we'll see you once you're done."

"Ready?" I ask, pocketing my phone.

"Yes," Austin answers, slapping her hands together to knock off what was left of the ashes. "What about their wallets?" she asks. "We don't wanna put those with their phones. It all needs to be separated."

Agreeing with her, I pat my back pocket that doesn't hold my shirt. I've got both of them. "We plant the wallets in the glovebox of the Maserati, then drive it about an hour out of town and put it in a river with the windows rolled down. If it's ever found, the cops will think they drowned and washed downstream," I answer.

It's the best option we have, given our timeframe. This isn't our first rodeo committing murder, but every time is a different situation.

"I'm taking you to the hospital," Cole tells her.

She looks up at him. "I'm fine, Cole."

He fists his hands down by his side at her refusal. "You have a pretty good size knot on your head. You may have a concussion—"

"Let's get this over with," she interrupts him. "It'll be daylight soon, and I need to go get Lilly once we're done." She places her hands in the front pockets of her now filthy skinny jeans and starts walking down the hill, not giving him a second to argue.

"What are we doing with her?" Bennett asks, looking down at Becky. "We can't leave loose ends lying around."

Becky begins to rock back and forth; her hands still tied behind her back.

I walk over to her and kneel. Gripping her face, I force her to look up at me. "I'm not gonna kill you, Becky." She whimpers. "Death would be too easy for you. No, instead, I'm gonna spare your miserable, pathetic life." My fingers tighten, gripping her cheeks. "Instead, you will watch your sister get the love that you always wanted." Her bloodshot eyes widen. "You've already seen me fall in love with her. And you'll live to watch me marry her and her have my children. You'll watch her be everything you wanted to be."

I release her, stand, and look at Shane. "She belongs to us, but at this point, you're the only one who will touch her."

Cole has Austin, I have Demi, and Bennett has my sister. Shane is the only one who can get any use out of her. So she's all his.

He gives me a smile, and I turn and walk down the hill back toward the house and Austin. She was right. It's time to get this shit wrapped up.

EPILOGUE

DEMI

DEKE AND THE rest of the sharks killed David and Maxwell. I wish I could say he killed my sister too, but he told me that death was too easy for her, and I understood what he meant. The more I thought about it, the more I understood his decision. She'll have to forever watch us together. She'll watch us live happily in love. Get married. Have children. I love Deke Biggs, and I don't plan on going anywhere without him.

Plus, she was theirs now. No matter what she did or where she'd go, she would never escape them. And I understood exactly how scary that would be for her.

I was released from the hospital the following day. We all got together and had lunch with my dad, sans Becky. She made up some excuse about feeling bad. The sharks didn't force her to join us because none of us wanted her around anyway.

We all went back to Texas and fell into a routine. I went to school, and Deke and Cole went to their classes. The guys were busier than ever with swimming, but I saw Deke every day, even if it was just for an hour. I loved him even more for it. And no one knew anything about what happened in the Lowes estate. I feel like it brought us all even closer. A secret that we will all take to our grave.

"Are you ready?" I ask Austin.

She nods. A huge smile on her face. "Yes."

It's New Year's Eve. Eleven fifty-five to be exact. The middle of the night. Cole and Austin are getting married. In five minutes, the date will change to midnight. It'll be their one-year anniversary. A new year and she'll no longer be Austin Lowes. She'll be Austin Reynolds.

"You look absolutely stunning," I tell her, running my hands down the black silk dress. It's got a corset back laced up with a red ribbon. She looks like she belongs on the front cover of a magazine. Cole and Austin aren't your average couple. And that's what I love about them so much. They say that opposites attract, but they are a lot alike.

They chose to get married on the hill behind where the Lowes estate once stood. The one that leads up to the abandoned cemetery. Where they first met one year ago tonight.

Austin doesn't know it, but Cole paid a company to come in and clean the property for their special night. Whoever said he isn't romantic doesn't know how much he loves her.

I cried. She cried. I even saw Cole blink rapidly at one point. The guy has a shell that can't be broken until it involves his sweetheart. The overcast night was dark, and you couldn't even see the moon, so we decided to light the way with tiki torches. And when they kissed, it started to rain. That quickly turned to snow. It looked like something out of a hauntingly beautiful fairy tale. Her in her black dress and him in his matching tux. And Lilly wore a red dress that made her look every bit of the princess she is. Afterward, we all went back to the clubhouse, and they danced to a song that they chose. It was so them. I'm not sure I've ever met someone else who would dance to "I Will Follow You into the Dark," by Yungblud and Halsey for their wedding song. It was perfect.

My mother asked me to wait until I was twenty-one to marry Deke, but I said fuck that. He proposed the night of my eighteenth birthday, February twenty-third. I married him a week after high school graduation. That was as long as I was willing to put it off. We eloped to a little bed and breakfast. No blood relatives were present, but all the sharks were there. They're my family now.

We spent two days in bed together. I called and told my father first. He asked us to come home and stay with him for the summer. I told him we would come for a few weeks. I didn't inform my mother of our nuptials until six months later. She said she hoped it didn't end like hers to my father. That was as much as I was going to get out of her.

Her marriage ended to my father because she couldn't stay faithful. She was like my sister. I'm nothing like them. I understand what I have, and I won't ever give that up. Deke Biggs is my forever, and I'm his.

THE END . . FOR NOW

ACKNOWLEDGMENTS

First I would like to thank my assistants, Christina Santos and Kelly Tucker. These two ladies are amazing. Without them. I would be lost.

I would like to thank Jenny Sims, my wonderful editor. I've been working with her for six years now and she's awesome!

And a big thank you to my proofreader, Amanda Rash for helping me out with such short notice.

To my cover designer, Tracie Douglas with Dark Water Covers. Thank you for making me another gorgeous cover for the Dare Series.

A big thank you to my formatter and friend, CP Smith. Thanks so much for your help!

I want to thank Candi Kane PR and all the blogs that signed up to help promote and review the Dare Series. You guys are amazing.

I want to thank my lovely betas, Rita Rees, Sarah Piechuta, Sophie Ruthven, Desire Jordan Wright, Brandi Zelenka, and Nakita Early Loudermilk. Thank you so much for taking the time to read If You Dare. And for all of our suggestions. I truly appreciate it.

I want to thank my Sinners; the ladies on my street team are amazing! Fay Moore, Lauren Lascola-Lesczynksi, Amy March, Sarah Piechuta, Sophie Ruthven, Heather Brown, Tara Hartnett, Rita Rees, Kat Strack, Brandi Zelenka, Michelle McLellan, Melissa Gaston, Aliana Milano, Amanda Marie, Brenda Parson, Ashley Estep, Tiffany Johnson Mauer, Kara Rotella, Jenny Dicks, Mary Dbo, Elizabeth Clinton, Catherine J Lawrence, Book Bre, Heather Creighton PA, Luetta Lyons.

And last but not least, my readers. Thank you for taking a chance and wanting to read my books. I hope that you all love them as much as I do.

OTHER TITLES BY SHANTEL TESSIER

The UN Series
Undescribable
Unbearable
Uncontrollable
Unforgettable
Unchangeable
Unforeseen
Unpredictable

Seven Deadly Sins Series
Addiction
Obsession
Confession- Coming soon

The Selfish Series
Selfish
Myself
Selfless

Dare Series
I Dare You
I Promise You
If You Dare

Standalones
DASH
Donut Overthink It
Slaughter
Just A Kiss